# PRAISE FOR THE NOVELS
## OF SAMANTHA YOUNG

### *Down London Road*

"Ridiculously incendiary chemistry."  —Dear Author . . .

"A deceptively complex romantic contemporary romance that will have you laughing, crying, and swooning with delight."

—Smexy Books Romance Reviews

"Just as hot and sexy as the first book. . . . Smart and sexy, Young writes stories that stay with you long after you flip that last page."

—Under the Covers

"Passion, romance, angst, LUST, major heat, mistakes, personal growth, and the power of love all combine perfectly in *Down London Road*."

—Bookish Temptations

"Heartwarming, sizzling, and captivating. . . . [Young's characters] are complex, a little flawed, and at their core good people struggling to make it in this crazy world. . . . Young creates steamy scenes that sizzle with just the right amount of details."  —Caffeinated Book Reviewer

"Ms. Young dives deep into the psyche of what makes a person tick emotionally, what stirs their vulnerability, and ultimately provides them the courage to be better individuals as well as partners. . . . The one thing you can count on from Ms. Young is some of the best steamy, sexual chemistry."  —Fiction Vixen Book Reviews

*continued . . .*

## *On Dublin Street*

"This book is fun. Sexy. A little dark. While the hero is extremely dominant, he also shows his softer side just when she needs it."

—Smexy Books Romance Reviews

"Every page sizzles when these two get together, but this book is so much more than a hot romp. This book has heart—and lots of it. . . . If you want a book that will lure you in, grab you by the scruff of the neck, and never let you go until you finish reading the last page, then *On Dublin Street* is the book for you."
—Totally Booked

"Brilliantly written with just the right amount of hotness, sexiness, and romance and everything else in between."
—Once Upon a Twilight

"The chemistry between Jocelyn and Braden was on fire. The characters were believable and more importantly they were lovable . . . one of the best books I have read in 2012!"
—Rainy Day Reads

"This book has it all . . . romance, fabulously written heat, family, friendship, heartbreak, longing, hope, and an ending that is completely satisfying."
—Bookish Temptations

"Lots of heart makes this book an absolute page-turner."
—*RT Book Reviews*

ALSO BY SAMANTHA YOUNG

*On Dublin Street*
*Down London Road*
*Until Fountain Bridge* (novella)
*Castle Hill* (novella)

# BEFORE JAMAICA LANE

## Samantha Young

NAL NEW AMERICAN LIBRARY

New American Library
Published by the Penguin Group
Penguin Group (USA) LLC, 375 Hudson Street,
New York, New York 10014

USA | Canada | UK | Ireland | Australia | New Zealand | India | South Africa | China
penguin.com
A Penguin Random House Company

First published by New American Library,
a division of Penguin Group (USA) LLC

First Printing, January 2014

REGISTERED TRADEMARK—MARCA REGISTRADA

LIBRARY OF CONGRESS CATALOGING-IN-PUBLICATION DATA:

Young, Samantha.
Before Jamaica Lane/Samantha Young.
pages cm
ISBN 978-0-451-46668-6 (pbk.)
1. Americans—Scotland—Fiction.
2. Man-woman relationships—Fiction. I. Title.
PR6125.O943B44 2014
823'.92—dc23
2013032444

Printed in the United States of America
1  3  5  7  9  10  8  6  4  2

Set in Garamond

For Tammy Blackwell

*Because if it weren't for you, Olivia might never have
become a librarian . . . and also because I had to get the phrase
"Let me Dewey your Decimal" into this book somewhere . . .*

*Dear Readers,*

*Often I receive tweets and messages from you, including pictures of your travels to the real streets of Edinburgh. Whether you've been captured on film on Dublin Street or goofing around beside the London Road sign, the proof of your love for this series, its characters, and its location blows me away. If, after reading Nate and Olivia's story, you decide to take to the streets of Edinburgh to find Jamaica Lane, I'll make it easier for you. You see, for the sake of title continuity I took some creative license and changed the street name. Jamaica Lane doesn't technically exist. It's really Jamaica Street North Lane, and that's where readers can find the wee one-bedroom flat where this next ODS couple are about to discover that life, more often than not, can take you where you least expect it . . .*

# BEFORE JAMAICA LANE

# CHAPTER 1

Every time we turned a corner the icy cold wind hammered into us, almost spitefully, like it was mad when a building buffered us. Its icicle-spiked fingers pricked my rosy red cheeks and I wrapped my arms tighter around myself, my shoulders hunching as I braced against the attack.

"For the fifth and final time . . . where are you taking us?" Joss asked, burrowing deeper against her fiancé, Braden. He'd opened his wool coat and huddled her inside it, his arm wrapped around her waist, holding her close. She wore a short, stylish jacket with a red dress that fit her like a second skin. Like all of us, she was wearing stilettos. In fact, the only thing she wore that shielded her against the Scottish winter was a scarf.

Ellie and Jo were in pretty much the same condition—wearing dresses, heels, and light jackets. I was only marginally warmer in a pair of black dress pants, but my silk top and lightweight tuxedo-style blazer were doing eff all to protect me. Not quite as used to walking in stilettos as my girlfriends were, I made slower progress at the back of our group as Jo led us to our mystery destination. "It's not far," she promised, glancing over her shoulder at us as she led the way through the city center high street. Cam, her fiancé, had his arm wrapped tight around her, keeping her as warm as possible, and behind them Braden's sister, Ellie, and his best friend, Adam, were cuddling into each other for heat too. They were also engaged. Very recently, in fact.

I, on the other hand, did not have a fiancé to protect me from the taunting wind. "It's not far?" I scoffed at Jo. Since my arrival in Edinburgh a little over nine months ago, Jo and I had grown as close as sisters, so I felt it was okay to scoff at her after she'd dragged our asses out of Edinburgh without much explanation. Hence the poor clothing choices. "You lost the right to say 'it's not far' when you directed our cabs to Waverley train station."

Jo's apologetic smile suddenly wilted into a frown as she stopped us at a street junction. "Okay, I think we're down here."

"Are you sure?" I asked, my teeth starting to chatter.

"Eh—" Jo glanced across the street at a road sign and then pulled out her phone. "Just a second, guys."

My friends huddled together and I stood back a little, taking them all in. I realized that despite how cold I was, I didn't truly mind. I was simply content to be there with them, still surprised, even, by how close I'd grown to them. They'd accepted me so fully into their lives, partly because of Jo, but also because of Nate, Cam's friend, and my newly adopted best friend.

As I reminisced, Nate turned around from speaking to Adam and Ellie to direct his beautiful smile my way.

I blinked, distracted by the flush of attraction I felt. I'd gotten so good at ignoring the feeling, it had caught me off guard. That was the problem when you were friends with a guy who totally got you and just happened to be the hottest man you'd ever met in real life.

That flutter, that rush of unexpected feeling, sent me reeling back to the first time Nate and I had met. Honestly, I deserved a medal for ignoring my attraction to him . . .

*Seven months ago . . .*

Ellie's mom, Elodie Nichols, and her husband, Clark, had welcomed me and my dad into the fold as if we'd always been a part of their family. It was nice. It made fitting in with Jo's friends easier. It made fitting in with Jo easier, and since my dad and I had decided to make Scotland our home, it would be good to fit into Jo's life. She was kind of awesome. She'd also been through a really difficult time these last few years. She deserved to be taken care of, and I knew that Cam was the one person who could do that for her.

I'd let myself and Cole into Cam's apartment. While he and Jo were at the store getting snacks, I'd decided to take Cole off their hands and give them some time together. That night we were all planning to hang out with Cam's friends Nate and Peetie, whom I'd be meeting for the first time, and I thought it would be a nice thing to give Jo and Cam some alone time before their friends appeared. As soon as I'd let us in the door, Cole headed straight for the game console in the sitting room while I headed to the back of the apartment. In the kitchen I puttered around, finding bowls and plates for the snacks. I was just washing the dishes when a low, Scottish, and very masculine voice said, "Eh . . . you're not Cameron."

When I whirled around to face the intruder, any words that might have descended from my brain to my tongue tripped up at the bottom of that staircase and suffered a concussion.

Oh.

Oh, my.

Leaning against the doorjamb, his arms crossed over his chest, was the sexiest man I'd ever seen.

My heart started beating ridiculously fast.

He quirked an eyebrow at my speechlessness. "Has someone pressed your mute button?"

That was funny, so I managed a semi-deranged smile as I drank him in. My eyes roamed him from head to toe, and as I took in all his glory I felt this funny little dip low in my belly, so low it was quickly followed by a shock of aroused tingles between my legs.

*Oh.*

*Oh, okay.*

*That was new.*

*Desperately trying to ignore the tingles and failing, I attempted to force myself through the arousal and my shyness to interact with the stranger. The stranger who I was guessing was Nate. Jo had told me all about Cam's super-hot friend Nate. She had not exaggerated.*

*Movie-star gorgeous, Nate had a natural tan that you just didn't expect from a Scottish person, and eyes so dark they were practically black—though right now they were glittering with mischief. He was smiling too, showing off a pair of sexy dimples and perfect white teeth. All this plus a straight, strong blade of a nose, lips I was staring unashamedly at because they reminded me of a certain swarthy, off-the-wall actor's, and from what I could see of the lean, muscled biceps revealed by the T-shirt he wore, the guy was also roped.*

*Miracle of miracles, his T-shirt actually distracted me from his muscles.*

*It had the words* RESISTANCE IS FUTILE *printed across it.*

*The paralyzing shyness that usually took me over when I was faced with a hot guy melted into the background as I burst out laughing. "Consider yourself one of the Borg, do you?" I gestured to his T-shirt, which referred to the catchphrase of an alien race on* Star Trek.

*He glanced down at the words, seeming surprised. When he lifted his gaze to me again his dark eyes were smiling. "You got that reference? Most women think I'm being a cocky bugger."*

*I laughed even harder, leaning against the kitchen counter. "I imagine it's a little bit of that too. And you can understand their mistake. You don't look like a* Star Trek *fan."*

*Something sharpened in his eyes, something intense. I shivered as he lazily ran his gaze down my body and back up again. His voice was lower, thick, as he replied, "Neither do you."*

*That intent look felt like a slow caress. If I was anybody else I'd think he'd meant to make me feel like that.*

*Still . . . my breath caught. The air felt suddenly too thin, broken by this weird electricity between us that I didn't quite understand.*

*"Are you one of Jo's friends?"*

*I struggled to fight the shyness that was starting to creep in again. "Didn't Cole tell you?"*

*"Peetie went in to see the wee man. I wanted a drink, so I came straight to the kitchen." His eyes were devouring me again, and apparently my body had been asleep until his eyes touched it because there was a whole lot of tingling, shivering, and overheating going on. "Definitely the best choice I've made in a while."*

*Um . . . okay?*

*"Oh, well, I'm Olivia."*

*Nate's eyebrows lifted and then he abruptly cleared his throat, his body jerking upright from the doorjamb. Just like that, the air in the room began to return to normal. "You're Olivia? Of course. The accent. Of course."*

*I nodded, confused by his reaction. "I'm guessing you're Nate?"*

*His smile was friendly. Platonic. That made more sense. "Aye, that would be me."*

*"Cam and Jo are on their way. I was just cleaning up for them."*

*"Right." He wandered farther into the kitchen and I watched him with open fascination as he got himself a glass of soda. "Want one?" He gestured toward me with a glass.*

*"I'm okay."*

*Once he had his drink, he smiled at me again and I realized that the reason I wasn't so tongue-tied around him wasn't just because of his nerdy shirt. It was his eyes. They were impossibly kind, and I just felt . . . not quite comfortable . . . but, yeah, not uncomfortable either. That was definitely unusual for me around guys I'd just met. Especially ones I was attracted to.*

*"Do you play video games, Liv?" he asked congenially.*

*"Uh, yes."*

*"Well, stop cleaning up the dishes and come play with us," he teased.*

*I chuckled. "Are you asking me on a playdate?" As soon as the words were out of my mouth, I regretted them. I wasn't being flirty. I didn't know how to be flirty! That was just my sense of humor, and now this guy was going to think I was coming on—*

*Nate laughed, cutting me off. "Only because you got the* Star Trek *reference. Otherwise, girls aren't allowed to play with us. They're icky."*

*Deadpan, I crossed my arms over my chest. "Well, boys are icky too."*

*He grinned huge. "Ain't that the truth." He nodded toward the door. "Come on, Yank. If I'm going to annihilate you I want it to be quick and painless. I'm merciful like that."*

*"Annihilate me?" I guffawed. "I think you must have me confused with someone who's not about to whup your ass."*

*"Do you even know what game we're about to play?"*

*I shook my head. "Does it matter at this point? I'm going to beat you whatever it is. So, first we trash-talk, then we commence the ass-whupping."*

*Nate threw his head back in laughter. "Oh, man! Come on, funny girl." He took hold of my elbow and I fought to hide my blush at his touch. "I have to introduce you to Peetie."*

*I followed him out of the kitchen, touched by how quick he was to include me. I also sensed I was to be indoctrinated as "one of the guys." I sensed this because it happened all the time. I was okay with that. It just meant squashing the fluttering in my stomach whenever I gazed at Nate. And by squashing, I meant I'd have to crush those little fuckers into nonexistence . . .*

"Liv? Liv, you okay?"

I blinked again, coming back to the sidewalk, to Stirling, to the cold.

To Nate, who was standing right in front of me now with a concerned line between his brows. "Where did you go?"

I smiled. "Sorry, I think the cold has numbed my brain."

"Well, come here, you"—he looped my arm through his, pulling me close—"before a finger drops off."

I relaxed gratefully into his strong side. "Couldn't you have done that earlier? Like, three streets ago?"

"And miss the horrified look on your face every time we turn a corner?" he teased, rubbing his hand up and down my arm.

I grimaced, but I was used to his teasing, so I let it go.

"I'm sorry, folks." Jo threw the comment over her shoulder, her quick glance filled with guilt. "I should have made sure we put on coats."

"W-w-we're Sc-c-ottish," Ellie chittered, her fingers curling into Adam's coat. "We c-c-can ha-a-andle it."

I squeezed Nate's arm as we started to walk forward again. "Well, I'm American," I reminded them. "*And* I'm from Arizona."

"I'm American and I'm okay," Joss said, sounding a lot more relaxed than she looked. Her weight wobbled as her stiletto hit a crevice in the cobbled street. Braden righted her as she cursed at the ground.

"That would be because of the six-foot-three shield you're huddled against," I replied dryly.

She laughed, cuddling closer into said shield. "Maybe."

"We're cold too," Nate put in. "We're just used to it, so we don't whine about it."

"No one is whining," Joss argued. "This is just our way of warning Jo that if she doesn't hurry up and get us to our destination, we're going to use her for firewood."

Jo laughed. "We're almost there . . . I think . . ."

We turned down a street that took us off the high street, and Jo frowned up at the buildings as we followed her. It was just an average street, with vans and cars parked all along it.

Today was Cam's twenty-eighth birthday, and while we all assumed we were getting dressed up for a night out in Edinburgh to celebrate, Jo had a secret plan up her sleeve. Somehow we'd ended up in Stirling, a beautiful city with a gorgeous castle and quaint little streets, but also quite possibly the tiniest city on earth.

I had no idea what Jo could possibly be up to by dragging us there.

Suddenly she broke out into a massive grin as she stopped on a corner facing a bar. "We're here."

We all looked at the bar and then shared puzzled expressions. There was nothing particularly glamorous about the bar. It was . . . just a bar.

"Where's here?" Cam asked quietly, his mouth twitching with amusement.

"Here." She gestured upward and we followed her motion to the street sign drilled into the brickwork above the bar entrance.

## CAMERONIAN PLACE

I burst out laughing as it all began to make sense.

"You dragged us to Stirling for a street sign?" Nate asked her incredulously.

Looking unsure, Jo nodded. "It's not just any street sign. It's Cameron's birthday. He deserves to have a birthday drink in his very own place."

The guys, with the exception of Cam, looked a little nonplussed by her thinking. Her fiancé, however, pulled her close and stared into her eyes in a way that made my chest compress with emotion. "I love it, baby." He kissed her softly. "Thank you."

A mixture of happiness and envy rooted me to the spot for a second. I adored the fact that Jo had someone in her life who worshipped the ground she walked on, but I often wondered to myself if there would ever come a day when a guy would look into *my* eyes as if there were nothing else in the world worth looking at.

Ripped from my musings by the group's teasing of Jo, I laughed with them all as we wandered into the warm bar together. We were perhaps dressed too formally for the casual atmosphere, but since we were a pretty laid-back bunch, not one of us was really put out by Jo's little adventure. In fact, I think even the guys secretly thought it was cute of her.

It was *definitely* cute of her. She was a sweetheart, so when she did stuff that was unbelievably cute—like hauling our asses to a different county just so Cam could have a drink on a street with his name on it—I was never surprised.

My dad had spoken of her since the moment I'd met him. At first I'd been resentful of this little kid who'd had my dad for the first thirteen years of her life while I'd grown up with just the specter of him. My mom had never said a bad word against Dad, and being a somewhat precocious kid growing up with friends whose divorced parents were acidic around each other, it struck me as kind of odd that Mom wasn't mad at the guy who hadn't stuck around when I'd come along. I'd begun an investigation, wearing down my mom for months until finally she broke.

I remember how incredibly angry I was at her that she had never even told my father that I existed.

After she met Dad while she was studying abroad at the University of Glasgow, they'd begun an intense affair that Mom abruptly ended by going back to Phoenix at the end of her program. It wasn't until she got back to the States that she discovered she was pregnant with me. She wouldn't confess until many years later that the reason she didn't get in touch with my dad was because she loved him so much, and she didn't want him coming into her life out of obligation. I loved my mom, but she wasn't infallible. She was young and she made a selfish decision. At thirteen I couldn't see past that for a while. It took us time to get back to a good place.

Time I would later regret ever wasting.

The fact that Dad dropped his entire life in Scotland to come and be a father to a little girl he didn't even know he had until I reached out to him was a testament to the kind of man he was. He uprooted his whole life to become a part of mine. But in doing so he left Jo behind.

When Cam first contacted my dad about getting back in touch with Jo, I thought about how much my actions had changed her life. With a father in prison and an alcoholic mother, my dad, who was a longtime friend of Jo's dad, had been the only stable parental figure she and her brother, Cole, had in their lives. Of course, Dad didn't know until we returned to Edinburgh that Jo's mom, Fiona, had become such a severe alcoholic, leaving Jo to raise her kid brother on her own. Dad and I were carrying around our own little weights of guilt because of that.

However, the guilt was eased whenever I spent time in Jo and Cam's company. After everything she'd gone through, Jo had finally found a guy who saw how incredible she was and treated her with the respect and love she deserved.

As I sipped the pint of lager Nate had bought me, I looked around at my friends. Here I was, surrounded by people who had been through hell and come out the other side to find the person they wanted to spend the rest of their life with.

Besides Jo and Cam, there was Joss, my fellow half American, half Scot, who fled to Edinburgh to escape an empty life back in Virginia. When I thought about all that Joss had lost, I honestly didn't know how she'd kept going. I knew how it felt to lose my mom when I was twenty-one, but I couldn't imagine what it must have been like for Joss to lose her entire family when she was only fourteen years old. From all accounts she was still pretty messed up about it when she moved in with Ellie and met Ellie's brother, Braden. Apparently they'd had their ups and downs because of Joss's issues, but had finally gotten through it all. They were getting married in three weeks.

Then, of course, there were Ellie and Adam. I was pretty close to Ellie because we shared a similar romantic idealism, and she'd told me the entire story of her and Adam. She'd been in love with her brother's best friend for years, but he hadn't noticed her until her eighteenth birthday, and he didn't make a move on her until a few years after that, and even when he did he said it was a mistake. Apparently he didn't want to ruin his friendships with her and Braden. There was a *lot* of back and forth until Ellie was ready to walk away from him for good, but when my beautiful and strong friend was diagnosed with a brain tumor, Adam finally stepped up to be with her. Luckily for us all, Ellie's tumor turned out to be benign, and luckily for Adam, he'd come to his senses just in time to win Ellie over for good. They'd been engaged for a while but had only recently told us, now that she had an engagement ring sparkling on her left hand.

I was surrounded by love, and not some cheesy, overbearing, faux in-your-face kind of love, but real, intimate, I-know-all-your-quirks-and-habits-and-still-love-you kind of love.

"You've got your final dress fitting on Monday, Joss," Ellie suddenly said, taking a sip of her mojito.

She was sitting next to Adam, who was squashed in beside Jo and Cam in the only available booth at the back of the room. Joss, Braden, Nate, and I were standing crowded around the table, and I was cursing myself for letting Jo talk me into the four-inch heels I was wearing.

Leaning into Braden, Joss replied, "Thanks for the reminder. I'll have to brace myself against Pauline's caustic remarks."

Cam frowned. "Why did you buy a dress from this woman if she's such a cow?"

"The dress," Jo, Ellie, and I answered in unison.

After having been in Edinburgh for only three months, I was honored when Joss asked me to be one of her bridesmaids. Her university friend Rhian had come up from London for the weekend, and we'd all gone on the hunt for Joss's dress and the bridesmaids' dresses. After a few arguments with Ellie regarding color, Joss had settled on champagne for her girls. We'd ended up in this bridal store in New Town where the owner, Pauline, made scathing remarks about our lack or overabundance of assets.

We were too busty, too flat, too skinny, or too fat . . .

We were about to head out of there when Joss stepped out in a dress the bitch had recommended and Ellie burst into tears.

Yup, it was that beautiful.

Clearly, Pauline knew how to dress brides—she just didn't know how the hell to talk to them. Or to people in general, for that matter. I'm not exactly the most confident person, and have more than my fair share of insecurities regarding my body, so I came away from that store feeling like a heifer of giant proportions. *Thank you, Pauline.*

Joss laughed and looked up into Braden's face. "Apparently the dress is good."

"I'm getting that," he murmured. "Still, I'm more looking forward to taking it off you than anything else that day."

"Braden," Ellie bemoaned, "not in front of me."

"Stop kissing Adam in front of me and I'll stop making sexual comments to my wife in front of you."

"She's not your wife yet," Nate reminded him. "No need to rush it."

I snorted. "Nate, your commitment phobia is showing again."

He turned to me in mock horror. "Where?" He patted his cheeks anxiously. "Get it off me."

Brushing my thumb across an imaginary speck on his cheekbone, I reassured him. "There it is. All gone."

"Phew." He took a swig of his lager and looked toward the bar. "I'll never get laid with that thing on show."

"Charming," I murmured.

He grinned cheekily at me and nodded toward a group of women standing at the bar. "Duty calls."

He sauntered casually across the room and came to a stop beside a girl standing with her friends. The friends shimmied to the side as Nate and the girl began flirting their asses off. The girl was gorgeous, of course—beautiful features, long dark hair, creamy skin, extremely curvy. Probably a little overweight, like me, but unlike me, she carried it well. I had to say that about Nate. He didn't really have a type—he didn't care if the girl was skinny, plump, busty, or athletic. As long as she was cute and a woman, he was attracted to her.

As soon as Nate smiled at the brunette she was a goner.

I wasn't surprised in the least. At five foot eleven, Nate wasn't exceptionally tall, but with his combination of a trim physique honed by martial arts, a gorgeous face, and the kind of charisma you just couldn't buy, most women wouldn't give a rat's ass if they towered over him in heels if it meant being on his arm for the night.

Not me, though. Nate would never see me in a sexual way, so there was no point in even allowing my thoughts to go there. I think I knew more about the real Nate than most people did, so it wasn't hard to put him in the friend zone. I could switch off whatever attraction I had to him because I knew it would never go anywhere. I'd rather have Nate in my life as a friend than not have him there at all. For all of his commitment issues and the unashamedly playboy mentality toward women, he was a really good guy underneath it all, and a really good friend.

"Well, she's a goner," Joss commented softly.

Turning toward her, I raised an eyebrow when I saw her smirking at Nate and the girl. "He never makes them any promises."

She laughed. "No need to defend him. I know Nate always makes himself clear, but we're talking girls here. Sometimes they just hear what they want to hear."

"Yeah, but Nate's got this down to an art. It's like a sixth sense or something. As soon as he feels even a slight change in their attitude toward him, he's out of there."

"I can't wait for someone to knock him on his arse," Ellie joined in, smiling wickedly in Nate's direction.

"Me neither." Jo flicked a pointed glance up at me before looking away, and I pretended I was too stupid to understand her meaning.

I changed the subject quickly. "Did you guys see Cam's new tattoo? Cole designed it," I told them proudly.

Cole Walker was the best kid ever. Jo had done an amazing job raising him and the best thing that had ever happened to the both of them, other than each other, was Cameron MacCabe. He and Cole were incredibly similar—both artists, both cool nerds—and Cam had commissioned Cole to design a new tattoo for him.

It was awesome.

A stylized "C" and "J" were hidden in the jagged vines and sharpened curlicues of Cole's tribal design.

"Ooh, let's see," Ellie begged with a grin.

Cam shook his head. "It's on my ribs."

"Oh, come on, it's not like we're going to pass out at the sight of your abs," Joss teased.

"They're good abs." Jo patted Cam's stomach proudly.

Braden took a sip of his whisky. "Personally, I don't want to see his abs. They might . . . provoke my envy."

Adam nodded in deadpan agreement. "Mine too."

"Fuck off," Cam muttered, his lips curled up in amusement.

"Oh, if he's going to be such a spoilsport . . . ," I grumbled, digging through my handbag. Feeling the paper between my fingers, I tugged and pulled it out, unfolding it to hold up the signed drawing of Cole's design. "Here, this is the tat."

As the others looked at it, Jo smiled up at me. "You're keeping that?"

"Sure, and I got Cole to sign it too."

She laughed. "You're only going to make his crush on you worse."

I shrugged, not caring. "He deserves to know how awesome he is."

"No arguments there."

We smiled at each other as the others complimented Cole's talent.

Nate soon returned to the group, and the brunette returned to her friends but kept her eyes on Nate.

"Are you not . . . ?" I asked curiously, pointedly looking in the woman's direction.

"Oh, aye." He grinned boyishly. "But I told her it was my mate's birthday and I wanted to hang out with him for a while."

True to his word, Nate stayed with us until closing. We were all getting ready to leave when his breath whispered across my ear. "I'm off."

I turned around to stare at him, spying the curvy brunette in my peripheral vision. "Okay. Have fun."

He winked at me and then kissed my cheek. "Always do."

After saying good-bye to the group, Nate took the girl's hand and departed the bar. Jealousy needled at me as I stared at the empty doorway. My friend was the master of seduction. If he wanted to get laid, he could.

Unfortunately, for some of us it wasn't nearly so easy.

# CHAPTER 2

*Edinburgh*

Dad and I came to the decision to stay in Edinburgh not just because of the empty black hole Mom's death had left for us in Arizona—although that sure was a big part of it—but because I'd lost my job, my way, and my enthusiasm for pretty much everything. Mom had been diagnosed with cancer when I was sixteen. She fought it, but it came back three years later. When I was twenty and a junior at the University of Arizona, I took a few months out from studying to go home and be with her.

She passed away two days after my twenty-first birthday.

It took a lot of persuading from my dad to get me to go back to college, but I did, graduating with a master's in Information and Library Science a few years late. I got a job back in Phoenix at our neighborhood public library, but three months before Cam got in touch with us our small library was closed due to lack of funding and I was out of a job.

It was really crappy timing, since I was just beginning to get back on my feet after losing Mom. The trip to Edinburgh couldn't have come at a better time.

"Uh, excuse me."

I blinked out of my daze and leaned across the counter of the library help desk, giving the exasperated girl in front of me a patient smile.

The library was split into two divisions—User Services and Library and Collections. I worked in User Services, on a staff of about forty-five people. Out of those forty-five people at least nine of us had a degree in library science. Only two were librarians—my manager, Angus, and my supervisor, Jill.

Ellie's stepdad, a professor of classical history at the University of Edinburgh, had given me a reference at the main campus library that helped me get an interview. Unfortunately, there were only so many librarian jobs to go around; I did get a job, but as a library assistant. I didn't feel too bad about that. I was just happy to have a job in my profession.

Normally I spent either the morning or the afternoon at the help desk in the forum of the library or in the reserve section, and the other half of the day in the office doing administrative work. I preferred being front of house and interacting with the students. I'd been there only eight months, but already I was familiar with a number of students, and had a great rapport with them and my colleagues.

"How can I help?" I asked loudly over the chatter of noise in the forum.

Beyond the security gates at the main entrance of the library was an area around the staircase that students had taken to using as a hangout. At the far end of the hall was the help desk, where they could manually check out their books, and beyond us was the reserve section, where they could check out material for either three hours or one week, depending on the proviso put down by the course head. The fines we made them pay if the reserve material was overdue were heavy, to say the least. We're talking two pence a minute, which is roughly three cents a minute. Doesn't sound like much, but if a student didn't return the material for a week, or two, or a month . . . Yeah . . . you see where I'm going with this. My least favorite part of the job was telling students what their fines amounted to in the reserve section.

The girl leaned in close, her cheeks flushed. "I'm partnered with a student who has an accessible room. Unfortunately, we can't get into that room right now because of . . . students and certain activities going on in there."

When she blushed harder, I instantly understood and glanced over my shoulder at Angus, who was taking a folder out of a filing cabinet. Angus, a bald, good-looking forty-something with kind eyes and a sharp sense of humor, overheard her comment, and his lips twitched with laughter as he said, "Your turn."

I grimaced but smoothed my face into perfect serenity when I turned back to the student. "Of course." Rounding the main desk, I caught up to the girl, whose whole body was rigid with embarrassment. God, I hoped I was walking into a little mild making out and not full-on sex. Horny little bastards. "I take it your friend forgot to lock her room last time she used it?"

The accessible rooms were small private rooms on the first floor, with lockable doors. They were reserved for any of our students with a disability. Those students were permanently assigned a room for the semester; however, more times than I'd like to count, I'd been tasked with kicking students out of the rooms not only for using them when they shouldn't have been but for utilizing them as hotel rooms.

Having caught two students going at it in the less-than-hygienic men's toilet, though, I was no longer surprised by anything.

As we rounded the staircase, I had to forcibly ignore the smell of coffee floating toward me from the student café. I would so much rather have been sitting down drinking a latte than playing whatever you called the opposite of a brothel's madam.

"She must have forgot." The girl pressed her lips together. "But that's not really the point."

I supposed I had to give her that.

When we reached the first floor, I flicked my long hair over my shoulders, threw them back, and marched into the main room, striding past study booths, study pods, and a bunch of giggling students who sat across from the accessible rooms. Attempting to look like I meant business, I looked back at the girl. "Which one?"

She pointed to room three.

Drawing in a breath I marched forward, gripped the handle, and thrust the door open, only just refraining from squeezing my eyes closed.

A girl squealed as a guy growled, "What the . . . ?"

I watched with my arms crossed over my chest as he quickly pulled up his zipper and she righted her dress. She slid off the desk, clinging to the guy, her eyes bright with laughter.

"This is not a hotel room," I told them calmly. "And the library is not a rendezvous point. *Capice?*"

"What are you, Al Capone?" The boy laughed, gently pushing the girl toward me and the door.

I sighed heavily. "Just have a little consideration for the general public, okay?" My eyes quickly looked him over as I raised an unimpressed eyebrow. "No one wants to see that."

The girl giggled while the guy laughed me off, brushing past me.

That would make it the fifth time since I'd started working at the university that I'd thrown someone out of one of those rooms for inappropriate behavior.

And they say a library is a boring place to work.

I'd returned from my tour of duty at the help desk to work in the reserve section. Tidying up and keeping an eye on the help desk, I was thinking about what to cook tonight for me and Nate, since he was coming over to work at my flat, when Benjamin Livingston showed up.

Trying to act cool, I slipped past the bookshelves and hurried behind the desk in case he required some assistance. A huge part of me hoped that he did, while the other part was terrified that he would.

The guy was beautiful—and not like Nate's obvious man beauty, but in this rugged, outdoorsy, I-can-chop-wood-with-my-bare-hands kind of beautiful.

I'd helped Benjamin out a few times. Of course, I hadn't managed to speak more than a few words to him, and they had been muttered under my breath in case they came out in the wrong order, which my words tended to do around a guy I was attracted to. From what I could tell by the resources Benjamin borrowed, he was a postgrad student in history. I usually saw him a few times a week, and lately I'd begun to really look forward to seeing him.

At six four, Benjamin Livingston was all broad shoulders, crooked smile, and light green eyes I could swim in. The last time I'd seen him, I'd fantasized about screwing him behind the book stacks. It occurred to me after he left that I may have developed a bit of a crush on him. I was trying to work through my shyness, in hopes of having an actual conversation with him.

I don't know where my inadequacy with the male species originated. Because Mom was sick for a good portion of my adolescence, I didn't have the same free time as other kids, since I tended to mother my own mom quite a lot. Plus, I was shy with boys at school. I had two dates in high school and only one of them ended in a makeout session that was memorable only for its sheer awkwardness

College was pretty much the same until after my sophomore year. I stupidly decided to get rid of my virginity by getting tipsy and sleeping with a senior I barely knew. It was awful. It hurt, it was awkward, and once he was done he rolled off me and left. I couldn't remember a time when I'd felt more humiliated, more empty, or more inconsequential, and I took a severe hit to my confidence. Really, I'd just been so afraid to try again after that, that I didn't. And then in my junior year it became clear that Mom wasn't getting better, so I left to take care of her.

By the time I went back to college I was so conscious of my inexperience with men that it just made me morph from an outgoing woman into a preadolescent with a speech impairment. Moreover, the fact that I was so body conscious played a huge role in my lack of seduction skills too.

"Hi there."

My eyes widened a little as Benjamin approached the desk, shuffling his backpack up, his biceps flexing nicely under his blue shirt as he did so.

He smiled at me, that adorable lopsided grin. "It looks like I've got a fine to pay." He passed resource material over to me and I took it while I stared into his eyes.

*You can do this.*

To function I was going to have to look away. It was like staring into the sun for too long.

Fingers trembling, I scanned the material and then flinched at the fine that appeared on the screen.

"Ouch. That bad, eh?"

Did I mention he had this divine Scottish accent that made me want to lick him?

I took a deep breath, shoving that thought aside. "It's overdue by three days, so that's eighty-four pounds."

He winced. "Won't be doing that again. What kind of rate are you guys charging?"

*It's not my fault! It's the library gods!* "Two pence a minute," I replied quietly.

"Ah, okay." He smiled reassuringly at me as he handed me his bank card. "My own fault for ignoring the reserve section rules."

It took less than a minute to pay his fine, but that forty seconds was forty seconds during which I could have asked him anything. Instead I worked mutely and couldn't even meet his eyes when I handed him back his receipt and card.

"Well, thanks."

My eyes were trained on his chin as I shrugged. *Shrugged? What the . . .*

" 'Bye."

My own chin lifted slightly in acknowledgment.

And then he was gone.

So much for that whole conversation thing.

Turning around with a deep groan, I slowly bumped my head off the wall, back and forth, back and forth.

"Uh, Liv, you okay?" Angus's voice spoke behind me.

My cheeks flushed at having been caught, and I jerked around to face my boss. "Just checking building stability. It's all good."

Angus raised an eyebrow at me. "How about your mental stability?"

"That's definitely next on the agenda."

## CHAPTER 3

Every week my dad, Jo, Cam, Cole, and I tried to meet up for a dinner together, and that night we were at my favorite Italian restaurant, D'Alessandro's, on India Street, right around the corner from my flat. Cam and Dad often fought over the bill, but Dad had height and age over Cam, so he usually won.

I loved these dinners. Not just because I loved the food at D'Alessandro's, but because Jo, Cam, and Cole had really become family for me and Dad, and us for them. Especially Cole. From everything I'd learned about his life before Cam, Cole really had only Jo. Now he had this makeshift family. A family he deserved. Jo had said Cole's instant camaraderie with me was a rare thing indeed, a camaraderie we all knew had turned into a bit of a crush. Cole was too cool to ever make the crush awkward, and I always pretended to be completely unaware of it. To the outside observer Cole could have passed for eighteen. He'd grown another few inches these past nine months, taking him to six feet at fifteen years old. His broad shoulders had filled out from training with Cam and Nate at judo, and his upbringing had given him this air of maturity that most kids his age didn't have. However, to me, and I knew to Jo, because we'd talked about it, he was just this little kid we adored. That could drive him crazy sometimes, since most people treated him like the young adult he appeared to be.

"Have you read any new books I might like?" the object of my musings asked as I took a sip of wine.

"Yes, I have actually. Angus recommended this sci-fi novel about this dystopian underground society. You'll love it."

"Cool. Can I get it in e-book?"

"Yup. I'll send you the link."

"Okay, cheers. By the way I finished *War of the Worlds*."

I raised an eyebrow. "Elaborate? What did you think?"

He shrugged. "I thought it was quite realistic for what it was and when it was written. It was pretty bleak. I liked it."

Catching my eye across the table, Cam smiled at Cole's review. "Keep coming with the bleak."

I put two fingers to my forehead and saluted him. "Gotcha."

Cole rolled his eyes at us. "It's not an emo thing or anything. Books with unhappy or grim endings just . . . make you . . . I don't know. Feel more, or something . . ."

He seemed embarrassed to have admitted that he had feelings (the horror!), and I felt the need to reassure him. "I understand. Unhappy and bittersweet endings have a tendency to stay with you, affect you long after you've finished the story."

"Ellie might argue with you on that," Jo murmured, exchanging a cheeky grin with Dad.

"No might about it," I cracked. "Still, I'd have to stand my ground on it. Although I love a good romance with a happy ending, I have to admit that unhappy endings have more of an impact on me."

I felt my dad's stare and turned to find him frowning at me.

"Put that away." I scowled, gesturing to the furrow between his brows. "I am perfectly okay."

"You prefer unhappy endings to happy endings," he argued.

"In literature. Not life. Lit-er-a-ture."

Dad leaned across the table to me. "You'd tell me if there was something the matter."

"Oh, my God." I shot a pleading look Jo's way.

"Of course she's okay," Jo said, rescuing me. "She's successful, she's gorgeous, she has her own flat, lots of friends, and an overbearing dad who loves her. Now leave her alone."

Dad was glowering as Jo teased him. After a few seconds he appeared to process her words and his shoulders relaxed. He turned to me. "I worry about you in that flat all by yourself, that's all."

"I'm rarely in it alone. Nate relocated his office there."

For some reason this made my dad scowl. That was immediately followed by Jo choking on laughter. I turned a swift glare on her and she choked harder.

Honestly, I didn't know what it would take to make her realize that Nate and I were completely platonic. When we'd first met, we'd hit it off. Sometimes you meet people who you're just comfortable with, and Nate was one of those people. We both felt free to be who we were around each other, and we'd bonded over two things. One was our sense of humor. We were both a little nutty. Second was our inner geek. We both embraced our inner geek.

Nate was a freelance photojournalist, but he made a nice second income as a film and video game reviewer for an international film and entertainment magazine. Whereas a lot of people would look at him and think movie star, in actuality he was closer to my species—geek. He'd started a blog when he was nineteen, reviewing movies, books, and video games. This blog grew so big over the years that by the time he turned twenty-five he had thousands of followers. This and his intelligent, funny, personality-infused reviews caught the eye of the magazine and they offered him a job. Luckily for me he'd taken to bringing the movies over to my flat to watch, and he could be pretty hilarious. I was known to have my moments too. Some of my commentary had even made its way into his reviews.

"So, Olivia, any funny library stories this week?" Cam asked, changing the subject for me.

I smiled gratefully. "I had to kick another couple of lovebirds out of the accessible rooms."

"Jesus, they really . . ."

But I didn't hear the rest of what Cam had to say because the door to D'Alessandro's opened and the world faded around me as *he* walked in.

Benjamin Livingston.

My breath caught as he walked to the host's podium with an older couple beside him. His parents maybe?

I didn't know. Frankly, I didn't care. All I cared about was that he was there and he might see me. If he saw me, he might recognize me and try to talk to me. Then again he might see me and not recognize me. I didn't know which was worse. All I did know was that I did not want my family and friends to witness the horrifying meltdown of Olivia Holloway Bumping into Handsome Man.

"Liv, are you really okay?" Jo asked, pulling my gaze from Benjamin to her. Her beautiful green eyes were wide with concern. "You look . . . buzzed."

"I'm sorry, Cam." I apologized quickly for blanking on him, my gaze flicking back over to Benjamin.

Shit! The hostess was taking him past our table.

"I must have—" I deliberately swiped my elbow across the table, knocking my dessert spoon onto the floor. "Oops. Excuse me." I pushed my chair back and dropped heavily to the floor, ducking my head under the tablecloth. Heart pounding in my chest, I stayed there, watching familiar walking boots stride past the table.

*He* was out of range. Or, more precisely, I was.

The tablecloth lifted and my dad's rugged face appeared in front of me. "Have you been smoking the wacky-backy?"

I pressed my lips tight to stop myself from bursting out laughing. Shaking my head, I reached out a trembling hand for my dessert spoon. I was going to need a replacement, since there was no way I wasn't having dessert. The tiramisu at D'Alessandro's was to die for. Of course I might die of embarrassment before I got the chance to charge to my death for dessert. "Just retrieving fallen cutlery."

"You're acting stranger than usual."

I huffed and the movement caused me to bump my head against the table. "Can we not have this conversation under here?"

His head disappeared and I quickly scrambled out after him, craning my neck to look for Benjamin. There was no sign of him as I pulled myself back onto my seat, and I slumped with relief as I realized the hostess had taken them into the other dining room.

I settled quite happily now that he was gone, smiling as I raised my spoon to a passing waitress. "Can I have a clean spoon, please?"

When she nodded, I grinned and turned back to my companions.

They were all staring at me. I flinched at their appraisal. "What?"

"Mick's right." Cam raised a speculative eyebrow. "You're weirder than usual."

I looked at Cole for help, but he just shrugged, and I took that to mean he agreed with them. Not wanting anyone ever to find out about my hopeless crush on Library Guy, I searched for an explanation. Finally I chose the creatively lacking "I had three Red Bulls today."

Creatively lacking it might have been, but it worked, and soon conversation was diverted from me and my absurdness.

To my chagrin, before dessert arrived disaster struck.

I needed to pee and I needed to pee badly.

Unfortunately, the toilets were down the corridor and opposite the other dining room, putting me in the possible path of Benjamin.

When my bladder couldn't take it anymore, however, I had to throw off my concerns and bolt for relief.

By the time I reached the restroom I wondered what I'd been freaking out about. I was moving so fast to get to the toilet in time that I was a blur. Benjamin would never recognize my bursting-bladder-induced blur. *Hmm, say that five times fast.*

Despite my growing calm, I had every intention of becoming a blur on my trip back to my table. Regrettably, I didn't factor in a collision with a wall as I came out of the restroom.

I stumbled back, blinking fast, as my eyes took in the dark blue wall. My brain very quickly processed that it wasn't in fact a wall . . . but a chest. A man's wide chest.

My heart began to thud in my own chest as my eyes drifted upward, my heartbeat escalating, sweat prickling my palms as the familiar and masculine beauty of Benjamin Livingston dwarfed my world.

I was pretty sure my mouth was hanging open unattractively as he grinned, his eyes alight with recognition.

*Oh, balls.*

"You work at the university library, right?"

Swallowing, I rehearsed my answer in my head. Then I managed a nod. "Assistant desk help." *No, that wasn't right.* "I mean help desk assistant."

So much for rehearsal.

His smile widened and he stepped a little closer, shutting off the oxygen supply to my already gasping brain. "Well, you're always very helpful."

And then somehow Maggie Smith possessed me. "It's what I do," I answered solemnly with a Scottish accent.

A freakin' Scottish accent.

Thankfully a pretty good one.

But that wasn't the point.

My cheeks burned with embarrassment as Benjamin chuckled softly. "Right."

I had to get out of there. I had to get out of there now! "Well, my table is waiting for me at the family."

Giving him a tight smile and ignoring his lip-twitching amusement, I shot past him, down the corridor, and into the other dining room. Plates and glasses tinkled as I collapsed gracelessly in my chair and announced loudly, "I think we should take dessert to go and hang out at my place. Like right now." I nodded encouragingly. "Yes?"

# CHAPTER 4

I was frustrated.

It was a few days later and I still hadn't quite recovered from my mortification. The object of my crush had made an appearance at the library, and as soon as I saw his blond head bobbing through the main reception area, I scurried into the admin office and persuaded my colleague Rachel that, yes, I would, in fact, prefer updating the Web site html and answering e-mail complaints instead of hanging out at the fun help desk.

Suffice it to say I was not in a great mood when I finished work that day, but as I turned the corner onto Jamaica Lane and saw a familiar figure leaning against the door to my building, my step lightened along with my mood.

Nate grinned, his dimples appearing as he lifted a white plastic carrier bag. "Chinese food and an alien invasion flick with some pretty-boy actor who will probably make me want to stick a pen in my eye."

I smiled at him in confusion, the smell of the takeout causing the greedy little growlers in my stomach to wake up. "Didn't you have a date tonight?" I asked as I shoved my key in the lock and led us into the dark, dank stairwell.

"She phoned me this afternoon to ask if I'd be okay with us going to her sister's engagement party instead of dinner. Apparently the party was 'impromptu.'" His unimpressed expression told me he didn't believe it for a second. So did the air quotes.

"A family event on the first date?" I gasped in mock horror. "How dare she?"

"You're funny."

"I know." I flashed him a quick grin and let us into my tiny one-bedroom flat. Tiny though it was, I loved it.

The kitchen and living room were one room. The kitchen was shaped like an L and took up most of the room, leaving space for a couch, an armchair, and a television. Fortunately, the bedroom was a good size and I could fit in a couple of bookshelves, but most of my books were scattered around the apartment. Also, I didn't have a bathroom. I had a toilet/shower room.

It worked for me.

It was cozy.

Shrugging out of my coat, I watched as Nate sauntered into the kitchen and began getting plates out and arranging our dinner for us. "Got you orange chicken, babe. That okay?"

He called me "babe" in that rumbly, rich voice of his all the time. I tried not to shiver each time. I failed. A lot.

"My favorite," I called to him as I headed into my bedroom to dump my coat and kick off my shoes. "There's beer in the fridge if you want one."

"Got it. Do you want one or will I pour you a glass of wine?"

"Wine, please."

"I picked you up a tub of Rocky Road too for later. I'll just stick it in the freezer."

Seriously, I could marry this guy. Strolling back out into the main room, I smiled gratefully at him. "I'm promoting you to best friend."

He frowned as he poured me a glass of Rosé. "I thought I got that promotion ages ago."

"You were promoted to best friend with equal friend status to Ellie and Joss. You've just graduated to Jo's level."

"Which is higher?"

"Yes."

Nate seemed to consider this. "Are there perks to this promotion?"

I answered gravely. "Yes. You get to bring me Chinese food and Rocky Road ice cream all the time."

He looked at me blankly.

"Don't worry. You can handle it. You're doing so well already." I rubbed his shoulder affectionately as I rounded the kitchen counter. "Do you want a coffee first?"

"I'll get it."

"No, no, go sit down, set up the movie. I'll bring it over."

Nate arranged my plate on the coffee table next to him and went about putting the movie on. He'd just relaxed back on the couch with plate in hand when I came out of the kitchen with his coffee.

"Would you rather die after being experimented upon by aliens, or be eaten by cannibals?" Nate asked casually, lifting a forkful of beef and rice to his mouth, his eyes never leaving the television screen.

I pondered his question as I placed his mug on the table and then curled up on the corner of the couch with my own plate. "Have I been given anesthesia?"

"Does it matter?"

"Well, yeah. If I've been given anesthesia then it doesn't matter which one I choose because I won't be aware it's happening to me."

Nate shook his head. "Not true. It does matter. If aliens experiment upon you they might find something from their research that they could use to destroy the entire human race. Or infiltrate us like in *Invasion of the Body Snatchers*. Cannibals, on the other hand . . . well, I'm guessing all they want is . . . to just eat you."

I couldn't fault his logic. I waved my fork at him in a gesture of agreement. "Good point."

"So? Aliens or cannibals?"

"Aliens."

"Me too. Fuck the human race—cannibals are creepy bastards."

I burst out laughing, almost choking on rice as I inhaled sharply with amusement.

Nate chuckled at me, his dark eyes bright with affection. "You've got a great laugh, you know that?"

I had a very unladylike cackle of a laugh, but if he thought it was great I wasn't going to argue. I shrugged somewhat shyly, as I always did when he threw out a random compliment, and then gestured to his bag to change the subject. "Aren't you going to get your pen and paper out?"

Nodding at his phone on the coffee table, Nate answered, "Voice recording."

He was recording our conversation? "I better shake out my sharpest wit, then."

"Just the usual commentary will do fine."

Ignoring the slight insinuation that I wasn't witty, I took another bite of chicken and moaned around it. "God, this is good."

"Yeah?"

"So good."

"You like that, baby?"

"Oh, yeah."

"How good is it?"

"I think this is the best I've ever had, actually."

"That good?"

"My God, yes." The chicken was so tender and the orange sauce was just that perfect balance of sweet and tangy. "Mmm."

"That's right. Take it, baby."

I'd closed my eyes to savor my dinner, but now they popped open to find Nate shaking with silent laughter. My eyes darted to his phone and I mentally replayed what we'd just said and how it would sound on the recording.

Grimacing, I held my plate in one hand and launched a sofa cushion at him. "Very funny."

Nate laughed out loud now, batting the cushion away while holding his plate well out of range. "You make it too easy."

"You're a bastard." I shoved his hip with my foot. "You better delete it."

He looked back at the screen, still smiling. "No way. That one's a keeper."

It turned out Nate was right. The pretty-boy actor really did make you want to stick a pen in your eye. "That sucked," I opined as he took the DVD out of the player. "But I guess not every movie can be *The Wizard of Oz*." My favorite movie. "Or *The Godfather*." Nate's favorite movie.

His lip curled up at the corners. "Is that your expert opinion? Remember, you're on tape."

"That is my expert opinion." I yawned and tipped my head back against the couch. "I came up with some choice phrases throughout that movie. You hereby have my permission to steal them."

"Well, when discussing the acting skills of the kid playing the hero's dying brother I think I'll definitely be using, 'Dying is supposed to be sad. I feel as sad as a high school virgin in a Japanese love hotel with a prostitute and a wad of cash.'"

Nate had almost choked on a prawn cracker when I said that. I wrinkled my nose as he quoted me. "I really need to work on my editing. 'Virgin with a prostitute' would have sufficed."

"And yet not been nearly so funny. Your waffling is what makes you funny."

"I do not waffle."

"You waffle, babe."

Deciding to let it go, I smiled wearily at him. "Are you really going to write that in your review?"

"What? That you waffle?"

I rewarded his deliberate obtuseness with a blank expression and he shook his head, his gorgeous soft, dark locks shifting with the movement. His hair was longer than usual, but it looked good. Really good. Great, even. "A lot of teens read the magazine."

As he pulled his jacket on, I eased myself up off the couch and handed his cell to him. "Did you get everything you need for it?"

"Enough to annihilate it with words." He leaned over and pressed a kiss to my cheek, the warm, spicy scent of his cologne comforting. "'Night, Liv."

I smiled and stepped back to let him pass, then followed him to the door. "Thanks for dinner and my Rocky Road."

Nate grinned back at me. "Thanks for the quotes."

The door was almost closing behind him when I suddenly grabbed the handle. "Nate."

Turning on the second step of my stairwell, he raised two questioning eyebrows at me.

Looking at his hair, I shrugged and leaned against the door. "Don't cut your hair, okay?"

His smile was slow, cheeky, and incredibly cute, and I totally pretended not to feel it in my long-neglected woman parts. "Like what you see, do you?"

Laughing, I leaned back, readying to close the door. "Just helping a bud out. I know you like to look your best for the ladies."

I'd almost closed the door when he said, "Liv."

I peeked back out at him.

His eyes were bright with mischief. "Don't stop leaving your red, wet underwear around the flat when you have a man around. We like that. Just helping a bud out, you know. "

*What?*

My eyes bugged out in horror as I turned to look around my apartment. Red caught my eye and mortification sank in. My lacy bra and panties were draped over the radiator, drying.

How did I not notice this?

"Kill me, kill me now," I moaned, my cheeks blazing with embarrassment as I winced at the sound of Nate's laughter echoing down the stairwell.

After I'd locked my front door I started to clean up, sporadically shooting lethal glares at the drying underwear, as if somehow it was the underwear's fault I was stewing over the fact that Nate now knew I had a taste for sexy lingerie.

Finally I rolled my eyes and told myself to buy a sense of humor.

As I undressed in my room, pulling my gray jersey pajamas out of the dresser, I caught a glimpse of myself in the mirror. I was wearing my favorite emerald green satin lingerie set today. In the bottom of my dresser and in a wicker box in my closet, there was plenty more where it came from. I liked nice underwear, but I didn't like looking at myself in it. I just liked the feel of it.

Frozen, I took in my wide-eyed expression as I indulged in a long look in the mirror. What I saw made me want to hunch my shoulders over. What I saw stole away the good mood Nate had put me in, and it reminded me why I would never end up with a guy like Benjamin Livingston.

It's not that I was ugly—I knew that. It was just that when I looked in the mirror I didn't see anything particularly special. I saw a plain face, with the exception of the high cheekbones Mom gave me and my dad's unusual golden eyes. I saw flabby arms. I hated those flabby arms of mine. At five seven I wasn't short, but I wasn't tall enough for my height to carry my ever-widening hips, pretty huge ass, and little rounded stomach. Thankfully I didn't have a thick waist, but you couldn't tell that to the little pouch on my lower belly that refused to be flat.

After losing my mother to cancer, I knew and I believed that having a healthy body was far more important than having a skinny, fashion-friendly one. I knew that.

*I knew that.*

Yet somehow I still didn't feel sexy or attractive. It was more than frustrating—it was painful—to *know* what was right but *feel* what was wrong.

Saddened that I, a smart, semi-funny, nutty, loyal, good woman, could feel so negative about myself under all the smiling and humor, I felt the sting of tears in my eyes. The way I felt about my physical appearance was *bad*. Really freakin' bad.

My fists clenched at my sides as I stared at my average figure.

I was so taking up Pilates in the morning.

The smell of dinner wafting into the room was causing overproduction of saliva under my tongue. After three days of cutting out food that was bad for me and painfully enduring a Pilates instructional DVD, I was more than ready to chow down on Elodie Nichols's hearty Sunday roast.

"I swear to God I'm going to gnaw off a finger," I muttered, examining my hand.

"Pardon?" Ellie asked absentmindedly as she looked at photographs of the flower arrangements Braden and Joss had chosen for their wedding. The arrangements had been selected months ago, as was everything else. After a disastrous start with Ellie as wedding planner (not because she couldn't do it, but because she and Joss had such different tastes), Braden had taken over organizing the wedding and Joss had helped with the decision making.

"Why are you staring at those photos? Again?"

"I would have gone with roses."

"Well, I went with lilies," Joss butted in from across the room where she was sitting on the arm of the chair where Braden was relaxing. He was talking about something with Adam. Clark was in the other armchair by the television, somehow managing to grade papers among all our chatter. His son, Declan, a twelve-and-a-half-year-old computer geek, was huddled on the floor with Cole, playing a Nintendo DS, while Mick and Cam sat on the other end of the sofa that Ellie and I were on.

Jo had disappeared upstairs with Ellie's sixteen-year-old half sister, Hannah. They were really close and tended to disappear to Hannah's room for a chat before dinner.

Ellie smiled at Joss. "They're still really pretty. I'll just go with roses in my wedding."

"Do you like roses, Adam?" Joss asked, grinning mischievously at Ellie.

Adam blinked as he was drawn out of his discussion with Braden. "Sorry?"

"Roses? For your wedding? Ellie wants them."

"Ellie can have what she wants."

Looking a little nonplussed, Joss asked, "You don't have a say in it?"

He frowned. "Nope. My only job is to turn up and say 'I do.'"

Joss made a face at Braden, who looked as though he was trying really hard not to laugh. "How come Adam gets the job I wanted in *our* wedding?"

Braden's mouth twitched. "You could have had that job. I did offer to do everything myself."

"But . . ." She glanced from him to Ellie to Adam. "There was definite emotional manipulation involved. Ellie's not doing that to Adam."

Now Braden was laughing. "What emotional manipulation? I do believe I said something along the lines of 'Well, I'll plan the wedding, then.' Nothing more. You were the one who got all mushy and grateful and decided to help out."

Joss's eyebrows hit her hairline. "Mushy?"

"Uh-oh," Ellie muttered under her breath.

I smirked and impishly added fuel to the fire. "Joss, you can be a little mushy. You try hard to hide it, but it slips out sometimes."

"Uh-oh," Ellie muttered. "Silly Olivia."

I shrugged, smiling, as I awaited Joss's reaction, which was almost always guaranteed to be funny.

Instead she just stared at me, seeming unable to come up with a response. Finally she slumped back against the arm Braden had wrapped around her waist. "I don't do mushy," she murmured. "I do tender. There's a difference."

"Tender?" Adam raised an eyebrow in disbelief.

Now she definitely looked affronted. "I can do tender. Braden, tell him."

Her fiancé grinned, and my chest did that achy, flippy thing again when he leaned over to press a loving kiss on her shoulder. God, I wanted what they had.

Joss turned to look over her shoulder at him. "Was that an affirmative?"

Braden laughed softly and looked up at Adam pointedly. "Jocelyn has her own brand of tender."

The way he said it was filled with innuendo and she rolled her eyes and straightened away from him. "Now you're just being annoying." She gave us an indignant stare and insisted, "I can do tender."

"I believe you," I replied, trying not to laugh.

Adam quickly turned the conversation back to whatever it was he was discussing with Braden while Joss pretended to ignore them by pulling out her phone and checking her e-mails.

I nudged Ellie. "So what do you think Hannah and Jo are talking about upstairs?"

Ellie glanced up at the ceiling and blew air out between her lips. "Hannah's been quiet lately—I suspect a boy is in the picture. She looks the way she looks and is absolutely hilarious and yet she's not been out on a date yet?" Els looked incredulous. "That just doesn't seem right. I think she's hiding a romance from us."

"You must be dying to know for sure."

"Oh, I am." Ellie's pretty pale blue eyes were wide with curiosity. "But the most important thing is that she has someone to talk to, even if it's not me."

I frowned in thought. "Why isn't it you?"

"I think she thinks I'd get caught up in it and fail to give her real advice. Hannah is more of a realist than I am. I think if it's a boy issue she'll feel more comfortable discussing it with Jo. Jo has a more practical outlook on these things, whereas I might get a little overenthused about it all. I mean, my wee sister's first romance—that's huge."

"You are so dying to know what is going on with her."

"Eh ye-uh, it's killing me."

"Dinner!" Elodie called from the dining room, and we all shot up as though we'd been starving for days.

We crammed into the dining room, inhaling the aroma of good food. Only three months ago Elodie and Clark had invested in a larger dining table because her Sunday dinners had rapidly grown in size since Joss's arrival into their lives.

"Work going okay?" Dad asked me as we settled into our chairs next to each other.

"Mm-hmm," I answered absentmindedly, handling the hot bowl of mashed potatoes as if they were made of pure gold.

Dad snorted. "You've got a wee bit of drool on the corner of your mouth."

"No, I don't." I slapped the mash on my plate gleefully and passed the bowl to him, then immediately reached for the gravy.

"What's with the cartoon hungry eyes? You not been eating right?"

"I'm on a stupid diet," I muttered.

I felt my dad tense next to me. "What the hell for?"

"To torture myself. I'm a masochist now."

"Liv, you know I don't like those fads. There's nothing wrong with you."

Oh, no. My confession had probably just bought me one of my dad's famous food-shopping trips. When I was at college, he'd turn up at the dorm every once in a while with brown paper bags loaded with food even though I had nowhere to put it. "I have a full fridge at home, Dad. Don't even think about it."

"Hmm, we'll see."

I took a forkful of buttery mash and closed my eyes in sweet relief and said, "So good, I don't even care," except I said it around a mouthful of potatoes, so it came out more like "Mu muu, u mmu mmm mmm."

"Mick, is Dee going to the wedding with you?" Elodie asked from the opposite end of the table. "Last time we spoke you said she wasn't sure."

I glanced at my dad, wanting to know the answer to that question too. I had to admit, even though I was a grown-ass woman of twenty-six, it was still weird seeing my dad with someone who wasn't Mom.

About four months ago, Dad started dating Dee, an attractive artist in her late thirties. Dad had reopened his painting and decorating company in Edinburgh, M. Holloway's, and hired Jo. He'd already built up a great reputation and had recently hired two more guys to join their team. Back when it was just him and Jo, they took a job for this wealthy young couple in Morningside who'd bought their first home. It was a fixer-upper. There they met Dee, a friend of the couple who had been commissioned to paint a fairy-tale mural in the nursery. Dad and Dee hit it off. She was the first woman he'd dated seriously since Mom died.

I was very much aware that I should be grateful to Dee. Since her appearance, Dad had less time to worry over me, which he did. A lot. When we decided to settle in Edinburgh, I made a point of getting my own apartment. We'd been in each other's pockets for a long time, and I really needed my space—I loved my dad to pieces, but sometimes his concern made me feel like there really was something wrong with me. The addition of Dee was at once confusing and a relief. I guessed I should get to know her a little better, because all I knew at the moment was that she was nothing like Mom. My mother was a dark-haired beauty with sharp cheekbones that hinted at the Native American heritage in her blood. Her fantastic bone structure and her dark hair were the only interesting physical attributes she gave me. Somehow a merciless God had not deigned to bestow upon me my mother's beauty. It was her beauty that caught my dad's eye, and then it was her dry, often twisted sense of humor—which I did inherit—and then it was the calm around her. Mom could soothe any room just by being in it. She was this incredibly peaceful, relaxing person, and it emanated from her to everyone around her. It was a gift.

Despite her faults—her inconsiderate choices as a young girl—Mom was unfailingly kind, compassionate, and patient, which was why she'd made a great nurse. She'd handled her illness with a grace that always brought a lump to my throat whenever I let myself remember. She was a pretty reserved person, not overly confident, but not insecure or shy. Just quiet. Innately cool. You can't teach that kind of cool. I should know because I'm pretty sure she tried to teach it to me and it *clearly* didn't stick. I had no intention of trying to browbeat my inner geek for the chance to be cool. No, thank you. Me and my inner geek were loyal to each other. We had been ever since I was eight years old and my mother told me it was okay to be whoever I chose to be.

*"Mom, Arnie Welsh keeps calling me a geek. He says it like it's a bad thing. Is being a geek a bad thing?"*

*"Of course not, Soda Pop. And don't listen to labels. They don't matter."*

*"What are labels?"*

*"It's an imaginary sticker people slap on you with the word they think you are written on it. It doesn't matter who they think you are. It matters who you think you are."*

*"I think I might be a geek."*

*She laughed. "Then you be a geek. Just be whatever makes you happy, Soda Pop, and I'll be happy too."*

God, I missed her.

"Dee was supposed to be visiting some family down south, but she's canceled so she can come to the wedding." My dad's answer to Elodie's question brought me firmly back to the present.

"Oh, that's nice." Elodie smiled. "I really need to have her back over for drinks. And I think I might have another job for her. A woman at work is looking to have a mural painted in her conservatory. She's converting it into her grandchildren's playroom."

"I'll tell her."

"Are you bringing a date, Liv?" Clark asked me casually, honestly just making conversation.

For some reason, though, the question pricked me. I was in a weird place about my long-suffering singledom. Still, that wasn't Clark's fault. Pasting on a bright smile, I shook my head. "Nate and I decided to forgo the hassle of dates and just go together."

I saw Jo smirk at her chicken.

"Don't," I warned her under my breath.

She glanced up at me, all innocent and doe-eyed. "I didn't say a thing."

"Your smirk said it for you."

"I just think it's nice how close you and Nate have grown."

Sighing heavily, I looked to Cam for help and hoped he wasn't in the mood to tease me too. "Cam, please tell her."

Cam slid his fiancée a regretful smile. "Baby, they're just friends. Let it go. It's not going to happen. Not in a million years. Never. Ever."

*Ouch. That was emphatic.*

"Nate is hot." Hannah suddenly spoke up, and when I looked at her I found Ellie's pretty sister frowning at me. "Why don't you go out with him? I mean, he's really, really, really hot. I'd go there."

"Please tell me she did not just say that," Adam pleaded with the table, looking green.

"*She* has a name." Hannah raised an imperious eyebrow at him.

Joss seemed to be trying not to choke on her food. "Oh, she said it all right."

"My ears are bleeding." Braden looked at Joss for help. "They feel like they're bleeding. Are they bleeding?"

Hannah rolled her eyes. "I'm sixteen, almost seventeen, I have boobs, a whole bunch of hormones, and I find guys attractive. Deal with it."

"Well, there goes my appetite." Clark shoved his plate away, looking so despondent that I felt sorry for him.

Seeing his expression, and most probably understanding it better than anyone else at the table, my dad pointed an admonishing finger at Hannah. "That was cruel, Hannah Nichols."

Rather than be cowed by Dad, Hannah made her face split into a gorgeous, cheeky, remorseless grin that made a low chuckle spill from Dad's lips.

"Well," Elodie said with a sigh, "since Hannah has successfully ruined the appetites of her male relatives, that means more dessert for us girls. We're having sticky toffee pudding and ice cream."

"Och . . . well . . . you know, I'm feeling much better all of a sudden." Adam gestured to Braden, whose cheeks had warmed at the mention of dessert. "I could go for some pudding."

Braden nodded solemnly. "Funnily enough, me too."

Determined to stock up on good food before I returned to my diet-food-laden fridge back at the flat, I wasn't sure I wanted to share pudding with the boys. No, I wasn't sure about that at all. I looked over at Hannah and asked evilly, "What was that about boobs and hormones?"

# CHAPTER 5

The Proclaimers were sing-shouting at me that they'd walk five hundred miles and then five hundred more just to be the man that would fall down at my door. Frankly, I was touched.

"See?" I gesticulated wildly. "That right there are two men who know what it's all about!"

Nate caught my hips as I stumbled slightly against the table. His handsome face was kind of a blur, but I could make out his smile. "And what's it all about?"

I rested my hands on his shoulders and bowed my head toward him. "Love, Nate. That's what it's all about. That's what *everything's* all about." I shrugged sadly, and yes, very drunkenly. "Which means I got a whole bunch of *nothing.*"

"Uh-oh. Happy drunk turning maudlin drunk. I think it's time we get you home, babe." He stood up, pressing me back.

"What about your girl back at the bar?" I swayed into him and he wrapped his arms around me, holding me steady.

After kissing my nose, Nate leaned away and gave me a squeeze. "I can get laid anytime, sweetheart. Right now I'm making sure you get home okay."

"How d'ya do it, Nate?" I asked on a sigh, the reception a blur of color and noise around me.

"Do what?"

"Get laid all the time?"

"What do you mean?"

"You just—" I gestured to the bar but instead whacked him on the chin. "Oops, sorry. You just get numbers. I don't know how to speak to a man, let alone get numbers. Or get laid. La-a-a-aid."

"Who's getting laid?"

I spun around and almost caught Joss in the face with my flailing arm, but she swung back in time. "Good reflexes, beautiful!" I grinned loopily at her.

Joss laughed, shimmering in shapes and swirls in front of me. "Nate, I think it's time you got my bridesmaid home, yeah?"

"I'm on it."

"It was such a beautiful wedding, Joss!" I threw my arms around her and hugged her tight. "But I didn't get laid!"

Her body shook with laughter as she gently released herself from my death grip. "Well, that doesn't seem right at all. The men at my wedding must be blind."

"Och," I said, imitating Dad, "you're just saying that!" I pushed at her playfully but obviously harder than I meant to because she stumbled back, chuckling at me.

"Nate, get some water in her first before you put her to bed."

His warm body pressed against my back. "I'll take care of her, don't worry."

"Dude"—I twisted my neck to look up into his face—"you need to teach me to get laid first."

.  .  .

*Nine hours earlier*

A guitarist and violinist played an instrumental version of Paul Weller's "You Do Something to Me" as I walked down the aisle. I flashed a reassuring smile at Braden, who looked tall and handsome in his kilt. He, Adam, Clark, and Declan wore what was called a Prince Charlie gray jacket and matching three-button waistcoat. Their champagne silk ties were intricately knotted against their dark gray shirts, and because the Carmichaels were associated with the Stewart Clan, they were wearing a subdued Stewart Grey tartan. They looked fantastic.

Braden smiled back at me, not a nervous tremor in sight. Grinning at Adam, who stood as Braden's best man, I took my place on the other side of the altar beside Hannah, Jo, Rhian, and Ellie.

The music seemed to swell as Joss made it to the halfway mark of the aisle, holding tight to Clark—who'd been honored to give her away—as her eyes locked on Braden. She was stunning, and when I moved my gaze from her to her soon-to-be-husband I almost expired on the spot at the look in his eyes.

Wow.

Was there ever a man more in love than Braden Carmichael?

He gazed at Joss in her ivory-and-white dress as though she was the only thing in this world that could or would ever matter. I sucked in a breath, feeling my nose sting with stupid, girly emotion.

I shot a look at Ellie, who had tears falling down her cheeks, and that made me feel a lot less of a goofball. Smiling at her, I watched her sniffle, her cheeks turning rosy.

Rhian, Joss's school friend, who was a bit of a straight-talker and, honestly, a ballbuster, surprised me by taking Ellie's hand and giving her a reassuring squeeze.

All of us wore champagne silk floor-length dresses. The dress was sleeveless with wide straps and a sweetheart neckline that draped with the fabric, and it nipped in at the waist, then fell in a straight waterfall to the floor without hugging the body too much. It was a classy design, and we all wore it well, including Hannah, who looked very grown-up, standing three inches taller than me even though we were both wearing kitten heels.

Joss's dress was simple elegance. It was strapless, with a heart-shaped neckline, and the upper half of the bodice was ivory with crystal beading and lace. The finest white silk chiffon pulled across the bodice in a tight drape, fitted to Joss's tiny waist. From her hips the layers of chiffon, shot through with silver, fell to the floor, floating around her—not too puffy, not too straight. Just right. She wore her hair in an almost Grecian-style updo of soft curls and French braids.

When Joss reached Braden, her smile was tremulous and vulnerable in a way I'd never seen before. She pressed a kiss to Clark's cheek and murmured something to him as he slipped her hand into Braden's.

Braden nodded at Clark and then his focus was back on his bride, his large hand engulfing hers as he pulled her into his side, oblivious to their audience.

He whispered something to her and she whispered back. Whatever she said made him chuckle and lean down to press a kiss to her lips. For a few seconds he just stood there murmuring secret words against her mouth.

The minister had to clear his throat to get their attention so he could start the ceremony, and the guests tittered in their wooden pews.

The music drew to a stop and the ceremony proceeded. I couldn't take my eyes off Joss and Braden, and I'd be surprised if anyone else could either. Of course, it was their wedding and most people would be focused on the bride and groom, but there was something about how they were together that took you to someplace else.

It was epic what they had.

*Everyone* should have what they had.

"Have you recovered from the speeches?" I asked Joss as she came over to our table. The speeches were over and dinner was done. Adam had cracked us all up with his best man's speech, keeping it funny and real and not sentimental. Clark was just as down-to-earth when he gave a speech on Joss's dad's behalf, but it *was* sentimental, and very kind and compassionate, and when Joss ducked her head to fight back tears and Braden squeezed the back of her neck in reassurance, I don't think I was the only woman blotting her eyes.

Finally Braden stood up and gave his speech and, well, if every woman in the room didn't end up a little bit in love with him, then my name wasn't Olivia Holloway.

Joss looked radiant, and laid-back. "Almost," she said in answer to my question about the speeches. "I have a feeling that Braden's speech is a get-out-of-jail-free card for at least the first year of our marriage."

"It *was* a good speech."

"Tell me about it." She smirked, her gaze turning introspective in a way that made me suspect she was thinking naughty thoughts about her husband.

"So how does it feel?" Jo asked, her eyes lighting up as she unconsciously rubbed her engagement ring. "To call someone husband?"

"Weird," Joss answered abruptly.

Nate snorted and Cam laughed. "Is that it?"

She shrugged. "It's the first word that comes to mind."

I laughed too now. "Not 'great,' not 'wonderful,' not 'right'? Just 'weird.'"

"'Weird' definitely wins out."

"Marriage to me is weird already. Good to know." Braden came to a stop behind his wife, a sardonic tilt to the corners of his mouth.

"Well, I wouldn't want normal," Joss replied.

I gave a sharp nod of my head. "Agreed. Normal's boring."

"You would say that." Nate smiled at me. "You wouldn't know normal if it bit you in the arse."

"Oh, like you would?"

"I didn't say I wasn't weird. I'm just better at hiding it than you are."

"Why would I hide it?" I asked the entire group, my expression deadpan. "I'm awesome."

"No one would dispute that." Nate's eyes glittered with amusement.

Joss chuckled. "If you'll excuse us, we have more rounds to make."

We waved Joss and Braden off, and settled into random conversation.

"Hey, kiddos." Dad approached, looking dapper in his dark gray suit. His arm was wrapped tightly around Dee's curvy waist. She looked stunning in a flowing light blue maxi dress, her long blond hair falling in waves around her shoulders. "Dee and I are going up to dance. Care to join us?"

"Perhaps in a bit," Jo answered, her eyes soft as she looked at the older couple. Her expression said she was happy my dad had found Dee, and as I took in how relaxed he was, I knew for sure I was too.

"Have fun," I said, and grinned at them.

Dee smiled down at me. "You look beautiful, Olivia." Her eyes swept the table. "You all do."

"Well, so do you," I replied, and immediately beamed happily under my dad's approving smile.

I watched them walk onto the dance floor, feeling something shift inside me.

Not long after, Cole decided to reduce his boredom by seeking Hannah and Dec's company, and Jo and Cam wandered off to find Ellie and Adam.

"Want another drink?" Nate gestured to my empty champagne glass.

"Yes. Beer."

"You got it."

I watched him walk through the wedding reception crowd, so at ease with himself. He'd shrugged off his jacket, leaving him in his shirt and waistcoat. The sleeves of his shirt were rolled up and he'd loosened his tie. I could see most women following him with their eyes, so it wasn't a surprise when a gorgeous young woman in a light blue, short, fitted dress pressed into his side at the bar and introduced herself.

I had to wait twenty minutes for my beer.

If I'd had Nate's confidence I wouldn't have had to wait twenty minutes for a beer. I could have just strolled up to a nice-looking guy, started flirting, and he'd have bought me one. If I could believe in myself like I knew I should, I could get up off my butt and do just that.

In fact, I was going to.

I searched the room for nice-looking men and pretended I couldn't find any.

Slumping back against my seat, I mentally kicked myself in the shin, once again frustrated with myself.

After Nate was done flirting his ass off, he came back to the table and shuffled his seat closer to mine as he handed me my beer.

"She was hot," I observed.

The left side of Nate's mouth curled up, his dimple flashing me. "Sorry I took so long."

"Did you get her number at least? Or just a promise to hook up at the end of the night?"

His look said *What do you think?*

We sat in companionable silence for a moment, looking around the room at all the guests. I barely knew any of them.

"What would you prefer?" Nate suddenly turned to me conversationally. "Being perpetually stuck at someone else's wedding reception or at the wake of someone you don't know that well?"

I mused over this. "Do I know the person whose wedding it is well?"

"No."

"Are both reception and wake inside or out?"

Nate took a swig of beer. "Is this a weather issue?"

"Yes."

"We'll give both an even playing field. Inside."

I turned slightly into him, ready to give him my answer. "Okay,

I'm going to go with the wake. At the wedding I'd continually have to pretend to be happy, and it is far more exhausting to pretend happiness than it is to pretend sadness. Also, I don't know the wedding people very well, so I'm not going to know many of the guests well either. At a wedding reception that's just awkward. Moreover, we're talking a perpetual sound track of cheesy music, so we're talking a perpetual migraine. No thanks. At the wake of someone I don't know I can at least spend some of eternity getting to listen to the stories about that person from each guest. Who knows, maybe the deceased was some amazing adventurer who lived to the grand old age of one hundred. We're talking lots of stories that are sure to be interesting. There'd be no awful music. I could be miserable if I wanted, but if I couldn't pretend misery then no one would blame me since I didn't know the deceased that well. There's usually a buffet at a wake, so I'm more likely to find something to eat that I'll actually like. Plus, death always makes people act weird, so there might even be a hot, grieving guy who wants to have sex upstairs in the bathroom with me. That would pass the time."

Nate had been sitting with his beer frozen at his lips the entire time I'd been talking, his eyes slightly rounded as my explanation rambled on. Finally he said, "You put a lot of thought into that one."

I shrugged. "You have to think it through when you're talking about forever."

"Good point."

"So what would you choose?"

"The wedding."

I wrinkled my nose. "Why?"

His smile was cocky as his eyes searched the room. His gaze stopped on the blue-dress girl. "Because there are always women feeling sad that they're single, and they're more than happy to quell that sadness with the first eligible man in the vicinity."

"You're vile."

"Hey, I'm not the one who's planning to take advantage of a grieving relative for sex in the bathroom at a wake."

"Yeah, well, at least I'd have the bathroom to go to. Where on earth are you taking these sad, lonely women if you're stuck at the reception?"

"I think the bathroom would work for me also."

"A public toilet?" I arched a brow at him. "Have you done that before?"

"Don't ask questions you don't want the answers to."

"Oh, I want the answer," I replied, eyeing him curiously.

Nate ignored me, staring off at the dance floor. "You want to dance?"

With an inner sigh of disappointment, I let him off the hook and shook my beer at him. "Get a few more of these in me and then maybe."

Grinning, he got up. "I'll be right back."

Suddenly the room shifted and the soft mattress of my bed was under my back, the ceiling of my bedroom in my line of sight. A feathery touch on my feet had me pushing up onto my elbows and I saw Nate taking off my shoes. After I almost knocked Joss off her feet with a serious lack of coordination, Nate had been as good as his word and had gotten my drunken butt in a cab and practically carried me up the stairs to my flat.

"I haven't had sex in seven years," I blurted out, not caring if Nate knew this embarrassing fact about me.

His head jerked up at my confession as he pulled off my right shoe. "Are you kidding?"

I shook my head, pouting a little.

"Seven years?"

"Seven years. I've slept with one guy, Nate, once. It was awful. I was awful. I'm crap at sex, I can't flirt. I'm a loser." I felt tears prick my eyes and flopped back against my pillow.

Nate finished taking off my other shoe. I felt the bed dip at my side as he sat. "Come here, you." He pulled me up and I melted into his arms, his chin resting gently on my head. His warm hands rubbed my back soothingly and in response my drunken tears fell silently.

"You are not a loser," he told me gruffly. "You could never be a loser, Liv, and I don't want to hear you call yourself a loser again."

"Okay," I mumbled.

We sat in the quiet for a while and then I decided since he knew so much he might as well know everything.

"There's a guy at the library. A student. Postgrad. I like him, but I sound like Rain Man every time I try to talk to him."

Nate made a choking noise in the back of his throat.

"Are you laughing?"

He cleared it and answered shakily, "Never."

He was so laughing.

"It's not funny," I told him grimly and pulled wearily out of his arms to fall back against my pillow, my eyes finally drifting shut. "I'm going to die alone, Nate."

And as unconsciousness pulled me toward it, I thought I heard him whisper, "Not on my watch, babe."

# CHAPTER 6

How had cotton balls gotten stuck in my mouth?

Smacking my lips, I pushed my tongue up against my teeth and attempted to rid myself of the dryness. As soon as my lips parted, my head jerked back against my pillow and pain shot across my forehead, around my temple, and down the back of my skull.

My breath did not smell good.

As I bravely forced movement into my limbs, the ache and wave of sickness that rose from my fragile stomach were just two more pieces of evidence pointing toward one conclusion:

I wasn't just hungover.

I was hung-the-fuck-over.

*Ugghhhhhh.* Groaning, I turned on my side and gently pried my eyes open. The hope was that I had been smart enough last night to leave a glass of water by my bedside before I'd passed out. As soon as my eyes hit the glass I knew smarter would have been to bring a *jug* of water to my bedside. I'd emptied the glass already.

For a few minutes I flicked my gaze back and forth between the glass and my bedroom door, hoping for a miracle every time my eyes swung back to my bedside table.

But no. It looked like I was going to have to get up off my drunken, smelly ass and get my own refill. I shuffled up to a sitting position, whereupon the room suddenly spun around, and with the spinning a memory slammed into my brain, knocking me back against the headboard.

Nate taking me home and getting me into bed.

That memory was like a key unlocking the rest, and as everything I'd said came flooding back in fits and starts, my cheeks burned with mortification. I grabbed at my phone in the hope that I'd find something there to prove that my brain was making up all those memories, but I found only a couple of texts from Jo and Ellie, asking me if I'd gotten home all right.

I slammed the phone back on my bedside table and then flinched in pain from the noise.

*Holy. Balls.*

I'd admitted to Nate I hadn't had sex in seven years, that I'd only had sex once, that I was shit at it, and that I had a whopping big crush on Library Guy.

"You. Are. An. Asshole, Olivia Holloway. *Ass. Hole.*" I glared up at the ceiling and felt the prick of tears in my eyes. I'd told Nate something I hadn't told anyone. Drunk off my ass, I'd ripped open my insides and shown them to the biggest player I'd ever met. Now every time I saw him, I would remember how I had laid myself bare to him.

I was a walking wound and I'd given Nate Sawyer total access to throw salt and anything else he liked on me.

Squeezing my eyes shut, I ignored the warm tears trickling down my cheeks and tried to reassure myself of Nate's loyalty. Even though I'd exposed myself completely, all I had to do was talk to him and make him promise not to tell anyone, or to talk about it. Ever again.

This was Nate. He was my friend. My good friend. I could count on him to just put this behind us.

The buzzer to my apartment knifed through my skull and I moaned, burying my face in my pillow. After a few minutes my phone rang.

Blindly, I reached for the cell, picked it up, and shoved it against my ear. "What?" I asked into my pillow, so it was more of a growl than a word.

"Open the door," Nate demanded softly and then hung up.

Heat rushed to my cheeks again. I'd thought I would at least get the chance to be sober and, you know, *clean*, when I got to face him again. Still in my bridesmaid dress, I rolled out of bed, fell, and then stumbled my way to my ungainly feet. Nate started ringing the buzzer again and I swear to God the noise was going to make me upchuck the delicious dinner I'd had at Joss and Braden's reception.

"All right!" I yelled as I picked up the entry phone and slammed my palm on the button to let him in.

To save the irritation of going through more banging, I swiped my hair off my face and clumsily unlocked the door, hearing Nate's footsteps ringing up the stairwell as I opened it. Through the jet-black strands of my wild hair I saw his face appear.

"You look like shit," he observed cheerily, looking way too sober and happy for someone who had been drinking the night before.

Skin prickling with embarrassment, I grunted at him.

He held up a bag. "I brought you aspirin, energy juice, and donuts."

I must have turned green, because he sighed, brushed past me toward the kitchen, and advised, "You need to eat something."

I grunted again and turned toward the bathroom. Seeing the crazy-haired lady with the globs of mascara around her eyes, pasty pallor, and lipstick smeared across her mouth, I gave a little shriek.

"You okay?" Nate asked warily.

My fingers shook with the hangover as I leaned across my sink. "I look like the Bride of Frankenstein with a massive hangover."

"I'd be hungover too if I'd just had to fuck Frankenstein."

Despite myself I giggled and then groaned when the sound ricocheted painfully through my noggin, as my dad called it. I took a couple of deep breaths and then fought through the hangover tremors and the nausea to wash quickly, brush my teeth, scrape my hair off my face, and scurry into my bedroom to change into a pair of jersey pants and a T-shirt.

Nate smiled at me from behind the kitchen counter as I approached. "There she is."

Unable to meet his gaze, I lowered my eyes to the glass of orange juice, bottle of energy drink, aspirin, and donuts he had laid out for me. Mumbling my thanks, I swallowed the aspirin and sat my ass down on a stool to nibble on a donut. After five minutes of total silence, Nate finally leaned across the counter and forcibly lifted my eyes to his by tilting my chin up with his fingers.

Everything from last night passed between us.

"Please," I whispered, my lips trembling as I fought the tears of vulnerability. "Please don't tell anyone, Nate."

His dark eyes widened slightly. "So it is true?"

Instead of answering, my gaze sharpened.

Nate sighed. "Who am I going to tell?"

"Nate."

He held up his hands in a gesture of surrender. "I promise, all right."

I went back to chewing on my donut, my skin burning from the heat of Nate's attention.

"How can it be possible, Liv? You're an attractive, outgoing woman . . . How . . . ?" He seemed flabbergasted. Honestly, that was kind of nice. Flattering.

Which was probably why I was finally able to meet his gaze as I replied, "I've always been shy around guys I'm into, but more than that I just wasn't really in the game. I never have been. My mom was sick when I was a teenager. When other teenagers were experiencing boys and kisses, dates, and sex, I was busy fussing over my mom. Then she got sick again when I was in college." My eyes burned into his. "*You* know, Nate."

And he did know.

An offbeat sense of humor and an inner geek weren't the only things Nate and I had initially bonded over. We'd bonded over a third thing: the Big C.

While I lost Mom to it, Nate lost his childhood sweetheart to lymphoma. They were only eighteen when she died.

Not a lot of people knew that about Nate, and I had the feeling I was among the privileged few who had gotten the whole story out of him. It explained a lot about him.

"It consumes you," I whispered. "You don't care about anything else. Nothing else mattered but spending every second I could with her."

He swallowed hard, his eyes dropping to the table. "I get it, Liv."

"By the time I got out of college I was—I *am*—constrained by my self-consciousness." I looked away from him. "Having such a lack of experience . . . it has shredded what little confidence I might have had."

We were silent a moment as Nate seemed to process this. Finally he turned my face back again so I had to look into his eyes. I found his expression solemn and thoughtful. "You were really sad last night, Liv. I've known you for almost a year and you know me probably better than most people, and yet last night I felt like I was getting to see a huge part of you that you've kept from me. From everyone."

Tears filled my eyes, my throat burning as I tried to keep them in. "I don't want to be the person who looks in the mirror and hates what she sees, or be the person that moans about how she can't interact with a guy long enough to secure a date. That's not a good person to be, Nate. I just want to be like everyone else. Have a relationship with the opposite sex. But I can't. It's pathetic. But at least I'm not pathetic enough to moan about it."

"It's not pathetic," he snapped, his eyes flashing. "Liv, you've been through a lot. You can't expect to be normal. And to hell with normal. Normal's boring. And you, babe, are anything but boring."

I smiled weakly, grateful that he was trying to cheer me up, but not really feeling cheered up.

"And this guy?" Nate continued gruffly. "This guy at the library. You like him?"

Nodding, I dropped my head to my hands and groaned at my crappy situation. "Yeah, I like him."

Nate contemplated this, and when it appeared he wasn't going to say anything, I lifted my head from my hands and stared at him questioningly. He smirked at me.

"What?"

"You have next to no experience, and I have too much."

My mouth twisted with annoyance. "It's not really a good time to brag about that shit, Nathaniel."

He grinned at me. "I'm not bragging. I'm helping."

"Helping?"

"Helping you."

"Helping me how?"

"Helping you get laid."

My cheeks grew even hotter. "Uh . . . what?"

Appearing quite happy with himself, Nate leaned back against the counter, crossing one ankle over the other and his arms across his chest. "I know sex. You don't. I'm going to teach you."

Feeling a flush of . . . *something* . . . I blushed to my roots. "How are . . . How does that . . . ?"

"First we work on your confidence. Next we work on your flirting. I'll get you to a point where you feel confident enough to approach this guy you like and ask him out."

My heart was racing at the thought. "I don't think you understand the magnitude of my ineptitude when it comes to men."

"Well, that's the wrong atti*tude* to start with." He shook his head and leaned, palms down, on the counter, his face ducking so our noses were only inches apart. "I may not do flowers, hearts, and all that shit with women, but you're my friend, and I consider myself the kind of person a friend can always turn to. Friends are important to me, Liv. And last night a friend cried in my arms and admitted she was unhappy." He brushed my cheek affectionately. "You deserve happiness, babe. What's the harm in letting me help you try to obtain it?"

"Nate," I whispered hoarsely, my throat clogged with emotion. That was so effing nice I was seconds from bursting into big goofy tears.

"We'll take it step by step. We'll start off by trying to work out why you don't feel confident enough to talk to men you're attracted to."

I nodded, and then winced when the movement caused a sharp streak of pain through my skull. "But not today, right? Because I might puke on you."

He grinned and straightened to his full height. "Sexy. But no. Be ready, though." He winked at me as he grabbed his jacket and readied to leave. "Lessons start tomorrow."

My mind was whirring with the turn the conversation had taken, so it wasn't until he was almost walking out the door that I realized I hadn't acknowledged what he was offering.

"Nate."

He stopped, his hand on the door handle. "Aye?"

My smile was slow but filled with appreciation. "Thanks."

Nate grinned and yanked the door open. "Anything for you, babe."

All throughout work I'd been a jittery mess, playing off my absent-minded clumsiness as a result of day two of my epic hangover. Angus was sympathetic and let me spend most of the day in the back office doing quiet admin work, but that still didn't stop me from messing up, and sooner rather than later, his sympathy waned. When adding html to the library Web site, I'd advertised our new student pods incorrectly. We already had pods on the first floor where large groups could sit in a booth and use the computer for working together on projects and tuto-rials. Additional pods had been set up on the second floor, and these accommodated fewer people. This was explained in the main text, and then there was a picture of the pod and a little tagline that should have read, "Maximum use: six." Instead of "six," I wrote "sex."

We didn't know until Janey, a young colleague of mine who was obsessed with checking out the Facebook page "Spotted: Edinburgh Uni Library"—a page used primarily for students to ask out students they'd seen in the library, but also a page for them to post about students who'd pissed them off in the library, or done one of a million disgusting things noted online—discovered it on the student page. It had greatly amused our student body. It had not greatly amused my boss.

He sent me home early, where I downed about six cups of tea in hopes of finding whatever harmony it was that British people thought tea provided. No harmony to be found.

Nate was coming over to start our lessons and I was ready to upchuck what little I'd eaten all over him.

About twenty minutes before the time he was set to arrive, my dad called me. He was over at Dee's and they were inviting me to dinner.

"I'd love to, Dad, but I can't. Nate's coming over."

"Nate's always over," Dad replied, not sounding happy about that.

"Nate's my friend."

"Hmmph."

"Dad."

"He's a player."

"We're just friends," I promised, although my skin was tingling with the anticipation of the possibilities for tonight. What on earth was he really going to be able to teach me? And how would he do it? I was going to die of embarrassment. I just knew it. Nate was all sex and charisma. He probably had a mouth on him. No, I knew he had a mouth on him. Would he expect me to talk to guys the way he talked to girls?

My eyes bugged out at the thought.

"Liv, you there?"

"Yeah, Dad."

"Dee's asking if you'd like to come over for dinner on Wednesday night instead?"

"Sounds great. I'll be there."

"How are you feeling today? Still hungover? You were pretty smashed at the wedding."

I nervously ran my fingers through my hair as I tried to think back to the reception. "Did I, uh, say anything embarrassing?"

Dad laughed. "No. You were a funny drunk, sweetheart. Who took you home, by the way? You never said when I texted you yesterday."

"Nate took me home. He's decent like that," I pointedly reminded him.

"If you say so."

My buzzer sounded and I flinched. "Got to go, Dad. Nate is here."

We said good-bye quickly and I hung up as I hurried to the door to let Nate in. I was standing tapping my foot impatiently as I waited for him. The sounds of his footsteps in the concrete stairwell seemed to match the rhythm of my heartbeat, and by the time he appeared in my doorway I was just about ready for passing out.

Nate reared back at the sight of me. "Christ, you look as though you're about to faint."

I gulped. Loudly. "Nervous over here."

He shut the door behind him, grimacing. "What the hell for? It's just me."

I glared at him.

"Okay. Be nervous." He strode past me, shrugging out of his jacket. He threw it on the couch and then walked into the kitchen to take two beers out of the fridge. I caught the one that he tossed to me. Uncapping his beer, he gestured to me with the bottle. "To calm your nerves."

When he didn't say anything for five minutes—five very *long* minutes—I sat down on the arm of my couch and took a sip of beer.

"Okay, talk me through it." Nate suddenly spoke up and I almost coughed on my beer at the seeming loudness of his voice in my little flat. "What happens exactly when a guy you're attracted to speaks to you?"

Trying not to be any more of a dork than I already was, I fought back the blush that was determined to stain my cheeks. "I get tongue-tied."

"Why?"

"I'm very tempted to insert a sarcastic reply here, but I'll just go with a simple shrug." I shrugged.

"Don't give me that 'I don't know, and if I did, I wouldn't need you' bullshit. Why do you get tongue-tied?"

I was really attempting not to get pissed at him. That wouldn't be a good start. Clenching my teeth, I answered as if it was obvious— which it so was—"I don't have a lot of confidence."

Nate considered me a moment. "In yourself? In your looks? In your sexual experience? What?"

"Do you know how mortifying this is?" I scowled at him.

Clearly annoyed, Nate narrowed his eyes at me. "I'm not here to make fun of you. I'm here to help you."

We were quiet again as I gathered together the confidence to be honest. After taking a shaky sip of my beer, I looked at the floor and told him quietly, "You already know I lack confidence because of my minimal sexual experience, but . . . I also just don't . . . don't feel sexually attractive."

His silence drew my gaze to him. He was looking at me incredulously again.

"What?"

He put his beer down and planted his palms on the counter like he meant business. "Let's start with how you don't feel sexually attractive."

I gulped. "All right."

"Are you fucking kidding me?"

I jerked back at his curse, confused by the angry tone of the question. "What?"

"Get up," he replied sharply. "Come on, get up." He rounded the kitchen counter and walked past me.

I got up slowly, wondering what the hell I'd done wrong.

"Follow me."

Follow him . . . all right. My legs trembled when I realized I was following him into my bedroom. With my heartbeat pulsing in my throat, I was unable to speak as I stopped in my doorway and gazed at him.

He stood before my full-length mirror and gestured to it. "Tell me what you see."

I swallowed past the heartbeat. "Nate . . ." I took a step back and my movement shot him into action. Lightning-quick, he had hold of me and was tugging me back into the room with him until he'd maneuvered me in front of the mirror, while he stood looking into it over my shoulder.

"Tell me. Trust me."

Taking a deep breath, I let my eyes focus on my reflection, sweeping them over my face and then down my body and back to my face again.

"Liv?"

"I see . . . I see an average-looking woman with . . ." I shrugged, so embarrassed it wasn't funny. "With fl-flabby arms, a belly pouch, and a fat ass."

When my answer was met by silence I finally gathered the nerve to look up into the mirror to Nate's reflection. He was glowering at me again. "Anything good?"

I glanced back at my face. My eyes were, as always, the only thing I liked. They were striking eyes, inherited from my dad. Unusual, pale hazel, with so many flecks of gold they appeared golden in a certain light. We both had dark lashes that set the color off. We'd been told on more than one occasion, and by quite a few folks, that our eyes were exotic, almost feline. My dad worked his eyes. They were flinty and perceptive in his ruggedly handsome face. On my average face they were the only thing to enliven my features. "My eyes," I whispered softly.

"That's a given, babe. What else?"

Tense, I searched for an answer and then said carefully, "Okay, my skin. I have good skin."

Nate smiled encouragingly at me. "You've got gorgeous skin." He heaved a beleaguered sigh. "Let's tackle the other stuff." I was pretty sure he then muttered under his breath, "Crazy fucking women," before he took hold of my arm. "Where are these flabby arms of yours, then?"

Skin flushing the color of raspberries, I pushed the fat around my triceps.

I was rewarded with a "what the eff?" look from Nate. "That's not flab. It's skin. Look, you've not got any definition, but you've also not got flab. Rule number one . . ."

I nodded at him to go on, my eyes wide, eager to learn.

". . . don't use the word 'flab' around a guy you want to shag. Now, if a guy's like me he can get past the self-consciousness and decide to think it's cute, but there are loads of guys out there who don't think it's cute. They want a confident woman in their bed. I don't know if this library guy is one of those guys, so we'll play it safe. No more flab talk."

For some reason that really made me want to giggle, but I also wanted Nate to know I was taking this seriously, so I pinched my lips together and nodded.

"Okay. Next."

I blinked in confusion again. "Next?"

"The supposed fat arse?"

The touch of Nate's hand on my ass caused me to jump about ten feet, but he didn't let go, smoothing his hand over my butt and giving it a gentle squeeze.

*Whoa, okay, then.*

My skin was prickling and there was a suspicious fullness in my breasts and lower belly that I adamantly tried to ignore.

"Not fat." Nate leaned close to my ear, speaking in a low voice that did nothing to abate the physical response in my body. "Curvy. And I'll let you in on a wee secret: There are still men out there that like a woman to be soft under their hands, to have curves, hips, tits and arse." He tapped my butt gently with the palm of his hand. "It's a good arse, babe. I don't want to hear you refer to it as anything else."

Shock rooted me to the floor. It wasn't just the very cool things he was saying; it was the rush of tingles that shivered through me as he caressed my butt and moved his hand upward, sliding it under my T-shirt, and around my waist to caress my stomach. I sucked in a deep breath.

There was no ignoring the fact that he was turning me on. I really needed him to *not* know he was turning me on.

Nate unwittingly saved me. His hand dipped downward, shaking me out of the little sensual haze he'd put me in when I realized where he was heading.

For my belly!

I clutched at his hand to stop him, but when our eyes met in the mirror his expression was admonishing. He gave me a little shake of his head. "Let go, babe."

I shook my head back at him.

"Liv."

"Nate . . ."

His expression instantly softened at the panic in my voice. "Trust me."

Trembling, I let go of his hand and sucked in another breath as he stepped even closer to me, the heat of his front brushing against my back. And suddenly I was sucking in my breath for an entirely different reason as the rough tips of his fingers glided slowly down my stomach.

I had never been more thankful for a T-shirt bra than I was at that moment. Nate's touch was turning me on so much that my nipples had hardened to little points.

*Oh, boy.*

He didn't need to know that his lessons were causing *that* kind of reaction in me. For the first time since we'd met, I really wished my friend wasn't so goddamn sexy.

Flattening his hand, Nate smoothed it over my belly, back and forth, learning my shape, until my cheeks could have guided a lost sailor home, they were so red.

"Is this the barely there pouch?"

I nodded, unable to speak, sure that if I did it would come out all Greta Garbo and sex. That would definitely give away my hormonally charged state.

Nate's hand slid back over my stomach to my hip, where it stayed. He gave me a reassuring squeeze. "Feels good. Soft. Sexy." He murmured in my ear again, and I tried and failed not to shiver in response. "Your skin is like silk."

In my head I was panting and in reality I was really close to panting, so when he pulled back abruptly it was almost like he'd thrown a bucket of ice water over me.

*Thank you. I needed that.* I shook myself, giving my cheek an inner slap. *Snap out of it!*

"Now," Nate began, his voice all controlled and back to normal, "I'm a man, and as you know, I don't say shit I don't mean. So here's what I see."

*Oh, God.*

"Great hair, stunning eyes, gorgeous skin, fucking knockout smile, great tits, nice arse, and long, sexy legs. Fuckable. Very, very fuckable."

My lips twitched with laughter, and I had to admit to feeling a rush of real pleasure sweep over me at his analysis. "Succinct."

Nate shrugged as he took in my bright-eyed expression. "Just trying to get the point across that there are not very many men who wouldn't want to fuck you. And this is from a man many *women* find attractive." He flashed a quick, arrogant grin.

I rolled my eyes at him. He knew damn well how good-looking he was. I imagined that when you looked like a movie star it was almost impossible not to know how good-looking you were. "Of course you're attractive."

"Really?" He crossed his arms over his chest, leaning against the footboard of my bed as his eyebrows dipped together in consternation. "I thought you got tongue-tied around men you found attractive?"

*Is his vanity pricked?*

Inside I was gleefully guffawing at the idea. On the outside I was a lot nicer. "You cocky bastard, you know every straight woman on the planet finds you attractive."

He rewarded me with another arrogant smile, his dimples popping in that delightfully sexy way that could be really distracting. "So you don't get tongue-tied all the time?"

"You're different. You and I are friends, so I try not to think about you that way."

"Back at you, babe."

*Hmm. Nice.* I immediately plummeted from the high I'd been on. I didn't know what to say to that.

Nate looked like he wanted to laugh. "It doesn't mean I don't."

"Don't what?" I frowned.

His eyes drifted slowly over my body in a way that had me clamping my legs together in denial. "Think about you that way."

My heart slammed against my chest. "Really?"

He snorted. "Last time I checked, I'm a man and you're an attractive woman. Just because we don't fuck doesn't mean I haven't thought about it. That's how men work."

Unsuccessfully hiding a smile, I nodded casually. "Back at you. But," I hurried to explain, "because you're my friend . . . I don't know. I'm just comfortable with you. There's no sexual pressure, so I can just be me around you."

Nate took this in and then straightened from his position against the footboard. "I'm working the next few days, but on Thursday night I'll come back over and we'll continue."

I bobbed my head in agreement.

"I hope you're feeling more confident." He shot me another cocky smile.

Sighing, I looked back at the mirror. "It's nice to know there are guys out there who might think how you think, Nate. But not all guys are like you. I've seen you." I smiled sadly back at him. "You find women, in general, attractive. It's not a bad thing. It's a great thing. I wish all men were as easy to please."

Nate shook his head, looking a little impatient. "I'm not attracted to all women. Believe me." He took a step closer to me, so close I had to tilt my head back a little to meet his eyes, eyes that now smoldered in a way that caused the breath to hitch in my throat. "If you were just some woman in a bar, I'd pick you out from all the others, take you home, and fuck you so hard you wouldn't be able to walk straight in the morning."

I gulped.

In fact, I think I might have had a little mini-orgasm.

"Olivia?"

"Got it." I managed a whisper. "You think I'm attractive."

His lips twitched again, his dark eyes bright with amusement. "But do you?"

Eyes wide, I nodded rapidly. "Oh, I'm definitely getting there now."

Breaking out into a huge grin, Nate smacked my ass playfully before heading for the door. "Good. See you Thursday, babe."

# CHAPTER 7

*Great hair, stunning eyes, gorgeous skin, fucking knockout smile, great tits, nice arse, and long, sexy legs. Fuckable. Very, very fuckable.*

Nate's voice kept ringing in my head during quiet moments. It had ever since Monday night. Every time I remembered his compliments I flushed with pleasure, smiling goofily, and then overanalyzed whether or not he meant it. Something I'm sure he'd be pissed off to learn. I couldn't help it. It wasn't like my confidence in my looks was suddenly going to grow overnight because the gorgeous Nate Sawyer said he found me attractive.

Okay, so I wasn't lying when I told him it helped.

It definitely helped.

Or at least it put me in a good mood for the next few days.

"Did you hear that Jude and Mari from Special Collections are getting married?" Ronan, one of my colleagues, asked me as we sat eating lunch in the staff room together.

Thinking about that harridan Mari, I replied dryly, "How nice for them."

"Jesus, you can hold a grudge," he chuckled, munching his sandwich while he texted his wife. I knew he was texting his wife because the two of them were addicted to texting each other throughout the workday. They'd been married five years and still acted like newlyweds.

My mouth parted in indignation. "She was horrible to me."

Special Collections was on the sixth floor of the library and could be accessed only by appointment. It was run by the rare-books staff—Jude, Mari, and a small group of colleagues who were trained in dealing with old and rare books. It was a pretty cool job, and by all accounts a pretty cool place. When I'd first started working at the library I'd asked Mari for a tour. I was promptly told that ordinary staff were not allowed in unless they had an appointment, and the appointment had to be for a legitimate reason.

"This isn't a small-town library, Miss Holloway," she'd sneered over her glasses at me. "And even if it was, what would a provincial like you find of merit in Special Collections?"

Ronan snorted as I reminded him what she'd said to me. "You've got to give her points for getting the word 'provincial' into the sentence."

"Oh, you know she meant 'American.' Elitist . . ."

"Elitist what?"

"Nothing," I mumbled, dipping my head to my e-reader again. "My mom always said if you can't say anything nice, don't say anything at all."

"My mum always said if you can't say something nice, say something memorable."

I laughed. "I might steal that."

The door to the staff room flew open and our colleague Wendy strolled in. She was grinning huge. "I just got asked out again by another student. This place is brilliant for my self-esteem. I can't believe I didn't think to come here sooner." She shrugged as she got a plastic cup of water from the water dispenser. "Of course, the fact that it's the third time I've been hit on by a woman is a little puzzling."

Sneaking a look at Ronan I saw him struggling not to laugh, which of course set me off. Once I lost control, he started laughing too. Wendy was a thirty-three-year-old wife and mother of two. She was attractive, friendly, funny, and just plain old nice. And apparently a hit with the ladies.

She watched us chuckle with a good-natured smile on her face. "What? Do you think I'm doing something to encourage it?"

I shook my head. "I don't know. Just take it as the compliment it is."

"You should know." Ronan smirked at me. "You're always getting hit on."

My eyebrows puckered together. "By barely out-of-their-adolescence boys who will screw anything as long as it has boobs and a vagina attached to it."

"We're using the word 'vagina' at work now?" Angus's voice jerked my head around from Ronan. My boss was leaning against the doorway, regarding us with cool amusement.

I smiled sheepishly. "We're talking about medical journals?"

Angus ignored that and wandered toward the coffee machine. "I met Michael here, you know," he suddenly offered up, which told us he'd been standing at the door for a while and knew exactly what we'd been talking about. "Fraternizing with the students isn't encouraged, but I was twenty-three and he was a twenty-five-year-old postgrad." He grinned at me over his shoulder. "Sometimes when you click you just click—you can't help who it's with. Have you never had that with anyone, Liv? A student, perhaps?"

My pulse throbbed in my neck at his pointed question. Oh, my God . . . did Angus know about my crush on Benjamin? I shook my head quickly. "No."

"Hmm." He smirked at me, leaning against the counter. "Well, I've noticed a postgrad or two checking you out . . . in the *reserve section*."

Was he saying he'd noticed *Benjamin* checking me out?

"Really?" I squeaked.

Laughing, Angus replied, "You're quite possibly the most oblivious person I've ever met in my life."

"Checking *me* out?" I asked for clarification.

"Yes. You." He frowned at me. "Why do you ask that like it's impossible?"

"Um . . ." Uh-oh. I didn't want my colleagues knowing that any self-esteem I had was clinging to my personality with a death grip.

Angus gave me a look that suggested he thought me more than a little nutty (he gave me that look a lot), grabbed his coffee, and strode toward the exit. "Try not to use the word 'vagina' outside of the staff room."

Ronan and Wendy laughed, but I was barely listening, diving inside my own head.

*If you were just some woman in a bar, I'd pick you out from all the others, take you home, and fuck you so hard you wouldn't be able to walk straight in the morning.*

Nate's delicious voice was echoing in my brain again, along with Angus's comments. Maybe Nate really was being one hundred percent honest with me. It was possible that *men*, actual *men*, not adolescent boys and young college boys, might find me attractive—might actually be okay with a woman who was a little overweight, had curves and an ass on her.

And here I'd thought Sir Mix-A-Lot wrote "I Like Big Butts" just because it was catchy.

"Huh."

"What?" Ronan's eyebrows rose in question.

"Nothing," I muttered. "I'm just having a possibly life-altering epiphany over here."

"Want to share?"

I shook my head with a smile and got to my feet. "Better get back to work." I cleaned up the small mess I'd made, rinsed out my mug, and headed toward the door, unconsciously singing out loud.

Just before the door shut behind me, I heard Ronan sigh heavily. "Great, now I've got Sir Mix-A-Lot stuck in my head."

As Nate leaned against my kitchen counter, drinking soda, I allowed myself to really look at him in a way I hadn't looked at him since cementing a close friendship with him. It was Thursday night and he'd just arrived to continue our lessons. Wearing a plain black T-shirt, black jeans, black boots, and a sports watch, he was glamorous without even trying. I knew he'd hate it if he knew I was thinking that word, but it just fit Nate. At any given minute he looked ready to walk the red carpet or pose for the paparazzi. When he'd been dressed up in his three-piece suit for Joss and Braden's wedding, he'd been absolutely beautiful. He could put Hollywood actors to shame.

And Nate wasn't just beautiful on the outside. Underneath the play-boy was a guy more loyal than most, earthy, compassionate, and—let's face it—giving. Here he was, taking time out of his life to help me with a pretty embarrassing situation. So far, he'd tried his best to make sure the experience wasn't excruciating for me. How many guys were that kind and patient?

He was beautiful all the way through, and it was only now sinking in that a man *that* beautiful had said he found *me* attractive.

"So did anything stick with you?" Nate asked carefully after taking his first sip of Coke.

"I've been singing 'I Like Big Butts' for the past twenty-four hours."

His laughter filled my tiny apartment and it hit me in my belly in a way that it hadn't in a long time. Stubbornly I squashed that feeling and continued. "Honestly, it has sunk in a little. At least it's put me in a good mood, and has made me think that maybe I do have a slightly skewed perception of my physical appearance. However, it's not going to make me confident overnight. The thought of flirting with Benjamin, doing anything with Benjamin, makes me nervous as all hell."

He shrugged. "You've got to be patient. We'll get you there. I just wanted to know you're at least thinking about what I said. I don't want this to be a total waste of my time."

I did my best not to wince at his comment. Nate was blunt. That's who he was. He didn't censor his words, and if you were feeling a little sensitive it was easy to take them the wrong way. "You're not wasting your time," I promised him.

The corner of his lip tipped up and a dimple flashed in his right cheek. "No, I'm not wasting my time."

Trying not to become mesmerized by that dimple, I exhaled a little shakily and asked, "So, what's next?"

"First flirting. Then clothes."

Blinking rapidly, I attempted to process the words in a way that made them make sense. I couldn't. "Uh . . . clothes?"

Nate ran his eyes down my body pointedly. "Do you own a skirt? A dress? Anything that shows cleavage?"

Suddenly I knew exactly what he was talking about. It wasn't that I wasn't stylish—at least I hoped not—but I was a little conservative in my clothing choices. Still, I had to have something that showed cleavage . . .

I took too long to think because Nate said smugly, "Exactly."

"My clothes aren't that bad."

"No, they're not. But the only time I've seen you in a dress was the bridesmaid dress you wore to the wedding. I've never seen you in a short skirt either."

Watching him take another drink, my eyes were glued to the movement of his strong throat. I shrugged absentmindedly. "I've never been that confident showing skin."

"Why?"

My eyes rose to meet his and I made a face. "You seriously have to ask that?"

His answer was aggravated silence. And yes, silence could be aggravated. It bristled around Nate as he waited impatiently for me to answer the question.

"Okay, okay." I slouched over to the counter, pushing at my own glass of cold Coke. "It meant the possibility of men looking at me, and if they're looking at me, they're judging me."

Nate contemplated this for a moment before replying, "Were you bullied as a child?"

"A little. Not in a way that would cause permanent damage. Why?"

"I'm just trying to work out why you're so afraid to put yourself out there."

I rolled my eyes. "Is this a therapy session now?"

"Does it need to be?"

"Nate"—my voice was stern so he'd get it—"there is no dramatic story here. I wish there was. Really. It would make me feel less of an idiot. I was teased at school like most kids are, but nothing major. My mom always made me feel special, and when my dad came into my life he worked his ass off to make sure I felt extraordinary." I gave him a small smile, feeling the emotion choke me a little. "I was shy. That was it. And with my mom's cancer, and minimal opportunities, sex and romance just passed me by. The older I've gotten, the more of a complex I've gotten about it, and I guess I've just lost any confidence in my sexuality that I might have had. That's it. That's all there is to know."

He sighed heavily, running a hand through his messy dark hair. "Sorry, Liv. I just wanted to make sure I wasn't missing anything. I really want you to get past this. I want you to see how gorgeous you are."

I grinned at him. "You keep saying sweet shit like that, and I might have to promote you to premier best friend."

Grinning back at me, Nate rounded the kitchen counter and headed for the couch. When he sat down he patted the seat beside him. "Come sit beside me."

Curious, I did as he asked.

His smile was teasing now. "Closer."

I didn't want to get closer. He smelled good—something that I was always vaguely aware of, but now I was extremely conscious of the fact that I was really, *really* aware of how good he smelled. "Why? I thought you were going to teach me to flirt."

"I am. Part of flirting is body language. If you sit three feet from a guy, he's going to assume you either farted or you think *he* did." I laughed and he continued. "If you're interested in a guy, start off by getting close. However, don't get in his face—in case *he's* not interested."

Feeling stricken and probably looking it, I asked, wide-eyed and panicked, "How will I know if he's not interested?"

"He'll make it clear."

"But I don't know anything. What if I don't pick up on his signals?" The telltale sign of Nate's lips twitching made me growl with irritation. "Don't you dare laugh. I'm being serious!"

"Okay." He laughed anyway, holding his hands up. "Calm down. I'll show you exactly what I mean. First, I'll get you to flirt with me and I'll react. You tell me if I'm interested or not."

My pulse had started to race, and my palms were already sweaty at the mere mention of flirting. "Yeah, but how do I flirt?"

I think he heard the trembling in my voice because he stopped grinning and gave me a small, reassuring smile. "Babe, we'll ease into it. Sit close to me. Start talking to me in a way that tells me you're interested in me."

"But—"

"Liv, just do it."

Sucking in a huge breath, I slid closer to Nate, deciding that my thigh almost touching his was a good place to stop. I looked up into his placid expression and . . .

I burst out laughing.

Shaking his head, Nate gave a huff of amusement. "Whatever you do, don't do that to a guy."

Then I started rapidly flapping my hand in front of my face in hopes that cool air would calm me and the idiotic laughing down. "I'm sorry," I apologized around a hard swallow of giggles. "I'll try again." With a couple more deep breaths I grew more composed.

"Ready?"

Throwing my shoulders back, I said, "Yes."

"Okay, go for it."

Taking a moment, I built the fantasy up in my head. I wasn't at home in my apartment with Nate anymore. I was in a bar with a guy I'd never met before, and he looked an awful lot like Benjamin Livingston. "Hi, I'm Liv."

His gaze flickered over me quickly before moving off across the room. "Nate."

Hmm, that seemed cold, but Nate could just be testing me.

"Is that short for Nathaniel?" *Really? That's the best you've got?*

Nate just nodded, not looking at me.

"That means you're not interested, right?" I winced, forgetting this was a lesson and taking it a little too personally.

As if he sensed that, Nate chuckled. "I told you that you'd be able to pick up on it. Guys make it fairly easy."

"Jesus, that would be embarrassing in real life."

He dipped his head toward me. "Babe, a guy responds like that to you, he's not worth shit, okay? You pick yourself up and go find a guy who's not a complete arse."

Smiling gratefully, I asked. "Okay. So what now?"

He smiled, wicked and seductive. "Now I'm going to flirt back. It gives you something to bounce off, so you'll find it easier this time around."

"You optimistic person, you."

Giving me another smile, he nudged me with his knee. "Start again."

Thinking I should have practiced how to smile seductively—there was probably a "how to" tutorial on YouTube—before Nate arrived, I quickly attempted to assemble that kind of expression on my lips. I had a feeling it came off weird, but Nate just went with it. "Hi, I'm Liv."

The smile he gave me almost melted me into the couch. Through lowered lashes, Nate's divine black-magic eyes traveled from my legs upward, lingering for more than a few seconds on my breasts, then migrating up to my face. He stared into my eyes, seeming transfixed, and I was pretty sure if he threw me back against the couch and took me wildly he'd find me unbelievably ready for him. "Hi, Liv. I'm Nate."

Somehow through the tingling and the sexual fog he'd cast over me I managed to smile back. I gestured to his soda and asked, "You drinking alone tonight?"

"Have a drink with me and I won't be."

"Ooh, that was nice."

"Don't break character."

I straightened my spine, chastened. "Sorry."

"Don't be sorry, just keep going."

Scrambling to think of a reply, I decided it was too much to try to imagine Nate as Benjamin, so I let that go, reminding myself that this was just me and Nate. We hung out all the time. Relaxing a little, I said, "I'll have a drink with you if you can guess my favorite drink."

"Good. Playful." He grinned again, going back into character. "Let me think." His eyes roved over me. "American. Casual. Laid-back . . . I'm thinking a beer."

I shook my head, trying not to smile, since beer was what I drank in reality. But that was too easy for him.

"Whisky?"

"Nope."

He told me with his eyes that he knew what I was doing, but he patiently asked, "What, then?"

"Rum and Coke," I lied.

"Guess my people-reading skills aren't quite up to scratch after all."

"No, I think it just means you're not psychic. For instance . . ." I gave him a little smile and shuffled closer so my leg was now pressed against his. Nate's cologne hit all my senses and my heart started to beat a little faster as I continued. "What are your people-reading skills telling you now?"

Nate's eyes dipped to where our legs were pressed together, and suddenly my palms were sweating again. Was I starting off too aggressively? Was this all wrong?

Oh, crap, I was never going to be good at this.

When his gaze rose to meet mine again, I was surprised for a moment to see how much heat was in his eyes. However, when he answered, "That I should buy you that rum and Coke," I remembered he was just acting.

I relaxed and let my eyes glitter as I got into it too. "It seems your people-reading skills are intact."

The right corner of his mouth tilted up in sexy amusement. "They're not my only skills, you know. I've been told I work wonders with my hands . . . as well as other parts of my body."

The blatant sexual innuendo caused a visible flush to spread across my cheeks. Nate groaned loudly, flopping back against the couch. "You were doing so well."

I tried to cool my cheeks with the power of my mind. "Sorry. I just didn't expect you to jump right into the sex stuff."

"I don't get it." He rolled his head to look at me. "We watch crude comedies together, we all crack sex jokes—you laugh, you join in. No blushing involved."

"But those aren't directed at me," I argued.

"So even the *thought* of shagging a guy turns you shy?"

"One, haven't we been over that? And two, don't say 'shagging,' Nate."

"I have to say *naughty* words if we're going to get you past this."

"And don't be condescending. I'm not a prude. I just don't like the word 'shagging.' I prefer 'fucking.'"

As soon as I said it Nate's eyes sparkled with humor. I could see the corners of his mouth tilting toward what I knew would be a massive grin. "Don't even . . ." I hit him with a cushion as he started to laugh really hard at me. "Stop being immature."

After what felt like at least five minutes of straight-out belly-laughing at me, Nate finally pulled himself together, wiping tears from the corners of his eyes. "We need to work on dirty talking," he said, still a little hoarse from all that amusement at my expense. "Some guys are subtle, but some guys will tell you what they want to do to you."

*I will not blush, I will not blush.* "Like you."

"I'm not exactly a subtle guy."

"What if I don't like that kind of talk?"

"If you don't, then he's not the guy for you. You just bow out of the conversation and find a guy who does subtle." Nate leaned into me, his eyes questioning. "But how do you know you don't like it? After all, it's just foreplay."

*I will not blush, I will not blush.*

*Damn, I'm blushing.*

Nate smirked at me again.

"Look, maybe we can just get me past blushing at innuendo before we see if I can handle dirty talking."

He contemplated me a moment. "Okay. It's your call."

I gave him a determined nod and then just sat there.

Nate raised an eyebrow at me.

"Should we go back to that part where you said you were good with your hands?"

He was laughing at me again, but this time only with his eyes. "Sounds like a good place to start."

# CHAPTER 8

After three hours of innuendo I finally reached a point where I wasn't blushing. I was even able to provide a fairly saucy rejoinder. This didn't convince me that I'd be able to approach Benjamin and start flirting with him. It only convinced me that I was so comfortable with Nate that my insecurities were taking a swan dive off the Mountain of Low Self-Esteem one by one while I was around him. Still, I felt better than I had in a long time—not only because Nate had begun to chip away at the weight of my physical insecurities, but because I felt like I was grabbing life by the balls and doing something about a part of my life that I was unhappy with.

Nate was nonstop busy on Friday since he had three photo shoots booked for the paper, one being an awards ceremony that had him working right up until midnight. As for me, I was having my usual weekly dinner with Dad, Jo, Cam, and Cole.

This meant no lessons.

Saturday was out too, considering that Nate, Cam, and Cole had judo class in the afternoon and usually hung out together afterward. However, I still got to see Nate.

Jo called to ask me over that evening, and when I got there I found the guys were there, including Peetie. Peetie's fiancée, Lyn, wasn't with them and I hadn't expected her to be. The few times we'd met I'd thought she was nice, but she never went out of her way to hang out with Peetie's friends. She had her own group, and both of them seemed cool with that.

Nate and Cole were playing a war game that Nate was in the middle of reviewing, while Peetie and I waited patiently for our turn. Cam sat in the corner at his desk, going over some work stuff, while Jo lay half snoozing on the rug in front of the fireplace.

I sat next to Nate, attempting not to feel weird hanging out with him in a normal situation with our friends after having spent all Thursday evening flirting with him. Despite it being friendly lessons, there was still something kind of naughty about the fact that none of our friends had any idea Nate had told me he thought about fucking me, or that we'd spent four solid hours lightly flirting until I'd begun to tingle between my legs.

"I'm rethinking my plan to become a tattoo artist," Cole announced, his thumb going into rapid motion upon the controller as an enemy target appeared on the screen.

Jo stirred and blinked sleepily up at her brother. "Why? You've been going on about it for months."

The game paused while Cole stared at her with a somewhat mulish expression on his face. "I don't 'go on.'"

Cam grunted from the corner of the room and murmured without looking up from his drawings, "He's got you there, baby."

"Okay." Jo yawned and sat up slowly. "You've talked about it. For you that is 'going on' about it."

Cole shrugged. "I want Nate's job now."

"Stick to the tattoos, mate," Nate replied. "One, this is a part-time gig. It doesn't pay all the bills. And two, I've seen the tattoo you designed for Cam. You should stick to it."

"Yeah?" Cole was trying not to look too pleased. "I could design *you* a new one."

"A new one?" Jo didn't look sleepy at all now as she brushed her hair off her face. Her eyes were bright with curiosity. I knew for a fact that she found Nate a bit of a mystery because she'd tried to pry answers about him out of me before. As much as I trusted her, Nate's story was not mine to tell, so she was left in the dark for the most part. "You've got a tattoo, Nate?"

On this, it would seem, so was I.

I'd had no idea Nate had a tattoo.

The room grew weirdly tense at Jo's question, and Nate's reply was tight and abrupt. "Aye."

"What is it?"

"Nothing." He shrugged and restarted the game.

"Well, it's got to be of something."

"I told you it's nothing."

"When did you get it?"

"Jo—"

"Where is—"

"Christ, I said it's nothing, all right?" Nate cut her off tersely and I stared at him in surprise. It wasn't like him to be moody or short with people. That meant one thing. The tattoo had something to do with *her*.

However, Jo didn't know enough about *her* to get it, so she looked a little wounded.

"Baby, do you want to help me put some snacks together?" Cam asked quietly, standing up from the desk.

She looked up at him and a silent conversation passed between them. "Sure." She took the hand he held out to her and he helped her up. Even after they'd left the room it was still thick with unease.

Cole cleared his throat and started playing the game again. "I think the reaction time on this is a little slow, by the way," he offered, trying to change the subject.

Nate nodded gratefully at him. "I think you're right, wee man."

They began discussing the game with Peetie. The whole time, I watched Nate, waiting for the tension along the back of his shoulders to disappear. It didn't. My chest ached for him. I needed him to know that if he was having a hard time, I was there for him just like he was there for me. I shuffled closer to Nate as Peetie disagreed with Cole over the graphics.

"Tattoo?" I asked softly in his ear, not sure whether I would get my head bitten off like Jo had.

Nate turned to me, his eyes soft as he gave a shake of his head. "Later, babe," he muttered. "I shouldn't have spoken to Jo like that."

"She's fine," I reassured him. Giving his knee a gentle squeeze, I got up with the intention of going to help Jo. As I was leaving the room, Cam was coming back in and he was scowling.

"You okay?"

He gave me a slight shake of his head. "She feels bad for pushing him."

"He feels bad for snapping, so don't give him a hard time," I murmured.

Cam gazed over at his friend and then whispered, "You forget I know, Liv. I wasn't going to give him a hard time. But I sometimes wonder if someone should."

Not really sure how to answer that, I gave him a sad smile and slipped past. I found Jo in the kitchen, pouring bags of chips—or crisps, as she and Dad called them—into bowls. I spotted packets of peanuts and empty bowls, and began to help out.

"So how's your week going?" I asked her quietly. "Has Dad worked you to the bone?"

Jo smiled at me over her shoulder. "We're really busy. But that's a good thing."

"And the new employees?"

"Good. I think Cam was a bit worried about it—how the guys would treat me—but Mick has chosen carefully. They're literally two more Uncle Micks, so I've got three of them to deal with now."

I smiled. "I gathered that much when talking to Dad."

"What about you?" Her brow puckered as she stared at me. "Are you okay? You seem . . . I don't know . . . Last night at the restaurant you were really quiet. Is it Mick and Dee? Are you okay about them? We haven't really spoken about it and they definitely seem serious now."

Last night I had been quiet, but it was mostly because I was replaying all the very complimentary and somewhat risqué things Nate had said to me during our lessons the night before. "Honestly, it's just been a tiring week. I think Dee is great. No problems there."

"You're still allowed to feel strange about it—you know that, right?"

I shook my head but felt that ache press in on my chest as I replied, "Dad adored Mom and he held her hand through it all. She spent a lot of their marriage sick. Too sick. So sick they were more like companions than lovers, but Dad didn't complain. I don't think he even cared—he loved her that much." I smiled through my suddenly blurry vision. "He deserves happiness now. Dee is really cool and she makes him happy. I'm good with it."

I wasn't surprised to see tears shimmering in Jo's eyes. She had a tendency to cry when her friends did because she cared enough to feel what they felt. "You can always talk to me, Liv, if you're having a hard time about anything."

Of course I knew this was true and I knew that Jo would be there for me anytime I needed her, if only just to listen. I knew I could talk to her if I was having a bad time about my mom, but the last time I did go through a hard time about it—which was Thanksgiving last year—Nate happened to be the one who was there to see me through it.

As for the problems I was having now . . .

I couldn't talk to Jo about them.

Starting over in Scotland, starting over with Jo, was a clean slate in more ways than one. I didn't have a close group of friends back in the States, but those few friends I did leave behind knew me long enough to know my history—or lack of—with men. They never said it outright, but they always spoke to me about guys with this hint of pity, sometimes even superiority, that made me feel even worse about myself.

But Jo . . . Jo didn't know any of this.

When we first met she was going through some pretty bad stuff with her mom and dad. For a long time I think she thought the abuse she suffered at their hands was somehow her fault. Meeting her at such an emotional time for her accelerated our friendship. I became a confidante for her, and somehow I found the right words to make her feel better about herself. Because of that and my sometimes cocky sense of humor, Jo saw me as this self-assured, strong, confident, and sassy woman. I knew this because she told me so all the time. She told me she admired me. With Jo, I liked myself so much more than I usually did. She was the only mirror I liked looking into.

I wasn't ready to let go of those moments when I felt about myself the way I should. Telling her the truth, about all these insecurities that Nate was helping me through, would put an end to that. I wanted to continue to grow into the person I wanted to be, and then I would open up to her. Not confiding in her was not a reflection upon how good a friend she was. Because she was the best.

"I know I can always come to you." I grabbed her hand and squeezed it affectionately. "You're the best non-sister sister I ever had."

Her green eyes widened with surprised pleasure at my announcement, and her lips parted as if she was about to say something in return when we suddenly heard a loud thump from upstairs. The smile was instantly chased from Jo's face as she stared up at the ceiling. On a heavy sigh she murmured, "I better go check on her."

Last year Jo had moved out of the apartment upstairs that she had shared with her mom, Fiona, and Cole. Upon discovering that her alcoholic mother hit Cole, Jo had attempted to keep her brother away from their mom as much as possible. They spent a lot of time downstairs in Cam's apartment. Finally Cam asked Jo and Cole to move in with him, not only because he wanted them there but because Cole needed to be out of that situation pronto.

"Do you want company?" I offered, knowing that dealing with Fiona was often unpleasant for my friend.

She shook her head and gave me an apologetic smile. "You know how she feels about you."

Indeed I did. When I first met Fiona she'd been ugly to me because she'd always had a thing for my dad and was jealous of my mom and resented me. She'd told me I looked like my mom, as though that was a bad thing. It was actually one of the nicest things she could ever have said to me.

"Go on." I waved her off. "I'll deal with the snacks."

Sighing again, Jo headed out of the kitchen and I followed, carrying a plate of little sandwiches she'd made up.

"I'm going to see if Mum's okay," she called out to the guys as she passed the sitting room.

Cam almost bumped into me. He let me pass, calling out to Jo, "I'm coming with you."

As I entered the sitting room, my eyes immediately went to Cole. Just as I expected, his handsome, boyish features were strained as he stared up at the ceiling. I hated seeing that look on his face. I worried what it meant, what was going on inside.

Cole never talked about it, but I couldn't imagine it was any easier for him growing up with a mom like Fiona than it had been for Jo. Not easy either to grow up without a dad, and then to discover that your dad was an abusive asshole. By all accounts Jo had been his mother, not Fiona. Still, their mom's abuse must have left its mark, and just the thought of that mark scarring Cole made me feel sick to my stomach. He was the best kid ever. I couldn't understand how anyone could hurt him.

Sensing my gaze, Cole looked over at me and I smiled gently.

He gave me a small smile back, but it didn't reach his eyes.

"Sandwich?" I asked, walking over to him with the plate. Before he could say anything I sat down next to him and thrust the plate under his nose.

Cole slowly accepted a sandwich.

I remained silent.

He looked up at me, as if he was waiting for me to say something.

Instead I gave him a slow, cheeky grin. Cole stared at me like I was a new species. Then he shook his head and burst into low laughter. His whole body relaxed and he bit into the sandwich.

I lifted my smiling eyes. They collided with Nate's and the smile almost faltered at his expression. The look on his face was so tender I felt it knock the wind out of me. I felt that now familiar, pleasurable ache in my chest as he winked at me.

I didn't think anyone could wink without it looking stupid or corny.

I was wrong.

Nate could.

Nate made winking panty-droppingly hot.

*Oh, boy, better be careful, Soda Pop.*

"You don't have to walk me home, Nate," I said as we hit Leith Walk.

After Jo had dealt with whatever was going on with her mom, she and Cam had returned to the flat and we'd switched the video game off to watch a comedy. Nate made a point of leaning down to kiss Jo's forehead when he got up to go the bathroom, and the tension between them melted away. The tattoo, however, was still on my mind because . . . well, I was just nosy like that. Mostly I was concerned about the reaction it had elicited in Nate. I got through the movie without bugging him about it, but when Peetie left we took that as our cue and announced we had to get going too.

Nate lived in Marchmont, a heavily student-populated area behind the Meadows—a large public park behind the University of Edinburgh. It was southwest of Jo and Cam's apartment on London Road, whereas I was just west. It was a good forty-minute walk from my apartment to Nate's.

"It's after midnight," he replied softly. "I'm not letting you walk home alone."

"I'm a big girl. I can take care of myself."

"That might be true if you ever decided to come along to judo with me."

Wrinkling my nose at the thought, I said, "I like watching it, but I'm not up for doing it."

"I hope that won't be your attitude toward sex." He smirked cheekily at me. "Then again, voyeurism *is* hot."

I punched him on the arm. "You're so immature."

"I can't help it if you don't think through what you're saying before you say it," he replied with an unapologetic shrug.

"Dude, there was nothing sexual about what I said. You just have a way of making everything sound dirty."

He grinned at me. "You, a grown woman of twenty-six years old, say 'dude' and you call *me* immature?"

"That's beside the point," I replied haughtily, ignoring his laughter. And in ignoring his laughter I stupidly decided to ruin his mood. Clearing my throat, I nudged him with my shoulder. "So the uh . . . the, uh, tattoo?"

Nate was quiet as we strode across the wide road to Union Street. By the time we turned down Forth Street he still hadn't said anything. I wasn't going to push. It wasn't my place to. But I was worried about his reaction to this tattoo and what it meant.

"It's a small stylized 'A.' I have it tattooed at the top of my ribs, across my heart," he suddenly piped up.

"'A,'" I whispered, and I understood instantly. "For 'Alana'?"

Nate nodded, his eyes on me as if he was waiting for my reaction.

"When did you get it?"

"Just after she died." Those deep dark eyes of his studied my face more intently. "Did you ever think about getting a tattoo for your mum?"

The familiar pressure on my chest accompanied my answer. "I don't need it."

"I'm glad I got it." Nate's voice was low, even hushed. "There are times I can go a whole day without her flashing through my mind. Then I catch sight of the tat in the mirror. So I remember."

I wanted to tell him it was okay to live his life, to have days that weren't weighted by her loss, but I'd feel like a hypocrite if I did. Whenever I went a whole day without thinking about Mom the guilt was almost crippling. Nate knew that. He knew that and I knew his story. Remembering everything he'd told me after he'd found me in my apartment last November, I wouldn't be the one to tell him that it was time to move on . . .

*Last Thanksgiving, Edinburgh*

*The turkey was in the oven and so were the roasted potatoes. My potatoes for the mash were boiling and my onions were chopped, ready to be mashed in with the potatoes, just like Mom made. The cranberry sauce was done. The vegetables were steaming.*

*Since I couldn't find a store anywhere in Edinburgh that sold pumpkin pie, I had to make one from scratch. I wiped sweat from my forehead because the heat from my kitchen had filled my little apartment to the boiling point. Windows were open, but I'd still had to change into a tank top on a Scottish fall day.*

*After spending an emotional morning with my dad, I'd told him I just needed some quiet time alone. I could tell he didn't want to leave me, but I was a grown woman and he gave me my space. I was using my space to do what Mom would have been doing if life was fair.*

*Finishing up with the pie, I opened the oven to see if I could make room for it. Smoke billowed out.*

*"What the hell?" I screamed at it, waving the smoke away to discover that the turkey was burning.*

*How was it burning? Didn't I put it in for the right time? I glanced up at* the clock and felt a wave of dizziness sway me. Seven o' clock. How did it get to be seven o' clock? That couldn't be right.

I felt tears prick my eyes as I looked at the massacred bird.

I'd ruined it.

"I fucking ruined it!" I shrieked, grabbing an oven mitt and pulling at the bird. Feeling the burning heat of the tray beneath my hand I yelled in outrage and dumped its heavy load in the sink.

My door buzzer went off, and I stopped and sucked in a breath.

What if it was Dad?

I hurried to the entry phone. "Who is it?" I asked tentatively.

"Nate. Let me up."

"Uh, now's not a good time."

"I just heard you screaming from your open window. You don't let me up, I'll break the fuck in."

Pushing a hand through my hair, I winced at the wetness in my hairline. I was a sweaty mess.

I buzzed him in and pulled my front door open with belligerent annoyance, then stomped into the kitchen to check my roasted potatoes.

"Fucking ruined too," I whimpered, my eyes filling with more tears.

"Liv?"

I whirled around to face Nate, and whatever he saw in my eyes made him stop in his tracks.

"Liv, are you okay?" he asked gently, taking a slow step toward me.

"I ruined it!" I yelled, flinging an arm out toward the turkey. "It's fucked! What's the point in me baking the fucking pie if the bird is fucked? I wasted my time chopping onions for the mash but there's no point because the roasted potatoes are burnt. You can't have Thanksgiving with just one kind of potato, Nate."

"Babe, come here." He approached me as though I was a wounded animal. I was so confused by his behavior that I let him curl a strong hand around my arm and pull me toward the sitting room. Realization that he was taking me out of the kitchen sank in and a misdirected rage tore out of me.

"No!" I screamed, trying to pull away from him.

"Jesus, Liv, calm down," he ordered through gritted teeth, grabbing hold of my other arm for better purchase. "Calm down and tell me what's going on."

"Don't!" I tugged my arms, and when that didn't work, I tried to force him away from me, tried to knock him off balance. "Get off! I have to fix it! I have to fix it!"

"Liv," he whispered, fear in his voice now. He shook me hard, so hard I stopped, wide-eyed, as his hands gentled and cupped my face. I stared into his dark eyes and what I saw in them frightened me.

I was acting like a crazy person.

My face crumpled as the familiar agony ripped through my chest. My body shuddered, hard, while I sobbed. "She's not here to fix it." I fell against him, trying to catch my breath.

His arms slid around me as I cried and in that moment I felt like his arms were the only thing keeping my insides from falling out.

"She struggled," I whispered, taking a deep breath, trying to find calm through the tears, "but she fought through it. Every Thanksgiving." I relaxed at his murmuring words of comfort, my head moving with the rise and fall of his smooth breathing. I let the rhythm take hold of me, and slowly my own breathing returned to normal.

When I finally became aware of my surroundings again, I discovered I was lying on the couch with Nate. He'd settled down on it and taken me with him so I was tucked into his side, my head still resting on his chest and my right hand clutched in his left.

"I'm sorry," I croaked out, my eyes swollen, my cheeks burning with embarrassment at my meltdown. Truth be told, I'd been going into a meltdown for the last few weeks as Thanksgiving approached. Much of the tension I was carrying had been coiled up tight as I tried to keep my meltdown from my father.

"Don't be." Nate reassured me. "Why today, Liv?"

"It's Thanksgiving back home," I told him in a hushed voice, afraid somehow that if I spoke any louder I'd become hysterical again. "No matter how sick Mom was, she always fought through it for Thanksgiving, trying to make everything normal when it wasn't." My mouth trembled as fresh tears spilled down my cheeks. "She was my best friend. My soul mate."

"Babe." I heard the pained empathy in his voice and took comfort from it.

"She died five years ago today, on Thanksgiving. It's the first year since her death that I haven't visited her grave." I cried harder. "I don't want her to think I've forgotten her."

He held me tighter as I continued to cry, soaking the already wet fabric of his shirt.

"Liv . . ." Nate squeezed his arm around me. "Babe, she wouldn't think that for a second."

"I was with her through it all, Nate." I wiped a hand across my snotty nose. "I missed out on being a kid, I left school, I did it all to help her fight. And we didn't win. Her life . . . gone. My teen years . . . gone. It should have meant something. It should mean something."

"It does mean something. She taught you to fight no matter how hopeless things look. That's a lesson not many people can impart to their kids, but she did. She taught you to be brave, Liv, and she taught you life is fragile. People say that all the time, but they never really understand until one minute they're laughing with someone they love and the next they're crying over their grave. I get it. I get it because Alana taught me about it. I think about her every day, and she knows that I think about her every day. I don't have to visit her grave for her to know that."

Confused and concerned, my heart pounding harder than before, I wiped at my cheeks as I lifted my head from Nate's chest to look into his eyes. "Alana?"

Grief I'd never seen in his eyes before, telling of a loss so deep I felt it seep from him to me, darkened them to pure black. How he'd managed to hide it all these months I would never know. "Did Cam tell you we're from Longniddry?"

I nodded.

"It's just a wee place outside of Edinburgh. A pretty place on the coast. Cam, Peetie, Alana, and I grew up together. We were all best friends until we turned thirteen and a kid I didn't like asked Alana out. I got really mad at her and we got into a fight." He smiled softly, remembering. "I hated fighting with her. She *was the gentlest girl. If you fought with her, she'd cry, and that just made you feel like shit. So we fought and she cried and I kissed her to say I was sorry." He shrugged, then laughed hollowly. "That was it. We were together. Childhood sweethearts."*

I swallowed past the massive lump in my throat, the pain inside me expanding for Nate. "You loved her."

Tears shimmered in his eyes, making the breath catch in my throat. "Aye. She was my best friend."

"What happened?"

He was silent a moment and then his eyes caught mine, and our connection only intensified as he replied, "Cancer. Lymphoma. She was just about to turn seventeen." He glanced away and his arm tightened around me again. "I stayed with her through every stage. Every dashed hope, every failed treatment. And I really believed that we'd beat it. That if I just kept breathing for her she'd make it." I heard the catch in his throat and tensed against him. "She was special, Liv. Pure. In the end the only thing that got me through was the belief that she was just too good for this place. When she died two days after her eighteenth birthday that was all that got me through. She was just too good for this place."

"Oh, God, Nate." I dropped my forehead to his chest and wrapped my hand tight around his arm. "I'm sorry."

"I'm sorry too, babe."

We lay there in silence for a while until finally I drew the courage to say something I really didn't want to. "I'll get up. Let you go."

I felt his lips in my hair and then he said quietly, "If it's okay with you, I'm quite comfortable here for the night."

I relaxed instantly. "I'm good with that."

We'd passed Dad's flat on Heriot Row and turned down Howe Street. We were less than a minute from my apartment and the entire walk home had been filled with comfortable silence born of the deeper connection we'd made last Thanksgiving. Still, there was a weight in Nate's silence that made me uneasy.

Finally, as we stopped outside my building, he spoke. "I've got a couple of deadlines this week, so I might not be able to drop around until after judo class on Wednesday night."

Shaking off the weird sensation that felt an awful lot like disappointment, I said, "No problem." I gave him a cocky smile that I didn't really feel. "I'll practice flirting with my mirror."

I was gratified at the low chuckle he emitted, a warm glow spreading through my chest as some of the darkness lifted from his eyes.

He pressed a kiss to my cheek. "See you soon, babe. Sweet dreams."

" 'Night." I let myself into the building and gave him one last smile over my shoulder before I shut the door and headed up the concrete stairs. Though I understood exactly where he was coming from, a heaviness grew in my gut as I changed into my pajamas. I knew that tonight Nate wasn't going to need to look in the mirror at his tattoo as a reminder to think of Alana.

No. She was inside him tonight; there was a haunted look in his eyes that I'd never seen before. Something was bothering him, and I was afraid that if I pushed too hard, I'd become just like every other woman in his life and he'd shut me out completely.

# CHAPTER 9

My worry for Nate gnawed at me for hours until I drifted off, my body finally too exhausted to wait my brain out. Worrying was never fun, especially when a solution seemed so impossible, which meant I was grateful for the Nicholses' Sunday lunch the next day.

Joss and Braden, honeymooning in Hawaii, were absent, of course, but I didn't get a chance to really feel that absence because of the drama. By "drama" I mean Ellie was giddy, and all because Hannah had gone on a date the night before.

While Dad, Cam, Adam, Cole, and Dec hung out downstairs, Elodie worked away in the kitchen with help from Clark, and I leaned against Hannah's dressing table watching her grimace at Ellie's excitement, often looking to Jo for help.

"I don't understand." Ellie threw her hands up in bafflement. "I remember being absolutely thrilled about my first date. Granted, Braden and Adam ruined it and I came home crying, but surely your first date went better than mine."

I was too busy smirking at Ellie and wondering what the hell Braden and Adam had done to ruin her first date to notice that Hannah was growing increasingly uncomfortable.

"Ellie, can you just drop it?" Her plaintive tone brought my head around and I frowned at her morose expression.

Oh, God. Had something happened? Had he . . . "I don't know about you, Els, but I'm beginning to worry."

Hearing the seriousness of my tone, Ellie stiffened, her wide blue gaze flying back to Hannah. "Hannah, did that boy do something to you?"

"Oh, for goodness' sake." Jo crossed her arms over her chest and gave Hannah an impatient look. "Just tell them."

"Jo." Hannah glowered at her. "No."

Jo looked at Ellie, seemingly ready to ignore Hannah's annoyance. "She's got this strange belief that if more people know about him it'll somehow jinx it. But, sweetheart"—she turned back to Hannah—"after last night, I don't think that's a problem now."

Ellie crossed her arms over her chest, frowning. "What's Jo talking about?"

We waited patiently—or at least Jo and I did—for Hannah to finally let us in on whatever secret she was harboring. "Just . . . don't tell Mum."

"Why not? Are you doing something illegal?" Ellie huffed. "I'm starting to get really concerned."

I knew Hannah well enough to know she was only *just* refraining from rolling her eyes. "It's nothing like that. I just don't want everyone to know. It's too depressing."

"Fine, I won't tell Mum. Now spill."

Exhaling heavily, Hannah leaned back against her pillows and stared up at the poster on her ceiling. It was a sexy black-and-white shot of the front man of one of the world's most famous rock bands. "Two years ago I met this guy. Marco. He's a few years older than me. He helped me out when a couple of boys at school were bullying me anytime I missed the bus. Anyway, I kissed him one day." She rolled her eyes at herself. "I thought he was kissing me back, but he pushed me off him and avoided me for a while. Then he started talking to me again, but he pretended like nothing had happened. He graduated last year." She turned her head on her pillow now to glance between Ellie and me. "We've stayed in contact. Texting. Facebook. Sometimes meeting up just to hang out and talk. Nothing has ever happened between us, although I think I've made it clear I like him." A pained expression, a deep hurt that caught me by surprise, entered Hannah's eyes, and I suddenly knew that this wasn't some silly little high school girl crush. She liked this boy. *Really* liked him. "I know there's been other girls, I'm not stupid. But it's different when you actually see it for yourself."

"What happened?" Ellie reached out to take her hand.

Hannah's lip trembled, her throat working as she fought to control her emotions. "A few weeks ago I saw him kissing this girl outside the cinema. Like, really, really kissing her."

Ellie sighed, a deep-seated understanding in her expression, and from everything Ellie had told me about her past with Adam, she *really* understood. "So you finally decided to move on and accepted a date. This is like déjà vu," she muttered, squeezing her little sister's hand.

"Scott"—Hannah flicked her gaze to me—"the date from last night. He's a nice guy. He's in the year above me. A lot of girls like him. So I said yes."

"What happened?"

"Wait for it," Jo murmured, her mouth twisted in annoyance. "It's bloody typical. Men," she huffed.

"Marco moved here from Chicago. He's living with his aunt and uncle. They own D'Alessandro's."

"Oh, my God, I love that place."

"Liv—" Ellie bugged her eyes out at me. "Stick to the program."

"Oh. Sorry." I winced. "Continue."

"Marco works for his uncle at the restaurant, something he never actually told me." She seemed perplexed by this. "He goes to Telford

College. He's studying to become a carpenter. I didn't know he was working too."

She was silent a moment as she got lost in her own thoughts.

"Hannah." Ellie shoved gently at her leg. "The rest of the story?"

"Scott took me to D'Alessandro's."

We all sucked in a breath, suddenly realizing where this was going.

"Marco was bussing tables. He saw us together and he looked . . ." She shrugged, seeming lost. "He looked furious. When Scott went to the toilet, I tried to talk to him, but he just . . . he barely looked at me and then stormed off. Disappeared."

We were all silent for a moment and then I offered unhelpfully, "Sounds complicated."

"Sounds *epic*." Ellie smiled at her little sister.

"This is why I didn't say anything." Hannah glowered up at Jo while gesturing to her sister.

"Hey," Ellie snapped, not something she did a lot, considering she was a pretty sunny person. "Stop treating me like some fluffy romantic. I can be useful, you know. In fact, I'm an expert on guys who push you away for inexplicable reasons when it's obvious they fancy you."

Her sister eyed her carefully. "That *is* true."

"I say let him hang." Ellie shrugged. "When I shut Adam out, that pushed him to make his move."

"Wasn't that your tumor?"

Els glared at her. "The tumor was a catalyst, but believe me I was wearing him down with my absence before all that."

Hannah bit her lip at Ellie's tone. "Sorry. I didn't mean to sound cavalier about your tumor."

"Forgiven." Ellie blew air out between her lips. "So? What are we going to do? About Marco, that is?"

For a little while we sat around debating the best move, all of us considering it seriously, since it was plain as day that this was no ordinary crush for Hannah. This mysterious Marco guy, whoever he was, meant something to her, and I wanted a description so I could go into D'Alessandro's and check him out. Hannah did not seem interested in playing games with him and was leaning more toward Jo's advice to try and get him to talk to her. As the girls left the room ahead of me at Elodie's call upstairs, I was suddenly hit with a realization.

Hannah, a girl who was yet to turn seventeen, had more of a love life than I did.

"And isn't that just depressing," I muttered, as I walked downstairs.

"What's depressing?"

I turned at the sight of Cole coming out of the toilet, his eyebrows raised in question.

"Tortoises," I answered immediately, lying because the truth was just embarrassing and way too complicated to explain to a fifteen-year-old boy. "They're so grumpy-looking."

Cole eyed me like I was nuts, which I might just be. "You're a little weird, Liv. You know that, right?"

I nodded in resignation and started walking toward the dining room.

"But you're wrong about tortoises."

Affection rushed through me, and I turned to him with a questioning smile. "I am?"

"They're not grumpy. They're just contemplating things. That's why they take their time getting places. They're constantly thinking things through."

My grin widened and he smiled back at me. "It's official. You are just as big a geek as I am, Cole Walker."

He grunted at me. "Aye, if cooler than ice is now being mistaken for geek."

Laughing, I followed him in to dinner. "You're spending too much time around Nate. His cockiness is wearing off on you."

"I don't suppose you're reshelving history books, are you?"

The familiar smooth voice surprised the heck out of me, and as I jerked my head back to stare up at Benjamin I felt my tongue immediately twist itself into a knot.

It was Monday afternoon and I'd taken a moment away from the quiet help desk in the reserve section to reshelve returned books. Benjamin had crept up on me as I sat on my haunches, putting a few books back on the bottom shelf of the last book stack in the room.

His green eyes were friendly and inquiring. "I'm looking for a book in this section."

Taking a deep breath, I tried to remember everything Nate and I had gone over, and yet sitting at this guy's feet I still felt incredibly inadequate. This was supposed to be my moment. I was supposed to start flirting and begin the first day of the rest of my life.

Instead I managed to unknot my tongue as I stood up, my hand reaching for the trolley of books and articles as though it would prop me up. "What are you looking for?"

He glanced down at a piece of paper in his hands and then gazed directly into my eyes. "*Sex Crimes, Honour, and the Law in Early Modern Spain.*"

As soon as the word "sex" fell from his mouth, my cheeks blazed.

His lips quirked up at my prudish reaction, and I ducked my head over the books on my trolley in humiliation and started searching through them. "Um"—my hands were shaking from the horror that I was still as socially awkward as I had been two weeks ago—"here it is." I grabbed the leather-bound book and quickly held it out to him, unable to meet his eyes.

"Thank you." He exhaled. "I thought I wasn't going to get my hands on it."

I didn't say anything, just nodded.

"Okay. Well, thanks."

I nodded again and waited for his shadow to move away. As soon as his footsteps faded I lifted my head and stared at the space where he'd been.

It was official. I was a loser.

And Nate was totally wasting his time.

For the next few days I avoided having to listen to my own thoughts. At work that was pretty easy because I kept myself busy, and was constantly in Angus's face asking him for more tasks. I wouldn't have been surprised if he thought I'd started a diet that consisted only of Red Bull . . . or crack. Considering he hadn't done a random locker check, though, I was guessing he was erring on the side of Red Bull. Or, you know . . . just plain crazy.

That night I had dinner with Dad and Dee and didn't go home until I was so tired I practically collapsed on my bed as soon as I got inside the apartment. Tuesday night I did a little shopping after work and bought a bunch of comedies on DVD. I didn't want depressing, maudlin, or angsty. I wanted my mind off anything that could possibly take me back to that one minute of absolute loserdom in the reserve section with Benjamin.

By the time Nate arrived for our lesson on Wednesday night just after eight o' clock, I was ready to quit.

So much for grabbing life by the balls.

Knowing Nate could eat an entire supermarket after judo class, I'd laid out a bunch of snacks on the coffee table and had a Steve Carell movie playing in the background. When he walked in, his hair still wet from the shower he'd obviously quickly taken before coming over, I studied his confident swagger as he entered my apartment. Nate didn't just walk; he prowled. This was a man confident in his body and he knew how to use it.

God, I envied him.

"Babe." He grinned at the food I'd laid out for him and quickly sat down on the sofa to be nearer to it.

"Beer?"

"Please."

I brought him the beer and flopped down beside him.

Nate instantly raised a questioning eyebrow, unsurprisingly reaching for a mini chocolate donut first. He had a bit of a sweet tooth. "What's with you?"

Watching him munch on the donut, I debated whether to tell him or not. Before he'd walked in I'd been ready to hold my hands up, apologize, and explain it had all been a waste of his time. Now that he was here, however, I started to wonder if he'd be disappointed in me. It didn't say much about me if I gave up on myself so quickly, especially when Nate was refusing to do so.

"Benjamin came into the library on Monday."

He gestured for me to go on as he took a swig of beer.

"It was a car wreck, Nate. He asked for a book called *Sex Crimes, Honour, and the Law in Early Modern Spain* and I blushed from the tips of my toes to the roots of my hair."

Nate winced.

"He tried to speak to me, and I was so mortified that I'd blushed I just kept looking at my feet like a five-year-old crushing on her ten-year-old neighbor."

"Crap, what is it with this guy?" Nate asked, settling back against the couch.

"I don't know." I shrugged. "I think it's a mental block."

"A mental block?"

A mental block indeed. It wasn't that hard to understand why I couldn't flirt with Benjamin. The reason why was the reason I'd been avoiding thinking about the whole thing for the past few days. It was just too depressing. "A mental block," I repeated. "It's the bit that comes after the flirting that is causing my mental block." I lowered my gaze, nervously twisting my fingers. "If the flirting worked and I somehow managed to get a date with Benjamin . . . I'd be terrified."

"Terrified?"

"It's the no-experience thing, Nate. It makes me feel inadequate, unsexy. It doesn't matter how much you tell me that I'm attractive, or how much we work on silly flirting, that inexperience is always there, taunting me. It's stopping me from doing anything." Feeling my cheeks burn, I prepared myself to explain to him just how bad the situation was. "I've kissed two guys, Nate. Two nights of kissing. That's it. And one of those nights I was spectacularly drunk and I lost my virginity. Two guys in my entire twenty-six years on this planet. I don't even know if I'm a good kisser or not."

The apartment was silent except for the murmur of the movie. I'd turned the volume down when Nate buzzed up, and now it was just an annoyance in a tense moment.

"Nate?"

He shifted a little closer, studying me carefully. "It's easy enough to find out."

"What do you mean?"

"Kiss me."

I jerked back. "What? No!"

He smirked. "I'll try not to take that personally."

"No." I hurried to reassure him. "It's not that you're not kissable, you know you are, you handsome bastard, it's just that you're Nate. We're friends. It might get weird."

He grinned at my answer. "Liv, we're grown-ups. I think we can handle an experimental make-out without freaking out and gabbing to all our friends about it."

I made a face at him. "Funny."

"Well." He gave me a "what are you waiting for" look. "Kiss me."

The pulse in my neck began to throb. "You're serious?"

"Completely."

My eyes dropped to his mouth. He had a great mouth. Kind of a perfect mouth, actually. "Now?"

"Now."

Trembling, I shimmied across the sofa so our knees were touching. "Just kiss you?"

I saw a dimple flash but ignored the fact that he was laughing at me. I was too busy hyperventilating over whether or not I was about to give Nate Sawyer the worst kiss of his life.

My chest began to rise and fall quickly as I scrambled to catch a proper breath.

"Calm," Nate murmured.

At his advice, I sucked in a huge breath and with it the fruity scent of Nate's shampoo. He wasn't wearing his usual heady cologne, and instead smelled fresh, clean.

For some reason it made me think of him naked.

*Oh, boy, Nate naked.*

Feeling my skin warm, I saw the question in Nate's eyes—as if he knew I'd had an indecent thought and wanted to know what exactly it had been.

To shut out his question, I leaned up and pressed my quivering lips to his.

His body tensed for a moment, seeming to want me to take the lead.

His lips were warm and soft as I brushed my own tentatively against them. Realizing he wasn't going to make a move until I *really* kissed him, I leaned closer, my breasts brushing his chest, and I pressed my mouth harder against his, my tongue running gently across the seam of his closed lips.

His mouth parted, letting me in. I flicked my tongue against his, and suddenly I wasn't in it alone. He moved his lips against mine, gently licked at my tongue until all I could taste was sugar and beer and Nate. Our kiss deepened.

Goose bumps rose all over my arms, and my breasts swelled against him.

He groaned, the sound vibrating in my mouth.

My fingers tightened in his hair. I couldn't even remember putting them there.

My chest was pressed against his. I couldn't remember him putting his arm around me to haul me close.

God, he could kiss.

And his tongue. Wow. He could use his tongue. The thought of him using his tongue on other parts of me added fuel to the already quickly-growing-out-of-control fire inside of me. My skin was ablaze. I felt like I was going to burst out of it any second, and I just couldn't care. All I cared about was the taste of Nate.

The pressure built between my legs, and frustration grew along with it. I needed more. More somehow. Clasping my hand around his neck I pressed my knee between his to bring me that little bit closer. Wanting a deeper taste, I sucked on his tongue.

A growl rose from the back of Nate's throat and suddenly I was pushed away from him. The absence of his mouth was almost painful. It took me a minute to come out of the fog of desire to realize Nate was staring at me wide-eyed, panting.

Reality settled around me.

For a moment I'd forgotten why we were kissing in the first place.

I clenched my hands into fists to stem the trembling in my fingers. "Was . . . was that okay?" I asked, my voice low and raspy.

Nate's expression changed, as his eyebrows lifted in disbelief. That I'd asked the question? Without saying a word, he reached for my hand, uncurled my fist, and then placed it on his thigh. Caught in his dark gaze, my heart still pounding from arousal, I pliantly let him graze my hand up his leg. I froze in shock when he slid my palm over the erection straining against the zipper of his jeans. "What do you think?" he asked, his own voice gravelly with arousal.

My eyebrows hit my hairline.

Feeling him hard beneath my hand and knowing that I'd got him into such a state sent a rush throughout my whole body. Not only was I completely turned on, I felt somewhat liberated to know that I *could* kiss. That my kiss could in fact make a guy as wonderful and as experienced as Nate Sawyer hard for want of me.

Reflexively I ground my palm against him and his eyes grew lidded, his breath stuttered. I felt that telltale flip deep in my lower belly. I wanted his hand on me. I wanted—

*I BELONG WITH YOU. YOU BELONG WITH ME . . .*

"Shit!" I gasped as the Lumineers blared through the room from my phone and brought me crashing back to reality. Wrenching my hand from Nate's lap, I couldn't meet his gaze as I knocked over the box of mini donuts trying to get to my cell. "It's my dad," I muttered, and lifted the phone to my ear.

I didn't have to answer, but Dad always worried when I didn't—and honestly, right now I needed an escape. "Hey," I answered, sounding out of breath, which I kind of was. My cheeks burned even hotter at the thought of talking to Dad after having been feeling up Nate.

"You okay? You sound out of puff," Dad asked, concern in his voice.

I scrambled for a lie. "You caught me in the middle of Pilates."

A tap on my knee brought my eyes reluctantly back to Nate. He gestured to the door and stood up. "I'm going to go," he mouthed.

I searched his eyes for any clue as to how he was reacting to what had just happened, but if he had any thoughts on the matter he was hiding them well. I gave him a little halfhearted wave, barely listening to my dad tell me about this television he'd seen on sale that would be better than the secondhand one I currently owned, as I watched Nate walk out of my apartment.

There was no way I could concentrate after that. I tried watching another movie and eating the snacks Nate had left behind, but my body was still taut from being left high and dry, and my emotions were all over the place. Mostly, however, I was just worried that I'd done damage to my friendship with Nate.

Finally, I caved and sent him a text as I got into bed.

### Did shit get weird?

I was staring at the ceiling in the dark when the Lumineers started "hey-ho-ing" at me again, and I lifted my cell to see that Nate was calling. Relief mingled with fear as I picked it up.

Nate was laughing on the other end of the line. "A little," he answered my text with no preamble. "But it doesn't need to be. Especially if it helped?"

My whole body relaxed into my mattress at Nate's reply. Despite still feeling a little anxious about the whole thing, I decided he was right. It was only weird if we let it be weird, so I snorted instead and answered, "I'm not worried I can't kiss, if that's what you're asking."

"Oh, babe." His deep voice rumbled in my ear and I was pretty sure my pupils dilated as the tingling started up between my legs again. "You can kiss. Believe me."

"Well, I certainly believe your dick."

His burst of shocked laughter did nothing to quell my suddenly burning cheeks. Did I actually say that out loud?

*Soda Pop, you're not in Kansas anymore.*

"Were you blushing when you said that?" Nate asked, and I could hear his wide grin in his words.

"Maybe," I mumbled, pressing a cool hand to my inflamed cheek.

His response was another hot, low chuckle that did funny things to my insides. As I lay there listening to him breathe, I couldn't believe how much my mood had been transformed from earlier that day. I'd felt out of touch with life. I'd felt lonely, pathetic, and inexperienced. I'd felt defeated.

Tonight I felt turned on, I felt alive, I felt a stirring of power inside me, and I didn't want that to go away. The only way I knew how to feel it again . . . was to ask Nate to help me. But that was really crossing a line, and I didn't know if he'd do it, and I didn't know if I was willing to risk our friendship just so I could feel sexually empowered.

"Liv?"

"Yeah?"

"What's going through your mind? I can almost hear it down the end of this line."

I closed my eyes, my heartbeat escalating as I readied myself to ask him.

"Liv?

"Um . . ." The phone actually shook in my hand. "Um . . . I was wondering . . ."

"Aye?"

"I was wondering . . ." I slumped as bravery deserted me. "What happens next?"

"Well, I was thinking you could practice flirting in a real situation."

Alert now, I asked quietly, "What does that mean?"

"We're going out for drinks with everyone on Saturday night, right?"

"Yeah? So?" I didn't know if I liked the sound of where he was going with this.

"Saturday morning before my judo class, we're going shopping for a dress. You're going to dress in something sexy, so you feel sexy, and then when we're out at night, you're going prove to yourself you *are* sexy by flirting with a guy and getting his number."

I was silent as I took this in, already feeling the butterflies in my stomach.

"Olivia?"

"Mm-hmm?"

"Babe, you have nothing to worry about. I promise."

Trying to be brave again, I put my faith in him. "Okay. I trust you."

# CHAPTER 10

Y awning, I shook my head when Nate held up a clingy red number.

His jaw clenched as he put it back on the rack. "Is there anything you like? And can you please bloody wake up?"

We were standing in the middle of a high street designer shop just off Princes Street, trying to find something sexy for me to wear that night. We'd been attempting this for two and half hours and although I was deliberately delaying it to torture him, I was unfortunately torturing myself in the process. I threw my hands on my hips. "You woke me up at seven thirty in the morning on a Saturday. I'm tired. I'm bored. I hate shopping. I'm one of those women that actually can't stand changing rooms, and mannequins freak me out. I own a T-shirt that says ONLINE SHOPPING IS MY SAVIOR. *Comprende?*"

Nate folded his arms over his chest, bracing his legs apart. He was wearing dark blue jeans, black boots, a slim-cut white T-shirt, a black blazer, and a beanie. He looked gorgeous and *awake* and everywhere we went women surreptitiously gazed at him, their eyes filled with longing . . . until they turned their focus to me—and the longing changed to envy as they assumed we were together.

I had to admit that part of the shopping trip was kind of fun.

"Do you think I want to be here?" Nate asked, irritation clipping his words. "I fucking hate shopping."

I grinned teasingly as I playfully punched his arm. "Then let's blow this joint, baby!"

A dimple appeared and I knew he was trying not to laugh and thus ruin his beleaguered countenance. He held it together. "Liv, we need to get this done."

Pouting, I clasped my hands together. "Please, let's just go."

His eyes dropped to my mouth for a moment before he lifted them to search my face. "Do you want to feel sexy tonight?"

Slumping at his question, I exhaled, gazed around me, and answered in the affirmative.

"And do you own anything that makes you feel marginally sexy?"

"Just underwear," I admitted with a shrug.

He was quiet at my answer, so I looked back at him. He was smiling. "That's good to know. However, I don't think you were planning on it going that far, so let's find you an outfit. I have class in a couple of hours."

"Excuse me." A young sales assistant approached, her smiling eyes eating Nate up, who was at least ten years her senior. "Can I help at all?"

Nate quirked an eyebrow at me and I answered with a long-suffering sigh before turning to the girl. "I'm looking for a dress. Nothing *clingy*," I said pointedly, my eyes on my friend. "Belly pouch," I reminded him and then turned back to the girl. "Do you have any peplum dresses?"

"Eh . . ." She shook her head. "We have peplum tops but no dresses."

"Do you have matching pencil skirts?"

"Oh, yes. This way." She turned on her heel and started striding away from us.

Nate was looking at me suspiciously. "Peplum tops? Pencil skirts?"

"What? I said I hated shopping. I didn't say I didn't know how to dress."

"I'm going to kill you," he muttered in my ear as we followed the girl. "You've been dragging your feet for two and a half hours."

I stopped and grabbed his arm to halt him. "Honey, you woke me up at seven thirty. On a Saturday."

"Are you saying the past few hours have been payback?"

I shrugged nonchalantly. "I didn't say anything of the sort."

"Here we are." The girl called to us and I hurried toward her to escape Nate's frustrated growl. I felt the heat of him at my back as I stopped in front of the clothes rail where she stood. "We've got three different styles of peplum tops and there are a few pencil skirts here that would work with each."

"Perfect." Nate slapped my ass heartily—so hard, in fact, that the noise of it ricocheted off the walls of the store. And it stung. Like, *really* stung. "My baby will look gorgeous in these."

The girl blinked in as much surprise as I did before murmuring her excuses to leave us to it. Once she was out of earshot, I slowly turned my head to look him in the eye. "What. The. Hell. Was. That?"

He patted the sore spot soothingly. "Payback for the payback," he murmured with an unapologetic smile. Without another word he grabbed a few tops in my size along with skirts and shoved them at me. "Try them on."

Snatching the clothes from him with one hand while I rubbed my sore backside with the other, I hissed at him, "You'll pay for that."

I spent the next twenty minutes stonily trying on outfits for his approval. Finally we decided on a low-cut black peplum top with a sweetheart neckline and a sapphire blue leather belt that looped around the waist, a skintight black pencil skirt that came to just below my knees and had a pretty pleat in the back, and a pair of blue suede stilettos and matching clutch. Nate was very happy with the outfit. I, on the other hand, was too busy planning my revenge for the ass slapping to really pay much attention.

It wasn't until we were at the counter and the girl gave me the total cost that I turned to Nate and sweetly asked, "Honey?"

He raised an eyebrow at me. "What?"

"I forgot my wallet."

His eyes narrowed. "No, you didn't." He gestured to the purse hanging from my shoulder. "It's right there."

"That's my purse. It's not got my wallet in it," I lied.

"I saw you put your wallet in there this morning, sweetheart," he reminded me through clenched teeth.

"Well, now I don't have it, sweetheart," I replied through my own clenched teeth.

We glared at each other for a while. Until I won.

Glowering at me the entire time, he took out his own wallet and pulled out his credit card. As the girl was putting my items into the shopping bag, I rested a hand against Nate's chest and pressed a soft kiss to his cheek, then brushed my mouth along his ear. "Payback," I murmured, leaning away as he turned his head to meet my eyes. His own smoldered hotly, and for a moment I lost my breath. Ignoring the thrill of desire that pooled between my legs at his expression, I whispered, "My ass cheek is throbbing."

A smile cracked his taut demeanor. "Fair enough. We'll just call this an early birthday present." He grabbed the bags and wrapped my hand around them.

"No." I shook my head, following him out of the store. "It's payback."

"Birthday present," he called over his shoulder.

"Payback," I insisted adamantly, almost tripping over my own feet as I hurried to catch up with him out on the street. "Dude, that is one of the coolest things I've ever done. You are not taking it away with some nonsense about a birthday present. It is payback." I lifted the bags to emphasize my point.

Nate shook his head as he grinned. "Babe, it was the coolest thing you'd ever done until you admitted it was the coolest thing you've ever done." He laughed at my mulish expression. "Fine," he conceded. "It was payback."

As we headed down Princes Street we were quiet in the slowly thickening crowds of pedestrians, until finally my good manners got the better of me and I said softly, "Thank you for my early birthday present."

A lot of women turned their heads to watch Nate Sawyer laugh hard at me before throwing his arm around my shoulders to cuddle me into his side.

I had to admit . . . it was a pretty good place to be.

The bouncer at Club 39 drank me in from head to foot and then murmured a flirtatious "Evenin', darlin' " as he moved aside to let me through the door. I did my best not to flush at the appreciative gleam in his eyes. Instead my legs shook as my heels clacked against the stone floor of the entrance. I was such a nervous wreck about tonight I'd ended up running late and had to text Jo to let her know I'd just meet her, Ellie, and the guys at the bar. It was the bar that both Jo and Joss used to work in, and we often went there socially because they still knew most of the staff and we could almost always get a table.

Honestly, it wasn't my favorite place to hang out. It was dark and crowded, and because it was a basement bar it was a little claustrophobic. The furniture was sparse and uncomfortably modern, and the dance floor was the size of my tiny kitchen. There was a hint of pretention to Club 39 that turned me off, and frankly I was worried I wouldn't be able to find someone here that I actually wanted to flirt with badly enough to pass Nate's latest test and win myself a phone number.

If the thought of this evening's goal wasn't enough to make me want to upchuck, what I was wearing and the admiring looks I was getting from guys definitely did.

Nate was right. I did feel sexy in this outfit. I had a goodly amount of cleavage on show, my waist looked tiny, and my hips über curvy. The top and skirt accentuated all the positive aspects of my figure and hid the negative. I'd also spent a lot longer on my makeup than usual, highlighting my pale eyes with smoky eye shadow and plumping my lips with dewy lip gloss. My hair was easy because I actually had good hair. It fell down my back in sultry dark waves that were perfect for the outfit.

Altogether I was feeling very Marilyn Monroe in it. That didn't mean I knew how to handle going from conservative to super vixen.

I ignored the attention my outfit was getting—something Nate would be pissed at, considering I was supposed to be throwing flirty smiles around—and my hand tightened on my new clutch as I searched the bar for my friends.

I found them in the corner, already sitting on the strange leather cuboid that was supposed to be a couch. Ellie was her usual sophisticated chic in a pale pink shift and silver stilettos, and Jo was her usual sexy glamour in a figure-hugging electric blue dress and matching high-heeled sandals. They were sitting with their fiancés, laughing at something Nate was saying as he leaned his elbows on his knees, cradling a beer in his hands. Adam was wearing a designer suit that fit him perfectly, while Cam wore dark jeans and a Ramones T-shirt. Nate was wearing a blue dress shirt and black slacks.

All three of them were droolworthy.

As I approached the table I kept expecting them to look up and smile and welcome me. Instead, Ellie, Jo, and Cam looked up, stared right through me, and glanced away before sharply turning back to me with sudden recognition. Adam's and Nate's eyes soon followed.

Jo's stunning face broke into a massive grin. "Oh, my God, Olivia, you look . . . amazing."

I fidgeted, completely uncomfortable under their perusal. "Uh, thanks. Moving on." I grinned goofily and was about to make my way to Ellie's side to sit down when Nate grabbed my hand and maneuvered me beside him. I smiled at him and then instantly shivered at the way he was checking me out. Finally our eyes met.

"You look insanely fuckable."

I laughed, trying not to flush. "As always, I'm charmed by you, Nathaniel."

"You have such a way with words, Nate," Ellie agreed dryly.

Adam grunted. "He's worse than Braden."

Nate shrugged and took a swig of beer before replying lazily, "I say it how I see it."

Attempting to let Nate's blunt compliment bolster my nerves, I began to search the bar for my victim.

Target?

Okay, that didn't sound any better.

*I need a drink.*

I gestured to their glasses. "Another round?"

Adam immediately stood up and edged past the small table we were crowded around. "I'm buying. Corona and lime?"

Usually that was my drink, but tonight I decided I needed something a wee bit stronger. "Talisker and ginger ale. On the rocks."

He set off to the bar, and I felt Jo's eyes on me.

"You okay?"

"Aye. Are you? Whisky?"

"I just feel like something a little different tonight." I looked away again, searching. There had to be a guy who elicited some kind of visceral reaction in me. Enough of one anyway that I'd want to strike up a flirtation with him.

The smell of Nate's cologne drifted over me as he leaned in to murmur in my ear, "See anything you like?"

It took a lot of self-control to stop myself from turning to him, raking my eyes over him pointedly, and purring back, "Definitely, baby."

However, I wasn't ballsy enough or cool enough to do that. Maybe later, with a few fingers of whisky in my bloodstream, I'd be ballsier.

"I'm looking," I told him quietly. "I feel like I'm going to throw up all over my new shoes."

"Please don't. I know how much they cost."

I grinned, my eyes roaming the bar. "I'll try not to, for your sake."

"Appreciated."

For the life of me I couldn't see anyone, but I wasn't actually concentrating too greatly. With Nate's thigh pressed alongside mine, and his cologne lingering in the air around me, I found myself distracted by how aware I was of him. Of course, I was always aware of him, but now I was aware of him in a way I was always aware of someone I was attracted to.

I stiffened at the sudden realization.

*Oh, boy.*

"What?" Nate's fingers curled around my wrist, drawing my gaze to his face again. He was so close I could probably count every single long thick eyelash that framed those seductive eyes of his.

I scrambled for a reason to explain the sudden tension in my body, my eyes flying back to the bar. They stopped on a tall blond guy who bore a mild resemblance to Benjamin. "I found him." I jerked my head in the guy's direction. He was standing just away from the bar, drinking a pint of lager and laughing with two of his friends as they checked out the girls around them. He wasn't amazingly gorgeous, but he had an attractive smile and nice broad shoulders.

"Good. Now, go up to the bar to retrieve your drink from Adam, and start flirting with the guy you've picked out."

Out of the corner of my eye I saw Jo studying the two of us carefully as Ellie and Cam chatted loudly over the music. Feeling the blood heat in my cheeks at the thought of Jo, or anyone, discovering what we were up to, instead of asking Nate for advice on how to start up a flirtation like I really wanted to, I just nodded mutely and stood up.

I smiled at the girls as I passed them, ignoring their inquiring eyes. I threaded my way through the crowd, trying to put a swing in my hips like Jo did when she was wearing heels. My heart was pounding so hard that the blood whooshed in my ears, and I was pretty sure if I said one word it would come out in a trembling garble. On shaking legs, I approached Adam, who was standing near the end of the bar and near my target.

"Hey." I slipped in at his side and spotted my glass of whisky on the bar. "Mine?"

"Yeah, I was bringing it over."

"No need." I grabbed it and tipped its contents down my throat, my eyes watering with the burn. I patted my chest and gave a little cough. "Woo!" The burn began to dissipate, leaving a nice heat that rose in my chest. Leaning over the bar and ignoring Adam, who was staring at me like he'd never seen me before, I tapped Alistair, Jo and Joss's ex-colleague, on the shoulder. He turned from pouring a pint and smiled in recognition.

"Olivia, what can I get for you?"

"Another Talisker and ginger ale on the rocks." I slapped the money on the counter. "Keep the change."

He took the money with one hand while he slid the pint to his customer.

"Eh, are you okay?" Adam frowned at me.

I nodded rapidly. "Never better." I cut a look at my target out of the corner of my eye to make sure he was still there.

Yup.

Okay.

I sucked in a deep breath, trying to tamp down the riot of nerves in my belly.

Turning my head as if I were casually checking out the club, I let my eyes pass over him and then come back. He caught the movement and looked at me, a spark of interest in his eyes.

That was good.

I smiled and he smiled back.

That was better.

Leaning around the bar so my cleavage became a bit of a focal point, I asked, "I've seen you around the library, right?"

The blond stepped closer to me and away from his friends, still smiling as he checked me out. His gaze dropped to my chest for a few seconds longer than was polite and then came back to my face. "Library?"

"The university. I'm a librarian there. You're a postgrad, right?"

His grin widened. "No, but now I wish I was. I don't remember librarians like you when I was at university." He had a sexy English accent and definitely seemed interested.

I might actually pass the test.

"Here you go, Olivia." Alistair slid my drink toward me and as he did I met Adam's eyes. He was looking between me and the guy as if unsure of whether I'd invited the attention or not. To reassure him I smiled, gave a flirty shrug, and deliberately turned back to my target.

"So it's Olivia?" He'd braced an elbow on the bar, bringing our bodies closer. So close that even in heels I was tipping my head back to look into his eyes.

"Yeah. And you are?"

"Will." He held out a hand for me to shake, which I did, quite liking the feel of his strong hand wrapped around mine.

Yeah, I could definitely do this.

"Is that an American accent?" His eyes searched my face with interest.

"Yeah. I was raised in the States, but my dad's Scottish, so we moved back recently."

"How do you like it?"

I grinned and answered honestly, "It's been great so far."

Will dipped his head, his blue eyes glittering with sexual intent that surprised me. It shouldn't have, since that's what I was hoping for, but still . . . I didn't feel that comfortable if I was honest with myself. I didn't know this guy and I didn't know how he'd react to harmless flirting. For some people there was a fine line between feeling flirted with and feeling like you were being sexually led on. Especially if you were in fact just an experiment . . . and were indeed being led on. "This is going to sound really forward and cheesy, but has anyone ever told you that you have the most amazing eyes?"

*Yes. Nate Sawyer did. And it sounded a lot better coming from him.*

I looked down and then glanced back up at him from under my

lashes. "Thank you," I murmured and then casually twisted my head to look back over at my friends.

Nate was standing near the table, but a short, slender and well-formed blonde was practically pressed up against him, and he dipped his head to her ear to be heard over the music, his lips brushing her skin.

I shivered, feeling cold, and the nerves in my stomach turned to ash.

He wasn't even aware that I was doing well on his test. There was a pretty blonde girl with slim hips and a gorgeous face pressing her body against his, so why would he be aware of anything *I* was doing? Heat, and this time I was pretty sure it was the heat of hurt and anger, burned under my skin, and I looked away, only to catch Jo's eye. She stared at me for a second and then glanced back at Nate. When she returned her attention to me, I could see the concern in her expression, so I smiled at her like I hadn't a care in the world and turned back to Will.

He was frowning.

Great.

"Is that your boyfriend?" he asked, tipping his chin in Nate's direction.

"No." I rushed to assure him. "They're all just my friends."

Relaxing, he said, "So you are single?"

"I'm single." So single it wasn't funny. "You are, right?"

"Hard to believe it, but yeah." He gave a little self-deprecating laugh, and I relaxed too, liking his answer.

"So, what is it you do, Will?"

"I'm an engineer."

Intrigued, I took a sip of my whisky, nursing it now that I felt more calm. "Tell me about that."

And as it turned out that was pretty much the way to a guy's heart. Or at least to Will's. For the next thirty minutes I asked about him, his interests, his work, his hobbies, all the while smiling and giving him the impression that everything he said was fascinating.

I had him eating out of my hand.

However, if it hadn't been a test I'd have given up ten minutes before then. I kept waiting for Will to ask me questions about myself, but for the most part he seemed happy to revel in my attention.

Getting bored, I shrugged with mock reluctance. "I really should get back to my friends . . . but . . ." *Be brave, Soda Pop.* "Can . . . can I have your number?"

Will grinned and held out his hand. "Give me your phone."

Opening my clutch, I pulled out my cell and felt the relief swamp me as Will typed his number into it. When he handed it back to me, he curled his hand around mine and gently tugged me forward, holding me to him as his head descended.

I stood frozen as he pressed his mouth to mine.

Then Nate and his blonde popped into my head and I angrily let my lips part.

Will kissed me, his tongue lightly touching mine.

It wasn't a bad kiss. In fact, technically he was a good kisser.

But I felt nothing.

Pulling back, I smiled a little shyly, which he seemed to like, and I said, "I'll call you."

Once he let me go, I ignored the grins his friends threw me and turned on my heel to head back to my table.

Nate, no longer with the blonde, was watching me with an unfathomable expression on his face. My eyes quickly darted over him to the others. Cam and Adam were grinning boyishly at me, Ellie was biting her lip to stem her own immature little smile, and Jo looked confused.

"What was that?" she asked, looking at my phone.

I waved it, and filled my voice with amusement and nonchalance as I replied, "I got myself a number." My eyes flicked to Nate and he gave a chin lift, silently beckoning me to him.

I sat down next to him and waited, but he didn't say anything until the others started talking among themselves. "Enjoy yourself?" he asked quietly, his eyes searching mine.

I shrugged. "I passed your little test."

His dark eyes flicked back to the bar, where Will was still standing with his friends. I waited for some kind of reaction, but his expression was blank when he turned back to me. "I didn't say you had to kiss a stranger."

"No. But I did."

"Seems I've got an overachiever on my hands."

I shrugged.

We were quiet for the rest of the night, I think mostly because I was lost in my own thoughts. When it was time to head home, as usual Nate insisted on walking me. I hugged the girls good-bye and said good night to the guys, then followed Nate down George Street in the gorgeous heels that were starting to pinch.

"So . . ." I tried for breezy. "It looked like you got a number tonight."

"The blonde."

I snorted. "Is that her name?"

He slanted me "a look." "It's the only name I need to know."

In that moment I really had to try to remember why he was the way he was so I didn't call him on his asshattery. Tonight he would drop me off at my flat and then he'd call up the blonde girl, go meet her wherever, screw her, leave her, and then delete her number from his phone.

It was not a good way to live, but it was the way he chose to live, and I had to respect his decisions. If he was just your regular old player I'd give him a lecture until his ears bled, but every time I thought of it now, I thought of the tattoo he had inscribed across his chest.

The closer we got to my flat, however, the more uneasy I grew, and as I remembered the hurt and fury that had ripped through me at the sight of him flirting with the blonde, it occurred to me that maybe it wasn't that I was uneasy at his choices, but at the thought of him leaving me to go screw some stranger.

I didn't even want to analyze that.

Yet, as we came to a stop outside my building, I found myself saying his name quietly.

"Aye?" he asked, shoving his hands in his pants pockets.

Staring into his handsome face, I reached somewhere deep within me for the courage I needed to ask him the question that had been burning inside me since we'd kissed. I led with, "When we kissed it helped."

He gazed back at me, waiting silently for me to make my point.

I cleared my throat, taking a mental bat to the swarm of butterflies that had erupted in my belly. "I felt better," I said, attempting to explain. "I felt . . . more confident."

"What are you trying to say, Liv?"

Where was another whisky when I needed it?

"Um." I wet my suddenly dry lips. "I want you . . . I want you to teach me how to be . . . good at sex."

Nate's focus sharpened and he asked with a surprising calmness, "In theory or in practice?"

"Practice."

The silence between us stretched so long that my butterflies were now multiplying at an unbelievable rate. Mortification and regret mingled as I began to feel awful for even asking, for putting him in that position. "Nate—"

"How much have you had to drink?"

A little affronted at the insinuation, I shook my head quickly. "I've only had a few whiskies. I'm not drunk." I took an apologetic step toward him. "Look, I'm sorry if I've made you uncomfortable. I didn't mean to. We can—"

Nate pressed a silencing finger against my lips and I abruptly shut up. "You are one of my closest friends. I don't want to do anything that might ruin that."

Ignoring certain feelings—and by "ignoring" I mean shoving them into the deep, dark depths of me—I concentrated purely on the thought of my own chrysalis as I hurried to assure him. "If I promised it wouldn't, would you think about it? I just . . . I want to feel like I know what I'm doing. If I do, I feel like I'd be able to approach Benjamin with confidence, knowing that if he said yes to a date and afterward, if the date went *there*, it wouldn't be this traumatic, nerve-racking thing for me. I trust you, Nate. And it wouldn't exactly be a hardship," I added with a small smile, which he returned with one of his own.

"So, let's get this straight. You want me to fuck you in order to teach you how to fuck another guy?"

"You make it sound so sordid."

With a sigh, he leaned forward and pressed a sweet kiss to my forehead. "Go to bed, babe. If you still feel the same way in the morning, ask me again."

"It was hard enough asking you the first time," I muttered under my breath as I turned to unlock the door to my building.

Nate heard and I felt his strong hand on my hip, his heat at my back as his breath whispered over my ear. "It was brave, Liv."

I looked back at him, a small grateful smile on my lips.

"Dutch courage or real courage, I guess we'll find out tomorrow," Nate said.

And then he was gone, and the cold wind rushed over my skin as he left me unprotected at the door. I hurried inside, my heart fluttering as though a thousand of the butterflies in my stomach had escaped into my chest to cause havoc there too.

Those butterflies kept me company the whole damn time I struggled to fall asleep that night.

# CHAPTER 11

I did drift off to sleep, waking up a little after noon, just in time to shower, get dressed, and wait for Dad to stop by the apartment and walk with me to Elodie and Clark's for Sunday lunch.

In the hours before sleep, though, I had time to really think, as Nate suggested.

I came to one conclusion: I wanted to see this through. I even felt I had to. But . . . what I hadn't considered when I blurted out my request to Nate was our friends. We were a pretty tight group, and although I was sure Nate and I could contain it, I was a little worried about any impact that this would have on the dynamics of our group. I was also more than a little worried that I was overly confident in my belief that Nate and I should jump into this deal and it would all be okay.

But I *really* wanted to see this through. The truth was I didn't believe I was ever meant to be an insecure person, and that was because for the most part I wasn't. I believed in my own intelligence; I believed in my own common sense; I believed that my personality, albeit quirky, was a good one; I believed that I was capable; I believed that I could do whatever I set my mind to. I wanted to believe that if someone didn't like me, then that someone wasn't worthy of my time.

I believed in *me*.

I believed in all the things written within me, I'd just somehow along the way stopped believing in my book jacket. I don't know why. But I don't think that was ever meant to happen. I don't think I was ever meant to be the kind of person who questions her own adequacy; who allows anyone to make her think she's lacking in some way.

But there I was. That's how I felt.

And I was tired of moaning and whining and complaining about it to myself. I'd watched my beautiful young mother battle through cancer and lose that fight. Life was short. Too short to spend it hating a part of yourself, and not doing something to get your confidence back. Too short to not be *living* it.

Sex was a massive part of life and living. I felt unqualified in it and there was someone who could give me a little practical experience to build my confidence and take me closer to that woman I believed I was always meant to be.

So, after lunch, I had every intention of calling Nate and asking him my question again. There was no fire from the whisky to keep my courage ablaze. There was just me and my determination to become a woman who liked herself . . . all the way through.

Turns out, I didn't need to wait until after lunch to ask my question.

Not only did Elodie have an extra person to feed in Dee, but Nate had dropped by Cam's earlier that day to hang out, and he ended up with an invitation to Sunday roast as well. Not that Elodie cared. With the Nichols family it was always "the more, the merrier."

It did mean, however, that I found myself standing outside on Elodie and Clark's tiny terrace at the back of their house, enjoying a warm spring day with Jo while the others were inside.

I was waiting for Nate, and my nerves were jumping all over the place. Thinking of the moment when I'd have to repeat my request to him, I nervously chugged an entire glass of water.

"Are you okay, Liv?"

I glanced, wide-eyed, at Jo. She was watching me, appearing concerned.

"You seem wired."

Taking in her expectant expression, I suddenly wanted to tell her everything. The words crawled up my throat and got stuck as my heart pounded hard.

"Liv?"

For all my determination, I grew very unsure as I gazed at my friend. What if Nate and I starting this thing really was a bad idea for us all? "I have this friend," I blurted out. "From work. He laid this dilemma on me and you know what I'm like, I like to have the right answer."

Jo grew thoughtful. "Okay. What's the dilemma?"

"He has this group of friends. They're all close, but there's a girl in that group that he likes and they both want each other, but with their histories they don't know where something between them could lead. They're also worried how it'll affect their group."

I tensed when I finished talking, attempting to pretend that Jo didn't look as if she didn't believe for one second the dilemma was the dilemma of a colleague. I waited for her to call me out.

"Well"—she heaved a sigh—"I think if your friend likes this girl he should go for it."

Relief flooded me and I felt myself relax. Jo wasn't going to out me. Great.

"You think?"

A reassuring little smile played on her lips. "If he really wants to go there and it feels right for him, then he should. No one knows where a relationship is ever going to lead. We go into these things blind and as it progresses, as you get to know each other, the light starts streaming in. As for the group of friends . . . well, if they're as close as you say they are, then they'll understand. They'll go with it and they'll handle it, whatever happens."

I drew in my breath as Jo reached for my hand. Her eyes told me she saw through my subterfuge, and the comforting squeeze she gave me told me she had my back.

I sort of, kind of, loved the heck out of her in that moment.

"There you are," Cam said as he slid open the French doors and stepped out onto the patio, followed by Nate.

I smiled in greeting, my nerves starting up again at the sight of Nate, and I let him, Jo, and Cam carry the conversation as they sipped chilled glasses of Coke.

"Peetie and I were talking about visiting home for a long weekend in a few weeks' time," Cam said to Nate. "We thought all of us"—he gestured to everyone—"could go. We could rent a house, split it six ways."

"Six?" Nate frowned.

"Well, me, Jo, you, Liv, Peetie, and Lyn. Of course Cole will be with us, too."

Nate turned to me. "What do you think? Fancy meeting my folks?"

Inside my head there was a small version of me jumping up and down with glee and excitement at the prospect of meeting Nate's parents, seeing where he came from, and delving further into the history that had created the man I'd come to know. On the outside I gave a nonchalant nod and an agreeable smile. "Sounds good."

"Great." Jo reached for the sliding doors. "I'll start looking into finding us somewhere to rent."

She and Cam moved inside to the empty dining room, Cam holding the door open for us. Nate shook his head. "We'll be in soon."

That meant he wanted to speak to me alone.

I sucked in a breath as Jo and Cam disappeared.

Nate didn't say a thing.

A minute passed.

Two.

Finally I huffed, "Are you going to make me say it?"

"Depends." He smirked at me, but I noticed there was something careful in his eyes, something a little like apprehension. "What is it you're going to say?"

Glancing back at the door, I made sure we were definitely alone before I spoke. "I wasn't drunk last night."

There was no hint of humor on Nate's face as he replied, "You trust me to do this with you, but I've got to trust that you won't try to make this into anything more than a friend helping out another friend."

Okay, so deep down in that dark place where I'd shoved it last night there was a little thing called jealousy that had reared its ugly head when Nate took that girl's number. But that was just a blip and I could get a handle on it. I was attracted to Nate, yes, and yes, I cared about him, but I had a big old crush on Benjamin, not Nate, and Benjamin was the goal here.

Trying to bring a little levity to the conversation, I said, "I'm sure I'll somehow manage *not* to fall for you."

His left dimple flashed in and out. "I'm sure that'll be easy for you."

"I'd like to point out something."

"Point away."

"I know you're used to getting laid. But I'm offering a chance here for *completely* hassle-free sex. It can't be too much of a hardship."

"No." He smiled suggestively. "Not a hardship at all." For a moment he was silent as he contemplated my proposition. He looked back at the door, making certain we were still alone. "Well, if we're doing this, I'll get myself checked out and I promise not to fuck around with anyone else during . . . our lessons." I knew I didn't keep my surprise at his offer off my face because he scowled immediately. "Babe, if you're going to start up a sex life, be smart about it. I get checked every three months, and when the time comes for you and this Benjamin guy, make sure he's clean before you start anything up. I'm not due for a checkup for a few weeks, but I'll move it up for you. Maybe you should think about going on the pill."

Now that we were discussing particulars my heart had joined in the conversation and it was *loud*. It thumped, thumped, thumped behind my rib cage, determined to let me know that it was freakin' out slightly. I willed it to chill. "I'm already on it. It regulates my . . . you know." I couldn't control the blushing.

Nate closed the gap between us so his chest grazed mine. "Not rethinking your proposition already, are you?"

*Uh . . .*

"No." I forced my courage back to the fore. "I just want to clarify that you understand what you're getting into. I mean, I know I was being all cocky about you getting regular sex and it not being a hardship, but the truth is this isn't a casual sex arrangement. This is you . . . teaching me . . . *stuff.*"

Nate's eyes instantly brightened with mirth and he repeated quietly, "Stuff?"

My cheeks burned. "Stuff."

"Stuff?"

I looked around us, watching for listening ears. Finding none, I looked back into his eyes, ignoring the awareness that tingled across my body as our chests brushed. "How to . . . how to please you," I muttered under my breath.

A glitter of heat entered his eyes as they dipped to my mouth. The air around us changed. I felt my breasts swell, and that all-too-familiar arousal between my legs.

My breathing hitched.

As did Nate's.

I felt his warm hand on my hip and he gave me a hard squeeze before stepping back, allowing the oxygen to flow freely into my lungs again. "This is the wrong place to tease you." His voice was low, thick with . . . sex?

He was just as turned on as I was.

Surprised, I gave him a nod, brushing my hair back from my face. "Yeah. We should . . . we should go in."

"You go on." He gestured to the door. "I'll be in, in a second."

My hand was on the doorknob and I was just about to step inside when his voice, wrapped around my name, stopped me in my tracks.

"Yeah?" I looked back at him over my shoulder.

"We'll start tonight." Nate's expression was filled with sexual promise that sent a shiver coursing down my spine as though he'd trailed a finger down my naked back. "I'll come by your place around nine."

I could barely eat at dinner.

And now it was eight fifty in the evening and Nate was due at my apartment in ten minutes. I was hoping that as soon as he walked through the door some of the nerves would at least give way to anticipation, because all I was feeling at the moment was anxious. Thankfully it was a massive step up from the fear I knew I'd be feeling if it was Benjamin I was expecting to walk through that door. With Nate there was an element of safety because I knew him so well. I knew he would never hurt me or make me feel stupid or ugly or anything negative. He was the perfect tutor to walk me through this because I trusted him completely.

I'd showered when I got home and then put on a light layer of makeup. Under my slacks and shirt I was wearing my favorite set of lingerie. It was white satin edged in lace and it looked nice against my olive skin. I was hoping it would distract him from my belly and my flabby thighs.

"Do not use the word 'flabby,' " I admonished myself, remembering Nate's warning.

Not really knowing how to act or what to do, I hurried around the apartment trying to tidy the piles of books and copies of Nate's review magazine I had lying everywhere. I wondered if perhaps we needed some mood music, and turned on the radio. Then I immediately decided that was a bad idea since it wasn't me, and Nate would know it wasn't me and guess how much I was freaking out over the situation. So I turned on the television instead. Five minutes later I decided it suggested indifference and I didn't want him to think I was indifferent either.

I was so busy flapping around like an idiot that when Nate rang my buzzer I ended up tripping over a pile of books, scrambled to my feet only to slide along my wooden floors on the socks I was wearing, and crashed against the buzzer. At least I hit the entry button. I opened my apartment door and took a deep breath.

Feeling sweaty and icky and not the least bit attractive, I frowned down at my socks and wondered why the hell I was wearing them in the first place. They were not sexy. I stooped to take them off, but the right one got stuck. I pulled and pulled, cursing the little mothereffer to hell as I hopped about on one foot. I'd just managed to peel the darn thing off when I hit my left ankle on the coffee table, taking a knock to a funny bone, and I went crashing down, whacking my head on the soft cushion of my couch.

"Jesus, are you okay?"

Pushing back my hair, I gazed up wide-eyed at Nate, who was now standing in my doorway. "I'm fine," I told him breathlessly.

He shut the door behind him, his eyes roaming my body—probably for signs of injury. "Are you sure?"

"Of course," I told him brightly and then realized I had a pair of sweaty socks in my hands. Not sexy. I stuffed them quickly under the couch and got to my feet, swaying a little with the rush of the movement.

Laughter curled the corner of his mouth as he shrugged out of his leather jacket. "Are you sure you're okay to do this? We don't have to."

I ran a shaky hand through my hair. "I'm good. Honest."

Crossing his arms over his chest, Nate braced his legs apart and studied me carefully. Finally drawing some kind of conclusion, he gave me a small nod. "Okay. Do you know how you want to start this thing?"

"Well . . ." I moved a tiny bit closer to him, finding some calm in his presence. "I was thinking we could work through the bases. We've already done first base and kind of second base . . ."

Smiling at me, Nate scratched his jaw in thought. "That's an American thing. You'll need to talk me through it."

*Say it out loud? Uh . . .*

Desperately trying not to look embarrassed—this was Nate, for God's sake!—I took another step toward him. "First base is kissing. French-kissing. Second base is touching, and thir—"

I pointed to his crotch.

He was struggling not to laugh at me. I appreciated the effort. "Liv, we're going to have sex. I think you need to get used to talking about it."

Stubbornness made me thrust my chin out. "Fine." *You can do this. They're just words.* "Second base is touching my breasts over or under clothes and third is touching me . . . between the legs." *Oh, my God, oh, my God.* "Or me touching you."

Nate's lids lowered and he dropped his arms to his sides. He took a step toward me so we were only a few inches apart. "Touching me where?"

*It's just a word.*

The blush stained my cheeks as I licked my lips and uttered, "Your dick."

His eyes flashed fire and I noted his shallow breaths as he asked, "And third base?"

"Oral," I answered instantly, squeezing my legs together at the thought of Nate's head between my thighs. I'd never received or given oral sex. I was at once intrigued and nervous regarding those particular acts. According to literature and the movies, I was in for a treat.

"And I can guess what a home run is." He cocked his head, biting his bottom lip as he considered the information. "Hmm, it's a plan. But I think the most important thing right now for you is to lose what you're wearing."

I felt the tremors start in my fingers at the thought of standing stark naked in front of Nate. "Now?" I squeaked.

He gave me a no-nonsense look. "You're going to have to stand in front of this guy naked. How are you going to be able to do that if you can't do it with me?"

"Completely naked?"

After a moment of silence, Nate offered me a patient and kind look. "Okay, we'll take it step by step. Strip to your underwear."

A shiver went through me at his demand, but I found myself replying, "You could ask nicely, you know."

His lips twitched. "Olivia, sweetheart, would you please strip down to your underwear for me?"

"Was that so hard?" I huffed under my breath as I started quickly unbuttoning my shirt.

"Is this a race?"

I stilled my finger on the third to last button. "Huh?"

Nate chuckled. "You're undressing for me. Hurrying through it makes it feel like an inconvenience rather than titillation."

My arms dropped to my sides and I nudged a shoulder toward the back of the apartment. "Maybe we should go to my bedroom."

"If you'd be more comfortable."

Exhaling, I fought through the belly flips and moved toward my room. I stood at the end of the bed and waited until Nate crossed the threshold and then, in what I considered a brave moment for me, I looked directly into his eyes and slowly began to unbutton my shirt. Nate grew still as I peeled it off my shoulders and let it drop to the floor, leaving me standing in my bra and slacks. I didn't mind that part so much. It was the next part that I'd dreaded, but I kept Nate's voice in my head, filling it with his compliments. Hopefully he would still think all those nice things once the pants were off.

I fumbled a little on the top button of my slacks, but Nate didn't comment on it. The sound of my zipper was incredibly loud in the quiet room, and I felt the tension between us mount. With a deep breath I placed my hands on either side of my hips and pushed the slacks down, dropping my eyes with sudden uncertainty as I carefully stepped out of them.

I didn't know what to do with my arms.

"Babe." Through my lowered lids I watched Nate take a step toward me. "Liv, look at me."

Arms hanging awkwardly at my sides, I slowly lifted my chin.

His expression winded me.

Heat and sincerity shone through it as he told me in a low, rumbling voice, "You're gorgeous."

My hand automatically self-consciously covered my belly, and I fidgeted as I thought about my thighs being on display. Nate took three determined steps toward me until I had to tilt my head a little to meet his eyes. He took hold of the hand that covered my belly and gently moved it back to my side.

"Don't hide from me." He bent his head to whisper over my lips. "Ever."

I glanced down at his shirt with a nervous smile. "Maybe you could lose something so I don't feel like I'm out to sea on my own here."

He grinned at me and stepped back to casually lift his T-shirt over his head.

I sucked in a breath.

This was the first time I'd ever seen Nate shirtless and I was kicking myself for not going to those judo classes with him like he'd asked. He wasn't the tallest guy, nor the bulkiest; in fact he was pretty compact, but every inch of his torso was roped with muscle. Between judo classes and weekly visits to the gym, Nate took care of his body, and I was enjoying every second of that upkeep.

Until my eyes drifted over the stylized "A" just under his left pectoral.

*Alana.*

A ghost in the room.

I ducked my head, pretending I hadn't been affected by the sight of the tattoo, and then glanced up at him from under my lashes with a faux-saucy smile. "I've seen worse."

Nate laughed and threw his shirt aside. "You know how to make a man feel good."

"Oh, come on, you know you're hot."

"It's nice to hear that *you* think so, though."

Hiding my surprise at his admission, I laughed lightly and replied, "I'll be sure to mention it often, then."

His mouth dipped toward mine again. "Appreciated."

As goose bumps prickled across the swells of my breasts, I gestured around the room. "What now?"

"Do you want to start with me or with you?"

I frowned in confusion. "Why would we start with me? I know what I want. This is about learning what you want, learning to be good at doing it to you."

Nate immediately shook his head, a frown marring his brow. "How can you know what you want when you've only had sex once, Liv? You not only want to be confident you can get him off, you want to be confident in your own pleasure." His fingers moved to the buttons on his jeans and he began to undress. Blood whooshed in my ears as I watched. "Know what it takes to get you off and then let him know. If he doesn't want to know how to get you off, then get him off you."

At that my eyes drifted back up to his face and I snorted, relaxing a little. "I'll keep that in mind."

"Make sure that you do. Sex is a two-way street."

"Okay."

"So . . . me or you?"

"Uh . . ."

"We'll start with you." He kicked his jeans off. I admired his athletic body. He was by far the best-looking guy I'd ever seen in real life and I was about to have sex with him.

"This is a little surreal," I murmured without thinking.

"It's about to get very real," came his deep, seductive reply.

"Oh, boy."

He laughed again and stepped back into my space, the back of his knuckles brushing down the curve of my waist and sending a lovely shiver rippling down my spine. "I'm going to take off your underwear," he whispered, his warm breath dancing across my mouth. "Are you ready for that?"

I'd already stood in front of him in my skimpy lingerie and somehow gotten through it without feeling like a heifer. In fact, surprisingly, Nate had made me feel kind of . . . hot. I nodded, a little tongue-tied, my eyes lifting to his as his fingers skimmed around my back to the clasp of my bra.

"You really do have the most stunning eyes," he breathed as he expertly unclipped my bra, his own beautiful dark brown eyes penetrating mine.

I almost purred, my chest rising and falling quickly now as I felt his fingers caress my shoulder blades before drifting over the straps of my bra.

As he smoothed the straps down my arms he traced little circles in my skin. "Like silk," he whispered.

My bra fell from my body and Nate's gaze dropped to my naked breasts. They swelled under his attention, my nipples puckering in the cold air. "Babe," he said appreciatively, and I shuddered at the feel of his warm hand cupping my right breast, his thumb sliding across the nipple. "Fuck me, you're gorgeous."

A light switched on inside me, its luminance shining from the very depths of me, and I knew Nate caught that light because when our eyes met again he grew very still.

"Thank you," I managed to force out. *For making me feel beautiful.*

I didn't have to say the words out loud. Nate got it.

In answer he crushed his mouth over mine in a hard, deep kiss, and cupped both breasts, thumbs gliding over the pebbled nipples. I gasped into his mouth as heat dove through my belly heading for my sex. Wanting to touch him but still unsure, I trailed my hands tentatively over his chest, learning the feel of him under my fingertips. He was warm, his skin smooth, and I felt his strength in the coiled, hard muscles of his body. I throbbed at the feel of him under my hands.

He broke the kiss and my swollen lips pouted in disappointment.

His grin was wicked as he edged his body into mine and kept going until I had to move with him. The back of my legs hit my footboard. "Get on the bed," he commanded hoarsely. "Lie back."

I did as he asked, leaning up on my elbows, waiting excitedly for his next move. My eyes lowered to his black boxer briefs and my breath stuttered at the sight of his raging erection.

*I did that.*

A triumphant smile curled my lips, and my belly flipped at his low, pleased chuckle. It flipped even harder as his hands coasted up my outer thighs and his thumbs hooked into the lace edging of my panties.

I froze, my eyes darting to his.

"Liv . . ." His tone was reassuring.

Nodding, I lifted my hips to help him and couldn't stop the blood heating my cheeks as he slowly peeled my panties down my legs and let them drop to the floor.

He took his time eating me up with his eyes. "I like the underwear, but I've got to say, I don't think you've ever looked better than you do right now."

*Oh, wow. That's so nice.* Telling him I thought so might have spoiled the mood, though, so instead, still blushing, I croaked out, "What now?"

"Lie back and trust me. I want you to tell me if you don't like something I'm doing and let me know when you really like something I'm doing."

The breath whooshed right out of me as I lay back, watching him as he got on the bed and settled his knees on either side of my waist. The heat from his body hit mine and he wasn't even touching me. His cologne taunted me, its heady scent affecting not only my sense of smell but my taste buds as well. I wanted to find its origin on his body and I wanted to lick and suck and kiss his skin until he was groaning underneath me.

It seemed Nate had a similar idea in mind.

Hands braced on the mattress on either side of my head, he bent to graze his lips over mine. Back and forth, back and forth. Teasing. Tingling. Frustrating. Just as I was about to complain impatiently, he kissed me harder. I moved my lips beneath his, our tongues stroking each other in a deep mating that brought me new understanding of the sexual promise of a kiss. The kisses I'd had before had been mechanical—a bit like Will's at Club 39—and I'd felt nothing, not realizing that a kiss with someone you were attracted to, a sensual kiss, was a prelude to what was to come.

I gripped Nate's waist as the kiss grew rough and breathless; I sighed into his mouth with pleasure as his erection stroked my belly. He groaned, his lips drifting from my mouth, across my chin, down my jaw. He kissed his way down my body, his mouth hot, hungry, and I held on, caressing his muscled back, sliding my hands up toward his shoulder blades as he moved downward.

When that hot mouth of his closed around my left nipple, my hips slammed against him in reaction. "Oh, God." My thighs gripped him as I urged him closer, my back arching for more as he first licked me and then sucked hard, all the while pinching my other nipple between his forefinger and thumb.

I felt a wet rush between my legs.

"Nate." My fingers dug into his shoulders. "Oh, God . . ."

He lifted his head, his eyes black as he undulated against me, his dick pressing between my legs now, only the fabric of his boxer briefs shielding me from its throbbing heat. "You like that, Liv?" he asked, his voice thick. "Like me sucking hard on your nipples?"

I flushed at his crude question but found myself nodding quickly. "Yes, I like it."

He groaned and dipped his head again, licking my other nipple now. I'd had no idea my breasts were that sensitive. As he continued to suck and tease and torment me, I felt the coil of tension tighten in my lower belly.

"Nate—" I was panting hard, clutching his head in my hands as he circled his tongue around my areola. "I can't . . . I don't . . ."

Suddenly he was moving, sliding down my body, his hands cupping and shaping my breasts as he descended, his lips trailing wet kisses down my stomach. I shivered at the touch of his tongue across my navel and then tensed when I realized his destination was the apex of my thighs.

Nate caressed my stomach reassuringly, and looked into my eyes. "Open up, sweetheart."

Biting my lip, I gazed down at him half in wonder and half in anxiety as I let my thighs fall open. Nate settled between my legs. His hand glided along the inside of my thigh and he asked, "You've never done this?"

I shook my head, too excited to speak.

A spark of mischief entered his expression. "I'm looking forward to this reaction."

He kissed me there.

I shivered. It was nice.

And then I felt his fingers slide inside me and a mew of delicious surprise escaped my lips, bringing Nate's eyes up to my face. They were intense, the mischief gone and replaced by sexual intent. His fingers slipped out of me and then back in. My hips pushed against them, trying to catch his rhythm.

"You're drenched, Liv," he groaned. "You're so wet and ready for me."

"Yes," I choked out, tilting my hips up. "God, yes."

With a growl of satisfaction, Nate dipped his head again. His fingers slipped out of me, but before I could mourn the loss, he parted my labia and I nearly came off the bed at the feel of his tongue on me.

He circled my clit, teasing it, pressing it . . . and then he sucked it.

I cried out, feeling my orgasm building quicker than I'd ever experienced before as he continued to lap at me, pushing me back up toward climax.

When he pressed his fingers inside me, I burst apart, crying out his name like a prayer as my eyes fluttered shut. I writhed against his talented mouth, my fingers curled into the bedding beneath me. The orgasm rolled through me in waves and I pulsed and pulsed against his mouth, until finally I was a limp rag doll.

I felt him move up my body and when I eventually pried my eyes open he had his hands braced on either side of my head again, his lower body pressed to mine. He was wearing this pleased, cocky smile on his face. He brushed his fingers across my cheekbone affectionately, his eyes searching. "I take it that was good."

*That* was an understatement.

The first and only time I'd had sex, I didn't come. However, I had been supplying my own orgasms since I was eighteen and I won a vibrator in a student raffle. Those orgasms had been good. A few had even been great.

None of them had been *sensational*.

Until now.

Lazily, I lifted my hands and clasped them around Nate's neck, my thumbs brushing along his jaw tenderly. "I'm going to let you keep that smug look on your face. You earned it."

Nate chuckled and kissed me, letting me feel his laughter tremble against my lips in a way that was incredibly hot. I smiled beneath it, but as it grew heated, as I tasted myself on his tongue, the smiles and laughter disappeared and I curled my fingers tighter into his hair.

I broke the kiss before he did and said breathlessly, "Your turn."

There was a flash of something in his eyes, something I didn't completely understand, but what I did know was that he was hungry. He shifted, moving off me to lie on his back, his arms crossed casually behind his head. "I'm all yours."

The butterflies returned to my belly, not as many as before, but they were there, cheering me on as I prepared to go down on a guy for the first time.

"I've never . . ."

Nate's countenance gentled and he reached out to smooth my hair behind my ear as he replied, "I know, Liv. And you don't have to. Ever. You only do what you're comfortable with."

My gaze flickered to his lap and his hard cock. "I want to at least try."

"Then I'll talk you through it," he answered. Quicker than a few blinks, he had shoved his boxers down his legs and kicked them off.

I stared openmouthed at him.

When I lost my virginity I didn't really get time to study my chosen asshat of a partner's penis. He'd just pulled down his zipper and pushed inside of me.

Nate's strained toward his belly. It was long and thick and it was throbbing. I was guessing it was impressive. The thought of it inside of me set off a new wave of arousal, but as I imagined wrapping my mouth around it, I began to feel apprehensive.

"How . . ." I looked back at him wide-eyed. "I . . ."

"Liv?" His brows creased. "Just say it."

It rushed out in a burst of geek. "Its size is a little problematic because despite my tendency to ramble, my mouth is pretty small and it won't all fit in it and I have a gag reflex that might be a problem so I don't know how—"

"Liv—" Nate was choking on laughter. "Take a deep breath." He closed his eyes and shook his head, keeping his inner thoughts to himself. I worried for a moment that my inexperience was suddenly a turnoff. But when his lids lifted he smiled, so I took that and his still raging hard-on as good signs. "Take me into your mouth and while you suck me off, pump the root with your fist. The key is to fist it hard but not too hard. Suck hard. Teeth sheathed."

I nodded, hoping I could do this.

"Liv, we seriously don't have to do th—ahh," he hissed as I cut him off by wrapping my mouth around him.

At first I was frozen by the foreignness of having him in my mouth, tasting him, feeling him as if he were all around me, as if there was nothing else in the world but him. It felt odd. It felt alien. And I was afraid I just wasn't cut out for this part of sexual intimacy.

Until I looked up at his face from under my lashes.

This was Nate.

I gathered my courage.

I began to do everything that he asked, and as I did I watched him—watched the color rise in his cheeks; watched the way his chest rose and fell in rapid breaths; watched his fists curl in the sheets around him; watched his mouth open on pants; watched the sheen of sweat build across his skin; watched his abs ripple. And I got off on it. I didn't expect to like going down on a guy, but I loved the sensual power that rushed through me at knowing I could make Nate feel so turned on that he huffed out my name in pleasured tones.

"I'm coming," he panted, sliding his hand into my hair, and I jerked back just in time to watch him shudder through a climax.

As his body relaxed, he dragged his hands over his face and into his hair, his eyes closed to me and thus his reaction closed to me.

I waited, unsure.

Slowly Nate opened his eyes and stared up at me.

*Well?*

"Did you enjoy that?" he asked roughly.

"Yes," I whispered back.

"Good, because I'd certainly like a repeat performance sometime." He blew air out between his lips and shook his head, grinning, before his bright eyes came back to me. *"Fuck,* girl."

Laughing softly in relief, I lay back on my bed and stared at the ceiling. "I take it I got a high score on my first lesson in seduction."

"Like I said before . . . you're an overachiever."

The bed moved and I turned my head to watch Nate sit up and slide his legs off it.

"Where are you going?"

He gazed back at me over his shoulder. "I think we've done enough for tonight. I don't want to overwhelm you."

I frowned, unhappy with this turn of events. "Isn't that up to me?"

Nate was reaching for his underwear, but I could see his shoulders shaking with amusement. Instead of answering, he strode out of the room, his muscled ass so biteworthy it took everything in me not to chase after it.

I heard the water running in my bathroom and a few minutes later Nate came back, cleaned up and wearing his boxers. He reached for his jeans and began pulling them on. Once fully dressed, he gazed at me, drinking me in, in all my flushed nakedness.

Strangely, I didn't feel like squirming.

I waited, wondering what he was thinking. Dying to know, in fact. Before, I would have asked him, but somehow the intimacy we'd shared had changed that. Now if I asked him what was on his mind, I might come across as some clingy, wannabe girlfriend. In that moment, I resented my decision to ask for his help.

As if he sensed my dark thoughts, he crossed the room and bent down to press a sweet kiss to my mouth. I felt his fingers in my hair as he pulled back and murmured his carnal promise: "Tomorrow, we fuck."

# CHAPTER 12

———————

Monday might as well have been devoured by fog. I was walking, talking, doing my job, and yet it was covered in this euphoric mist that didn't allow any of it to really sink in. Instead I was consumed by thoughts of the night before, of what Nate had done to me and what I had done to him.

I was consumed with anticipation for the evening to come.

When Nate called around my apartment that night I didn't bother with clothes. I put on another set of nice lingerie—emerald green this time—and wore a robe over it.

I opened the door after buzzing him up, and his eyes sharpened as they drifted over my ensemble. He shut the door behind him and immediately shrugged out of his jacket.

"I like undressing you," he said without even a hello, dumping his jacket over my kitchen stool. "Your Benjamin boy might not care, but since it's me you're about to fuck for the foreseeable future . . . I like to undress you."

Not knowing quite what to make of that except that I liked it, I replied, "Okay, I won't undress next time."

Nate bit his lower lip, studying me. "Tonight's lesson is all about discovering what turns you on. Do you like being in the driving seat, do you like him in the driving seat, do you like absolute control, absolute submission, or give-and-take?"

I hoped I understood what he meant and he wasn't about to reveal to me that he had a thing for St. Andrew's crosses and floggers. Better we found out now so I could run a million miles in the opposite direction. "Uh . . . what do you prefer?"

"Both." He shrugged. "Depends where the mood takes us." He began to prowl toward me, and with my mind still on kink I backed up until I hit the wall. Nate pressed in on me, his hands reaching for the ties on my robe.

"When you say control . . . we're not talking whips and chains, are we?"

He burst out laughing, shaking his head. "No, babe. Just good old-fashioned fucking." The belt came loose and my robe fell open, revealing my lingerie. "Did I tell you you have shit-hot taste in underwear?"

"It *is* nice to finally have it appreciated."

Pushing the robe off my shoulders, Nate's fingers lingered across the tops of them as the fabric pooled at my feet. Watching his hands the whole time, he caressed the skin along my collarbone while I stood shivering with eagerness.

His fingers trailed down my breastbone and over the swells of my breasts. Goose bumps prickled in the wake of his touch and my nipples tightened in expectation. Instead of giving in to their clear cry for attention, Nate let his fingertips drift back up over my chest and gently along my neck, touching a spot just under my ear that made me shudder with need.

The reaction made him smile and he immediately bent his head to graze his lips across the spot. I felt the wet touch of his tongue and the shiver rippled through me again.

"Sweet spot," he whispered in my ear, brushing his lips over it and scattering barely-there kisses along my jaw. When he stopped, hovering above my mouth, he looked deep into my eyes. "Tell me what you want tonight."

I blinked, wondering exactly what he meant.

"Don't think about it," he urged. "Just tell me what you want."

My eyes dropped to his mouth, so close and yet not quite close enough. Hoarse with arousal, I said the first thing that came into my head: "You inside me."

My words affected him. I knew because he braced his hands on the wall at either side of my head and pressed his erection against my stomach. "You want my cock, baby?" he murmured, letting his top lip catch my bottom lip before moving infinitesimally away as I nodded. His lashes lowered over his eyes. "I want to hear you say it."

All evidence was pointing to the fact that Nate liked dirty talk. He'd mentioned it in our earlier lessons, but I hadn't really processed it. Clearly, however, talking about what we wanted to do to each other got him off.

I was learning. And not just about him, but about me.

Because talking about what we wanted to do to each other turned me on too.

I tilted my mouth closer to his, kissing him lightly as I answered thickly, "I want your cock inside me."

"This is the point"—he kissed me softly, his tongue just touching the tip of mine—"where I'd ask"—he kissed me again—"if you want it slow or fast, gentle or hard"—another kiss—"but tonight we'll take it slow."

"It has been a while," I agreed, sighing happily as he began to dust kisses down my neck again.

His lips moved over my breasts, down my stomach, and his hands followed, squeezing my breasts gently before skimming down to my waist. He rested on his knees and I gazed down at him, breathless with anticipation as he sweetly kissed my belly before kissing his way to the edge of my panties. His lips pressed against the silk fabric and I whimpered, flattening my palms to the wall as my body took over, my legs parting. Nate continued to kiss me over the fabric of my lingerie, his hands curled around my thighs. It was a torment, a tease, my body vibrating with need.

My breath stuttered as I felt his tongue push the fabric against my clit. "Nate," I whimpered, my right hand moving to curl in his soft hair. "Please . . ."

He relented, leaning back to remove the panties. I tried to help, but my legs were shaking. After he peeled them off, Nate slid his hands around both my calves and glided his fingers upward. "You've got fantastic legs," he told me quietly. "I remember one night while we were watching a movie and you were wearing leggings. It was the first time I'd seen you in anything that showed the shape of them." He kissed the inside of my knee and looked back up at me with a fierceness that made me throb. "You stretched them out, feet up on the coffee table, and I couldn't stop staring. I couldn't believe you'd been hiding those long, gorgeous legs. I dreamt of your legs that night, Liv. I dreamt they were wrapped around my back while I fucked your brains out."

Need flipped in my belly at his admission. "God . . . Nate . . ."

"That's right, babe," he murmured as he lifted my right leg over his shoulder and parted me. "I'm taking you straight to heaven."

"Heaven. Hell," I panted, my fingers raking the wall. "Who cares as long as I ride there on an orgasm."

It was a strange but not unpleasant sensation to feel the huff of his laughter on my sex.

I smiled.

And then I cried out in relief when his tongue slid inside me at the same time his thumb pressed against my clit.

He worked me expertly. I came quick and hard.

Barely conscious I slumped against the wall as Nate got to his feet.

"Damn," I finally whispered as he undressed. "Your mouth should be illegal."

His answer was a deep, soulful kiss that had me swaying against him. When he pulled back, my bra went with him and he threw it over his shoulder. "Any other day I'd probably just screw you against the wall, but I think we'll ease you into this with the bed."

"I'm fine with the wall." I patted it lazily, still high on my orgasm.

Nate shook his head, his lips twitching. "This might be a bit uncomfortable for you, Liv. We'll take it slow." Gently he gripped my hand in his and I found myself smiling giddily as we walked naked through my apartment. Nate glanced over his shoulder at me and caught the look. "What?"

"We're naked." I grinned.

He gave a short bark of laughter and turned, tugging me against him so our bodies collided. He wrapped his arms around my waist and I gripped his shoulders tightly to stop myself from falling over with the sudden movement. Nate rendered that a fruitless action by spinning us quickly and pushing me down on the bed, falling with me but bracing his body over mine so he didn't crush me.

"Shit," he murmured, getting back to his knees.

"What? Where are you going?"

"The condoms are in my wallet. I still haven't been checked yet." He got off the bed before I could say anything and cool air wafted over my skin as he left the room.

I lay there, staring at my ceiling, feeling his mouth under my ear again and his soft murmur, "Sweet spot."

We'd started this because of my inexperience, but even to me, the inexperienced, this felt like a seduction, not an education in seduction. I bit my lip and stared at the doorway waiting for him to come back. Maybe I was wrong. Maybe this was what it was: all part of building my sexual confidence and experience.

*I dreamt of your legs that night. I dreamt they were wrapped around my back while I fucked your brains out.*

Or maybe it was an excuse to give in to the attraction that had always been there? Attraction we denied because of our friendship.

Nate appeared back in the doorway, his eyes devouring every inch of me as he prowled toward me.

Maybe. Maybe. Maybe.

As he crawled up my body, ripped the condom wrapper with his teeth and rolled one onto his impressive hard-on, I forcefully shoved the maybes to the bottom of my pit of denial. Right then I didn't care *why* we were doing this. I just cared *that* we were doing it.

His hand coasted up my torso and I arched my back into his touch, a blaze of heat lighting me up from the inside out as he rubbed his thumb over my nipple while his other hand slid between my legs. While he coaxed my clit to attention with his thumb, his erection strained, and I couldn't stop looking at it.

"Now." I tilted my hips against his touch. "Nate, come inside me. Please."

He groaned at my invitation, gently pushing my legs farther apart before bracing himself over me. His kiss was long and deep.

I felt him brush against me and to my surprise I tensed.

The last time a guy shoved inside of me it had hurt.

"Ssh," he whispered across my lips, his hand slipping between our bodies again, his thumb finding my clit. "Babe, it'll be okay. Just keep looking at me."

I relaxed, my eyes locked with his. And then he was pushing inside of me, hands on the mattress at the side of my head to hold himself up. His eyes darkened as he pressed through the tight resistance of my body, my muscles squeezing around him. I stifled a whimper. It was uncomfortable. Not painful like last time, but I wasn't sure if it was pleasant either.

Nate shut his eyes for a second, panting. His arms shook a little.

"Nate?" I rested my hands on his waist.

"I just . . ." His lids fluttered open and my inner muscles squeezed him again in response to the sexual heat I saw in his eyes. "You feel . . .

amazing," he breathed, eyes gleaming. "So tight. I'm trying to go gentle, but you feel fucking amazing."

Pleased, I caressed his back soothingly and realized that the discomfort was beginning to dissipate. I was suddenly eager to learn more. My hips automatically lifted, seeking movement, and Nate growled, pulling back out of me. Instead of pulling all the way out like I thought he was going to, he thrust back in. I cried out as I felt the stirring of a beautiful tension.

My eyes were locked on his face, mesmerized by his expression, by the mixture of lust and gentleness in his eyes, by the tautness of his jaw that told me he was clinging to his control.

And he did that for me.

He was slow and tender, his hands gripping my thighs lightly as he slid in and out of me, every stroke a gradual climb toward climax.

His eyes drank me in, watching me pant beneath him, watching my breasts quiver gently against his thrusts, and suddenly he was pushing that little bit harder, moving that little bit faster. "Liv, come for me, babe," he commanded, his voice guttural. "You've got to come for me."

"I am," I promised, lifting my hips against the pumping of his, the coil tightening, tightening, tightening—

Nate's thumb pressed down on my clit.

I shattered. Loudly. My eyes fluttered behind their lids as my lower body shuddered uncontrollably, jerking hard against Nate as he gripped my hips tightly to his and followed me into climax.

When I finally stopped coming, my muscles relaxed to jelly. I think I melted into my mattress, just barely able to lift my arm and curl a hand around Nate's nape as he collapsed over me, his head buried in the crook of my neck.

I delighted in the feel of his chest rising and falling quickly against mine, of his warm breath puffing against my skin. We were both slick with sweat and I didn't care. It felt wonderful.

"So that's what *real* sex is like," I breathed, in awe of it and in awe of the pleasure he'd elicited from my barely tried body.

Nate's lips pressed against my damp neck before he raised his head and pushed himself up. Our eyes met and I stilled. There was something stirring to life in his gaze, something important, possibly profound. Other than when he spoke of Alana, I'd never seem him look so serious. So grave. He stared at me a long moment until . . . his head jerked back as if I'd said something.

"Nate?"

His Adam's apple moved with a hard swallow before he kissed me quickly and rolled off of me.

I couldn't say anything. I didn't know what to say.

Instead I lay there as he walked out of the room. I listened as I heard the water running in the bathroom and then the toilet flushing. There was rustling in the living room and I heard a thump, like a boot against my wooden floor.

That got me up.

I tugged on my sheet, hauled it off the bed and wrapped it around me.

Wandering into the apartment, I found him shrugging his jacket on.

"Nate?"

He smiled at me, but there was something false in it and my heart immediately began beating faster.

"Nate?"

"I'll, eh . . . have to text you when I'm free again."

Something strange, solid and cold, settled in my stomach, but I attempted not to let it show as I shuffled in my sheet over to the glass bowl I kept my keys in. I lifted my spare and held it out to him. "To make things easier. For our lessons," I emphasized.

He gazed at it a moment and then eventually, just as my hand was beginning to tremble, he strode over to take it. He kissed me quickly on the cheek as though he might get burned if he lingered.

" 'Night, babe."

Watching him hurry out of my apartment, I couldn't force a reply past the lump of apprehension in my throat.

I'd been worried all day. Worried something had happened in my room last night that had made Nate rethink this whole lesson thing. Or worse, our whole friendship thing. When he didn't text in the morning, I gnawed my lip. When he didn't text in the afternoon, I snapped at a boorish student who somehow blamed me for his fifty-pound fine, and when Nate didn't text as I was walking home from work I began to despair that I'd seriously effed up our friendship.

The joy I should have felt after our first lesson, the relief of realizing that I'd feared sex only to discover how easy and natural it felt, was overwhelmed by the regret that waited in the wings just ready to be prompted to center stage by Nate's prolonged absence.

I ignored a text from Ellie and didn't answer a call from Jo as I picked at dinner, changed into an overlarge T-shirt that I wore to bed when the weather got a little warmer, and sat down in front of the television to not take in a word of the movie that was playing.

It was a total surprise then when a key turned in my lock and the door opened to reveal Nate carrying a DVD, notebook, and pen.

I didn't know what to make of it.

He smiled at me, a real smile this time, as if nothing had happened last night, and he strode forward, dumping his stuff on the coffee table.

I had my feet on the couch, my arms clasped around my bent knees.

Nate's gaze flickered over my bare legs as he took off his jacket. Our eyes met. And held.

He cleared his throat. "Lesson first and then I have a movie to review."

Part of me really wanted to question him and his weird, erratic behavior. But a bigger part of me was afraid of the answers. Or the consequences. "Tonight's lesson?"

He kicked off his shoes. "Tonight's about confidence. Taking control."

And just like that I realized I was mad at him for the way he'd walked out last night. Really effing mad.

It took over me, turning me into someone else.

Dropping my feet to the floor, I reached out and grabbed his belt, hauling him closer to me. "Sit down," I demanded, my voice cold even to my ears.

A spark of uncertainty appeared in his eyes at my tone. But he complied, lowering himself onto the couch beside me.

I lost no time in making my move.

Straddling him, I gripped his hair in my hands and kissed him hard. His arms banded around me and just as easy as that, Nate took back control of the kiss.

*Fine, no kissing.*

Pulling away, I gently pressed him back with a hand to his chest.

"Well?" he asked, his voice low, eyes questioning. "What now?"

In answer I began unbuckling his belt, quickly unbuttoning his jeans so I could slip my hand inside. Nate hissed as I fisted him.

"Feel good?" I purred across his mouth, a part of me floating on the outside of this little scene and wondering who the hell I thought I was.

"What do you think?" Nate narrowed his eyes, stroking his hands up my thighs and taking the hem of my nightshirt with them.

I released him so I could remove his hands from me. Shaking my head, I tutted at him. "No touching."

Displeasure darkened his eyes. He didn't like that.

*Good.*

I tugged at his jeans and he lifted his hips, helping me free his erection. I didn't bother pulling them all the way down. Instead I pushed down my panties, moving off him so I could kick them off before straddling him again.

"Take off the nightdress," Nate insisted. When I didn't move, he rubbed a hand over my thigh, his expression gentling. "Liv, I want to see you."

I stilled, tilting my head to the side as I studied him carefully. "You do?"

There was so much more in my question than I wished there was.

And just like that Nate understood completely. "I want you. I want you to ride my cock and I want you to ride it hard. And then afterwards I want to sit with my friend, eat some food, and watch a movie with her. I'm not going anywhere." His grip tightened. "Now take off your night-dress."

His assurance made the anger slowly ebb away and as it did I returned to my senses. I flushed at my actions, at my demands, at my cold confidence. Nate relaxed too, with a smug aspect in his eyes when he caught sight of my blush.

In an ironic effort to hide my renewed self-consciousness I lifted the nightdress up over my head and threw it behind me. I didn't even get a chance to say or do anything before I felt Nate's hand on my upper back between my shoulder blades along with the power in his body as he held me to him, his lips sucking on my nipple.

I arched into him, sighing as pleasure instantly coursed through me.

He played me for a while, thinking to make me pliant, but I still had his lessons in mind. He wanted me to learn sexual confidence, and although I had no intention of letting my anger fuel it again, I had every intention of retesting its waters.

As Nate had already pointed out, I was an overachiever.

I moved over him, pressing him back into the couch. "Put it inside me."

His lips curled at the corners. "You put me inside you."

So I did.

I whimpered against his mouth as he sucked in a deep breath.

And then I moved.

I tried to go slow, to take it easy, to build it, but I was too impatient, too desperate for it.

Too greedy.

Too inexperienced.

Yet Nate let me control it.

And by his doing so, we both came hard but much too fast.

I leaned against him, curling my arms around his shoulders as he wrapped his arms around my waist and held me close. "I guess I'm still learning," I admitted breathlessly.

Hearing my uncertainty, Nate gently lifted me away, his expression sincere as he confessed, "No woman has ever ridden me that hard. Believe me, babe, I'm not complaining."

Smirking through my embarrassment, I asked, "Really?"

Nate grinned as he swept a strand of my hair behind my ear. "Really."

It wasn't until I lifted myself off him that the mood changed dramatically. A single expletive fell from Nate's lips.

"What?" I asked, wide-eyed, glancing down at his lap to make sure I hadn't hurt him.

"No condom," he bit out.

"It's okay, I'm on the pill."

He frowned at me as he pulled his underwear and jeans back up. "Liv, I only went to the clinic yesterday. I still haven't gotten the results back."

At that I pulled my panties up and hurried around the couch to go clean up in the bathroom. "I'm sure you're fine," I threw over my shoulder, my heart pounding. I *hoped* he was fine. *Shit.* I shut the bathroom door and leaned on the sink, staring into the mirror in front of me. My cheeks were flushed and my eyes were golden bright. I looked thoroughly fucked. I was. And I'd been in such a rush to get a taste of what was clearly becoming an addiction that I'd forgotten about protection.

Now, if I had kids, I'd forever be a hypocrite when I lectured them about it.

I admonished myself to hell and back, and then it occurred to me that it wasn't just my fault. Nate had forgotten too. I glared at the door and instantly grimaced. I could argue that he was supposed to be the experienced one here, but that didn't really wash when you were twenty-six years old and knew better.

Hearing the noise of the television, I wandered back out of the bathroom to find that Nate had the DVD playing while he was in the kitchen putting together bagels. Suddenly my stomach growled.

Nate glanced up at me. "I'm sorry I forgot the condom."

"I forgot too. But it'll be okay. Right?"

"I've never forgotten protection before tonight, so we should be fine. But we really need to be more careful." He licked cream cheese off his thumb and turned to the fridge for some soda.

Deciding I didn't want another weird ending to our evening, I thought it best not to say any more, so I changed the subject. "What are we watching tonight?"

Nate handed me my bagel and I thanked him, then followed him to the couch. To my surprise he sat closer than usual, putting his feet up on the table and settling in at my side. "It's a musical."

I choked on a bite of the bagel and quickly swallowed so I could ask incredulously, "Are you kidding me?"

Smirking, he shook his head. "It's a satirical musical."

"Does that make it any better?"

"Let's hope so."

As it turned out, the musical was pretty funny at first, but it soon started to go downhill. Clearly bored, Nate took a sip of his Coke and with his eyes trained on the screen, asked, "Would you rather live in a musical or a post-apocalyptic world?"

I immediately smiled, so unbelievably relieved to be hanging out with my friend just like always and answering his weird questions. "What kind of post-apocalyptic world?"

"Think *The Book of Eli.*"

"Harsh."

"Aye."

"So what kind of musical, then?"

He rolled his head on the couch to grin at me. *"Grease 2."*

I spluttered on the sip I'd just taken, and it took me a minute to breathe freely enough to ask, "You've seen *Grease 2?*"

Some of the spark went out of Nate as he shrugged and turned back to the screen. "Alana made me watch it."

Oh. The ghost in the room.

Nudging him with my shoulder, I tried to pass over the moment and bring back his good humor. "I'm definitely going with post-apocalyptic world. Especially if there are men in it that look like Denzel."

His left dimple popped. "I'm going with post-apocalyptic world too."

"Because of Mila Kunis, right?"

"Well, there's that, but mostly it's because I'm anti-violence."

I wrinkled my nose in confusion. "I don't get it. Post-apocalyptic worlds unfortunately tend to go hand in hand with violence."

"Aye, but I'm much more likely to be the one that's killed in a post-apocalyptic world. However, if I have to live in *Grease 2*, there's more than a ninety-five percent possibility that I'll shoot the next fucker that bursts into song." He glanced up at me, all deadpan. "It's just the wrong life for a pacifist."

Giggling, I bobbed my head in agreement. "We're going dystopian, then."

He nodded and then asked with a small pucker between his brows, "So why are you against living in a musical?"

I shook my head, watching the couple on-screen take a shot at a well-known musical. "It's not that I'm against living in a musical per se. I just like the idea of living in a post-apocalyptic world more. I think I'd be badass."

I wasn't looking at him, but I could feel his shoulders shaking.

I slanted him an un-amused look. "Stop laughing at me. I would be so badass."

"Badass how?"

"I . . . I . . . uh . . . Well, I'm smart. And witty. I'd be, like, your witty, quirky, book-smart sidekick while you went around kicking everybody's ass and giving them judo smackdowns."

Laughing, Nate relented. "Okay, that could work." His eyes flicked over me with interest before returning to the screen. "You might be a bit of a distraction, though."

Trying not to show how pleased I was by the compliment, I replied, "That could work in your favor."

"Aye, if we cover your legs up."

I nudged him with my knee and he casually put his hand on my leg, curling it into him. "I think someone likes my legs."

He caressed my skin, almost absentmindedly. "They're great legs, babe." He reached for the notepad at his side. "This is quickly deteriorating."

"The movie?"

"Aye, what else?" he murmured, scribbling something down on the paper. "Any witty comments, O Sidekick?"

Musing, I stared at the screen. "There's a crack about erectile dysfunction in here somewhere."

He huffed in amusement. "And how's that?"

"Well, the plot and songs start off well, each one better than the next, until you hit midway through and realize it's not going anywhere. This proves true toward the final half, where the plot worsens, the songs make your ears bleed, and all the anticipation just—" I raised a hand and let it flop to make my point.

"E-rec-tile dys-func-tion," Nate said slowly as he scribbled it down. He glanced back up at me with a smile. "Anything else?"

# CHAPTER 13

Arter we spent the rest of the evening joking around like old times, I felt much lighter when Nate left for home. Even though we made no plans to meet up again the next evening, I didn't find myself worried sick over it. Nate seemed fine. I knew I was fine. It was all fine.

Any niggling concerns were shoved forcefully back into my pit of denial.

At work the next day my colleagues commented on my good mood, and not just because I'd been in an uncharacteristically bad mood the day before, but because I was in a *gooood* mood.

"If I didn't know any better, I'd say she got laid," Ronan joked as he stood beside me at the help desk.

Thankfully, the wide-eyed look I got on my face was attributed to the fact that he'd made his crack in front of a student, who was now laughing his ass off.

"Funny," I hissed at Ronan when the student walked away.

"It was, actually." Angus chuckled behind us.

"You"—I pointed at him—"are a mean boss."

He laughed harder. "Oh, come on, Liv. You're walking around as though everyone is farting roses and pissing champagne. What's up?"

I blinked rapidly at his observation, making what I'm sure was a "what the fuck?" face. "Farting what and pissing what?" I looked over at my colleague Jill. "Are you listening to this?"

She shrugged, smiling. "He has a point. You've been telling every student to have a 'freakin' awesome day!' all morning."

"So? I'm being polite."

"I'm just saying . . ." Ronan eyed me carefully. "Yesterday you were in a terrible mood and today you're on some kind of natural high."

Blowing them off, I turned away and rested my chin on my palm. "I had a bit of a falling-out with a friend Monday night," I lied, but attempted to keep my story as close to the truth as possible. "We sorted out our misunderstanding. Now I'm in a good mood."

"Well, what a bloody boring explanation that was," Angus said teasingly. "You're a librarian, Liv. You're surrounded by books and material for a good yarn. And you stick to the truth." He tutted. "Have I taught you nothing?"

I smiled sweetly. "I'm quickly learning how to become a drama queen."

"Well, that's something, I suppose. I'll be in my office, then, where in five minutes a dashing stranger who looks an awful lot like Ryan Gosling will shackle me to my desk and do completely inappropriate and naughty things to me for the next two hours." Angus arched an eyebrow at me. "Now didn't that sound better than 'I'll be writing this month's rota'?"

I laughed. "Point taken." I heaved a contrite sigh. "Well, if you must know, Monday night I had wild, amazing sex with this hot guy but shit got weird and I was in a really bad mood about it but he surprised me by appearing in my apartment last night where we had more hot wild monkey sex before we snuggled up and watched a movie. Hence my good mood today."

All three of them looked at me incredulously and then Angus made a face. "My Ryan Gosling story was far better."

I grinned and turned to serve the student approaching my desk, Nate and my secret still . . . well, a delicious secret.

Later that day I was still in a fantastic mood and more than happy to see my dad standing outside my building with a shopping bag in hand. As soon as I reached him, he bent his massive frame so he could press a kiss to my cheek.

"Hi, baby girl. Hope you don't mind"—he lifted the bag—"I brought some food over. Thought I could cook you dinner."

I unlocked the building door and let us in. "Of course I don't mind. It's great to see you."

Once we were inside, Dad immediately set about cooking and soon my apartment smelled like home. Like old times, we chopped vegetables together and I stirred the sauce while Dad boiled the pasta. You wouldn't think there was an art to boiling pasta, but there was. Apparently. Just ask my dad.

Our conversation as we cooked was light. Dad told me about this new contract he'd just signed to work with Braden's company again, while I told him about the sock I'd found in a returned book last week only to come upon the matching sock in the reserve section on Monday. They were dirty socks. I was all for weird. But there was weird, and then there was just *weird*. Angus had this theory that we had a crackpot Harry Potter fan in our midst and this person had somehow confused library assistants with enslaved house elves and by giving us socks thought he was doing a humanitarian act.

I thought it was a pretty good theory.

Better than my theory that some immature freshman was stashing his dirty socks everywhere, laughing his ass off while he filmed me finding them and then put the video up on YouTube.

We ate sitting on stools at my counter, and I was having a great time just chilling with my dad when our conversation took a more serious turn.

"So you've been quiet lately?" He eyed me, his eyes sharp, searching.

I shrugged, feeling guilty as hell about keeping my shenanigans with Nate from Dad. "I've just been busy."

"Did you know Joss and Braden are back from their honeymoon?"

Another pang of guilt. Wonderful. "No, I didn't know that." I swirled a piece of pasta around my fork. I didn't know that because I was too lost in my selfish sexual world with Nate Sawyer to give a shit what was going on outside of it. That would have to stop. "I should call Joss."

"This . . . absence . . . Is it because of Dee?" Dad looked deep into my eyes for answers. "Because I think we should talk about that. About me and Dee, I mean."

My breath caught at his expression, at his words, and I felt my pulse speed up. Sweat coated my palms as I shakily exhaled. "Are you . . . are you going to ask her to marry you?"

Dad frowned and gave a slight shake of his head. "No, baby girl. No. Though I'm going to take all the color draining from your face at the mere thought of it as a bad sign."

"No." I hurried to assure him. "Dad, I like Dee. I don't know her as well as you do, but I like what I do know."

He studied me, not convinced. "Then why do you look ill at the thought of me marrying her?"

Pushing my food around my plate, I shrugged. "It's silly. Immature. I just . . . still think of you as Mom's."

Dad's fork clattered against the plate and his huge hand covered mine, drawing my gaze back to him. His eyes were bright with emotion as he told me in a low, thick voice, "A huge part of me will always be your mother's. I was from the moment I met her. What I have with Dee won't ever change that."

"Is that fair to Dee?" I asked, trying desperately not to cry.

He squeezed my hand. "I'm a different man now, Olivia. Life changes us, second by second. Who I was before Yvonne passed was a man who was right for her. Who I am now is someone I hope is right for Dee. But the most important person in my life is, and always will be, you. I need to know that you're okay with me moving on with Dee. And I'd especially like it if you got to know her better."

I smiled teasingly through the shimmer of tears in my eyes. "Dad, I'm a grown woman. You don't need to be worrying about what I think."

"See"—he shook his head with a grin—"to the world you're a grown woman, but to me you're still my kid. You'll understand that when you've got your own."

"Then if it makes you feel better, I want you to know that I'm glad for you. Dee makes you laugh. She makes you happy. That's all I care about."

"Will you meet with her? Spend some time just you two? I know she'd like that."

Honestly, it's something I should have thought of doing without having to be asked, and I realized that I really had been locked up in my own insecurities and problems for so long now that I hadn't been a very good daughter lately. "Of course, Dad."

Satisfied, Dad changed the subject again, talking about Cole and how Dad and Jo were thinking of getting him a dog if he passed his exams at the end of the school year. Cole had made a comment about how he'd always wanted a puppy and Jo had felt bad that she hadn't known that, and now she and Cam were discussing it with the landlord.

It was funny, but Jo's behavior with Cole reminded me of how Dad was with me. Smiling lovingly at my father, I was feeling all mushy and happy for Cole that he'd been blessed to have Johanna Walker as a makeshift mom.

And it was in that moment of perfect contentment that Nate used his key and walked into my apartment.

The sexy grin on his face froze when my dad slowly turned his head and raised an unimpressed eyebrow at Nate's appearance. They stared at each other for a moment, and then my dad slowly turned his head back to me. He was not happy. "He has a key?"

When I closed the door behind my dad I finally let go of all the oxygen I'd been holding inside me and turned to Nate, my eyes bugging out half in horror, half in amusement. He was sitting on my couch, drinking a cold beer and laughing.

"That wasn't funny."

Okay, so maybe it kind of was. But it also kind of wasn't. We'd just spent the most uncomfortable half hour with my dad as he not very subtly cross-examined us about our friendship. The funny part was watching him try to make Nate squirm. The not-so-funny part was the part where I lied my ass off to my dad about the nature of my relationship with Nate.

Nate put his beer down on the table and stood up, kicking off his shoes. "Your dad is bloody scary," he commented, still amused. I watched, questioning him with my eyes as he began to undress. "Are you sure he's not the reason you haven't had a man in seven years?"

I laughed, my eyebrows rising as he stood before me in nothing but his boxer briefs and a raging erection. "Why? You're clearly not scared of him."

"I'm made of sterner stuff than most men." He strode toward me and grabbed my hand, pulling me toward the bathroom.

"Tonight's lesson?" I asked, since he'd just gone into it without so much as a word.

Nate shut the bathroom door behind us and took the hem of my shirt in his hands to tug it up and off. "Spontaneity. Nothing hotter than a woman who wants to fuck you all the time, no matter where you are or what you're doing."

I unclipped my bra as Nate worked on my jeans. "I'm beginning to think these lessons are personalized lessons on how to please Nate Sawyer."

"You don't realize that all men think that way?" he teased, removing my jeans and panties.

"I don't know." My heart was racing now as he reached into my shower and switched it on.

"Well, most men I know think that way. So . . . tonight? Shower sex. I didn't manage to have one after my class, so I thought we'd share one together." He grinned and dropped his boxers.

I licked my lips and eagerly followed him into the shower. "You know I have a feeling that women like men who want to have sex with them all the time no matter where, too."

Nate's smile was heated as he pushed me under the spray of water and up against the tiles. "It's good to know the shower does so much for you, babe. In the grand scheme of things, shower sex is pretty vanilla. I can't wait to see how you react to me fucking you in the university library."

My eyes widened. "You can't do that," I breathed, growing hot and wet just at the thought of it. "I throw kids out for that."

"But you like the idea . . ." He grazed his lips over mine and lifted my leg. "Admit it."

Before I could answer he thrust into me hard and I would have smacked my head against the wall if he hadn't curled his hand around it to cushion it in expectation of me arching back in pleasure.

"Never mind," he purred in my ear. "I'll take how wet you are as admission."

"Are you sure you don't mind me crashing here?" Nate asked, skimming a finger down my naked spine as I lay on my stomach beside him on the bed.

After the delicious shower sex I'd dried my hair while Nate reheated some of the pasta for himself. By the time I wandered out of the bedroom, he had finished eating and was ready for our lessons to continue. I knew this because I walked out of the bedroom only to have him maneuver me back inside immediately. Three orgasms later, I was thoroughly sated, it was late, and there was really no point in Nate heading home when I had a comfy bed big enough for the both of us.

With my head resting on my arms, I'd been staring at my headboard, my body so relaxed that I was almost purring like a kitten. I turned my head to answer him, my hair rustling across the pillow. "At this point you can have anything you want."

I watched his dimples appear and decided that one day I was really going to have to kiss those sexy little indentations. "Do you really want to make my ego bigger than it already is?"

"Hmm, good point."

We smiled at each other before my eyes drifted closed.

I was dozing when I felt the touch of his lips against my bare shoulder. "Liv?"

There was something in his tone, something solemn that made me instantly alert. Opening my eyes, I searched his face and found his expression equally grave. My stomach flipped with uncertainty as the blood rushed in my ears with the sudden pounding of my heart. "Yeah?"

Nate rolled onto his back, his hands clasped behind his head as he studied my ceiling. "You really are one of my best friends, you know."

My pulse slowed a little as warmth rushed through my chest. Touched, I reached out to skim my fingertips affectionately down his stomach. "Back at you, babe."

"So promise me something."

I stilled. "Okay?"

"Promise me, no matter what, this . . . what we're doing . . . it's not going to ruin that."

I didn't understand the sharp, serrated pain that cut across the warmth that had flooded my chest, but I did understand why he was asking what he was asking. Flattening my palm across his stomach, I moved it until it rested over the "A" tattooed on his skin. "I promise."

His whole body relaxed under my hand and when he turned his head to look at me I saw tenderness and gratitude in his eyes. We smiled at each other again, and I ignored the jagged pain.

After a moment he moved his head back and returned to staring at my ceiling.

I couldn't look away from his face, my eyes committing the sharp cut of his jaw, the perfect profile, straight nose, sooty lashes, beautiful lips, to memory. I was no longer surprised by the way my body prickled to life at the mere sight of his handsome face. For now I put that feeling aside, sensing that his mind was somewhere else, somewhere a little darker than usual.

My fingers circled the "A" on his chest.

"Nate?"

"Mmm?"

"When you're having a hard time about it, you know you can talk to me, right?"

He gave a slight shake of his head. "I'm okay, Liv."

"Really? Because when Cole mentioned your tat, you seemed a little off for a few days afterwards."

Nate slanted a look at me and gave a long, shaky sigh. "I don't know if I can admit it out loud."

"Hey, as if I'm going to judge you about anything," I teased, trying to relax him again and remind him he was safe with me.

I wanted to follow the little sad smirk curving his lips with the tips of my fingers, but I refrained.

And I waited.

Until he said, "I got the tattoo so I'd remember Alana every single day."

"Yeah, you told me," I reminded him softly.

"I sometimes wish I hadn't gotten it." Shame entered his gaze as he looked at me, and I hated that he felt it. "Sometimes I think it would be easier to forget her most days."

"That's understandable, honey."

Nate shook his head in denial. "I promised her."

"Promised her what?"

His voice was hoarse now as he confessed, "I promised I'd never leave her." He cleared his throat, trying to bury the emotion, but he couldn't. My friend was still carrying around so much history and I knew that for a fact as he continued. "When we were kids I protected her from everything. Crappy stepdad, kids who'd tease her because she didn't have a lot of money, nightmares, even sad stories. But I couldn't protect her from the cancer. I couldn't protect her, so the least I could do was never leave her."

A new ache wrapped its bruising hands around my ribs, and I leaned over to press a comforting kiss to his chest. "Nate, moving on with your life doesn't mean forgetting her, or leaving her."

Eyes narrowed, he wasn't impressed with my comment. "How can you say that? You of all people know it doesn't work like that. I should want to see that tattoo in the mirror every day, Olivia. I shouldn't resent it."

The hands around my ribs squeezed as the voice inside me told me to speak up, confess my own deep buried secret, the real reason behind all of this. I should. For my friend, I should. I pressed my cheek to his chest and struggled to find control of my breathing, tears pricking my eyes as I forced myself to be brave for him.

"Do you want to know the real reason I asked for your help?" I choked on the last words, the tears falling from my eyes. Nate tensed when he felt the splash of salt water on his skin.

He moved beneath me, but only to release his arm from behind his head so he could wrap it around me. "Liv?"

Looking up at him now through my tears, I whispered my own confession. "I was scared of resenting my mom. I was scared that somewhere deep inside of me I blamed her for the fact that I'd never had what everyone else had—first love and sex, and time to explore it when everyone else was. I thought"—I brushed away my tears—"I thought if I could just do something about it, it would take the chance of that resentment building away. Because resenting her for that would just make me the worst person ever, and I don't know if I could have handled that dark part of myself that blamed a woman who was kind and gracious until the very end." I wiped at my tears and braced myself over him, running my fingers tenderly through his thick hair. "You're not alone, Nate."

I pressed a comforting, tearstained kiss to his lips.

And promptly found myself flat on my back, my hands pinned above my head as he braced himself over me, his eyes burning. "Nate?" I gasped at the sudden movement.

His answer was to kiss me deeply, roughly, almost desperately as he nudged my legs apart. He let go of one of my wrists only to grab a condom off the bedside cabinet, and once he was ready, he held me down again.

I tried to move my arms, but they wouldn't budge, and I was wickedly surprised to feel swift arousal move through me at the feeling of being completely under his control.

His to do with as he pleased.

With a growl of need he slammed into me and all I could do was take it as he pounded me into the mattress, my cries growing louder and louder until an eyes-rolling-to-the-back-of-my-head orgasm shattered my insides and I screamed his name upon beautiful release.

After Nate came just as hard, out of breath, out of control, he pulled out of me, but this time he didn't get up to go to the bathroom. Instead he took off the condom and threw it in the trash can by my bed and then wrapped his arms around me, resting his head in the crook of my neck, leaving our legs tangled together.

We lay like that for some time, not saying a word, until finally sleep began to lull me. Feeling the pull of sleep Nate turned us on our sides, my back to his chest, his arm around my waist, his legs entwined with mine, and together we fell into a temporary state of absolute peace.

# CHAPTER 14

There was a lot to be learned from what was happening between me and Nate, but unfortunately I was determined to learn the least important things. Waking up with him that next morning, feeling his arms around me, feeling this wonderful mixture of being thrillingly alive but so comfortingly safe, I didn't allow myself to take the time to read the signs.

Instead, we woke up, Nate in a hurry upon realizing he'd slept in and had a photo shoot early that morning for one of the local high schools. I discovered that laid-back, charming Nate did not like to be late. He relied on the use of grunting to reply to me as he rushed around trying to get ready. It was kind of cute.

Before he left he told me he was working that night so he'd have to call me to arrange our next lesson, but there wasn't any weirdness about him like on Tuesday morning, so I took it to mean he really was busy and we'd arrange something later.

I'd gotten a couple of texts from him since then, but they were just to crack jokes about work, not anything about our lessons. I was cool with that. There was no rush, no immediate need to see him or anything.

Nope.

Uh-uh.

Still, I was looking forward to the distraction of Friday dinner with my dad and company. Jo had chosen D'Alessandro's because we had two extra guests that evening. Dee, and also Hannah. She was having a wee bit of bother getting Marco to talk to her, so we'd decided the only way to see what the hell was up was to create a situation where she could see him without looking like a total stalker.

We had no idea if he was working that night, but we'd decided it was worth a shot.

I sat at the table with Dad, Dee, Jo, Cam, Cole, and Hannah and did my very best to be there and be present, but every now and then a memory from the past week would cross my mind and I'd get lost in a little Nate-and-Olivia fantasy until one of my companions dragged me out of it.

Jo was talking to me about Joss and Braden's photos from their honeymoon in Hawaii when I felt Hannah tense beside me. Both Jo and I looked at her and then followed her frozen-rabbit stare across the room to the young man who was bussing a table in the corner.

Our girl had good taste.

A little young for me, of course, but I could see the attraction.

"Is that him?" I asked under my breath.

She nodded quickly, licking her lips nervously. That surprised me, since I'd never known Hannah to be anything but forthcoming and confident. Apparently she'd been a shy little kid, but I could never quite picture her that way. It wasn't that she was particularly outgoing or boisterous; in fact she was a pretty chill person, quiet, reserved. But she also spoke her mind and was hilarious when she did so.

"Go talk to him."

Hannah's jaw hardened with determination and she immediately got up. She was wearing skinny jeans and a fitted T-shirt that showed off her curves. She was casual but she was gorgeous. This kid didn't stand a chance.

Feeling a niggling in my bladder, I realized I was going to miss the show. "I'll be right back," I muttered and made my way to the toilet, trying not to look obvious as I saw the boy's eyes widen in surprise to see Hannah walking toward him.

I hurried into the restroom, and when I came out, I was right behind Hannah and Marco, hidden by a tall faux plant. I eyed my table, knowing I should go back and give them privacy. Then again, this was a girl I cared about, and if the little idiot was mean to her I wanted to be there so I could sort his punk ass out.

"I told you I've been busy," he said with a shrug, his American accent throwing me for a moment until I remembered Hannah telling me he was from Chicago.

Hannah eyed him suspiciously, a stubborn little jut to her adorably pointed chin. "So you're not avoiding me?"

Marco scratched his cheek, his lips curling at the corner. "No. Why would I be avoiding you?" His eyes flickered over her shoulder and there was something proprietary in the way he said, "It looks like you've been keeping busy anyway. New guy already?"

She stared at him for a second, and I was mighty impressed by how cool she was. Way cooler than I would have been. Especially if I'd been confronted with a guy as hot as Marco at her age. He was a good couple of inches over six feet, athletically built, and his mix of African American and Italian heritage had lent itself beautifully to his light caramel skin tone, high cheekbones, cut jawline, and sensual mouth. His blue-green eyes were a striking contrast to his skin and dark lashes. All of this was only made more appealing by his quiet but intense presence. I had a feeling Hannah had found herself a broody boy to crush on.

"That's Cole," she finally answered, tilting her head to the side to give him a questioning yet cocky smile that told him she thought his words belied his jealousy. "He's a family friend. Why? Would it bother you if he was my date?"

Marco frowned. "No, Hannah, it wouldn't. You can do whatever you want."

She was good at hiding her disappointment, I'll give her that. "Well, what I want is to hang out with my good friend Marco, but he's been hard to find lately."

It was his turn to stare, and I recognized the moment when he crumbled under the gaze of her wide velvet brown eyes. He shook his head as if he couldn't believe he was giving in to her. "I'm off Tuesday night. We could hang out then."

"Okay. Do—"

"Eavesdropping is rude, you know," a familiar voice told me quietly.

Surprise, and I wasn't sure if it was good surprise or bad surprise, spun me around and I gazed up, probably looking a little stupefied, into Benjamin's face. "Benjamin," I wheezed, my heart taking its time to slide down my throat and back into the chest where it belonged.

His gorgeous eyes brightened as if he was pleased I knew his name. "Hi again," he said with a grin, jamming his hands in his pockets.

"Uh, hi." I quickly glanced back at Hannah to see that she was walking to our table, looking over her shoulder with a frown line between her eyebrows. It appeared as though a tall, good-looking Italian man was quietly chastising Marco. "Uh"—I turned back to Benjamin—"I know her." I gestured to Hannah. "Hannah. I was just making sure she was okay." I shrugged sheepishly. "And maybe eavesdropping a little."

To my relief he laughed and it suddenly occurred to me that I'd spoken to him without fumbling up the words. It made me smile, and my smile made Benjamin's eyes drop to my mouth.

After swallowing hard at the interested gleam I saw there, I said wryly, "I take it you like D'Alessandro's."

"My favorite Italian restaurant in the city."

"Mine too," I agreed and then glanced past him, trying to see into the other dining room. "Are you with your family?"

Just like that, Benjamin appeared uncomfortable. "Um, no. A first date. I saw you and thought I'd come over and say hello."

Admittedly, I'd felt a little disheartened at the words "first date," but knowing he'd left that date to come talk to me obliterated most of the disappointment. "The date must be going well."

He leaned into me and whispered in mock horror, "She ordered salad."

I gaped back in *actual* horror. "In D'Alessandro's?"

"A salad and water. It's painful to watch."

A rush of giggles bubbled out. "I'll bet."

Benjamin chuckled too now, his eyes roaming my face in a way that was nice but also that suggested he was taken aback by me. That wasn't so surprising. It was the first time he'd gotten a conversation out of me. "Well," he said, seeming reluctant, "I better go back. I told her I was going to the loo."

"Okay." I smiled giddily. "I'll probably see you at the library then."

"Definitely," he murmured sexily and I grinned wider watching him walk away.

As soon as he was out of sight, I made my way back to the table, feeling warm flutterings in my chest. That had gone well. Really well. My lessons with Nate were paying off!

*Nate.*

I frowned suddenly as the warm flutterings disappeared and I landed heavily in my chair.

"Who was that?" Jo asked.

They were all staring eagerly at me.

Even Dad.

"A guy from the library."

Dad tilted his head to the side, a curious look in his eye. "A colleague?"

"No, a postgrad. He's nice."

"Postgrad," Dad repeated, thinking this over. "Smart fella, then." He grinned cheekily at me. "He's definitely interested in you, sweetheart. Do you like him?"

Something unpleasant squeezed my stomach as I considered my dad's observations. Benjamin had indeed seemed interested. He'd left his date to come talk to me. Did that mean . . . if I saw him again . . . what would happen?

And . . . Jesus effing Christ . . .

. . . what did I want to happen?

*Nate.*

I shrugged again, struggling to breathe through the sudden tightness in my chest. "I don't really know him."

My legs felt heavy as I walked up the concrete stairs to my door. Luckily I'd gotten through dinner by pestering Hannah with questions and laughing while she held her own against Cole's teasing.

However, as soon as I was on my own, walking toward my apartment, the headache that had been dying to make itself known sprang to life between my eyes. I rubbed my sinuses, wishing my brain wasn't all mushy and messed up right now.

Lines were being blurred, and other lines were actually being crossed. There were a whole lot of lines and none of them were of a solid consistency.

Mothereffing lessons.

With a huge sigh I let myself into my apartment and came to an abrupt halt at the sight of Nate leaning against my couch, his arms crossed over his chest, his legs crossed at the ankles.

God, he was beautiful.

He didn't even have to say a word and my heart was pounding.

I shut the door behind me, leaned against it, and turned the lock. Our eyes met across the room and clung. "New lesson?" The words came out all husky and needful.

Nate straightened up to his full height. "Tonight's lesson: Use your initiative."

Without saying a word I shrugged out of my jacket and began to undress.

Nate's eyes smoldered as he prowled toward me. "Good initiative."

# CHAPTER 15

———

The Lumineers were singing to me. Usually that was a good thing, but the previous evening had been pretty physical and I wanted my Saturday lie-in.

Nate's warm body was pressed against my side as I lay on my stomach, my face buried in my pillow. I felt him shift against me as my ringtone woke him up.

"Babe," he said, rubbing my back lightly, "your phone."

I mumbled incoherently into my pillow.

The delicious heat of him up my left side disappeared and I grumbled a little more. He rolled back into me, kissed my shoulder, and deposited the phone on the pillow near my ear. Wincing at how loud it was, I lifted my head and fumbled for it. "Hey," I answered sleepily, not even checking the caller ID.

Joss's husky voice replied, "Hey, you. How's it going?"

More alert now, I leaned up on my elbow, enjoying the feel of Nate's fingers stroking my spine. "Joss, it's good to hear from you. How are you? How was the honeymoon?"

"It was great. You know Braden." She gave a low, intimate laugh. "It was fun."

I shot a look at Nate, who was lying there watching me, all sexy and stubbly. I finally got what that low, intimate laugh meant. "Was it beautiful?"

"Stunning. I recommend Hawaii to all. If it weren't for the weirdos I sort of, might, kind of care about, I would never have come home. Speaking of, Ellie and Adam are house-hunting and are looking at a property on my street. Els said she wanted to check it out again, so I'm going with her this afternoon. We thought we'd come back to my place afterwards for a few drinks. I know Jo can't make it because she's working, but I hoped you'd want to hang out with us."

"I'll be there. What time?"

"Noon."

I frowned. "Uh, what time is it now?"

"Quarter—" Nate began to answer, but I cut him off immediately, slapping my hand over his mouth. I glared at him as I felt his lips curve beneath my palm. His eyes danced with mirth.

"What was that?" Joss asked curiously.

The last thing I needed was my friends finding out about my situation with Nate—because the last thing I needed was a concerned lecture. "The radio. My alarm."

"Well, then, I guess I don't need to tell you it's nine forty-five. That's a weird time to set your alarm."

"It's a Saturday," I answered quickly, flustered. "I sleep in a little on a Saturday and, uh, you know, nine thirty seems too early but ten seems too late so . . ." My hand tightened over Nate's mouth as he laughed harder at my lame rambling.

"So you're weird," Joss finished for me. "I already knew that. See you soon." She hung up and I immediately took my hand off Nate's mouth, fisted it, and punched him in the arm.

"Dude, are you trying to get us caught?"

His laughter died down on a huff as he rubbed his arm. "I could give a shit."

"Liar." I shoved him playfully. "If I don't want to be subjected to the concerned 'ooh do you think that's a good idea?' crap, then I know you certainly don't."

In answer Nate sat up, grabbed my hands, and forced me to my back, cocky seduction curving his lips as he pushed my legs apart with his.

"What are—"

I was interrupted by his masterful mouth and soon found myself melting into the bed as he kissed me into submission. When he drifted his lips down my chin, sprinkling shivery little brushes over my neck, I managed to find my voice. "What are you doing? I've got just a little over two hours to get showered and dressed and haul my ass to Joss's."

"Hmm." He traveled lower, freeing one of my wrists to cup my breast to his mouth. I sighed, involuntarily arching my back as he licked my nipple. "I've got judo in a few hours too. I'll make this quick." He grinned up at me from beneath his lashes, wicked and seductive as his hand slipped between my legs. "I promise."

Delicious sensations rolled through me. "Uh . . ."

And then he abruptly got up, leaving me lying there with my back arched off the bed. "Where the hell are you going?" I snapped.

His warm chuckle hit me low in my belly as he began searching through my dresser. "Don't worry, I'm coming back. I'm just looking for a pair of tights."

Confused, I replied, "I don't have any. I've got a pair of stockings in the bottom of my underwear drawer."

"Even better."

"Do I even want to know why you're looking for stockings?"

Without answering, Nate found the stockings and climbed back up on the bed. With efficiency and deft that took me completely by surprise, he tied one end of the stockings around my wrists and the other around the slats of my headboard.

Makeshift handcuffs.

I tugged on them, feeling the material stretch but not loosen. "What the hell?"

Nate was no longer smiling as he braced himself over me. "When I held you down the other night . . . it made you so wet, babe, it makes me hard just thinking about it." His voice thickened as his eyes darkened. "You got off on it."

I flushed, remembering how much I'd enjoyed the fact that Nate could do whatever he wanted with me and my hands weren't free to stop him. It was altogether a surprising feeling, but one I didn't think I'd have with just any man. I allowed myself to be intrigued by the notion of being Nate's captive, allowed the fantasy, because . . . I trusted him. Behind the fantasy was the knowledge that he'd only do things I liked, loved, and that he would never hurt me.

Still, I didn't know I'd made it so obvious.

I tugged on the stockings, growing steadily more breathless. "So what now?"

He caressed the backs of my thighs and then curled his hands around them, pulling my legs up around his hips before pressing his hard, hot erection to my entrance. "Now you're completely at my mercy . . . while I fuck you senseless."

Staring at the stripped-out kitchen, I wondered if Ellie and Adam were nuts.

"Guys, we're talking a lot of work here," I murmured, taking in the loose wiring and a damp patch in the lower left-hand corner of the room.

Ellie glanced back at me and Joss regretfully. "Adam said as much, but I wanted another look." She stroked the wall. "I love these buildings."

"Ellie, you know if you want the flat back, Braden and I are happy to look elsewhere," Joss offered.

But she might as well have offered to drown someone's cat. "Joss, no! That flat is special to you guys."

"It's special to you, too."

"Not as much." She shook her head with a heavy sigh. "Let's go. Staying here is depressing."

We shuffled out of the flat on Dublin Street, Ellie looking back at it longingly as we climbed the hill toward Joss's place. "It's such a massive renovation job. We just don't have the time."

"It's a money pit," Joss added. "There was damp and cabling issues. Els, it would be a constant headache."

"You're right, you're right, I know you're right," Ellie grumbled, and pouted at me as Joss let us in at her flat.

I rubbed Ellie's arm in reassurance. "You'll find a place."

Braden was working at his nightclub, Fire, so we had the flat to ourselves. In preparation for us coming, Joss had already made up little snacks and bought a cocktail mix. We laughed and joked in the kitchen as we sipped mojitos and ate tiny sandwiches.

"So will you treat us to details about the honeymoon?" I asked, grinning cheekily at Joss.

Joss smirked at me. "With Braden's little sister in the room? No. All I will say is that a delicious time was had by all. And Braden only growled at one guy."

I laughed. "Growled?"

"He was staring at my boobs, and I mean staring, while Braden was right there." She wrinkled her nose and shook her head. "I thought Braden was going to pop a vein."

We laughed, but my amusement froze up under anxiety when Joss suddenly threw me a mischievous grin. "So, Ellie said you went all Lady Sass at Club 39 while I was gone. Got some guy's number?"

I snorted, trying to cover up the fact that my heart was pounding hard and I was starting to sweat. Lying was horrible, shitty, and excusing it by telling myself that I wasn't lying, I was merely withholding, was just a crock of crap. I was lying to my friends and I didn't like it. "Lady Sass? It was just a number."

"I've never seen you so interested before." Ellie turned her wide eyes on Joss. "You should have seen her flirting her arse off. Speaking of"— she looked back at me questioningly—"how would you feel about going on a date with a guy Adam knows?"

The heart pounding became more of a sickly fluttering. "You've been talking about me?"

"Only since that night at the bar. We thought maybe you were taking time to get settled before you started dating, so we never said anything before. But then on Saturday you seemed to show interest. And Dougie is lovely."

"Doogie?"

"Douglas. Dougie."

I snorted. "He sounds charming."

Joss laughed. "I'm picturing Doogie Howser."

"Right." I giggled immaturely.

Ellie frowned at us both. "Um. Who?"

"It was an American TV show."

"About what?"

"A kid genius doctor."

Ellie gave us a long-suffering look. "Dougie is not a kid. He's a very nice and very good-looking architect."

"Don't let Adam hear you say that."

"Liv, I'm serious. Please consider going out with him."

"I don't do blind dates."

She eyed me carefully. "Did you call the guy whose number you got?"

Uh-oh. How did I tell her I didn't want to date this Doogie guy because I was too busy screwing Nate? I racked my brain for an excuse that sounded plausible, becoming increasingly nervous as the silence stretched thin between us. My eyes sought Joss for help since she was the queen of not doing anything she didn't want to do and not giving a rat's ass if you didn't like her explanation. Instead of help, I watched as her face turned a sickly color.

"Joss, are you okay?" I leaned forward, touching her arm.

She pressed her lips together and turned toward the sink. Ellie was watching her sister-in-law in concern.

After a moment Joss sucked in a breath. "Do these mojitos taste okay to you guys?" she asked weakly.

"Fine."

Joss shuddered, taking another breath.

"Uh—" I backed off warily now. "Are you going to upchuck?"

She grimaced at me. "No, I'm not going to upchuck."

"Here." Ellie shoved a plate of sandwiches toward her. "You've barely eaten anything this morning."

"Ellie, if you don't get that plate out of my face I will eat *you*."

"I think she's going to upchuck," I murmured, pulling Ellie back.

"Stop saying 'upchuck,'" Joss snapped.

I raised my eyebrow at Ellie. "Someone's crabby when she's sick."

"Yup," Els agreed. "She got the stomach flu last year and hissed at anyone that came near her."

"I'm standing right here," Joss huffed, slanting a dangerous look our way. With her tip-tilted gray eyes she really knew how to give good glare.

"And we'd like you to remain there if you're going to be sick."

Ellie giggled at me. Joss did not.

"You're lucky I like you, Olivia Holloway."

I grinned at her and replied meaningfully, "Don't I know it."

She flicked her gaze up at me. "I can't be crabby when you're being cute."

"And my genius plan works."

Joss snorted and then immediately clamped a hand over her mouth.

We waited as she took deep breaths until finally she turned to us. "I'm fine." She moved over to the table in the corner and settled into a chair. "Those mojitos are definitely not working for me."

Without having to be asked, Ellie poured Joss a glass of water and we joined her at the table. To my chagrin, the first thing Ellie said was, "So? Dougie. Yes?"

"No. I'm . . ." I shrugged, deciding to give them a little of the truth. "There's a guy at the library. I like him."

Ellie grinned, curiosity sparking bright in her pale eyes. "Fair enough. Do you work with him?"

"He's a student. Postgrad." My tone said, "I don't want to talk about it" and, surprisingly, Ellie let it go.

Instead of giving me the Spanish inquisition on him, she asked, "How is work?"

"Good. It'll be hard to get promoted but, you know, it's a good atmosphere and I like my colleagues. I don't think I'll be leaving anytime soon. What about you?"

"I've almost finished my PhD and the university is discussing giving me a year contract with them as a course lecturer. They're impressed with me and my thesis, so they pulled me aside yesterday to let me know that they're considering me."

Ellie was a scholar in art history. I didn't know much about it, but I did know that she'd dreamed of a career in academia just like her stepdad, Clark, so this was huge news.

"You didn't tell me that," Joss said softly, delicately picking at a sandwich.

Ellie shrugged modestly. "I wasn't sure whether to mention it or not in case it falls through."

"It won't, Els," Joss replied firmly. "I'm proud of you."

"Me too."

She smiled gratefully at us. "Thanks."

"It means I'll probably be consulting with you on research materials for the library."

"Yup. Maybe you can point out Library Guy while I'm there."

I nodded, then took a large gulp of my mojito. Why, when I thought of Benjamin, did I no longer feel butterflies and a rush of possibility?

# CHAPTER 16

I was happy.

Truly, peacefully, happy.

And I had no intention of analyzing it.

Analyzing it was sure to kill all the happy.

Lying with my head on a cushion, my legs stretched out across Nate's lap, I looked at him out of the corner of my eye as he watched the movie and absentmindedly stroked my ankle.

Our sexual relationship had only escalated over the last two weeks, until nearly all of my inhibitions were gone. Sex with Nate was easy. I didn't feel self-conscious. I wasn't constantly worrying if I was doing it wrong.

My confidence had grown, yet still I was avoiding Benjamin. Instead I was lost in this world of sex and laughter and fun with Nate. We still hung out, but now it was intermingled with sexy time.

Freakin' awesome sexy time.

We never hung out at Nate's—I'd never even seen his place—because he said he preferred my apartment, so he often used the key I had given him. Today I was especially pleased to come home and find him on my couch, eating my potato chips and watching TV. I'd just had "the dinner" with Dee that Dad had suggested a few weeks ago, and up until I saw Nate in my space I'd been feeling a little raw.

I bent to kiss his temple to let him know I was happy to see him and then I got changed into a silky nightdress Nate had bought me. When I came back into the room he took one look at my face and patted the couch beside him. I sat down and let him enfold me in a hug.

"You okay?" he asked, pressing a kiss to my hair.

"It was just . . . It's fine. We just talked about Mom. It always takes it out of me."

In response he cuddled me for a while. It felt wonderful.

Nate's phone buzzed on the table and I pulled my legs off his lap so he could reach it. He flicked the screen, his eyebrows drawing together as he read the text message he'd just received.

"Everything okay?"

"It's Cam," he murmured. "I think he's getting suspicious. Wondering why I'm busy all the time."

"Just tell him you're busy getting busy. He doesn't need to know who with."

"I've been getting busy so much lately, he's bound to know it must be with just one woman and he'll want to know who. Even I can't find a new sexual partner every day."

"We're not having sex every day."

"Almost."

I shrugged, acquiescing to the truth. "Fine. But we're trying to cram years of experience into a few weeks here."

Nate grinned and suddenly grabbed my ankles, pulling me down the couch before crawling over me. "I know, it's so exhausting," he teased. "I'm utterly sick of it."

He was so sick of it he yanked my nightie off and sat back to pull his shirt off and unbuckle his jeans. My thighs were already quivering with excitement as he pulled my panties off and threw them over his shoulder.

The apartment was soon filled with my pleading whimpers as he buried his head between my legs and brought me to climax with his tongue. I was barely coherent when he suddenly gripped the backs of my calves to lift my legs over his shoulders.

This was new.

His lips grazed mine. "You'll feel me so deep this way, baby. Hold on."

"Nate!" I cried out, feeling every inch of him as he pumped in and out of me.

He was right. His cock thrust in at the most beautiful angle and the pressure inside me was building, building, building—

"Ahh!" I yelled, clamping a hand around my thigh and gritting my teeth in pain.

"What? What?!" Nate stopped, panic in his voice. "Liv?"

"I've got a leg cramp," I whimpered.

Nate immediately pulled out of me, his panting sounding really loud in the small room. "Which one?"

"My left," I managed to answer through the ugly discomfort.

Nate coasted his hand up my leg and found the cramping muscle in the back of my thigh. My fingers bit into the couch as he began to massage it for me.

After a while the cramp began to ease, and as Nate felt the tension start to drain out of me the couch started to shake a little with his laughter.

Mortification instantly hit me.

I got a leg cramp during hot sex.

That was not cool. That was not sexy.

Blushing furiously, I slapped my hands over my face. "Oh, God."

Nate laughed harder.

I was so embarrassed that I was on the verge of tears. I sat up, ducked my head, and pushed him off me.

"Liv." No longer laughing, Nate grabbed for me, but I pushed harder, trying to crawl past him. "Olivia."

"Get. Off." I shoved an elbow in his stomach, but that just made him fight harder. And he was stronger than me. In a tangle of shoving limbs I ended up flat on my stomach, the left side of my face pressed into the couch and my hands held captive above my head.

Nate kissed my cheek. "Will you calm down, please?"

"I'm humiliated," I whispered, closing my eyes.

I felt Nate's chest on my back as he rested his chin on my shoulder, his lips close to mine. "Why would you be humiliated? Fuck, Liv, it's just me."

I shrugged, not very successfully, against his weight. "I took leg cramp. Interrupting sexy time."

"Babe"—humor entered his voice—"please don't make me laugh, because I'm sensing laughter is not good right now."

I glared at his mouth. "You'd be right."

"It was funny, though." He kissed my cheek again. "And not funny in the way that you should be humiliated. Just funny. The Liv I know can laugh at herself."

I pushed my face into the cushion as if it would somehow hide me. "I guess I'm just still not confident about this stuff."

"What? You think a bit of leg cramp will turn me off you?"

I half shrugged again.

Nate's weight lifted from my back, but as he sat up his hands gripped my hips. He jerked my body up so I had to bend my knees to steady myself. I rested on my elbows, the breath whooshing out of me as I stared at him over my shoulder. "What are you doing?"

He caressed my ample bottom, his eyes filled with a dark intensity as *his* knees nudged *my* knees apart. Without a word he slid inside me.

I gasped, watching as he closed his eyes as if savoring the feel of me. He pulled back and this time he slammed into me. I bit out a cry, watching as his eyes opened, his grip practically bruising on my hips. Through clenched teeth, he asked, "Does this feel like I don't want you?"

I reared against him, silently begging for more. "No." I shook my head, and then arched back as he thrust into me. Just like that, Nate began to screw the mortification right out of me.

My head fell forward, my hair spilling across the couch, my cries mingling with Nate's grunts as he rocked into me with increasing desperation. When his movements suddenly slowed, thus delaying my encroaching orgasm, I glanced over my shoulder at him through the strands of my wild hair. "Why?" I moaned.

"I want to feel you," he responded, his voice rough as his hand slid up the damp skin of my stomach. The pressure of his hold forced me back against his chest, changing the angle of him inside me.

"Nate." I sighed in pleasure, my head resting against his shoulder.

He cupped my breast lovingly in his right hand while his other tickled back down my stomach. My hips jerked in reaction to the press of his fingers against my clit. As he worked me with his fingers, he began to work me again with his cock.

I moved against him, finding rhythm to his sensuous torture, sliding up and down on his dick, feeling out of my mind with sensation. I wrapped my arm behind me, my fingers biting into the back of his shoulder as I held on to him for dear life.

"This is me and you," he panted, driving faster and harder into me. "Don't ever run. Not from me."

"Okay." I shook my head against his shoulder. "Okay."

He stilled his fingers on my clit. "Promise me."

"Nate, don't stop, don't stop," I whispered hurriedly. "Please, I'm so close. I'm so close."

He rocked up into me and stilled.

"Nate!" I keened, my hands dropping to his hips, gripping him behind me. "Please!"

"Promise me. Tell me you won't run." He bit my ear, the nip almost painful. "Tell me you won't run from me ever. And then beg me to fuck you."

My brain was too busy firing neurons for me to even question it. "I won't ever run from you," I gasped, urging my ass down on his lap. "Now please, please fuck me. Make me come."

Suddenly I was on my stomach, Nate's chest to my back, his animalistic grunts and growls filling my ears as he thrust into me over and over, pounding me into the couch, and pounding me toward an orgasm that blew my head off.

My scream of release filled the apartment, muffled only somewhat by Nate's own hoarse shout as he came at the first clench of my climax.

# CHAPTER 17

The following Saturday I huddled under an umbrella with Jo as we waited for Ellie and Joss to step out of the house on Scotland Street. The estate agent, Ryan, an ex-colleague of Jo's from when she'd worked at Braden's estate agency, Carmichael & Co., began talking to Ellie as Jo threaded her arm through mine.

Adam and Ellie had found a place they liked. The spacious Georgian flat had stripped wood floors, high ceilings, and period details. Any work that needed done was merely cosmetic. Ellie was in love, Adam really liked it, and Els wanted our opinion.

It was a resounding "yes" from us girls.

Once Ryan left, Ellie grinned at us excitedly. "I'm so glad you guys like it. I really appreciate you coming out to see it." She started down the stairs and Joss rushed to get under her umbrella with her as we followed. "Especially you, Liv." She smiled curiously over her shoulder. "You've been so busy lately."

I smiled back in response, hoping it wasn't a slightly startled, panicked smile.

Jo squeezed my arm against her ribs. "It's funny," she murmured so only I could hear, "but Nate's been busy lately too."

Forcing myself not to react, I couldn't say anything. I didn't want to lie outright, so that meant I was left with ignorant silence. In truth, we were five weeks into our lessons—could we call it lessons anymore?—and now I was getting a little desperate to talk to someone about what was going on with me and Nate. Jo was more experienced than I was about relationships, and men in general, and now I was at a point where I was so in need of advice that I wondered if I should let that need over-shadow all the reasons I had *not* to go to her.

We came to an abrupt stop on the sidewalk as Joss's cell rang. She fumbled in her purse for it and smiled apologetically at us as she an-swered.

Watching her was disconcerting. It was disconcerting because something I didn't understand but definitely didn't like entered her eyes. Growing pale, she muttered her thanks to whoever was on the other end of the line and let her phone dangle in midair as she stared off into space.

"Joss?" Ellie shook her gently, sensing what both Jo and I did.

Something was seriously wrong.

"Joss, what is it?"

She blinked suddenly, and looked over at us, her eyes glassy with fear. "I have to go."

"Joss?" Ellie took a step toward her as she began to back away. "Jocelyn?"

"I have to go."

"Go where?"

"I . . . just"—she touched a hand to her forehead, turning paler by the second—"I have to go."

"Seriously, you're scaring me. What's going on?"

"Ellie," she snapped, but as soon as her eyes clashed with her sister-in-law's she softened. "Just . . . I need to be alone for a little while."

After a moment's thorough contemplation Ellie finally nodded. Si-lently, we watched as Joss turned on her booted heel and slowly walked away from us, her arms crossed over her chest, her chin tucked.

Ellie, Jo, and I shared concerned looks. "What. Was. That?" I asked, feeling my stomach shift with unease.

Ellie didn't answer as she pulled out her own cell with shaking hands. She flicked the screen a few times and began typing quickly.

"What are you doing now?" Jo looked down at Els's phone, then turned her gaze back in the direction of where our friend had taken off.

"Texting Braden to let him know."

I burrowed closer to Jo to comfort her. "Does anyone know what that phone call could have been about?"

"Not a clue." Ellie hugged herself, almost causing her umbrella to hit a person walking by. But Ellie wasn't aware of anyone else at the moment, and her panic was making my unease increase. "But I haven't seen Joss so guarded in a long time. It's definitely not good."

"She'll be okay," Dad reassured me, pulling me into his side for a hug.

After Ellie texted Braden she'd jumped in a taxi to go home to Adam, and Jo and I jumped in a taxi to head back to her flat. When we got there, the boys were back from judo class and we told them all what had happened with Joss. No one had a clue as to what it meant.

It was only afterward, as we were sitting around the living room, that I realized it was the first time in two weeks that Nate and I were in the same room with our friends. This time it felt weird. It felt weird because after I'd been watching four loving couples for the last few months it seemed to me that what Nate and I had wasn't that different. Not only were we having *mind-blowing* sex, but we hung out, we talked about things that bothered us, we laughed . . . we snuggled. Nate joked and teased with me and stole my phone to take random snaps of me all the time.

We cared about each other.

A lot.

Hiding what we obviously had behind the excuse of lessons in sexual education and keeping it a secret was beginning to gnaw at my gut. Mostly because I knew Nate.

He wasn't over needing to see that "A" on his chest in the mirror every day, and I didn't know if he'd ever be. It was becoming increasingly obvious to me that I was in danger of getting hurt.

Yet somehow I wasn't smart enough to extricate myself from the situation.

A few times that afternoon I felt his eyes on me and it made me squirm uncomfortably, as if he could see inside me to exactly what I was thinking.

*Soda Pop, if he knew what you were thinking he'd be out the door faster than a fugitive.*

So when my dad called and invited me over for an early dinner I jumped at the offer, hurrying out of Jo and Cam's with barely a good-bye to Nate.

Dad had thrown together marinated chicken, potatoes, and salad, and I sat on the stool next to him, picking at my food while he reassured me after I told him about the Joss incident.

I shook my head at his assurances. "You didn't see her face. She looked . . . haunted."

"Braden found her, right?"

"Yeah. Els texted to say he found at her at the castle, where he thought she'd be."

"Well, we'll just need to wait and hear from them."

I nodded but kept pushing my food around my plate, my thoughts consumed by Joss and Nate.

"You've lost weight," Dad commented. "Eat up."

That was another upside to constant and active sex. I really had lost a few pounds and even toned up a little. Not that I could tell my dad the reason why. My cheeks burned just at the thought. "I've been really busy. Not a lot of time to eat."

Dad raised an inquisitive eyebrow. "I have noticed these last few weeks you've been a little distant. Is it work keeping you busy?"

"Yeah, work . . . and, you know, sometimes I help Nate out with his job as a reviewer."

I caught the curl of his upper lip out of the corner of my eye. "Surely he's getting paid to do that himself."

"He's my friend, Dad," I warned.

"I can't help it. He's twenty-eight years old and hasn't bloody well grown up. He swans around taking photos and playing video games and watching movies, *and* he takes to bed anything that moves. That's not a man, Olivia. That's a boy. One that's trouble. And I don't like him sniffing around you."

"Hey, that's enough!" I snapped, my fork clattering to my plate.

Dad stared at my angry, flushed face in surprise.

"You don't know him," I said before he could reply. "You don't know anything about him."

"Then enlighten me. What is it about this guy that you find worthy of your respect and time?"

"He's a good friend. A loyal, caring, compassionate friend."

"How? Why? What has he done?"

Crossing my arms over my chest, I leaned back, staring at the beautiful bay window that looked out over Heriot Row. I couldn't quite meet my dad's eyes as I admitted, "Last Thanksgiving I lied to you. I said I was okay, but I wasn't." I felt the air around him thicken as he tensed. "When I left you I went home and went into a crazy meltdown. I cooked a turkey, potatoes, everything, but I burnt it and started to freak out. I mean . . . *really* freak out. Luckily, Nate was just dropping by and he caught me in the middle of it and he sat with me while I sobbed all over him about Mom." I chanced a glance at my dad and saw his jaw was taut, his eyes bright with sadness. "Nate was really there for me, Dad. And he got it. He got me. He lost the love of his life when he was eighteen." My voice cracked on the words "love of his life." "She died of cancer."

"Jesus." Dad bowed his head, drawing his hand down in his face as though exhausted by the news.

"They were childhood sweethearts and by all accounts she was pretty special. He hasn't been the same since. You can't tell anyone, Dad. He doesn't talk about it."

Dad looked at me, his gaze sharp. "Are you seeing him?"

My pulse started racing, my limbs shaking as I lowered my eyes. I couldn't lie to my dad. I just couldn't. "We're not in a relationship, if that's what you're asking."

"Oh, baby girl." He groaned as if he was in pain. "I hope you know what you're doing."

Feeling tears inexplicably prick my eyes, I looked away and picked up my fork to play with my food again. "You can't say anything. No one knows about us."

"And who am I going to tell?"

I smiled weakly at my plate. "Are you disappointed in me?"

"No." His hand came down around mine, stilling my nervous movements. "But my girl deserves more than whatever you two are up to. You deserve to start making a life with someone. *You* deserve to be the love of some man's life."

Somehow I managed not to cry. Instead, I smiled brightly at him, pushing all the negative stuff into my deep, dark pit. "Believe it or not, Nate has taken me a hundred steps closer to finding that."

"I don't understand."

"You don't need to, Dad. Just know that I'm better than I have been in a really long time."

He studied me for a moment. "Okay. I'm glad, sweetheart."

My phone rang, interrupting our heart-to-heart. Seeing Jo's face on my screen, I reached for the phone hurriedly, as I realized she was probably calling about Joss. "Hey."

"Ellie just called," she said without preamble.

"And?"

"Joss is pregnant."

I froze, frowning as I looked over at Dad. "Isn't that good news?"

Jo sighed heavily. "I think it's stirred up some ghosts, Liv."

Understanding, I squeezed my eyes closed in empathy. "Her family?"

"Aye." Jo's exhalation was shaky. "Ellie says Braden's pretty upset by Joss's reaction. It's supposed to be one of the happiest days of his life."

I felt terrible for them. "They just got married. This whole time is supposed to be amazing for them."

"Yeah. Anyway, I knew you were worried, so I thought I'd let you know."

"Thanks, Jo. We'll talk later."

After we hung up, I turned to my waiting father. "Joss is pregnant."

Dad looked just as confused as I'd felt at first. "That's not a good thing?"

"From the sounds of it, it's opened some old, very painful wounds . . . about her family."

"Sometimes that happens. It's just . . . something . . . triggers it. And you're feeling everything all over again."

I guess we understood that too. "I just hope she can get through it."

"She will." Dad sounded certain. "Braden's her family. She'll fight through it for him."

I could only hope my optimistic father was right, because if anyone deserved happiness it was Joss and Braden Carmichael.

# CHAPTER 18

The trip to Longniddry could not have come at a better time. For Joss it meant she had a valid excuse to be antisocial, since more than half of her social crew had gone out of the city for the weekend, and for me it meant the hope of some much-needed clarity.

Spending time with Nate's family, in an entirely different environment, would allow me to see him in a different light too. It also meant we would have to spend time without any shenanigans, and honestly I thought I was in need of a breather from it. Not because I wanted a breather, but because I was hoping that being free of his sexual spell would give me the courage to end what we'd started.

I really needed to end it.

Since Peetie had a car, he and Lyn drove there together, while Nate rented a car for him, me, Cam, Jo, and Cole to share. We'd all gotten the Friday off work and Cole had permission to take a day off school. Just after noon we set out, with Nate driving, Cam in the passenger seat, and Jo crowded in between Cole and me. By the time we drove through the main street of Longniddry with its cottages and flowers and traditional pub, I was dying to get out of the car. I'd rolled my window down and I could smell the sea air.

We pulled into a well-maintained housing estate and Nate drove up to a whitewashed house with a red roof. Peetie's car was already parked on the drive. According to Nate, the house we were renting was only a few streets behind Cam's parents' home.

"Nate did not consider the size of my ass when he hired this . . . whatever it is." I winced as I climbed out, the right side of my thigh and butt aching from having been squashed against the door.

Nate got out the driver's side and grinned at me. "It's a Nissan, because we're on a budget."

I raised an eyebrow. "A budget? My ass says there's budget and then there's just cheap." I rubbed my sore backside.

"It wasn't your arse that was the problem," Cole grumbled, rubbing his left side. "It was the bag that wouldn't fit in the boot."

We all stared at Jo as she fumbled around in the backseat, then hauled out a massive duffel bag. She glanced over her shoulder at us. "What? I didn't know what the weather would be like, so I had to bring clothing choices."

"Tell that to my ass."

Nate snorted at me and guided me to the trunk of the car. "Did I mention I appreciate how light you pack?" He grinned at me as he lifted my backpack out of the car.

"It's two nights." I leaned around the car to see Cam helping Jo with her bag. "Did you hear that? *Two nights.*"

She scowled at me. "Look, Uncle Mick increased my wages and I may have gone a wee bit nuts buying some new clothes. I got a little overexcited about what to bring." She eyed Cam a little apologetically. "Sorry."

He kissed the apology right off her lips. "Don't apologize to me, baby. I could give a shit. Bring what you want." He grinned teasingly at me. "I'm not the one crammed in the back of the car with you."

"Shotgun!" I shouted, perhaps more loudly than I needed to.

They all gazed at me like I was crazy.

"Shotgun," I reiterated. "On the drive home, I call shotgun." When

I got no answer, I huffed, "The rule is, the first person to say 'shotgun' gets to ride in the front passenger seat."

Cam frowned. "Oh, that rule doesn't translate here. Sorry."

I narrowed my eyes at him. "But apparently some misogynistic silent rule that the eldest men in the group get to ride in front does?"

Cam slanted a teasing look at Jo. "You had to make friends with a feminist?"

Jo grunted. "You're the one who tracked her down on Facebook."

"Nice. I'm feeling the love, guys, I'm feeling the love." I brushed past them and shoved at Cam. "I'm riding shotgun."

"No. You are not."

"Oh, yeah?" I stopped and turned back to look at Nate, who had gotten all the bags out of the trunk and was locking up. "Nate?"

He glanced up at me casually but stilled at the smug little smirk on my lips. "Yes?" he asked warily.

"Who is riding shotgun with you on the trip home? Cam . . . or me?" *If you don't say me I will forget you even have a penis.*

He got the message and threw Cam an apologetic look as he walked past us toward the house. "Sorry, mate. She called shotgun."

Triumphant, I followed Nate to the house and as he let the two of us in he whispered in my ear, "Sexual manipulation . . . pick that up on your own time, did you?"

I gave him a wide-eyed look of mock innocence as I wandered inside. "I have no idea what you're talking about."

He slapped my ass playfully and I turned, giggling up into his face as he grinned down into mine. A throat clearing pulled us up short and we glanced sharply over my shoulder to see Peetie and Lyn standing in the doorway to the sitting room. Lyn's curious gaze shifted between me and Nate, while Peetie's stone-faced expression was focused solely on his best friend.

Cursing myself to hell for not being more circumspect, I pretended the intimate moment between me and Nate was nothing and hurried forward to give Peetie and Lyn a hug.

Cole, Jo, and Cam followed us inside the house, and the "incident" was thankfully forgotten as we looked around the cozy rental and chose our rooms. There were four bedrooms, so Jo and Cam, Lyn and Peetie each took a double room, Nate and Cole took the double twin room, and I took the small twin room. Cole disappeared into their room to dump his bag while Nate pointedly looked between their room and mine and pouted comically.

"No sex for you," I mouthed.

"Aye, well, that means no sex for you either." He did not mouth it; he just said it out loud.

My eyes bugged out as he laughed and darted into his room to escape my wrath.

Was he trying to get us caught?

The pub on the main street of Longniddry was typical—exposed brickwork, massive open central fireplace, solid wood tables that had seen many a year, matching chairs, and wooden benches trimmed in red fabric hugging the perimeter of the room. Seated around one of the larger tables, with a Tudor-style window behind us, I found myself happily situated between Nate and Cole on a bench. At the head of the table was Nate's dad, Nathan. Nathan was an older version of Nate—same thick, unruly hair, once dark, now salt and pepper, same twinkling dark eyes, same olive skin, same dimples, same build. Same overall charm and masculine beauty. Across the table from Nate sat his mother, Sylvie. I could tell Sylvie must have been a knockout when she was my age because she was still very pretty. She had dark hair that she kept long, bright blue eyes, and soft features. She was small in stature and slender.

Nate's behavior with his parents somehow surprised me. When we walked into the pub and they stood up to greet us, Nate threw his arms around his mom and lifted her off her feet. Once he was done with her, he and his dad hugged each other hard, grinning happily into each other's face as they pulled back. Nate introduced us, and Cam introduced us to his parents, Helena and Anderson, before Peetie introduced us to his aunt and uncle, Rose and Jim—they'd raised him when their too young niece had decided to give him over in adoption.

Once we were seated, it became clear to me that Nate was incredibly close to his parents. This was something I hadn't known. I knew he loved them. I knew there were no problems there, but considering he rarely went home to see them . . . well, I didn't know what I thought. I just didn't think they were best friends. Clearly I was wrong.

The two of them were especially kind to me, asking me lots of questions. His dad in particular was possibly even more charming than Nate. There were so many of us at the table it was hard to carry on just one conversation, so we'd split into separate conversations. I, for one, was happy to get a little more insight into Nate.

"He used to have this toothbrush he took everywhere," Nathan divulged as Sylvie laughed.

"A toothbrush?"

Nate groaned. "I can't believe you're telling her the toothbrush story."

Nathan ignored him, grinning devilishly and so much like Nate that I was mesmerized. "You know, with most kids it's a blanket or a teddy bear. With Nate it was a toothbrush. And not the toothbrush he used. Just a toothbrush he cried and begged his mum to get him from the supermarket."

I was choking on my laughter now. "A toothbrush?" I repeated, shooting a look at Nate, who was now pretending not to listen. I wondered how it was possible a man could be so sexy and yet so adorable all at the same time.

"It had a yellow handle with a smiley face on it," Nathan continued. "He took it everywhere with him. He even took it to bed with him. He'd fall asleep with it clutched in his wee hand. We have photographic evidence."

I laughed and Nate turned to me, shaking his head. "He *thinks* he has photographic evidence."

Sylvie gasped. "You better not have done anything with those photos, Nathaniel Sawyer, or you've had it."

Nathan saved his son by turning to me. "Nate told me your dad is Scottish."

"Yup. He's originally from Paisley."

"Has he shown you much of Scotland?"

"Some. We visited a few years ago and he took me north, I think past Inverness. Since we moved here we've been to a couple of places. The western highlands. Oh, and I wanted to see where Robert Burns was from, so he took me south to Alloway, and then we drove right to the border, to Gretna Green. I read a lot, so I'd read about it being the place where abducted heiresses and young English couples forbidden to marry would flee because the marriage laws in Scotland allowed them to marry without parental consent. I wanted to see it. It sounded pretty cool."

"You're a librarian, right?" Sylvie asked with a smile.

The food arrived at that point, so it wasn't until my hearty fish and chips—that would do nothing for my belly pouch but add a little more cushion—had been served that I answered her. "Yeah, at the university."

"Do you have a boyfriend then, Olivia?" Nathan asked, a glint of mischief in his eyes.

Trying not to squirm at the question or the feel of Nate's leg tensing against mine, I shook my head quickly and took another bite of food so I would have an excuse not to answer.

"You're a beautiful girl." Nathan frowned, seeming flummoxed. "There's no one?"

"She's choosy." Nate saved me. "As well she should be."

"Well, there's no such thing as perfect. Sometimes you just have to take what's there. Isn't that right, sweetheart?" Sylvie winked at her husband teasingly, and suddenly I knew where Nate had gotten the ability to make a wink look cool.

Nathan gave her a droll look and turned back to me. "Sylvie's right. You'll end up living a lonely life if you're waiting around for perfect."

I was about to laugh at the well-meaning but overly personal interest they'd taken in my love life within thirty minutes of meeting me
when Nate said quietly, "Liv's perfect. She's deserves perfect. She won't
be settling for anything less."

It could have been funny. Sweet. Teasing. But there was an intensity
about the way he said it that drew the three of us up short. Nathan and
Sylvie studied their son with curiosity before turning that attention to
me. I dipped my head, my cheeks burning, wondering if we were going
to get through this weekend without Nate giving us away.

I was angry with him. And not about his little slips here and there.

I was angry because what he'd just said was utterly beautiful. Looking at him caused a dart of pleasure-pain to hit me in the chest. My
blood heated, my fingers curling into little fists. He was making me fall
for him.

That wasn't supposed to be part of the deal.

In an effort to slow my descent, I turned to Cole and started chatting with him and thus found myself in conversation with Cam's dad,
Andy. Andy was a quiet, reserved man who got along really well with
Jo's little brother. As soon as I showed interest in local history, Andy
opened up, a veritable font of information. I was glad for it, glad for the
distraction.

The meal wore on, and as conversations collided and beer kicked in, we
got louder and louder. It soon became clear to me that Nate, Cam,
Peetie, and their families were all very close. There were bonds here that
I'd already witnessed from spending time with the guys, but seeing
them with their parents made it clear that those bonds were solid. They
were forever. I didn't know if the fact that the guys didn't have siblings
factored into that somehow. It certainly factored into their friendships
with each other.

I'd never had anything like that. I'd had my mom, and she had a
few close friends. Then Dad came along and all I needed was him and

Mom. For some reason or other I'd never had a best friend the way the guys had each other. There weren't any family get-togethers, although there had always been someone coming in and out of the house because Mom was always helping someone and Dad was always doing a favor for someone else.

Still, I'd never thought I needed anything like this until I moved to Edinburgh and was enfolded into the lives of these warm, down-to-earth people. They'd done the same for Joss, and Joss had done the same for me, even going so far as to make me a bridesmaid in her wedding.

I decided then as Nathan, Andy, and Jim split the bill that when I got back from Longniddry I was going to pay Joss a visit. She'd been there for me. I needed to be there for her too.

Overall, the meal had left me feeling strangely melancholy, so I was relieved that the guys were in such high spirits. They'd had a few pints with dinner, and after saying good night to their families, they'd walked us back to the house, where they immediately pulled beers out of the fridge.

Two hours later they were still enjoying their freedom from the usual responsibilities and were a little drunk. After Peetie proclaimed that there was no way either Cam or Nate could take him down using a judo move, the two of them had looked up at their massive rugby-playing friend and taken on the challenge. I should have stopped them. Someone was going to get hurt, but since Jo and Lyn were sitting laughing in the corner and not doing anything about their men, I decided I wasn't going to intervene on Nate's behalf either.

I wandered into the kitchen and found Cole putting out some snacks.

"Hey." I nudged him as I sidled up next to him. "Have they made you one of the catering staff now?"

Cole smirked. "I thought I better get out of Dodge."

"Smart kid." I picked up some peanuts. "I'm surprised you haven't asked one of us to sneak you a beer yet."

As soon as I said it, his face got all pinched and I cursed myself for being such an idiot.

"I'm not really that interested in the stuff, to be honest."

Of course he wasn't. He had an alcoholic parent.

*Way to go, Olivia.*

"Sorr—"

"While Cam is pounding Peetie's face into the rug *I* would like some food." Nate wandered in, his eyes a little brighter from the beer, his cheeks flushed. His eyes dropped from me to the snacks, and he skirted the table, pressing against my side as he reached for a bowl of chips. With his other hand he caressed my bottom.

I tensed, my eyes darting to Cole, whose own gaze was fixed on my ass. He glanced up at me, caught my look, and immediately scowled.

*Shit.*

Nate grinned at us both, completely unaware that he'd been caught. He sauntered out of the kitchen without a care in the world, leaving me and Cole in a staring match.

I suddenly felt like the teenager in the situation.

Exhausted, I lowered my gaze and sighed heavily. "I'm going to bed."

Lying in bed that night I stared at the ceiling, listening to the laughter filtering up from downstairs. The noise, plus my stressing, was a kind of hindrance, and it took me a long time to fall asleep. Eventually, I assured myself that Cole wouldn't tell anyone what he saw. The caress wasn't evidence of anything but Nate's inability to not flirt with an available woman.

Right?

# CHAPTER 19

---

The sun was shining brightly the next day, a lure for Cam, Jo, and Cole, who had decided to meet up with Cam's parents and their dog for a picnic on the beach. That sounded like heaven to me. However, while Peetie and Lyn were spending the day with Peetie's aunt and uncle, Nate wanted me to spend the day with him, Nathan, and Sylvie.

It was a tough choice. Spend the day frolicking on a beach or learn more about Nate.

Okay, so it wasn't really a tough choice, but for the sake of pride I'm going to pretend I mused over it for more than ten seconds.

I also really wanted to get away from Cole's eagle eyes. The whole morning, while we all ate breakfast together, he watched me and Nate closely for, I imagine, any signs that we were up to no good.

It was to my relief that I soon found myself out on the back deck of Nate's parents' home. The day started well. Nate complimented me on my body-skimming maxi dress, something I would have never have felt comfortable wearing before our lessons, and when we were stopped at traffic lights he kissed me softly for the first time in what felt like forever. In actuality it had been only a few days since our last mouth-to-mouth. We'd taken the car, since Nate's parents lived on the other side of the village, and Sylvie and Nathan had come out to greet us as we pulled up to their beautiful cottage. Nate had certainly grown up in a lovely place.

Sipping lemonade, I laughed as Nate and his father teased each other. I shared smiles with Sylvie and felt very at home there.

"I saw a picture of you with a dog," I said to Nate, smiling quizzically. I'd passed the photo of him as a child with a Lab puppy as we walked through their entrance hall. "You didn't tell me you had a dog."

Nathan immediately snorted as Nate groaned.

I grinned. "What am I missing?"

"The dog"—Nathan laughed and then composed himself so he could continue—"was called Duke and we only had him for about fourteen months, until my son decided that Duke had more value in trade than as a family pet."

"Oh, God." Nate groaned again and shot me a dirty look. "You had to ask about the dog."

Sylvie was almost crying with tears of laughter.

My intrigue grew. I giggled. "What did you do?"

"Do?" Nathan leaned back, shaking his head at his son. "Well, he'd been bugging his mum and me for a surfboard for months, and we kept saying no because we both weren't comfortable with him being out in the water without someone experienced with him. So when he went with Cam and his parents to the beach, we let him take Duke. He was out of Lena and Andy's sight for a few minutes and he decided to make things happen for himself."

Nate's expression was pained.

"He came across some surfers and started chatting to them. Eventually he asked them if they'd consider trading one of their boards."

My eyes widened in horror. "Nate, you didn't."

He grimaced. "I was eleven years old."

"Aye, meaning you knew exactly what you were doing." Sylvie wiped her eyes.

"As you've surmised," Nathan continued, "the guy said he'd trade his surfboard for Duke."

"You gave them Duke? Did you get him back?"

"Nope." Nathan shook his head. "Once Andy realized what had happened, he went back to find them but they were gone. I went looking every weekend for a while, but I never found the group of surfers again."

I tutted. "That's cold, Nate."

"Hey—" He pointed his finger at me. "I'm not a complete shit. I realized later that night that it was a stupid bloody idea and I felt awful."

"Felt awful?" Nathan harrumphed. "You cried your eyes out."

I pinched my lips together to keep from laughing.

Nate scowled. "Manly tears. Manly tears of regret."

"I take it getting another dog was out of the question?" I teased.

Sylvie chuckled. "We were afraid what he'd trade it in for."

Slapping his hands on his knees, Nate ignored our laughing and stood up. "Right, if you're done torturing me, I'm going to show Liv the prison you guys kept me in for eighteen years." He tugged on my hand, pulling me out of my seat and I grinned conspiratorially at his parents as I let him lead me back into the house.

The prison was in fact his bedroom. And it wasn't a prison. It was just a typical teenager's room. Posters of indie bands on the wall, books and comics still scattered here and there. My eyes looked past the dark blue walls and dark blue comforter on the queen bed and shot straight to the photographs. It was clear that from an early age Nate liked to take photos. There were some beautiful shots of Longniddry and the beach, but mostly shots of his parents and lots of his friends. I grinned, seeing younger versions of him, Cam, and Peetie fooling around . . . at the beach mostly.

As I moved from one picture to the next, a girl started to appear in most of them and my heart pounded as Nate leaned quietly against the doorway and let me look my fill. Finally my eyes dropped to the one photograph that he'd actually framed. It sat on his bedside table. I sat down on the bed and reached for it, a crack of pain lancing through my chest.

It was the same girl.

She was sitting on a low brick wall, and her long strawberry blond hair blew out behind her as she squinted against the sun, smiling into the camera. She was small, pale and slender with fine, delicate features and a beautiful smile. Wearing a white summer dress, she looked like the angel Nate had described.

Somehow I found my voice. "Alana?"

When Nate didn't answer, I glanced up from the picture in my hands and he nodded, taking a step inside the room. "Alana."

I put the photograph back where I'd found it and whispered sincerely, "She was beautiful, Nate."

"I took that picture just a few weeks before we found out about the lymphoma."

Struggling to find something to say, I asked, my voice quiet, "Does her family still live here?"

"Yes." He walked toward me. Sitting down beside me, he stared at the wall opposite us, where lots of pictures of her were pinned. My own gaze fell on one that someone else had taken. A gangly-limbed teen version of Nate, boyish but no less handsome, was standing behind the young Alana, his arms wrapped around her waist. She leaned back against him, her hands clutching at his arms, holding them to her. They both were smiling. Seeming so happy. So innocent.

They had no idea what was coming for them.

Choking back tears, I hurriedly glanced away from the picture, unable to rid myself of the burn in my chest.

"Aye, her family still lives here. I don't have anything do with them."

"Why?"

Nate shrugged moodily, his eyes narrowing in thought. "I spent most of Alana's childhood providing her with a safe place away from her stepdad."

"Did he hit her?"

"No. We could have done something about that. No, it was emotional and verbal abuse. All the time. He did the same to her mum, and her mum just let it happen. When Alana was diagnosed, it stopped. He distanced himself. But the damage was done. Alana was quiet and unsure, and she could never stand up for herself. I was always fighting her battles. He did that to her. And her mum let him. I'd say Alana was meek, but the courage she showed when she was dying . . . She was brave in the way that matters. When she died, I washed my hands of her parents."

I rubbed his shoulder in comfort. "Alana was lucky to have you."

He smiled softly, his expression far away. "We had this spot on the beach, near the golf club, where we'd meet when she was having a bad day because of him. We'd just sit." He shrugged. "Just sit in this perfect silence. She didn't need me to say anything to her. She just needed me beside her. It made me feel like I had purpose."

The tears were choking me again so I couldn't say anything.

When he looked up at me, his expression softened at the shimmer of unshed tears in my eyes. "I never slept with her," he told me gruffly.

Surprise slackened my features and Nate laughed humorlessly. "We were both virgins. Can you believe it?"

"You? No," I answered honestly.

"Alana's mother was devoutly Catholic. Alana didn't believe in sex before marriage."

"That's such a rare principle these days."

His mouth quirked up at the corner. "She was a rare girl."

"An angel."

"Aye, an angel." His grin got a little cocky now. "Not an angel all the way through. We messed around a lot, but I didn't push her for more. I only wanted what she wanted to give me. Then she got sick. It wasn't until about three months after she died that Peetie and Cam decided I'd been wallowing enough. They took me into the city, got me shit-faced, and I went back to a flat with this French exchange student and got laid. It was so easy. It was free of feeling. It was free of everything." His gaze turned intense now, his eyes searching my face. "And that works for me, Liv."

I felt like he was making a point and with his point the crack in my chest split open until there was a gaping hole over my heart. Attempting to hide how much he'd unintentionally hurt me, I smirked and said, "As does having clueless friends who recruit you for help that involves free and easy sex."

*No sex is free, Soda Pop.*

I flinched inwardly.

Nate gave me an unfathomable look. It slowly turned into an answering smirk.

"Speaking of—" I bit my lip nervously. "I think Cole knows what we're up to, thanks to you feeling me up last night."

Confusion clouded his features. "When?"

"You touched my ass in the kitchen when you came through for snacks. Cole caught the whole thing."

Nate's brow cleared. "Och, I'm sure Cole doesn't think anything of it. He knows I'm a flirt."

I had actually thought the same thing myself, but hearing him say it—the suggestion that I was no more special than a random woman he'd meet at a bar—was a lash across the wound he'd opened in my chest. The angry pain it elicited caused me to speak without thinking. More like use "a tone" without thinking: "Does he see you flirting with other women a lot?"

I was rewarded with a blank look. "That sounds suspiciously like the accusation of a jealous girlfriend." He got up off the bed and headed toward the door.

The blank look, the casual way he blew me off, lit an angry fire under my ass.

"Don't flatter yourself," I snapped, hurrying past him. I took the stairs two at a time.

Sylvie caught me making my way to the bathroom, where I was hoping to take a minute to collect myself. Openly concerned by the thunderous expression on my face, she asked me if I was all right and I reassured her quickly, hearing Nate's footsteps coming down the stairs.

For the rest of the day there was a strain between us. While I laughed and joked with his parents, I avoided his eyes and spoke to him only when the conversation forced me to do so.

We'd finished up dinner and spent hours chatting into the evening when things took an even more awkward turn.

Nathan smiled at me, relaxed and seemingly content. "It's so good to see Nate with such a lovely girl, Olivia."

"Dad, Liv's just a friend," Nate replied, a warning note in his tone that hurt me, and clearly made his parents uncomfortable.

His dad shot him a dirty look. I thought he was going to reprimand him for being rude, but instead his expression softened and he reached for his beer. That seemed to be the end of it, until he took a sip and then quietly said, "I'm not blind."

*Awkward.*

Nate got us the hell out of there.

I hugged his parents good-bye, wishing I could stay with them while Nate hoofed it back to the rental by himself. He had such a good family, such a happy family, and I knew he appreciated it. This, unfor-tunately, was a catalyst for my growing lack of understanding. When he had two parents who loved him and each other, when he could see what was possible . . . why didn't he want the same things for himself? Alana was haunting him, preventing him from moving on, but he was letting her. He was actively holding her specter up as a shield against . . .

Well . . .

Me.

The car pulled away from Nathan and Sylvie's, and I stubbornly faced away from Nate, my cheek pressed against the cool glass of the passenger window. My eyes followed the smattering of stars in the dark sky and I did my best to control my breathing so I didn't sound as nervous as I felt. Nate and I had never argued before. Not seriously, anyway.

To my surprise we didn't take the route back to the rental. Instead Nate kept driving, taking roads I didn't recognize, until finally he pulled off into a dark, empty parking lot surrounded by the tall yellow grass of the sand dunes. I could hear the waves crashing ashore beyond the dunes.

Reluctantly, I turned to him as he pulled to a stop. "What are you doing?"

He eyed me warily. "Earlier you said you wanted to go to the beach."

"But won't the tide be in?"

"Low tide at this time of night." He abruptly got out of the car, not waiting for my answer.

I got out too, shivering in the cool salt air. My eyes followed him as he made his way toward the sand dunes, but I didn't move. The slumped line of his shoulders got to me, and when he turned, the moonlight caught something in his eyes that looked like defeat. And I hated that he felt that way. No matter how mad I was at him.

"Nate, what is it?"

Sucking in a huge breath, he shook his head, stuffing his hands in his jeans pockets as he stared off into the distance.

"Nate?"

My heart was pounding so hard.

"I feel like I'm disappointing him."

I tensed. "Who?"

His eyes came back to me. "Dad."

"Why?"

"He's not a man who fucks around with people, Liv. He's always been steadfast. Loyal. He knows how I treat women, and he doesn't like it."

"'Treat women'? Nate, it's not like you're awful to women. You just go through a lot of them. And you . . ." I squeezed my hands behind my back in an effort to curb the pain. "You never make them any promises."

"Don't," he whispered hoarsely. "I've hurt women by not giving a shit what happens after I've fucked them. Let's not pretend I'm something I'm not."

My blood heated. "If you don't like what you're doing, then stop it. Your dad isn't disappointed in you, Nate. He loves you and he's proud of you. That's plain to anyone who spends time with the two of you. He just wants you to move on. And you know what?" I threw my hands up. "Maybe he's right. Maybe it's time to move on from Alana. Find a nice girl. Settle down."

It was the wrong thing to say.

Nate's lip curled as he eyed me disdainfully. "And what? I find a nice girl and you finally fuck the unwitting Benjamin—*Library Boy?*"

Not liking this side of him one bit, I glared at him, crossing my arms over my chest as I leaned back on the hood of the car. "I'd say I'm ready. You've got me all trained up. Lessons learned. I'm pretty fuckable now, right? I think he'll enjoy it."

I only had a moment to see the anger flare in his eyes before he rushed me. I found myself gripped by the nape of the neck as he hauled me up against him and started kissing me. It was rough, bruising, nipping, biting, and I gave as good as I got.

Breathing harshly, Nate pushed me back on the hood, insinuating himself between my legs. Shoving my dress up, he leaned over me, eyes black as the night around us, and I arched into his mouth as he pulled the straps of my dress, and the bra underneath, down to allow his lips access to my naked breasts. His hand slid along my inner thigh, his fingers dipping under my panties and pushing inside me.

I cried out as he cursed hoarsely at finding me wet and ready.

And then it was all about desperation.

My panties were gone. His zip yanked down. My hips in his hard grasp as he pulled me down the hood of the car to meet his cock. He pumped into me, feeding my frenzy, and our surroundings no longer mattered. I didn't care that we were outside. I didn't care that I was on the hood of a car. All I cared about was that he wanted me. I took that, my inner muscles squeezing around his hard thrusts, extorting his release from him.

He relaxed against me, both of us lying across the hood, his warm breath on my neck, my legs wrapped around his waist. I could feel his heart thudding against mine. The skin of his back clammy and warm beneath my hands. I took it all.

I took it all and held on to it for a while.

And he let me.

Because I think he knew that it wouldn't be long before he yanked it all away from me.

# CHAPTER 20

Nate was tender, almost apologetic after the wild sex on the rental car. It was only later that I realized he hadn't said a word during the sex. It wasn't like him. He usually said something hot, dirty, to spur us on. That he hadn't made me feel like he was as angry and as confused as I was. Too caught up in pushing that confusion away—just needing to connect, not to think, let alone speak. At least that's what I let myself believe.

We drove in silence back to the rental house, but I could feel his gaze on me every now and then. Searching. As soon as we arrived at the house, I left him to mingle with our friends while I headed for bed. Jo followed me upstairs. Concerned. I convinced her I was okay. Not so much my pillow. I think it was the tears that soaked it through the night that gave me away.

The next morning I almost gave up my spot in the front passenger seat on the ride home, but I knew that would raise suspicion since I'd been loud about getting it in the first place. However, I was quiet and Jo noticed. She sent me a text from the back of the car telling me she was worried about me.

I was breaking.

I so wanted to tell her everything.

But I held my silence and was grateful when Nate dropped me at my door so I could hurry inside away from all of their questioning looks.

There was no word from Nate for the rest of the day, and no word all day Monday. I left work, going over everything in my mind, trying to make sense of it all. To understand how I could have let myself fall.

When I couldn't do that, I sought distraction . . .

"Liv?" Joss stood in her doorway, surprise slackening her features.

My brow furrowed at her appearance. She had dark circles under her eyes, her olive skin had a sickly pallor to it, and altogether she did not look like a healthy pregnant woman.

Before she could come up with an excuse to keep me out, I barged into her flat. "Is Braden here?" I threw over my shoulder as I marched toward the kitchen.

"No, he's at work."

She appeared in the doorway as I set about making coffee. My eyes washed over her. "You need to take better care of yourself."

Joss smoothed a strand of hair back into her ponytail. "I've been busy. A literary agent in New York now represents me."

A teaspoon of sugar froze over my mug. "She loved your book?"

"She loved my book."

I grinned excitedly. "Joss, that's amazing."

Her smile was bright, but it didn't quite reach her eyes. "Yeah."

My gaze dropped to her stomach. "So what's—"

"She thinks I should start working on another." She interrupted me, almost frantically.

I knew deflection when I saw it. I let her get away with it. Just for a little while. Coffee made, biscuits on a plate, I carried them into the sitting room for us and settled back on her couch while she curled up in an armchair. Her words were hurried, breathless, so lacking in her usual composure that I could feel the unease growing in my gut. It was clear she was willing to talk to me about her books until she was blue in the face if it meant I wouldn't ask about the pregnancy.

Finally, just when I was about to stop her and cut to the chase, we heard the sound of the front door opening. I watched Joss tense, as if she was a fragile pane of unsupported glass, bracing against a harsh wind.

My heart pitter-pattered on her behalf as she chewed on her lower lip, her eyes on the sitting room door as heavy footsteps made their way toward it. Braden's large frame filled the doorway. His eyes were tired and the corners of his mouth were turned down. "Liv." He gave me a chin lift in greeting before his gaze moved to Joss. They narrowed at the sight of her. "Did you sleep today?"

Joss shook her head. "I couldn't."

Annoyed, he said, "You need to get some sleep." Without another word he turned on his heel, tugging at his tie as he wandered out of sight.

The tension between them was obvious. The apartment was thick with it. "Joss," I whispered. "Girl, what are you doing?"

"Don't."

So I shut up, not sure what to say, or how to help. A few minutes later Braden walked past the door, calling out, "I've got a late meeting with Adam." The front door shut behind him.

Joss flinched and I saw her throat working as she tried not to cry.

"Oh, honey." I moved to get up to hug her, but she held up a hand, warding me off.

Tears glimmered in her eyes. "You hug me and I won't stop crying. And I need to not cry."

I stayed where I was.

"It's not me," she promised. "I haven't shut him out. I'm just having a really hard time right now and I ruined it. I ruined this for him."

"He's the one not talking to you?"

"He talks," she answered dryly. "But it's . . . it's like he can barely stand to be in the same room as me. He hasn't asked me how I feel about it now that the shock has worn off. He doesn't want to know. He doesn't want me to touch him . . ."

"I'm sorry, Joss."

"He's never been like that. I think I've fucked up." She laughed hysterically and immediately burst into hard, shaking sobs.

There was no way I wasn't hugging her.

Cradling her against me, I held her until she cried herself out.

When her body stopped shuddering, I heard the soft whimper of her breathing and realized that she'd fallen asleep on me. I couldn't move. I daren't.

Fifteen minutes later, the front door opened and Braden came striding back into the sitting room, looking like a man who meant business. Clearly, he'd decided not to meet Adam. I don't know what his purpose was in coming back—whether it was to shout at Joss or try to bridge the distance between them—but I instantly glared him into silence.

"She cried herself to sleep," I whispered.

The muscle in his jaw ticked as he looked down at her. "She doesn't cry a lot," he answered me quietly.

For some reason that made *me* want to cry. The pain my friend was feeling seemed to seep from her into me. "You have to forgive her."

"It's not about that," he replied hoarsely, his eyes trained on her sleeping face. "I'm not angry. I'm just disappointed."

"That's worse."

He ran a hand through his hair. "This is our kid, Liv. Problems with us I can handle. But this is our kid. She should be happy."

"You know it's not that easy. You also don't know what's going on in her head, because you won't give her the time of day," I hissed, knowing I shouldn't get angry at him but still shaken from Joss's meltdown.

Braden gave me a look that would have a cowed a lesser woman. Okay, who was I kidding? I was cowed. "Are you done?"

I didn't answer, thinking a smart-ass comment wouldn't go over so well right now.

Without another word, Braden approached me and I tensed, wondering what he was going to do. Carefully he leaned down and scooped Joss up into his arms as if she weighed nothing. Joss roused long enough to wrap her arms around his neck and snuggle into his chest.

My throat closed as I looked up at them. They had to work this out. They were *that* couple. If they couldn't work out their problems, what chance did the rest of us have?

I got up quickly, giving Braden's arm a squeeze of affection before I left. I hoped to God when Joss woke up the two of them would start communicating.

Being around them had done nothing to lessen my own heartache, and so, not wanting to be alone, I went to my dad's. Like old times, he cooked me dinner and we hung out, watching TV, just keeping each other company. He knew something was wrong, but for once he didn't ask questions. He was just there for me, like always.

I didn't go home. If Nate used my key I wouldn't know about it.


Avoiding Benjamin had become a challenge these last few weeks. I locked myself in the staff toilets the first time, I hid behind book stacks—moving from one to the other as Benjamin moved around them—the second time, and I'd even hidden in a coat stand. There was a coat stand behind the help desk and it was the first hiding place I seized upon when Benjamin came through the front entrance of the library.

Praying that the coast was clear, I'd stepped out of the coats to four curious gazes.

"What the hell was that?" Angus had asked.

I'd blinked, not sure there was any explanation on earth that would work. "Bee?"

He had stared at me for a moment and then abruptly strode off into the back office without another word.

The day after my visit to Joss and Braden's, my pattern of avoiding

Benjamin changed. Whether it changed out of circumstance or because of the weirdness between me and Nate, I wasn't sure.

I was standing at the help desk, flicking through a book in between assisting customers, when a shadow fell over me. I looked up to find Ellie smiling at me.

"Did you have a nice weekend away?" she asked brightly.

"Hey." I grinned and then turned to Jill. "Can I take five?"

"Sure." She smiled at me and then at Ellie. "Hey, Miss Carmichael. I heard it'll be Dr. Carmichael soon."

Ellie flushed as I walked around the counter toward her. "Soon, yes. It'll be strange, though."

"It's awesome." I pulled her into a hug before leading her toward an empty couch near the main staircase. "What are you doing here?"

"I came to thank you." She turned to me, her eyes bright. "I heard you popped around Joss and Braden's last night."

"Yeah?"

Ellie shook her head. "The last few days have been awful. I couldn't bear to be in the same room with them and I didn't know which one of them to be angry at, so I just decided to be sad for the both of them, which was really no help." She smiled sheepishly. "I'll stop babbling and get to the point. I don't know what you did or what you said, but it helped. Adam just called me to tell me Braden is in a much better mood. I called Joss and she sounds good too. I'm heading to see her next."

"I'm glad." Relief whooshed through me. "But I didn't do anything."

Ellie shrugged. "Braden mentioned you to Adam, so I think you did something."

"I think they were close to fixing things themselves. I just happened to be there at the right time. That is not a couple who can be mad at each other for long."

Apparently I was wrong, because Ellie laughed. "Jesus, you should have seen them when they broke up. That is a couple that can do mad at each other and do it well. That's what I was worried about. Anyway, it doesn't matter now. They're sorted and Joss seems tentatively excited about the pregnancy, so I'm going to seize upon that. I'm going to be an auntie!" she squealed as if it had just suddenly hit her.

I laughed, glancing around us to find students smiling in bemusement at us. One of those students caught my eye and the laughter fell from my lips as he began to make his way across the foyer toward me.

"Liv?" Ellie asked.

"Olivia?" Benjamin stopped, towering over us. He grinned down at me, his friendly, gorgeous smile flickering to Ellie and then back to me. "I haven't seen you in a while."

There was no avoiding him.

And for the first time in weeks I wasn't sure I should. I stood up, and Ellie did also. "Hi. Benjamin, this is my friend Ellie. Ellie, this is Benjamin."

"Call me Ben." He smiled at me before turning to shake Ellie's hand. I felt the heat of Ellie's burning curiosity on my face.

"Have you been on holiday?" he asked, his focus entirely on me, which was really nice considering that Ellie was a tall, stunning blonde.

"No. I think we must just keep missing each other," I lied.

"That's a shame," he murmured. "But it's good to see you now."

"You too," I replied with a smile.

We stared at each other a moment too long.

Ben cleared his throat. "I suppose I better get on," he said, seeming reluctant.

"You know," Ellie said, "a group of us will be hanging out at Club 39 on Saturday night. Maybe we'll see you there."

Understanding flashed in his eyes and he grinned at me. "Yeah, maybe."

As soon as he was gone I turned to her. "What was that?"

"I'm just helping along a courtship that was going as slow as mine and Adam's. I don't want you to have to wait five years, Liv." She patted my shoulder. "It's not fun."

Ellie's news that Joss and Braden were okay and Ben's obvious interest in me brightened my day a little, helping me to bury the increasingly excruciating hurt and uncertainty I was feeling over the whole Nate situation.

It was understandable, then, that when I got home from work that night I didn't know how to react to the fact that Nate was sitting on my couch, drinking my coffee and watching my TV.

I know how my body reacted.

It liked his lean, muscular form on my couch. It liked the stubble on his handsome face, and the gleam in his gorgeous, dark chocolate eyes.

I know how my heart reacted.

It loved that he was in my sitting room, waiting for me.

"Hey?"

He sat forward, reaching for the remote to switch off the television. "I came by last night. You never came home."

"I stayed with my dad."

Tension seemed to melt from the line of his shoulders. "Are you okay?"

"I'm fine."

He scratched his jaw, a question in his eyes. "Did we fuck up at the weekend?"

Moving toward him, I exhaled heavily. "I don't know. Did we?"

Nate stood up, coming toward me. He put his hands on my waist and drew me to him. I was a goner. "I think it was a strange weekend. I think we should forget about it."

*What the hell does that mean? Find out!*

"Okay," I acquiesced, hating myself for it, but loving the feel of his lips whispering across my jaw.

His warm breath puffed against my ear as his hands pulled the back of my shirt into his fists. "I feel like I haven't been inside you in forever."

I leaned into him. "It's only been a few nights," I reminded him softly.

"That's what I said." He pressed an open-mouth kiss to my sweet spot. "Fucking forever."

At first he was rough, wild, hot. I let him kiss me. I let him undress me. I let him lead me into my room. I let him caress every part of my body.

Somewhere along the way he turned tender.

I let him slide inside me and take me slowly, beautifully. I closed my eyes.

"Don't," he said gruffly, grasping the back of my thigh to change the angle of his deep, slow thrusts. "Look at me. Give me those eyes."

So I let him look into my eyes while he made love to me, until I came with tears in them.

I let him push my uncertainty aside.

I let him back in.

Nate came hard, his grip on my body almost bruising as he threw his head back and groaned his release. Once his hips stopped jerking against mine, a strange stillness came over him. An alertness. Our eyes met, and whatever Nate saw in mine had him rolling off me as if I was on fire.

Quickly he took off the used condom and threw it in the trash can. He immediately started pulling his jeans back on.

Something was very wrong.

"You're not staying?"

He didn't answer, and that line of tension was back in his shoulders. I waited as he put his shirt on. Not meeting my eyes at first, he dragged a hand down his face, and then finally looked at me.

My heart pounded as I sat up. I swallowed a wave of nausea.

"I'm ending this, Liv. I can't do it anymore."

I felt like my rib cage was closing in on my lungs. "You—" I shook my head. "You make love to me and then . . . end it?"

"That's why." He clenched his jaw tightly. "Make love to you? That was never what this was about."

Anger tore through me as I got out of the bed, reaching for a night-shirt so I wouldn't feel so vulnerable. I yanked it on over my head and then spun around, hands on my hips. "Why did you come here tonight? If you were going to end it?"

"Because I wasn't sure it needed to be ended . . . but after that . . ." His voice trailed off as he gestured helplessly toward the bed.

I stared at the bed, where he'd been so tender only moments before. "I was just following your lead."

"Don't," he snapped at me. "Don't give me those wounded eyes and that hurt tone. We agreed that this was just sex. And you promised." His eyes softened now, almost pleading. "You promised it wouldn't ruin us."

"You want me to hold to that promise? Nate, don't lie to yourself! For the past six weeks we've been in a relationship, and I'm sick of pre-tending it isn't. You're here most nights and it's not just sex. It's friend-ship and affection and tenderness." I didn't want to cry, but I could feel the tears burning behind my eyes. "We make each other laugh and we *get* each other. What's so wrong with that?"

"I can't believe you," Nate whispered hoarsely, sounding and look-ing betrayed.

Ice slivered over my heated skin, making me shiver in a cold sweat.

"I've told you over and over that I don't want that and you sat there and murmured your understanding and gave me your fucking assur-ances and all the time you were manipulating me!" He ended on a roar that made me flinch.

He was shaking.

I'd never seen him like this.

When I didn't say anything he turned to leave.

That's when I found my voice. "I wasn't the one who asked you to sleep over after sex. *You* did that. I didn't ask you to be here almost every night. *You* did that. I didn't cuddle you on the couch. *You* did that. I didn't ask you to come home and meet my parents. *You* did that."

Nate stopped, his jaw locked, glaring at my carpet.

The realization that I was about to lose him forever hit me.

I couldn't breathe as invisible hands ripped me open.

Blinded by tears, I told him softly on shallow breaths, "Looking back, I think you knew that there was more here. There were moments when I felt you pull away and I thought that was it—this, between us, was over. But then you'd come back. Why?"

This time when his eyes met mine I knew I recognized fear in his.

"Liv, don't."

"Don't? Don't, why?"

"Because . . ." He bit the word out, his tone ugly. "If you say any more I'll be forced to say things I don't want to."

I curled my lip in disdain. "Just say them. Come on. Just say it! I'm a big girl."

"Don't make this ugly."

"You've already made this ugly with your goddamn mixed signals, so just say it!"

"Fine. I don't love you. I can't and I won't and you knew that, so don't stand there like some victim."

I laughed harshly through the agony of his words, hating him so much in that moment. "Last week I thought you might just be the best person I ever met in my life. Last week I loved you like I've never loved anyone." It was a bitter relief to finally admit it to the both of us. "You taught me to be brave again, Nate." I swiped at the tears, my heart catching painfully as his eyes seared into mine. "How can such a coward teach someone to be brave?"

He flinched.

Good.

"You know what else you taught me?"

He didn't answer.

"You taught me to believe in myself all the way through. You taught me that I'm worth more than what I see in the mirror. So today, as you try to teach me the opposite lesson, I say fuck you." I smiled humorlessly, licking the salty tears off my lips. "I deserve to be loved. All or nothing."

As if he realized where I was going with this, a flicker of unease entered Nate's expression. He took a step toward me. "Liv, I never made you any promises, you know that."

"Stop playing dumb. You've been in this with me for the last six weeks! This wasn't just a casual fuck, Nate. It's me!"

"You promised . . ."

Exhausted, I stumbled back from him. "You're right, I did. I didn't expect you to blur the lines, though. *We* blurred the lines. At least I can admit it. But if you admit it, you have to admit what a selfish bastard you've been, and I don't think you're going to do that."

"You're wrong," he growled. "I admit it. I thought we could be best friends and have sex. It didn't work. And I kept coming back and making it worse because I didn't want to lose your friendship. I'm sorry. But you know me. You know I don't do relationships. You know that. Don't hold it against me. Just be . . . my bloody friend."

I looked at him incredulously. "I just told you that I've fallen in love with you."

I started to cry harder as he flinched again.

"You expect me to be able to be around you now?"

"Liv, don't do this."

"I have to. I'm sorry. For the sake of my sanity I have to. You walk out that door, Nate . . . if you walk out that door . . . don't *ever* come back."

The muscle in his jaw ticked. "You don't mean that."

"Oh, come on," I replied sadly. "You just told me you don't love me and you never will. I doubt you'll even miss me."

There was so much pain in his voice when he whispered his plea. "Olivia, don't."

That obvious pain stopped me in my tracks. The hope being that beneath all the confusion and anger and uncertainty, Nate really cared . . . and he was just frightened. So I gave him one last shot to be brave.

"I love you, Nate. Do you love me?"

I knew it was over when tears glimmered in his eyes. "I never meant to hurt you, babe." His voice was thick with emotion.

My own tears spilled quicker. "I guess that was good-bye."

# CHAPTER 21

I found myself in a staring match with the bird outside my window again. I didn't know what it was, but it was tiny. Some kind of tit probably. He or she had brown feathers, a white neck, and this really cool jet-black Mohawk. We'd been staring at each other on and off for the last few days.

I'd decided it was a "he" and named him Bob.

"Hey, Bob," I whispered, my chin resting on the back of my couch. He was sitting on my window ledge, his neck moving in tight little jerks from me to the world outside. "It still hurts today."

He stilled, cocking his head at me.

"Yeah. Are you sick of me yet?"

His head cocked to the other side.

"I'll take that as a yes. Don't worry." I heaved a sigh, feeling my lips tremble. "I'm sick of me too."

That awful night Nate had walked out of my apartment for the last time, I'd been somewhat hysterical. I couldn't stop crying, and no matter how hard I attempted to squeeze my arms around myself I couldn't numb the pain.

It was a singular kind of pain. A pain I already knew well.

Loss.

Somehow, somewhere, maybe even long before we started a physical relationship, Nate had crept inside me until he flowed in my blood and rested in my breath. He'd become integral to a life that I looked forward to living each day, and the knowledge that I would no longer hear him laugh, or feel his lips on mine, or feel complete when I looked in his eyes, was insufferable to my body. It reacted as if someone had ripped off a limb or removed a vital organ. I'd felt something similar upon losing Mom, but with Nate it was different in that he chose to leave me. That added a different hurt to the pain—a sting, like a paper cut across the heart.

"Does it sound melodramatic to you, Bob?" I whispered, dry-eyed from having cried an ocean's worth of tears in the last few days.

Bob looked away as if he was bored.

"Yeah, that's because you've never been in love. Don't do it. You might as well put yourself through a meat grinder."

The crying jag that first night was so bad I had to call in sick to work the next day. I managed to pull myself together enough to go in on Thursday, but my colleagues knew right away that something was majorly up. I was quiet—not sullen, but just trying to keep the pain in lockdown. As soon as I got out of there I headed straight home, ignoring texts from Jo and a call from Joss. When Dad called, I answered. I didn't convince him I was okay, but I convinced him to let me have space. Friday was much the same. Saturday I stayed home all day, only taking time to answer Ellie's text about going to the bar that night. I was in no state of mind to go anyway, but the knowledge that Ben might be there put me in full panic mode. I told her I was sick and couldn't make it.

Jo called. I ignored her. Finally she sent me a text.

If you don't answer I'm coming around. Cam spoke
to Nate. Cam thinks you guys had a fight. Are you okay?
Xoxo

I sucked in a teary breath and texted her back.

**I'll explain later. I'm not feeling well. I'm in bed. Xoxo**

**Okay. Let me know if you need anything. xoxo**

I didn't do that.

Instead I wallowed on my couch for the rest of the night and well into Sunday morning.

When Dad called again to ask me if I was attending Sunday lunch with the Nicholses, I made my excuses. He started to get a little more concerned.

I wouldn't know how concerned until my attention was ripped from Bob the bird at the sound of a key turning in my lock.

My heart jumped in my throat. For one second the fleeting hope that it was Nate absolutely paralyzed me.

The sight of Jo's worried face was like a big-ass rusty nail popping my balloon.

"What—" I cut off as Jo walked in, followed by Ellie and Joss.

Jo waved a key in her hand. "Uncle Mick called and told me he was worried about you. He gave me his spare key."

"Aren't you supposed to be at lunch?" I pulled my nightie over my knees while smoothing my other hand through my ratted hair. I was a mess. My apartment was a mess. There were empty food packets all over the kitchen counter, dirty plates on my coffee table, crumbs on my hard-wood floors, and a musty smell that could only be the result of a human inhabiting one space for too long.

Shrugging out of their jackets, the three of them stared around at my place and then at me, little matching furrows appearing between their brows.

"Okay, first things first." Jo quickly began tidying up my mess while I watched, blinking stupidly as Ellie helped and Joss wandered into my kitchen to switch on the kettle.

Five minutes later the place looked marginally better, although it still needed cleaning. Jo sat down on the couch next to me as Ellie kicked off her shoes and curled up beside her. Joss put a tray of tea, coffee, and biscuits on the table and settled into my armchair.

They all stared at me, waiting.

I immediately burst into tears.

So maybe I wasn't completely dried out.

Tears shimmered in Jo's eyes and she gently pushed my legs aside so she could pull me into her arms for a hug. "I totally smell," I sobbed. "I'm so sorry!"

"Ssh." She shushed me and rubbed my back soothingly.

After a while my tears subsided to sniffles and Jo eased me back, tenderly tucking strands of my unwashed hair behind my ears.

"Do you want to tell us what's going on?"

I lowered my gaze. "I think you know."

She sighed. "Nate."

I looked up at her, my gaze flickering to a concerned Ellie and Joss. "It started as a favor . . ."

Tuckered out from telling them the whole story, I slumped back on the couch and stared at the ceiling. "I feel like if I move, all my insides are going to fall out. I hate it. I hate him for making me feel this way."

"Liv"—Joss leaned forward, elbows on her knees—"I want to be able to tell you that he'll come around, because it sounds like he's going through what I went through. But I can't tell you that. I don't know how he feels about you or what it was like between you. I do know that if I didn't love Braden so goddamn much I wouldn't have come around. I just wouldn't have. So without the one hundred percent certainty that Nate is as crazy about you as I am about Braden, my advice is to move on. I know you probably want to punch me for saying it, but I can't help but feel it's the best advice."

Ellie's eyes filled with sincerity and sympathy. "I agree, sweetie. I think as much as it hurts, you're going to have to start moving on."

I looked at Jo, but she wasn't looking at me. She was sipping her tea quietly.

Too quietly.

"Jo? What do you think?"

"The girls have a point," she replied.

"Jo?"

Sighing heavily, Jo met my eyes. "Cam and I have been suspicious of the two of you for weeks. I saw how you are together. It was . . . it's special." She gave me an almost apologetic smile. "I'd like to believe that there's a chance for the two of you. I don't know . . . maybe you should just give him time to miss you."

Ellie smirked at Joss. "Didn't Braden have a similar plan?"

Joss rolled her eyes. "Yes."

"And did it work?" Jo asked.

"Well . . . yeah . . . but—"

"But Joss is right," I whispered. "Nate might miss me at first but not for long. He cared about me. He didn't *love* me. He told me he didn't love me."

"So . . . ?" Jo's eyes dimmed with disappointment.

I shrugged, the tears threatening to fall again. "I guess I better buy a giant-ass bandage to wrap up my insides . . . I've got to find a way to move on."

Musical therapy. My first attempt at moving on.

Creating a playlist on my iPod Nano, I decided that the independent musical roars of Kelly Clarkson, Pink, Aretha Franklin, and other ladies who refused to be broken by an ill-fated love affair might just be the best way forward.

At work that Monday I went all out with my hair and makeup, wearing my favorite skinny jeans and purple silk blouse. It was part of the therapy. If I wanted to feel good on the inside, I had to start with the outside.

Since I was splitting my morning between the office and reshelving the reserve section, I approached Angus to ask a favor.

He looked down at my iPod with a frown. "You want to what?"

"It's just in the morning. When I'm working front of house in the afternoon I'll of course take the earbuds out."

Angus searched my face before taking the iPod none too gently out of my hands. "What are you listening to?" His thumb moved over the screen quickly and as he scrolled through my playlist his features softened with understanding. When he looked up at me his blue eyes were concerned. He handed the iPod back to me. "Okay. Just for this morning."

"Thank you. I appreciate it."

I turned and started to put the buds in my ears when Angus said my name. I looked back at him as he asked, "Was it anyone I know?"

My heart turned over in my chest. "It was Nate."

And since Angus knew how close I was to Nate, I wasn't surprised when he blanched and whispered, "I'm sorry, honey."

I smiled sadly back at him. "You're a great boss. You know that, right?"

"Best ever," he agreed softly.

A while later, with Pink singing "So What" in my ears, I was tucked in the back of the reserve section shelving new articles and taking out ones that were no longer being used. While I concentrated on doing my job and letting the female vocalists' words of wisdom seep into me, I tried my hardest not to sing out loud.

That's probably why I didn't catch his approach out of my peripheral and why when I felt a hand clamp down on my shoulder I got such a fright that my knees gave out. I caught the end of my shriek as I yanked my earbuds out in midfall.

Ass on the floor, I gazed up at my frightener.

Ben stood over me, struggling not to laugh. "Olivia"—he reached out a hand, his shoulders shaking with mirth—"I'm so sorry. Let me help you."

So far beyond the point of being mortified at this kind of thing now, I let him pull me to my feet. "It's okay." I beat at the dust on my jeans. "We're not usually allowed to listen to music and now I know why."

He grinned. "I am sorry."

I gave him a tired smile. "No, you're not, but I wouldn't be either. It was funny."

Still smiling, beautiful green eyes twinkling, Ben shifted the strap of his backpack as he stared at me. Not too long ago, being the focus of his attention would have put butterflies in my belly, so it was to my chagrin that I discovered . . . *nothing*. I felt absolutely nothing when I stared at him.

My shoulders slumped.

"I went to that bar on Saturday, but I didn't see you or your friend there."

"I'm sorry. I was sick."

"Oh." His brows drew together. "I hope you're feeling better."

He was so nice. So, so nice. And so cute.

"I am, thank you."

He glanced nervously over his shoulder, and then turned back, taking a step closer to me. "Look, I would really like to have dinner sometime. With you." He smiled, all rugged and handsome. "Can I have your number?"

It was impossible. I'd broken up with Nate only a week ago . . . if you could call it breaking up. My heart was in tatters. Clearly all my sexual feelings had fled when Nate had. And . . . you know . . . I'd only just begun musical therapy. I needed to give it some time to kick in and start working.

I couldn't go on a date.

I just couldn't.

"Yes," I answered, nodding and smiling as he pulled out his phone so I could recite my number to him.

A smaller version of myself slapped me upside the head. *What is the matter with you?* she yelled, but I ignored her, gazing up into Ben's face and praying that in time the butterflies I used to feel for him would come back.

# CHAPTER 22

Musical therapy did not work.

Like I didn't know that was coming.

I blamed it all on my apartment.

After work on Monday I opened the door to my place and just stood there, gazing around the room. Every part of it reminded me of him. The couch where we'd hung out for hours over the last year. We'd had really great sex—*God*, no, out-of-body-experience sex on it too. More than once. More than a handful of times actually. Then there was the kitchen, where we'd eaten dinner and chatted. And yes . . . we'd christened the counter. The wall by the door. The wall by the window. The shower. My bedroom.

It was all him. Everywhere.

I ached. I ached so much that even my gums and teeth ached for want of him. I kicked my door shut and slumped against it. The only hope was that this feeling would pass. Eventually I had to start functioning like a normal human being again. Right?

Either that or I needed to start looking for a new apartment. Yet the thought of leaving the place where all my memories of him were . . .

I needed to see him.

I pulled my phone out of my bag with trembling hands and held it up, my thumb brushing over the screen. I'd deliberately avoided doing this since the breakup.

My breath left me as I opened the picture gallery on my cell and started flicking through it. The last picture I'd taken of Nate was him smiling as he drove the rental toward his parents' house before things got weird that day. The next was of us both. Nate was giving the camera this sexy, low-lidded smirk as I held it over us while we were lying in bed. My head rested on his shoulder as I smiled happily. The next one was worse because we were kissing in it.

It was like a knife in my gut.

I quickly flicked past it.

There was another shot of him with his head buried in the pillow, hiding from me. And then there were plenty of me, because if you put a camera in Nate's vicinity he was sure to overuse it.

Rage rushed through me.

My cell went sailing across the room and smashed against the far wall. I slid down the door, drawing my knees to my chest as I cried away all my efforts to move on.

"So are you going out with him?" Ellie asked me casually as we congregated in Hannah's bedroom.

The week had passed as though it had been taken over by the spirit of a slug. A particularly slimy one that secreted mucus all over the goddamn place.

It wasn't a good week.

After smashing my phone, I quickly found a replacement. I kept my old number with all my data . . . hoping what? That Nate might call? Ha. Nate still did not call.

Ben did, though. He called on Tuesday night to tell me he had a hectic week ahead of him but he wanted to know if I was free for dinner next Monday. I said yes, because frankly I was hoping for some kind of miracle that would bring back my enthusiasm and zest for life. If a tall, handsome Scotsman couldn't do that, then I was seriously *fucked*.

Finally it was Sunday again and this time I'd mustered up the courage to face my friends—including the guys, who I now assumed knew everything that had happened between me and Nate—and join them for lunch. As had become routine the last few times, we disappeared into Hannah's room while Elodie and Clark cooked and the guys talked.

I'd just told them about Ben's call.

"Yes. I said yes."

"I think that's great," Joss said. "I think it'll help."

"Yeah, so enough about me." I directed the conversation elsewhere by pinning a lounging Hannah to the bed with my eyes. "How's Marco?"

I don't think I'm mistaken when I say I thought I heard her growl.

I looked at Ellie for help. "I take that as a negative?"

Ellie patted her sister's leg. "He's playing hard to get."

"He's not playing hard to get. He just doesn't want to be gotten," Hannah muttered. "No, he wants to be gotten. He just doesn't."

"Did that make sense to anyone else?" Jo scrunched up her nose in confusion.

Hannah's eyes swept us all. "There are moments when I think he wants more, but he pulls away anytime I make a move. At this rate I'll be in my forties before I lose my virginity."

Ellie snorted. "I doubt it."

"I'm not losing it to anyone but him," Hannah answered rigidly, absolutely serious.

Her sister took in her demeanor and her eyes narrowed. "You will wait until you're at least eighteen."

Hannah made a *pfft* sound. "Okay, I'm sure you waited that long."

"I did, actually."

Seeming surprised, Hannah asked, "Really?"

"Yes, really. It was the night of my eighteenth birthday party."

"With Liam?"

"Who's Liam?" I asked curiously.

"My boyfriend at the time. We had been dating for a few weeks. I thought he'd help me get over Adam." She smiled ruefully. "I hadn't planned to have sex with him that night, even though I knew he was pushing for it. No, I found Adam out the back of the hotel with one of the catering girls. I was so hurt I went back inside, grabbed Liam's hand, left the party, and we got a room. I thought it would help. It didn't. I mean, it was okay." Ellie shrugged, her mouth turning down at the corners. "But it wasn't what it should have been. It should have been with someone I loved. Someone I trusted. Liam ended up cheating on me with one of my so-called best friends."

"Wow." Hannah slumped. "That's crap, Els. I'm sorry."

"I was sixteen." Jo suddenly piped up. She smirked, and it was not a happy smirk. "He was nineteen, a student, and he came from a wealthy family. It was the first time anyone had tried to take care of me—buying me nice presents, even paying my rent when I was struggling. I thought when I gave it up to him that I was giving it up to someone I was in love with. But things turned ugly when I continually prioritized Mum and Cole over him. He dumped me." She shook her head, disdain curling her lip. "He knew he was going to dump me, but he slept with me that night. As soon as we were done, and I mean *as soon* as we were done, he got out of the bed and dumped me as he pulled his clothes on."

I winced at the somewhat familiar situation.

"Jo," Hannah breathed, "that's awful."

Jo smiled at her. "Don't feel bad, Hannah. I ended up with Cameron and that more than makes up for John and all the idiots that came after him."

Hannah's teenage curiosity was still piqued, and so her gaze moved to Joss. "What about you, Joss?"

Joss shook her head. "I was way too young, Hannah." We all stared at her, our expressions asking for more than vagueness. She blew air out between her lips and confessed, "Okay, it was a few months after my parents died."

Ellie's mouth dropped open. "But you were only fourteen."

I felt the same shock ripple through me. When I was fourteen I was sticking posters of pretty boys to my ceiling and envisioning us setting up home in a real-life Barbie dream house and having fabulous parties and sweet kisses. I had not been sexually awakened yet.

Seeing the shadows in the back of Joss's eyes, I realized that she was well aware of the innocence she had given up by having sex too young.

"Was it with someone you liked at least?" Hannah asked softly, clearly hoping for some kind of happiness to lighten Joss's past.

"No, Hannah. He went to school in the next town over. We met at a party. We got wasted. The rest is history. And not one you should ever repeat."

"Don't worry, I won't," Hannah promised.

After a minute's silence Ellie's little sister's eyes came to me.

I'd been waiting on it. I heaved a massive sigh. "Well, at least I was nineteen when I made my mistake. Honestly, there is nothing romantic here. I was sick of being a virgin, so I got tipsy at a college party and lost my virginity in a room upstairs to a drunk senior. There was no finesse. Nothing. It hurt. And afterward he rolled off of me and left me there."

Hannah now looked traumatized. "Not one of you has a good 'losing my virginity' story?"

We gazed back at her apologetically.

"Well, that's settled it. I'm not doing it with someone I don't love."

The four of us shared a look, and I smiled. "Well, at least something came out of it."

Their laughter was cut off as a knock came at the door a millisecond before Braden popped his head in. "What's going on in here, then?"

"Clothes," Ellie answered quickly. "We're talking clothes."

We all agreed for the sake of Hannah. I'd heard the stories from Ellie. The last thing Hannah needed was for Braden and Adam to find out there was a boy she liked, because they'd end up making her life an utter hell with their overprotectiveness.

Braden didn't look convinced, but it seemed he was too preoccupied to care about what we were up to. He walked into the room, a small smile playing on his lips as he came up to Joss, who was sitting on the edge of Hannah's dressing table. He bent and pressed a soft kiss to her mouth, his hand automatically drifting across her belly. "How are you?" he murmured, staring deep into her eyes.

My chest squeezed, but this time in a good way. It was the first time I'd gotten to see them together since the last awful moments in their apartment.

I knew from talking to Joss that she was tentatively excited about the pregnancy and had managed to explain whatever was going on in her head to Braden until they came to an understanding. They were back on track, and it was great to see.

"I'm good," she answered softly, a wry smile on her lips. "You don't have to keep asking me that, baby. You know I'll be vocal if any issues arise."

He rubbed her stomach again.

"You can stop doing that too." She huffed in amusement. "There's no bump yet." She looked around him, eyeing us with humor in her expression. "He's looking forward to the bump part."

"Why?" Ellie asked, bemused.

The question caused Joss to color and Braden to chuckle in this deep, intimate way that suggested, whatever his reason, it was not something he wanted to share with a group that included his little sister.

Ellie looked ill. "Okay, definitely don't answer."

Braden chuckled again and then turned to us, his arm sliding around Joss's shoulder. "Did Jocelyn tell you her agent has found a publisher who's interested in her book?"

"No!" Jo cried out excitedly. "That's amazing!"

Joss squirmed, uncomfortable because she was modest. "They read the first three chapters and came back and asked to read the rest of the book. It doesn't mean anything."

I had to disagree. "It means a lot. Pity you can't drink, because this is a reason to get shit-faced." I glanced over at Hannah. "Sorry, Hannah."

"Sorry for saying 'shit-faced' or sorry because I can't get drunk with you?"

Ellie snorted. "I'm so glad Mum isn't in the room."

An Italian woman sang a lively, frolicking tune through the speakers as the waiter poured red wine into the glasses on the table before me and Ben. We'd met at D'Alessandro's since we both loved it so much and also because it offered us a familiarity that I imagined we both hoped would help with any first-date nerves.

Ben was wearing a purple shirt and dress pants and he looked very handsome. It occurred to me that I'd never seen him wear black—and that only occurred to me because it was Nate's favorite color. Black or dark red. Nate had looked good in both.

"I have to admit," Ben said as the waiter walked away, "I've wanted to ask you out for months."

*"Really?"* I asked incredulously, and then immediately scolded myself as I heard Nate's voice tutting at me for my lack of confidence. "I mean . . . really?" I asked again, going for nonchalant this time.

It made Ben smile. "Really. But . . . you didn't seem that interested before . . . ?"

"I'm very focused at work," I lied. "Sometimes I don't even realize someone is flirting with me because my head is somewhere else."

He nodded as if that made sense. "True. You were different when we met here."

I smiled in answer, my eyes dropping to my plate because I couldn't think of anything to say to that.

"You seem distracted."

"I'm not," I lied again.

"I thought maybe the other reason you were resistant was because there was someone else?"

Tensing, I lifted my eyes to meet his. "There was."

"How recently?"

I gave him a wry, unhappy smile. "This is not how I wanted to start this date, but you're right . . . I'm distracted. I just got out of something. Something really serious, and I don't know if I'm ready to . . . I mean I know I should be. And you should know that I like you, I do, I just—"

"Olivia." He leaned across the table and took my trembling hand into his, his beautiful green eyes sincere. "I get it. I've been there." He sat back, his smile patient. "Let's just enjoy our meal together. Forget about this being a date. This is just two people enjoying a good meal and conversation."

And so that's what we did, and afterward, once we'd split the bill (I insisted, since it wasn't a date), Ben walked me around the corner to my apartment. On the sidewalk he pressed a kiss to my cheek and said, "I like you, Olivia. So when you're ready . . . give me a call."

# CHAPTER 23

———————

$S$taring at the rolling credits, I sat in the now-lit-up movie theater as my fellow moviegoers got up and shuffled out of the screening.

I'd chosen a comedy because fake laughing at fake stuff helped a little.

It had been three weeks since I'd last seen Nate, and I still hadn't heard from him. He'd definitely taken it to heart when I told him to never come back. My friends, with the exception of Jo, did a good job of not mentioning him, although his absence when we went out for drinks was felt by all. It made me feel terrible. Nate was Cam, Adam, and Braden's friend, and now whenever I was around they couldn't hang out with him. Not that Nate was up to it apparently. According to Jo, anyway. She would casually let information slip into our conversations every now and then. Cam was worried about Nate. He hadn't seen much of him lately with the exception of judo class. At their last session Nate had been so intense, bordering on outright aggressive, that their teacher had thrown him out of the class by suggesting he walk off whatever was bothering him.

I didn't want to know this. It would be much easier for me to pretend that Nate had no feelings about the dissolution of our relationship. Jo wanted me to know, though. She thought it meant something. She thought there was still possibility.

She just didn't get it.

"Oi, movie's over," a belligerent voice said.

I glanced up at the young cinema worker. "Yeah, so?"

"So . . . you have to leave now," he replied irritably.

Slowly I got up. "You just love your job, don't you?"

His look would have quelled Death. I grabbed my bag and got out of there.

I pushed my hair back off my face as I entered the lobby of the Cineworld. I'd come to the Omni Centre at the top of Leith Walk on a Friday night because sitting home, remembering how many Friday nights I spent watching movies with Nate, was not a good way to get over him.

"Liv!"

I glanced back over my shoulder before I hit the stairs and saw Cole standing at the concession stand with a group of friends. Being so tall, he was easy to spot. He smiled at me, murmured something to a friend, and strolled over. I had to tilt my head back to look up into his face. "Hey." I smiled at him. "You okay?"

He shrugged. "Just going to see a film with some friends." His eyes searched my face. "You okay?"

"I'm fine. Just heading home."

"You were here alone?"

"A person can go to the movies alone, you know."

Cole's eyes narrowed. "Right." He glanced over his shoulder before returning his focus to me. "Let's go back to the flat. Jo and Cam are just hanging out tonight. We can all watch a movie together."

"Cole, no, go be with your friends."

"Nah, it's cool. They're going to see a film I've already seen. Jo bought those little chocolate cupcake thingies you like . . ."

I groaned. "You know me too well."

He grinned. "Come on, then."

Maybe it would be nice not to go home to an empty apartment just yet.

"Okay."

We turned toward the stairs. "Hey, Cole!" Looking back over our shoulders we saw a pretty blonde step away from the group, her large eyes questioning. "Where are you going?"

"She's pretty," I murmured under my breath. "Sure you want to leave?"

Cole shrugged. "She's not really my type," he murmured back.

"Pretty's not your type?"

"She's kind of annoying."

"Coh-ul?" the blonde whined, and the sound was incredibly irritating.

"Oh, yeah, I get you now."

He snorted and looked back at his friends. "I'll catch you guys later, all right?"

One of the boys glanced over at that, his eyes flying to me and widening instantly. "Fuck, Cole, are you tapping that?"

Cole glared at the kid. "Del, why don't you turn around and start talking through your arse? That way we'll forgive the shit you come away with."

While their friends laughed, shoving and teasing this "Del" person, Cole gripped my elbow and started walking me down the stairs.

I was choking on laughter. "I know I'm supposed to admonish you for cursing, but . . . you are getting so like Cam, it's too funny."

Cole was pleased with my assessment. He tried to hide it, but I saw the flush of pleasure on his neck and the little twitch to his mouth. I understood why. Cam was this hero who had swept in and saved him and his sister from a crappy life. Cam was everything Cole wanted to be.

We were silent for a while as we strolled down Leith Walk side by side until the thought of the pretty blonde who'd stared at Cole with open fascination came to mind. "So, if you're not into the whiny blonde girl, is there someone else you like?"

In answer Cole flushed but surprised me by saying, while gazing at the ground, "There's someone, but I'm too young for her. And I think she likes someone else anyway."

A pang of deep affection echoed in my chest. "Dude, you really know how to boost a woman's self-esteem."

He smirked, but his eyes were searching when he finally gathered the courage to look at me. "I overheard Jo and Cam talking. I know about you and Nate and what he did. I told him I don't hang out with idiots or assholes, and seeing as he's both, I was done."

For some insane reason I felt bad for Nate. "Cole, while I appreciate your loyalty, and I really do, Nate is your friend. He cares about you. Don't shut him out because of me."

"But he hurt you."

"Yes. And I'm angry at him. But he didn't hurt you. So please don't *you* be angry at him."

Cole was quiet for a moment and then he said, "I think he feels bad. He's been looking like shit lately."

I pretended not to hear that. "That's the third time you've cursed— you realize that, right?"

He shrugged.

"Okay, I'll leave the admonishing to Jo. Let's talk about something less depressing. How's school?"

"You think that's less depressing?"

"It can't be that bad."

He shrugged.

"Okay, how about art?"

That topic immediately opened him up. "I'm getting a tattoo on my eighteenth birthday. I've been drawing loads of different ideas."

"Oh? So, are you still thinking about becoming a tattoo artist?"

"Aye, didn't Jo tell you?"

"Tell me what?"

"Adam's friend's cousin owns a tattoo parlor down in Leith. He's going to let me spend a couple of days a week there over the summer.

After high school there might be a possibility of an apprenticeship with him. If he likes me, that is. He told me to keep all my drawings. Create, like, a portfolio."

"That's brilliant. Wow, you are way more organized about life than I was at fifteen."

He grunted. "Tell that to Jo. She wants me to go to college first."

"Maybe you should."

"We'll see. Despite what she thinks, I have still got time."

"She just wants you to have choices in life, Cole."

"Aye," he said, his eyes softening. "I know that."

The walk passed quickly as we talked about school and movies and books. He was a kid who was kind of taciturn with most people, and it was nice to be counted among the circle of friends and family he was willing to open up to.

Arriving at Jo and Cam's flat, Cole shoved the door open. "I'm home!"

"We're in the kitchen!" Jo called back.

Cole grimaced. "I'm not going in there," he whispered. "Sometimes when they think they're alone they're all . . . affectionate."

I chuckled under my breath and followed him into the sitting room. He stopped abruptly and I had to sidestep his tall frame to see past him.

If a bus had driven through the wall and slammed into me, it wouldn't have had any less of an impact than when I saw Nate sitting there. Our eyes collided and Nate slowly stood up from the couch. After a moment of helpless staring, my gaze drifted over him. Sporting a short beard and dark circles under his eyes, he looked exhausted and unkempt. It was so not like him.

"Sorry, Liv," Cole apologized quietly. "I didn't know he'd be here."

"It's okay."

"How?" Nate took a step toward me and I automatically took a step back. He stopped, swallowing hard as his eyes took me in, almost hungrily. "How are you?"

Before I could muster up some kind of reply to that stupid-ass question, the loud clack of heels in the hall grew in crescendo as they came toward us, and I turned, my eyes narrowing, as a tall redhead in a low-cut tank top and skinny jeans sashayed into the room in five-inch sandals. "That bathroom is gorgeous." She smiled politely at me before sidling up to Nate. Her toned arm slid around his waist and she pressed her breasts against him. "Your friends have a really nice flat."

Heat unlike anything I'd ever felt before flooded me. A fire blazed in my chest, the flames licking my throat and forestalling any words. Instead I just stood there glaring at them in impotent jealousy and heartbreak.

"Liv?" I turned at Jo's voice and found her standing in the doorway, her features slack with surprise. "What are you—"

"Just leaving." I cut her off and pushed past her hurriedly, ignoring her calling my name in concern as I slammed out of the apartment and raced for the stairs. I heard the door opening behind me, but I just kept moving, desperate to get somewhere quiet where I could brood and rail and curse Nate Sawyer to hell.

"Olivia!"

*Oh, God.*

"Olivia, stop," Nate growled behind me. Close. Too close.

His hand clamped around my arm and I found myself hauled to a stop and turned about to face him.

He stood, a few steps up from me, breathing heavily, his expression panicked. "Liv, don't go."

I wrenched my arm out of his grip, and immediately felt the phantom of his fingers wrapped around it. "Go back inside, Nate." My expression was pure disdain. "I should have known nothing would keep you down for long."

To my surprise, his eyes hardened with what I would almost call indignation.

What the hell did he have to be indignant about?

"Pot calling kettle," he bit out, taking a step down, bringing him closer to me. "I heard you got your library boy." He raked his eyes over me. "I assume you fucked him well and he's enjoying the benefits of my lessons."

A punch to the gut would have been just as effective. And probably would have hurt a whole lot less.

He flinched at my expression and ran a hand through his too long hair, his fingers turning into a fist. "Shit, Liv, I'm sorry," he whispered hoarsely. "I didn't mean that."

I turned to leave and promptly found myself caught in his hold again. "Let me go," I hissed.

Instead he pulled me toward him. The familiar smell and feel of him made me ache. "Just tell me you're okay."

I relaxed, in the hope that it would make him release me. "I'm fine," I answered quietly. "Go back to your girl, Nate."

Nate's grip tightened. "She's not my girl."

I shook my head. "I wasn't talking about the redhead. I was talking about the ghost tattooed across your heart."

My words loosened his grip.

Lowering my lashes so I didn't have to see the haunted expression on his face, I turned and descended the stairs, back out of his life.

# CHAPTER 24

Seeing Nate again was like straining a recent injury. When I left him I had to start packing ice on it again.

That's why when Ben called the next week while I was having dinner with Dad and Dee, I was glad of the distraction.

"I know we don't know each other *that* well, but I'm going to selfishly pretend that's not true in order to ask a massive favor."

Amused, I leaned my elbow on my dad's counter and relaxed into the conversation. "What kind of favor?"

"My sister has somehow managed to rope me into babysitting my niece, Zoe, on Saturday. Now I love my niece, but she's eight years old, a total girly girl, and when I asked her what she wanted to do, she replied that she wanted me to take her to see some Disney pop princess musical movie at the cinema. Zoe is used to getting what she wants, so this *is* going to happen. I was hoping you'd do me a favor by coming with me so I don't appear to be some creepy guy at a Disney movie, but—"

"One-half of parental obligation?"

"Exactly."

I laughed. "It sounds like you'll be owing me majorly."

"So you'll come with us?"

"Sure. As a favor. Not a date."

"Not a date. I completely agree. Nothing kills romance more than a teenybopper musical."

After a minute of confirming details of when and where, I hung up. My dad stared at me curiously.

"What?"

"Are you sure that's a good idea?"

"We're just friends," I assured him.

"I've heard that before."

"Mick," Dee admonished, scowling at him on my behalf.

Dad grimaced. "I'm sorry, sweetheart, but it's the look on your face right now that tells me that going on a date with some other man is not a good idea. And you know"—he pushed his fork around on his plate as he avoided my eyes—"Jo told me Nate is not doing well at all. She says he looks like hell. And apparently he's been trying to contact you."

My eyes narrowed. "I thought you didn't like Nate."

"I didn't. Until you told me all those things about him."

"Dad—"

"He was very young when he lost that girl," Dad interrupted, pushing his plate away and leaning toward me conspiratorially. "I can't imagine how difficult it is to go through the loss of a woman you love at such a young age. But I can understand how it might paralyze you. Nate never got a chance to experience enough of life to learn how to put loss into perspective. Or the fear of loss even. He might just need time."

Not surprised by my dad's understanding and empathy, I placed my hand over his, my heart hurting. "Dad, even if Nate turned around tomorrow and told me that he wanted to give us a chance . . . I'd say no."

"I thought you loved him."

"I do. I'm very much in love with him. But he won't ever allow himself to love me the way he loved Alana. She was his big love. I want to be someone's big love, Dad. I think I deserve to have the man I love love me back just as much."

·  ·  ·

Saturday afternoon I met Ben and his adorable niece outside the Omni Centre. Zoe was a bundle of excited energy and Ben looked more than a little relieved to see me. He had this permanent crease in his forehead, which I would soon learn had come from listening to Zoe talk on and on about her painful decision to demote a certain world-famous boy band to the status of her second-favorite band, in favor of this new, cooler band that had just hit the charts.

I could speak boy band, since I went through my own boy-band phase until I hit thirteen, so I listened attentively to Zoe as we walked into the cinema together. As she hemmed and hawed over what kind of candy she wanted, Ben squeezed my shoulders and murmured, "Thank you," in my ear in a way that I felt across my skin.

I smiled, feeling relief that maybe, just maybe, I could get over Nate after all.

The movie was as bad as Ben and I thought it would be, but Zoe loved it and was giggling and singing as we walked out of the theater. With the innocence of the young, Zoe took my hand and her uncle's hand too, walking between us so we made a picture of the perfect family.

It was more than awkward for me, since Ben and I still didn't know each other that well, but when I caught his mischievous grin I knew he didn't feel awkward at all. In fact, I got the feeling he was enjoying himself. My suspicious side wondered if this had been a ploy from the beginning. Had good old boy Ben gotten a little sick of waiting on me to call him for a date and decided to move things along faster?

I squeezed Zoe's hand but shook my head at Ben as we strolled up the street toward McDonald's, where we'd promised to take Zoe for lunch.

"Using your niece to turn this into a date?" I semi-whispered over Zoe's singing.

Ben laughed at me. "I did no such thing."

"Oh, you did too." I rolled my eyes. "You knew the adorableness of this situation would tug at me."

Ben threw his head back in laughter, causing Zoe to stare up at us and ask, "What's going on?"

Before I could explain in a bumbling fashion, a very familiar voice froze me to the spot.

"Olivia?"

The three of us stopped, our hands still clasped, and stared at Nate, who'd come to a halt on the sidewalk in front of us. People pushed past us in irritation, swerving around us as we just stared at one another. I took in his unshaven face, his messy hair squashed under a beanie, and the dark circles that were still under his eyes since last we'd seen each other. My heart flipped over painfully in my chest.

It flipped even harder when the color leached from Nate's cheeks as he processed the sight of me with Benjamin and Zoe.

"Ben, this is Nate. Nate, this is Ben and his niece, Zoe."

"Hi!" Zoe chirped.

Nate, the inherent charmer, would usually have flashed his dimples at her adorableness and responded to her. But something was happening to him as he looked from me to Ben to Zoe to our hands clasped tightly together. There was something akin to horror in his expression.

"Nate?" I whispered, taking a step toward him.

"I, eh, I . . ." His eyes caught mine now, his chest rising and falling in shallow breaths. "I . . ." He lifted a shaking hand.

"Nate?"

"Excuse me." He pushed past us and strode down the sidewalk as if the hounds of hell were nipping at his heels.

I stared after him, hating that I was worried for him as I wondered what the heck had just happened to him.

"Well, I'm guessing there's a story there," Ben said softly.

"Maybe."

"Do you fancy telling me about it?"

I glanced down at Zoe, whose head swung from one to the other of us in confusion. "Not really."

"Okay, that's fair enough. But how about we put whatever that was behind us and go to McDonald's, eat some processed food, and then I'll persuade you to accompany me to my cousin's wedding. As a date."

Reeling, I could only stare at him.

Zoe's excited laughter and jerk on my hand pulled me out of my daze. "Say yes! I'm Flower Girl. I want you to see my dress."

I threw Ben a dirty look as his mouth twitched in amusement. "You are an evil genius."

I didn't understand what had gone through Nate's head when he saw me with Ben and Zoe, but what I did know was that he wanted to talk about it. I knew this because he started calling me. Now I felt like I was *continually* icing the injury he'd left me with.

That very night he called me. When I didn't answer he sent me a text, asking me to call him back. The next day he called me. He left a voice mail, which I refused to listen to. He called me the day after that. And thus began a daily dose of Nate.

So many times I had to catch myself. I wanted to pick up. I wanted to pick up because he was obviously sorry he'd hurt me. I got it. I understood. However, it didn't change anything. It didn't change the fact that being around him was too hard.

So I decided to go to the wedding with Ben that next Saturday.

Seemingly a staple of every Scottish wedding, the Proclaimers filled the wedding tent with their promises while I sat huddled beside Ben at our table. I'd told him countless times to go off and mingle with his family, but he'd told me that the whole point of bringing a stranger to the wedding was to have an excuse not to have to do that.

More and more he proved to me that he was funny and charming, and that I'd be a complete idiot not to give him a shot.

"Can I get you another drink?" he asked, nudging my nearly empty champagne glass.

Ruefully, I shook my head. "The last wedding I was at I got shame-fully drunk and ended up saying things I now regret."

He smiled mischievously. "Now I definitely want to get you drunk."

I laughed. "No, you don't."

"So . . . what was it you said that you regret?"

"It's not really what I said, it's what saying it led to."

"And what was that?"

"A broken heart." I winced as soon as I said it. "God, Ben, I'm sorry. I'm the worst wedding date in history."

He gave me a sympathetic smile. "You know what might make it up to me?"

"What's that?"

"Tell me about him. Nate." He guessed correctly. "What happened? It might help."

I shook my head. "You don't want to listen to that."

"What if I go first?"

Of course my curiosity got the better of me. I wanted to know about Ben's big heartbreak. Just as I was about to agree, my cell rang. With an apologetic smile, I reached for my clutch and pulled out the phone.

I got goose bumps all over when I saw the caller ID.

Nate.

Did he know I was on a date? Was that why he was calling? Angry that he kept interrupting my life, I shoved the phone back in my purse.

Ben gestured to it. "Was that him?"

"How did you guess?"

"Because I'm fairly certain I get that look in my eye anytime my ex tries to contact me."

"What look?"

"That 'if-I-could-tear-you-to-shreds-with-my-incisors-I-would-why-won't-you-get-out-of-my-life-you-crazy-bitch' or in his case 'crazy bas-tard' look"

I laughed humorlessly. "Close. It's more like . . . I keep trying to get back to who I was before this happened, and every time someone says his name or he calls, it reminds me that I probably won't ever get back to that person because . . . he was a part of who I was then."

We sat in silence for a moment.

Finally Ben took my hand and rubbed his thumb over my knuckles. "One day you'll wake up and he won't be the first thing you think about."

"Promise?"

"I promise."

My cell rang again, jarring the sweet atmosphere between us. Growling in frustration, I reached for my purse, ready to switch off the damn phone, but then I saw it was Jo calling this time.

For some reason I felt an unpleasant dip in my belly.

"I'm sorry," I told Ben. "It's my friend. I should answer her."

"Of course."

"Jo?" I asked as I put the phone to my ear.

"Liv"—she sounded out of breath—"Liv, Nate tried to call you. Something's happened."

"What is it?" I asked, instantly panicked. "Is he okay?"

"He's . . . His dad's been rushed to hospital."

I got a taxi from the wedding as quickly as possible, but it took me almost an hour from the time Jo called to get to the hospital. The whole time I was begging and pleading with whatever divine being might exist in this world to help Nathan. Jo said they thought he'd suffered a heart attack.

I practically threw the cab fare at my driver and dashed out of the car, hurrying inside the main entrance of the hospital.

*Please, please, let Nathan be okay. Please.*

He was such a good man.

*And Nate cannot take more loss.*

As I hurried toward the main reception to ask after Nathan, his son's voice called my name and I stopped, my eyes following it. Nate stood in the middle of the crowded waiting room, looking pale and haggard.

I moved toward him, drinking him in. The beard was gone, but the eyes were still dark, and now his mouth was pinched with worry. Sitting behind him were Sylvie, Cam, Cole, and Jo. Sylvie was tearing a Kleenex into pieces. She reminded me of a frightened animal, the way she kept staring round-eyed at the doors beyond.

"Nate—" I stopped hesitantly before him, not sure if I should hug him but wanting to. "Is there any word?"

He shook his head, his eyes bleak. "They took him into surgery. No one's come out yet."

Breaking, I took one last step toward him and wrapped my arms around him.

Nate instantly sank into my embrace, his strong arms locking around my waist as his head bowed into my neck.

We stayed that way for a while.

"Nathaniel Sawyer's family?" a doctor called.

Nate and his mother quickly stood up from their chairs and hurried to him. I glanced around at Jo, Cam, and Cole before looking over at Peetie and Lyn, who had arrived a little while after I had. We'd been waiting for hours and hours, and now all of our expressions were the same.

Hopeful.

Desperately hopeful.

At the sounds of Sylvie's sobs my lungs ceased to work and I watched in horror as Nate pulled her into his arms. Cam, his eyes hollow with grief, moved toward his friend. He rested a hand on Nate's shoulder and Nate gave him a small smile, shaking his head.

Cam's body slumped, as if with relief, and my lungs started working again. He strode back to us, running a shaky hand through his hair. "Nathan made it through the surgery. He's stable."

. . .

"Knock, knock." I leaned around the hospital door, wearing a huge grin.

I'd left Nate to be with his mom and dad for the last few days, but on Monday I cut out of work to make visiting hours.

Nathan was alone in his room, watching television. He blinked in surprise at the sight of me and then smiled widely as I walked in. Having dealt with a very sick person, I was a master at schooling my reaction to the physical toll sickness could take. Nathan's frame looked so much smaller as he lay in the hospital bed. His cheeks were drawn and there were a few more wrinkles around his mouth than there had been when I'd last seen him.

"To what do I owe this pleasure?" he asked, sitting up, careful of the wires connecting him to monitors hooked up by his bed.

Laying the flowers I'd brought with me on the bedside table, I pulled up a chair. "I was worried."

"*Pfft.*" He waved me off. "What's a little coronary disease?"

I glared at him.

"Aye, Sylvie didn't think that was funny either."

My lips twitched. "Don't make me laugh. I'm trying to be stern."

"Stern?" He huffed. "Stern? I'm going to be on medication for the rest of my life and I have to cut out my favorite food. My entire life is going to be stern from now on. I don't need stern from a pretty girl too."

"Fine," I agreed. "I won't do stern." I glanced around the room in confusion. "Where is Sylvie?"

"Och, I sent her home. She's absolutely shattered. She wouldn't leave me." He tutted. "Had to get my doctor to make her leave so she could get some rest. I'm going to pay for that later."

I snorted. "I'll bet."

"Nate's downstairs getting coffee, if you were wondering . . ."

My gaze was sharp as our eyes met. "You know, don't you?"

"The two of you didn't exactly do a bang-up job of hiding it when you came to visit. I am sad to hear it didn't work out, though . . . Which begs the question . . . What are you doing here?"

I answered belligerently, "Is a person not allowed to be worried about another person?"

"Aye, of course. You being a nice girl, I think you probably were worried about me and that's appreciated, but I think more than anything you're worried about my son. Which makes two of us." His brows dipped in concern. "He misses you."

"I miss him too," I confessed softly.

A throat cleared behind me.

Turning, I discovered Nate standing in the doorway, stirring a cup of coffee. He pinned me to my seat with the weight of his stare.

"Nate." I finally found my voice. "I just wanted to stop by and see how Nathan was doing. I should get going." I stood up.

"Nonsense." Nathan stopped me, gesturing to me to sit down. "There's still half an hour left. Sit. Talk." He looked up at his son. "Sit down."

Nate looked like he wanted to laugh as he casually took the seat beside me.

My eyes, with a will of their own, traveled over the long sprawl of his legs. Tingles hit me unexpectedly as I lifted my gaze to his hands, continuing to stir his coffee. He had beautiful, masculine hands— graceful, strong fingers that were callused from work and judo. The soft roughness of his hands had always felt wonderful. And the T-shirt he was wearing showed off his strong forearms. I looked quickly away from the thick vein that ran up his muscular arm. I'd licked the entire length of that vein with my tongue.

Hurriedly, before I expired on the spot, I turned my attention to Nathan.

He was smirking at me.

Great. Even sick, the guy could tease.

"So how have you been, Olivia? Nate says you're seeing someone." His tone had turned disapproving.

"I'm not seeing someone," I answered irritably. Technically, I wasn't seeing Ben. Yet.

Nate sat up. "You're not?"

I flicked a look at him before directing my answer to his dad. "It's just been a couple of dates."

Nathan frowned. "That constitutes as seeing someone." He looked at his son. "What do you think?"

"Agreed," he answered tersely. "And it definitely looked serious."

Starting to feel uneasy, I exhaled. "Can we talk about something else?"

"Why? Nothing else is as interesting."

I groaned. I was *so* not ready to do battle with two Sawyer men. "Fine, then I should definitely go. Nathan, I'm so happy you're going to be okay." I leaned down and pressed a kiss to his cheek, ignoring his bemused expression.

Not looking at Nate, I quickly exited the room.

"Olivia, wait," Nate called as I hurried down the hospital corridor.

I did not wait.

That's why I found myself caught in his hard grip and unceremoniously hauled into a dark janitor's closet.

"What are you doing?" I hissed, feeling his breath against my cheek as he pressed me back against the door.

His answer was to kiss me.

I froze in shock at the move, but soon the shock wore off under the feel of warm, coaxing lips. Perhaps it helped that he wasn't aggressive or fierce. His kiss was soft, yearning. My lips answered to that and I found myself kissing him back.

Nate pulled away first, panting heavily as he nuzzled my cheek, his hands iron bands around my biceps as he breathed me in. I was surrounded by him. The familiar strength of him, his scent, his taste on my tongue, even the slightly bristly feel of his cheek on mine.

I closed my eyes, tears clinging to my lashes.

Maybe I was wrong. Maybe the loss of him wasn't the most painful thing in the world. As I stood there in his arms, knowing that he would never really be mine, it occurred to me that more than loss, it was the longing that hurt.

"You're the first person I thought of," he told me hoarsely, his words vibrating against my ear and causing an involuntary shiver. "The only one I wanted here with me."

Swallowing past the burning, choking ball of unshed tears in my throat, I whispered, "I'm sorry I ignored your call."

"Don't be. You came. That's all that matters."

Needing some kind of distance, some kind of break from the intensity between us, I cracked, "I think there's an inappropriate joke in there somewhere."

He laughed against my skin before pulling back. "Fuck, I've missed you, Liv."

"Nate." I pushed gently against him until he got the message. His hands dropped from around my arms, leaving me bereft. "I'm glad your dad is going to be okay, but I have to go."

"Liv, please—"

"Ben's waiting," I lied impulsively. I had this sudden fear that Nate's calls and his confession that he missed me were leading somewhere. And I didn't know if I was strong enough to do the right thing, so I wasn't going to give him the chance to mess with my head. "I'm meeting him."

He was quiet in the dark for a moment.

And then . . .

"We need to talk."

"No. We really don't." I fumbled for the door handle and managed to slip outside. He didn't follow.

I took that to mean that he understood there was no point.

# CHAPTER 25

Apparently Nate didn't take it to mean that at all.

I shouldn't have been surprised really to find him waiting for me in my apartment when I got home from work that night. I slammed the door behind me and held out my palm. "I want my key back."

Nate had stood up as soon as I walked in, and now he was prowling toward me with this playful look in his eyes. The way his dimples played peekaboo had my face scrunching up like a five-year-old preparing for a tantrum. I did not need him to be gorgeous and charming right now! I definitely did not need the dimples.

"I swallowed the key."

"You didn't swallow it. If you'd swallowed it I'd have come home to a corpse."

Nate stopped with one eyebrow raised. "Should I be worried by how *not* upset you are at that prospect?"

My nostrils flared. I knew it. He was here to be charming.

I had to get him out!

"Give me my key."

Nate shrugged. "I can't do that."

"You have to," I huffed indignantly. "It's *my* key."

"Why are we still talking about the key?"

"We've barely even started talking about the key." My right foot moved back as Nate moved forward, his lids lowering sexily over his eyes. It was his hunting look. "Nate—"

"I love you."

I froze, almost gasping from the words, words that were fists punching gaping holes in my chest.

While I was in shock Nate took advantage. He stopped, inches before me, not touching me but not really needing to. The heat from his body licked my skin.

"My life has been hell without you," he confessed, his voice rough, his expression morose. "I thought I could do it. I thought I could lie to the both of us. But seeing you on the street last week with that guy and the little girl . . . It was a glimpse into the future. It didn't hit me until right in that moment that walking away from you, from us, meant having to watch you be with someone else, have kids with someone else." He closed his eyes as if in pain. "It cut me to the quick to see you playing happy family with that guy. Christ, Liv, I couldn't breathe."

And I couldn't do this. It wasn't enough.

Shaking my head, I stepped to the side so he couldn't back me into the corner. "Nate, you have to leave."

Instead he studied me carefully. "You're not ready to hear this yet," he concluded. "But I do need you to know that I'm going to fight for you. I'm not making the mistake of walking away from you again. The only man in your future is me, Liv. The only kids in your future are mine." Nate opened my front door, dug into his pocket and produced my key. He held it out to me and I took it tentatively, confused by the action. "I don't need to break into your life. You've put up a locked door between us and I understand why. But I'm going to stand outside it, bugging the absolute shit out of you." He smiled wryly. "Until you let me back in." His expression changed like a black cloud rolling in unexpectedly. "I'll warn you, though—you let that Ben guy in the door . . . I'll start fighting dirty."

Before I could respond, Nate slipped out, leaving me split in two.

Part of me was desperate to call him back, to savor those three little words that spilled from his lips. Savor them over and over again.

The bigger part of me, however, knew it wasn't enough. Maybe it was selfish, but I didn't just want Nate to love me. I wanted him to love me the way I loved him. The kind of love that's so big it would last beyond a lifetime.

The kind of love he had for Alana.

I don't know what I expected. Nate always had such a laid-back approach to life that I wasn't sure if he would really fight for me. Honestly, I was kind of hoping he wouldn't because it would make it easier for me to keep saying no.

The day after his little visit to my apartment, however, a basket of chocolates from my favorite chocolate boutique in the city was delivered to my work with a note from Nate:

> *We have a date with melted chocolate waiting in our future . . .*
> *I'm going to paint you with it and lick my fill until you . . . Well,*
> *what is it the French call it? La petite mort. I love you.*
>     *Nate*

Not only had he had no qualms about writing something like *that* on a gift card that the delivery person could see, but I also had to deal with my colleagues, who'd ripped the card out of my hands before I could stop them.

Angus grinned as he handed it back to me. "He used a French phrase for orgasm. That's classy. I say he's a keeper."

"He wrote about orgasms on an apology gift," I said, pointing out the obvious. "That's classy?"

"No, but it's bloody hot," Jill chimed in, frowning at me. "Get back with him, you silly cow. Do you know how many men do stuff like this?" She poked at the gorgeously wrapped basket of goodies. "Not many."

I spent the rest of the day scowling at my basket of chocolates.

The next day a large gift-wrapped box arrived at work and I took it into the staff room to open in private. Of course as soon as Jill saw the box, she told Angus and Angus told Ronan and all privacy was obliterated. They'd stood behind me as I pulled off the black satin ribbon and opened the pale pink box. Under layers of tissue I found a beautiful and very expensive black lace and satin bustier, matching high-cut panties, and silk stockings. They came with a card:

> *Beautiful, sexy, sensual. The underwear is nice too. I hope one day you'll wear it for me, but if you don't, I hope at least when you put it on you'll see what I see in you when you look in the mirror. I love you. Nate.*

I'd ended up crying in the bathroom after that, cursing Nate Sawyer to hell and hoping that tomorrow wouldn't bring another gift that would push me closer to opening that goddamn door. In a stupid effort to somehow outmaneuver him I called Benjamin that night and arranged to meet him for coffee after work the next day at his favorite café, not far from the library. The hope being that his presence would remind me that life didn't begin and end with Nate and I *could* move on. *I could, I could, I could, I could.*

The day after, I was manning the help desk when security came over with another package for me. This time it was a small parcel with an envelope attached. My heart thumping, I ignored Wendy, who was working beside me, and opened it.

A Blu-Ray disc of *The Wizard of Oz.*

Tears pricked my eyes and I felt strangely nervous as I fumbled for the envelope. Taking a deep breath, I began to read the handwritten letter from Nate.

> *Dear Liv,*
>
> *It's time we upgraded your favorite movie to this century, even if it is* The Wizard of Oz.
>
> *And just so you know: If you were a movie you'd be* The Godfather—*I could watch you over and over and over and over again because . . . well, you're my favorite.*
>
> *I miss you.*
>
> *I miss our Would You Rather conversations and your hilarious answers. I miss your laugh. I miss the way I feel when I make you laugh. Like I just won something really important. I miss just sitting with you in perfect, silent understanding. I miss the way you never judge anyone. It's such a rare find, Liv. And I miss watching how kind you are with everyone. I miss being able to call you and talk to you about random shit and important shit.*
>
> *I miss my best friend.*
>
> *I miss you.*
>
> *I love you.*
>
> *Nate*

Shaking, I pulled my cell out of my pocket, hoping Angus would understand that I needed to make a personal call and make it pronto.

Jo picked up, sounding out of breath. "Hey, Liv, can I call you back? I'm in the middle of pasting wallpaper and I need to get it up on the wall quite quickly."

"Well, I'll be quick. Tell Nate to stop sending me gifts. We're over."

She was silent a moment. "Can't you tell him yourself?"

"No, he's . . . I can't be around him. Please tell him to just back off. Please."

"Liv, the reason you don't want to see him is because you care about him and being around him makes you less hurt and more susceptible to giving him a shot. And I don't think that's a bad thing."

"You're wrong," I told her haughtily. "I've moved on. I'm meeting Ben for coffee after work at Black Medicine."

"The one on Nicolson Street?" Jo asked sharply.

"Yes. I think I might even suggest we take things to the next level."

"Well, I hope for Ben's sake you're not just trying to piss Nate off. Because he actually sounds like a nice guy and he doesn't deserve to be messed around." Jo sighed. "I've got to go."

She hung up, clearly annoyed, and that only made me feel like shit.

I'd feel less bad about the fact that I'd disappointed her roughly five hours later . . .

"What the hell are you doing here?" I hissed up at Nate.

He stood between me and Ben with his hand on the back of my chair and I saw the hardness in his eyes before he shook it out to turn to my friend with a congenial smile. He held out his hand to Ben. "I'm Nate. We met briefly before."

Tucked in the back of Black Medicine, this quirky, gorgeous little café with naturally cut wooden furniture that wouldn't be amiss on the set of a *Lord of the Rings* movie, I'd been in the middle of telling Ben about my Nate woes when the handsome bastard had suddenly appeared as if conjured.

But I knew he wasn't conjured.

Jo had given up my location.

I was going to kill her.

Ben blinked, clearly as surprised as I was to see Nate there. He took in Nate's offered hand and slowly reached forward to clasp it with his own. "Good to meet you," Ben answered quietly, his expression assessing.

"So—" Nate made a *tsk* sound with his teeth "I'm going to have to ask you to leave. I need to talk to Liv."

My mouth fell open at his audacity. "Are you out of your mind?"

When his gaze slid back to me, the hardness was in it again and I realized quickly that it was annoyance. *He* was annoyed with *me*? Was he kidding me? "You and I have unfinished business," he replied softly. "I don't think it's fair to drag Benny boy here into it."

Ben cleared his throat. "With the exception of the condescending nickname, he has a point." Ben shifted, pulling his wallet out. I stared in horror as he put a five-pound note on the table to cover his coffee.

"You're actually leaving?" I hissed.

His lips curled up in beleaguered acceptance. "You've just spent the last fifteen minutes telling me about all the ways this guy has spent the past week trying to convince you that he's in love with you. I think you need to talk it out with him instead of me." He smiled kindly before shooting Nate a warning look. His green eyes flicked back to me. "Call me later to let me know you're okay."

My eyes narrowed on him. "I don't talk to traitors."

Ben snorted, shaking his head at me. "Just call me." And with that he left me.

Nate didn't bother to watch him leave. He just slid into the chair Ben had vacated and shuffled it so close to mine that our legs were touching. I pushed my chair back, readying to leave. Nate's arm shot out, his hand taking hold of my wrist. "Liv, please."

Our eyes clashed in a war of wills, and unfortunately my will was severely dented by the pleading warmth of his gaze. Sighing, I tugged my hand gently out of his grasp and shifted back toward the table, but made sure that we were no longer touching. "You have five minutes."

His eyes searched my face for a moment, like he was cataloguing every feature, and there was something so vulnerable and open about his expression that my heart immediately began to pound. Nate leaned forward, his voice low as he said, "That night at Cam's . . . the redhead."

I flinched, my expression shuttering.

I didn't really want to talk about the fact that while my heart was breaking Nate was out there getting over me by getting other women under him.

"I didn't sleep with her," he hurried to assure me, his words almost desperate. "Liv, I haven't been with another woman since you."

Snorting, I casually took a sip of my coffee even though I felt anything but casual about our conversation. "Right," I muttered sardonically, setting my cup back on its saucer.

"I would never lie to you about that."

At his hard, indignant tone I looked up at his face and found he was angry. I raised an eyebrow at his expression. "You're mad because I don't believe you? Really, Nate? I asked you point-blank if you were in love with me, you said no, and now weeks later you're saying yes. And you wonder why I'm struggling to believe a word you say?"

For a moment I thought he wasn't going to answer. Clearly attempting to keep his impatience in check, Nate exhaled heavily before replying. "That night was the only night I've ever lied to you. More than that, I was lying to myself. I didn't want to fall for you. You, more than anyone, know that. But I did. And I'm man enough to admit that it scared the absolute shit out of me. It still does." He reached for me, his hand resting gently on my knee as his eyes bored into mine. "There's been no one since you because I don't want anyone else. You've ruined me for anyone else." His hand coasted lightly up my thigh, and unfortunately that mere touch elicited a hundred memories of sensual caresses. Lust must have flared in my eyes, because I saw Nate's gaze sharpen as he caught it. "I miss you, babe. I miss everything about you." His fingers started tracing circles on my leg and I felt trapped, unable to move as my body began to hum with the memories. Nate's eyes darkened with heat as they scanned down my body and back up to my lips. "I miss your mouth," he confessed hoarsely. "I miss your tongue. I miss the feel of it against mine. I miss the feel of it on my skin." He leaned in even closer so all I could see and smell was him. "I miss your mouth wrapped around my cock."

My breath left me, blood rushing in my ears as his words cast a sexual spell over me.

His fingers continued to draw their lazy pattern on my thigh. "I miss your breasts, Liv, and the feel and taste of your nipples. I miss the way they pucker up for me, for my thumb, for my tongue . . . and how me just touching your tits makes you so fucking wet." He groaned at the thought and his hand suddenly tightened over my thigh. "I miss that. You drenched and hot and tight around me as I pump into you. The feel of your nails digging into my back, your thighs gripping me tight, your eyes on mine."

I think I whimpered.

Nate's eyes flared. "You screaming my name as you come around my cock. I miss that most of all."

Breathless, I gazed into his eyes, my cheeks flushed, my breathing unsteady. I couldn't believe he'd said all that to me in public. I couldn't believe my body's reaction.

His hand smoothed over my thigh. "If I slipped my hand between your legs right now, I'd find you wet, wouldn't I, babe? I'd find you as wet as I am hard."

I sucked in my breath, trying to clear my desire-fogged brain.

Somehow, somewhere, I found the strength to push his hand off my leg. Trembling, I reached for my bag. "Sex . . . it isn't love."

"For Christ's sake, I know that." Nate grabbed my wrist, stopping my flight. "Don't walk away, Liv. You walk away now . . . it's about pointless stubbornness."

Anger engulfed me and I ripped my hand away from him. "You left me," I growled. "You treated me no better than one of your random hookups, and suddenly because you've decided that no, wait, you *do* love me, I'm to come running back?" I stood up, my chair clattering behind me with the force of the movement. "Your words are nice in the moment. But at the end of the day it means fuck all. I don't trust you with your own feelings, Nate. Why the hell would I trust you with mine?"

Before he could say a word I hurried out of there, my throat choked with the tears I held back the entire walk home. It had taken an enormous amount of strength to walk away from Nate. A strength I hadn't even known I had.

# CHAPTER 26

Even though I felt like Ben had left me to the slaughter, I was also flattered that he was concerned enough to want me to call him when I got home. However, when I did call him I was surprised to hear what he had to say.

"You're that couple," he told me softly.

"What couple?" I snapped.

"That couple who are a couple even when they're not being a couple."

"You spent five seconds with us," I argued.

"Yeah, and it was enough to know that you and Nate aren't over. You're unresolved, and until you know whether or not you're going to go back to him, I think I'm less likely to get hurt if I stay completely out of the cross fire. Look, I really do like you, Olivia, so if I'm wrong and you decide he isn't for you, give me a call."

And then he hung up on me.

I spent the next few days seething at Nate. Not just for the emotional damage he'd caused me but because my body had been strung taut like a guitar string twisted to near breaking point ever since his little word seduction in the dark corner of Black Medicine. My vibrator barely took the edge off.

*Jerk.*

The only good news to come at me that week was Jo's casual mention that Nathan was home and recovering well, and that Elodie and Clark were hosting a party to celebrate Joss's pregnancy. Jo suspected Joss was only going along with it to prove to everyone that she was happy with the pregnancy. I wasn't so sure. I thought the only one Joss really cared about was Braden, and from what I'd seen, he was happy and he knew that Joss was happy. I thought that more than anything they were just going along with the party because it meant something to Elodie.

The other good news—and I was determined that it was good news—was the fact that Nate had stopped calling. Saturday came around and it was time for the party and I hadn't heard a peep out of him since our conversation at the café. That was good. It meant I was right.

Nate didn't love me.

He'd given up easily.

He didn't love me.

That was good.

*Yeah, that's convincing, Soda Pop.*

Okay, so it would suffice it to say I wasn't in the greatest mood when I turned up at Elodie and Clark's on Saturday evening. Even the pink and blue balloons, the decorative baby gowns with funny quotes on them, the mammoth white cake with pink and blue buttercream frosting, the chilled champagne and delicious-looking finger food couldn't pull me out of my funk.

But I pretended it did. Or I tried to . . .

"You look better." Joss wandered over to me as I settled myself in the corner of the crowded sitting room with a glass of champagne. She, on the other hand, was holding a glass of water.

"As do you."

And she did. She looked well rested and happy.

"I feel good," she said, a small smile flirting with her mouth as she glanced across the room at her husband. He was standing talking to someone I didn't know, but his eyes kept flicking back to her. "Braden's a little overprotective at the moment, which I thought I'd find annoying." She grinned at me. "Not so much, though. You'd be amazed at the lengths he's willing to go to to make me happy."

I gave her a sly look. "Are you using your pregnancy to extort irrational favors from your husband?"

"I wouldn't call making him get up at two o'clock in the morning to find a twenty-four-hour supermarket that stocks chocolate peanut butter Häagen-Dazs ice cream irrational."

My eyes bugged out. "You didn't do that to him?"

Joss snorted. "No." She took a sip of her water, her eyes twinkling with mischief. "But I'm going to."

I burst out laughing, drawing the gazes of several people in the room, and one of those gazes turned me to stone.

Nate had arrived. And he looked good. His hair had been trimmed a little and he was sporting stubble. He wore a dark red T-shirt and black jeans. Nothing special, yet still he managed to look good enough to eat. I really hated that about him.

Seconds after our eyes locked across the room, his expression grew blank and he quickly turned back to Cam and Jo.

What? My eyes narrowed in heated indignation. *He* was ignoring *me*?

Joss hissed in her breath. "Did we forget to mention Nate was coming?"

Attempting to control my anger, I turned back to Joss, smoothing out my own expression. "He is your friend. I can't expect you guys to not talk to him."

"Still . . . it's awkward. I should have told you."

"It's fine. We're ignoring each other." I swallowed past the lump in my throat. "There's no reason why we can't both enjoy our friends' happiness without one of us wanting to stick a fork in the other's eye!" I snapped, and gulped down the entire glass of champagne.

Joss stared at me for a second. "Okay then. I'll just leave you to . . . your violent musings."

She was gone before I could apologize for my insanity.

"Fuck," I muttered.

"Charming."

I spun around at Ellie's wide-eyed, smiling regard. "Hey, Els. Sorry about dropping the f-bomb. I forgot to check my bitterness at the door and Joss got whiplash from it."

Ellie waved me off. "Oh, Joss won't care. She knows all about it. She's just in this little happy bubble at the moment and it deflects all misery."

"She shouldn't have to deflect my misery. My misery should have been checked at the door along with my bitterness."

Ellie took a step closer, her expression conspiratorial and yet still sympathetic. "So you're still miserable?"

I just blinked at her.

"I'll take that as a yes." Without another word she scurried off.

"Oh, God," I mumbled under my breath, as I realized I was successfully driving my friends away with my attitude. "I'm that cousin who stinks of pee."

I was more than grateful, then, when I saw my dad striding through the party toward me. However, as soon as I caught sight of his grim countenance, the gratitude was quickly replaced by concern.

"What's going on?" I asked softly, as he gently took hold of my elbow.

"I need to speak to you," he replied gruffly.

Mystified and troubled, I let him lead me out of the sitting room and all the way upstairs. To my surprise he opened the door to Hannah's room and gestured for me to go in ahead of him.

Throwing him an inquiring look as I passed, I walked inside, only to come to an abrupt halt at the sight of Nate standing with his back to me. I swung around, wide-eyed, to question my dad, but the door was already slamming shut behind me.

My mouth agape, I whirled around to find Nate frowning at me.

"You're not Cam," he observed quietly.

"You think?" I snapped. "We've been had. My dad led me up here on false pretenses."

He raised an eyebrow, amusement glittering in his dark eyes. "Mick was in on it? When did he take my side?"

I knew exactly when my dad had switched to the dark side, and it was all my fault. Idiot child. "Before you turned into a total asshat, I made the mistake of convincing him that you're a good guy. Unfortunately, what I told him seems to have overridden the fact that you stop being a good guy once your dick is involved."

Instead of being offended, Nate laughed. "I remember a time not too long ago when you would have blushed from head to toe saying that."

"I remember a time when I thought there was no one else like you."

That bled the amusement right out of him. We stared at each other in tense silence for a moment until Nate shook his head sadly. "I hate that I'm the one who's done this to you. The Liv I fell for is the kindest, most compassionate and understanding woman I've ever met. I've made you lose her."

Although I don't think he intended it as a barb, it hurt like one and I couldn't hide the tears that sprang to my eyes. Choking on the crushing sensation around my throat, I turned away, heading for the door.

I heard the sound of his quick movement behind me as I pulled the door open and suddenly his heat was flush against my back, and his hand was above my head, forcing the door shut again. I froze as Nate pressed against me, his hard body so achingly familiar.

"I know you think I've given up, babe," he whispered against my ear, and I closed my eyes against the feel of him. "But I haven't. I'm just giving you time to find her again."

It came to me on swift feet—the knowledge that I would never move on as long as Nate held out hope of a reconciliation. I needed this to be final and yet I wanted just one more taste, so I spun around in his arms, cupped his nape in my hand, and pulled him down to my mouth. I'd forgotten what the taste of him could do to me—I was lost for a moment, drowning in sensation. Nate instantly wrapped his arms around me, hauling me tight against him as he kissed me back, desperate, a little rough, the wet, hot, deepness of our kiss like a euphoric drug taking effect.

I suddenly found myself pushed against the door, Nate's hands roaming my body like he didn't know where he wanted to touch me first. When he took hold of the back of my thigh and lifted my leg around him so he could press his erection against me, the heat roared through me. I growled into his mouth and his grip grew bruising.

It was a good thing too, because that slight nip of pain wheedled its way into my consciousness and I somehow found the strength to pull away from him.

Pressing hard against his chest, I forced him back and he released his hold on me.

Tenderly, I caressed his neck, sweeping my hand around and across his jaw, before brushing my thumb over his lower lip. Once my breathing began to even out, I lifted my eyes from his mouth to meet his burning gaze. The tears were back and he became a blur as I whispered, "Stop waiting, Nate. I forgive you, okay. I get it, and I'm not angry at you. Not really. Because it's not your fault. I'm just kind of mad at the situation and I've been taking it out on you."

Nate's brow creased with confusion. "Liv, I don't . . ." He shook his head, squeezing my waist in question.

So I explained.

"I want a love like what my dad had with my mom. I want what Joss and Braden have. Jo and Cam. Ellie and Adam." The tears flowed freely before I could stop them. "You already had that with Alana."

As if I'd shot him, Nate jerked back from me.

"This may sound selfish and childish, but it's how I feel. I want to be the love of someone's life. I can't be second best. And I definitely can't be second best for you." I reached behind me, turning the door handle. "I'm sorry, Nate. I really am. But I can't spend the rest of my life loving a man who can't love me back in the same way." I opened the door, trying to block out the pain in his eyes. "So stop. For the both of us. Please."

I didn't give him a chance to speak because I was a coward and I didn't want to hear the transference of pain in his eyes to his voice. So I left—hurrying down the stairs and out of the house before anyone could stop my retreat.

Later that night I let my dad into my apartment, shooting daggers at him the whole time. His eyes washed over my face, taking in my swollen eyes and puffy nose, and I saw a flicker of guilt pass over them.

"I thought I was doing a good thing," he said quietly and immediately engulfed me in a mammoth hug.

I clung on for dear life. My dad did good hugs. "I know," I said, sniffling against his wide chest.

He squeezed me tight and kissed the top of my head. "Nate didn't look so good when he came back downstairs."

Tensing, I squeezed him back. "Dad, don't."

"I just want to make sure you're not throwing away something good out of stubbornness."

"You sound just like him."

"Maybe he has a point."

Pulling back, I looked up into Dad's face with a calm I wasn't sure I felt. "He can't love me the way I want him to. It would be disastrous for the both of us."

Dad's expression softened. "Baby girl, you're not even giving him a chance to prove you wrong."

"You don't know how he talks about Alana. You don't know," I whispered fiercely.

At that, Dad said no more. He gave me one last squeeze and then proceeded to potter about my kitchen, throwing together hot cocoa and a late-night snack.

He stayed until I fell asleep, and the next morning I woke up tucked safe and tight in my bed.

My pillow was damp with tears.

---

# CHAPTER 27

Determined to convince everyone I was okay, I spent the next ten days going through the motions. I got up, I got dressed, I went to work, I smiled when I was supposed to, laughed when it was required, was serious when seriousness was appropriate, and hoped to God that my pretense was working. The truth was I felt as lost as ever without Nate, and I was scared and angry with myself. I was terrified that I was never going to find my way back to who I used to be. I felt like I'd lost a limb and hadn't quite come to terms with it and how different my life would be from now on.

So in pretending otherwise, I felt less of a whiny coward.

Maybe things would have been easier if Nate had given up like I'd asked him to.

But he insisted on calling.

I ignored him, and along with him I ignored Jo. Kind of. I talked on the phone with her, as I did with all my friends and family, but after they'd set me up (and I knew that they'd all been involved in getting me and Nate alone that day) I didn't trust them not to try it again. So I was avoiding spending any actual time with them.

Four days after the party I'd turned the corner onto Jamaica Lane and spied Nate sitting on my stoop, his head bent as he stared at the

ground. I'd fled before he saw me, going to my dad's, the one person I
trusted not to try to set me up again.

Under the pretense of indifference I felt my anger begin to build
again. Why couldn't Nate just leave well enough alone? He'd heard what
I had to say and he couldn't argue with it.

Thankfully, by the seventh day of avoidance Nate seemed to get the
picture and the calls stopped. All was quiet for a few days, while I attempted to get my head together. I buried myself in work, doing over-
time since the library was chock-full of students preparing for their
exams. Ben came into the reserve section and we talked amiably, but I
didn't let on that I hadn't chosen Nate. I didn't let on because not choosing Nate didn't mean I was choosing Ben.

I was choosing me.

And me needed some peace and quiet, away from any potential
added heartbreak.

As I stood at the quiet help desk, sorting mail while I wasn't busy,
my brain was determinedly ignoring any Nate-like thoughts. I had a
whole life outside of Nate. Concentrating on that should be a cakewalk.

Or so you'd think.

"Olivia"—Angus hurried toward me, a stack of files in his hand—
"can you do me a favor?"

"Anything," I said a little desperately, eager for distraction.

He gave me a concerned look but didn't comment. "There's a . . .
situation in one of the accessible rooms. Room five. Can you handle it,
please? I'm snowed under." He raised the files in explanation.

I wrinkled my nose. "Another situation." I shook my head, rounding
the help desk. "Why can't they just keep it in their pants?"

Angus grunted and shuffled past me.

Bracing myself, I threw back my shoulders and hurried up the
stairs, brushing past the busy throng until I got to the first floor. You
would think during exam period these kids would have more pressing
things on their minds, but oh no, sex was never off the table.

Literally, in this case.

Sucking in my breath, I threw open room five and charged in.

I hit an invisible wall, my body tensing at the sight of Nate leaning against the table, his arms crossed over his chest, his ankles crossed casually.

The door slammed shut behind me, jerking me out of my stupor.

"What are you doing here?" I demanded, my hands clenching into fists at my sides.

"Angus helped me out."

*That traitor!* "Oh, he is *so* off the Christmas list," I fumed.

Nate's lips twitched. "Don't do anything drastic. I was quite persuasive. The poor guy couldn't help himself."

"Oh, I'm sure." Angus had probably melted under Nate's warm, chocolaty gaze. "Now if you don't mind, you need to leave." I gestured to the door, trying not to visibly shake. I felt like I hadn't seen him in a hundred years and I did not like the warm fuzzies I was getting in my stomach from just being in his presence.

"I can't. I need to explain something first." He stood up and to my utter shock he began to pull his T-shirt up and off.

"What are you doing?" I snapped, reaching forward to stop him, until my eyes caught sight of his tattoo.

My heart began to thud. Loudly.

His eyes never leaving me, Nate dumped his T-shirt on the desk. "I made the change to the tattoo a few weeks ago. What you said during our breakup . . . it got inside me, Liv. I've had a lot of time to think, to process. To move on. And this"—he gestured to the tat—"I wanted to talk to you about it, what it means, since the day I got it."

The stylized "A" on his chest had been expanded to the word "After."

A lump the size of Mexico formed in my throat.

Nate took a step toward me, his gaze intense, raw, and his words were low and rough with emotion as he said, "Before you, there was Alana. I can't change that, Liv, and I don't want to. She was my first love. It was a simpler kind of love. It was the love of two children." He searched my face, apparently trying to gauge my reaction to this, but I was stupefied. Nate continued quietly, "I always thought that I kept a distance from women because I knew I'd never be able to love someone the way I loved her. I was wrong. I kept my distance because I was afraid of finding the kind of love my parents have, and I was afraid of what it would do to me if I lost that kind of love." He took another step toward me and with each step he stole another breath from me. "I never meant to fall in love with you. But I did. I felt it the first night I made love to you. I tried to walk away then because I've never felt so lost and yet so fucking found as I felt that night looking into your eyes as I moved inside you. I thought I should walk away . . . but I couldn't stay away from you." He smiled. "Totally fucking addicted at the first taste of you. I'm so sorry I put you through hell. I'm sorry I was selfish. I'm sorry I ever made you doubt what you knew was between us from the start. Because it *has* been there since we met, Liv. The sex lessons just pushed it to the fore. Since we met, I've enjoyed being around you more than anyone else. I laugh harder with you. I feel more myself with you. I trust you with me—the real me. When something goes wrong, or right, or I hear a funny joke, or I see something bizarre, you're the first person I want to talk to about it. Fuel all that with the best fucking sex I've ever had in my life, and it's no wonder I'm a goner." His voice deepened again as he took one last step toward me. "I want you all the time, Olivia. The past few weeks have been torture without you. And despite what you might still think, I promise there has been no one else. How could there ever be?"

I didn't even realize I was crying until he cupped my face to catch my tears on his thumb.

"Alana was my first love and I'll never forget her. She's a part of me and always will be. But I know it's time to move forward, it's time to start living in the after. You're that for me, Liv. You're the love of my life."

The sob burst forth before I could stop it and Nate caught me, leaning his forehead against mine as he rubbed his hands soothingly down my arms.

"Please, Liv. Please tell me what I need to do to make sure you believe that."

I swallowed, trying to calm the ache in my chest that was causing the sobs. Sucking in a deep breath, I gazed down at his chest and gently touched the new tattoo.

*After*

I tilted my head back to give him a watery smile. "You've already done it."

Nate's arms slid around me, his head dipping so he could growl against my lips, "I love you so fucking much."

My heart jumped and I closed my eyes in pure relief. "I love you, too."

He kissed me.

Hard.

And I clung on for dear life.

We stumbled back against the table as we kissed each other as if it were the last time we'd get the chance. Turning us, Nate lifted me onto the table without breaking our connection and I immediately wrapped my legs around him, urging him closer. My hands pressed deep into the muscles in his back as he gripped my hips. I sucked on his tongue and felt his answering hard-on nudge insistently between my legs.

A loud burst of laughter from outside managed to force its way between us, and I jerked back, shaking my head dazedly. "We can't," I panted breathlessly. "Not here. Do you know how many students have gotten up to no good on this table?"

His eyes bright with lust, color high on his cheeks, Nate looked a little nonplussed at first as he gazed past me to said table. Finally, he lifted his hopeful gaze. "My place is a five-minute walk from here."

Surprise shot through me and I smiled slowly. "I've never seen your place."

Tenderness softened Nate's expression as he tucked a strand of hair behind my ear. "I'd really like you to see it now, babe."

I bit my lip, musing over it. I didn't muse long. "Angus does owe me some vacation time. I'm sure he won't mind me taking a half day."

Nate's hand was warm and strong in mine, and since his strides were eating concrete I had no choice but to hurry along with him or have my arm pulled out of the socket.

After Angus grinned knowingly at my half-day request and then quickly granted it, Nate had grabbed my hand and hauled ass out of the library. Without saying one word he pulled me along with him over the Meadows and into Marchmont.

I was now being ushered up the stairs in his building at super speed. On the second floor, without letting go of my hand, I might add, Nate dug his keys out of his pocket, opened the shiny black door one-handed and dragged me inside.

Before I could take anything in, Nate was blocking my view, slamming the door shut over my shoulder a second before crushing his mouth down on mine and pushing me up against the wall.

I caught on fire pretty fast.

I salivated over the feel of his bristly stubble against my cheek, his tongue teasing mine, his soft hair drifting over my fingers as I clenched them in it in an effort to fuse myself to him. Nate pulled back to rip his shirt off and then he reached for mine.

Helpfully I lifted my arms and I was soon divested of my T-shirt.

My bra was gone seconds later.

A pleasured whimper fell from my lips when Nate wrapped his mouth around one nipple, laving and sucking it with his tongue while he pinched the other between his finger and thumb. I closed my eyes, arching against his mouth, clutching his head to my chest in sheer sexual delight.

"I've missed you so much," I gasped as arousal coursed between my legs.

My words brought Nate's head up and he was kissing my mouth again before trailing hot, openmouthed kisses down my neck. I jerked in delighted surprise at the touch of his fingertips on my sex. He rubbed me through the fabric of my pants and I moaned his name, pushing my hips into the contact.

"I almost came out of my skin," Nate suddenly said, his voice cracking with sexual anticipation, "when you first asked me to teach you . . . when you asked me to fuck you." He groaned and dropped his head against the crook of my neck as he continued to rub me torturously. "It took every ounce of willpower I had not to grab your hand, haul you up to your flat, and fuck you until we both died of exhaustion."

"Seriously?" I panted, my hands sliding down his warm, naked back to clutch his hips, to draw him closer.

"Seriously." He lifted his head to stare into my eyes and I almost climaxed at the expression on his face. Nate *wanted* me. Like, seriously, seriously *wanted* me. "It was the excuse I'd been waiting for, for nine months."

Our heavy breathing mingled for a highly charged moment, and then I reached up and kissed him. I kissed him with every ounce of love I had in me. Pulling back, we both panted a little as I cupped his face with my hands and let down every single defense I had. My soul was in my eyes, and I knew the moment Nate felt it because his grip on my waist tightened. "No one," I whispered, my lips trembling with the emotion, "has ever made me feel like the person I've always wanted to be until you. You make me feel beautiful, Nate. All the way through. No one else has ever given me that. No one."

"I'm glad," he murmured against my mouth. "Not just because you deserve to feel that way . . . but because it makes you mine."

"Nate . . ." I shivered at the possessive purr in his voice.

"You're going to scream that for me tonight." He brushed his lips gently over my mouth as his fingers worked the zipper on my pants.

"You're going to scream that you're mine." His hand slipped inside, his fingers pressing beneath my panties and pushing gently in.

I arched into his touch, sighing. "Come inside me," I begged. "I've missed you inside me."

"I am inside you," he answered, teasing me as he added another finger.

I groaned at the fullness but despite the pleasure, it wasn't enough. "Not . . . I want your cock. I want your cock inside me. And I want it deep. So deep, Nate."

He crushed my mouth beneath his, his kiss as uncontrolled as his movements as he pushed my pants down until they fell to the floor. We broke apart just long enough for me to toe off my shoes, divest myself of the pants and my panties. I felt an indecent ripple of arousal wash over me at Nate's reaction to the sight of me naked and trembling with anticipation against his wall.

"Fuck." He stopped, his hands on the zipper of his jeans as his eyes washed over me. "Do you know how insanely sexy you look right now?"

His expression was hot, and it turned me on to the point of combustion, so suffice it to say I was done being stared at. I wanted to be taken. "Nate, hurry."

Burning eyes drinking me in, Nate slowly unbuttoned his jeans as his chest rose and fell rapidly. "Say it again. Say it standing there with your legs spread, waiting for me."

The flush of self-consciousness I felt under his perusal was more than eaten up by how excited I was. I was soaked. "Say what?"

His lip curled at the corner. "You know what, babe."

Dirty. Nate liked it dirty.

Who was I kidding? We *both loved* it dirty.

Shoulder blades pressed against the wall, my breasts heaving with breathlessness, I widened my stance, causing Nate's nostrils to flare. "I want your thick, hard cock inside of me now and I want you to fuck me against this wall until we can't breathe."

I barely got a chance to see the way his lower abs jerked at my words before he was on me. His kisses were bruising as he slammed into me, pushing his jeans down to free his dick, seconds before he wrapped his hands around my legs, sliding me up the wall, angling my body just right.

He thrust into me.

Hard.

Deep.

We both cried out as my sex clenched around his invasion. I wrapped my arms around his shoulders, my legs around his waist, hanging on for dear life as he pounded into me.

"You're drenched," he said on a harsh breath. "So wet for me, babe. I love how hot and wet you are."

"Just for you," I promised on a pant and that made him pump into me harder, faster.

I yelled out to God and the heavens as the delicious, rough friction quickly created the right pressure inside me.

And then suddenly I was moving through the air, falling against Nate as he took us to the floor. With him still inside me, he flipped us, now with my back on the floor. He lifted my right leg higher, pushing my left leg gently, spreading me wider. His eyes burned into mine as he moved above me, this new position allowing him to thrust deeper.

The pressure in me built and built.

"Nate!" I cried, unable to move against him since he held me so tight. It only made the tension coil, my climax nearing . . .

"That's it," he panted, his eyes never leaving mine. "Let me take you there, baby."

"I'm coming." I scraped my nails into his hardwood floor. "I'm coming."

Then suddenly his movements slowed and the pressure stabilized.

"No!" I gasped frantically, reaching for him. "Don't stop."

His eyes glittered at me. "Say you're mine."

"What?"

"Tell me you're mine."

What the hell was he doing?

"Nate, don't stop, I'm so close."

He circled his hips against me, teasing me. "Tell me you're mine."

"Of course I'm yours," I snapped. "Now bloody well fuck me!"

Nate's grin was quick, melting hurriedly beneath his own growing need as he began to pump into me again, his movements gaining speed as my breathing stuttered.

"Oh God!" I slapped my palms against the floor. "Oh God, oh God! Nate!"

The pressure blew and the orgasm that tore through me was so epic my eyes actually rolled to the back of my head. My lower body shuddered against Nate's thrusts, my inner muscles clamping hard around him. Nate came with a shout of release rather than his usual groan. His hips jerked in hard shudders against me as the orgasm rolled through him, setting off little aftershocks in my body.

He braced over me, his eyes wide as we stared at each other in blissed-out shock.

It was safe to say . . . best sex ever. Ever!

Gently releasing his hold on my legs, Nate fell to the floor beside me, and we lay with our heads together, panting hard, slick with sweat, staring up at his white ceiling.

"So," Nate said once he had his breathing under control, "this is my place."

Smiling, I said, "I like the wall. And that's a good ceiling."

We turned our heads to look at each other and instantly burst out laughing.

I was still giggling as Nate rolled into me, his hands shifting through my hair as I wrapped my hands lightly around his back. "Want to see the rest of it?"

I pretended to contemplate this for a moment and then asked, "Do you have a slatted headboard?"

His answering grin was slow and wicked. "Are you asking me to tie you down?"

I nodded my affirmative. "In every way you possibly can."

Nate's expression softened to absolute tenderness and he leaned down to press a soft kiss to my mouth. "That," he whispered, "I can definitely do."

# CHAPTER 28

I t was a warm spring evening, a slight breeze whispering over my bared arms as I stalked toward Club 39 in my stilettos. Two guys passed me and I felt their eyes drift over me. Glancing up at them out of the corner of my own, I found them staring appreciatively at my legs.

A few months ago I would have somehow managed to convince myself that they weren't staring appreciatively—that they were staring in bemusement at the fat girl who had dared to wear a dress. I knew that wasn't true anymore. I had good legs. I was showing them off.

But not for these guys.

No, my pins were out on display for Nate Sawyer and Nate Sawyer only.

*I'm happy for you, Soda Pop.*

I smiled to myself. Yeah. I think my mom would be really happy for me.

My heels had just hit the end of the line to get into Club 39 when my cell rang. Pulling it out of the black clutch with the ruby clasp that matched the scarlet red dress I was wearing, I saw my dad's name and instantly answered.

"Hey, baby girl. Dee and I were wondering if you and Nate wanted to pop by the flat for a beer?"

"I'd love that, Dad, but how about tomorrow night instead? I'm meeting Nate and the gang for drinks."

"Not a problem. Sounds good. Is Nate there? I wanted to ask him if he'd talked to his journalist friend yet about doing a piece about the business."

I grinned, looking at my stilettos. They were suede and they were dark red. They were awesome. I'd chosen my outfit carefully for Nate. Nate, whom I'd officially been seeing for only the past week. Already my dad was trying to extract favors out of him. "I'm meeting him inside. You can ask him tomorrow."

"Okay, sweetheart." He was silent a moment and I moved along the line, now descending the stairs to the basement bar. "So things are good?"

"Things are great."

"I'm happy for you. Your mum would have been so happy for you."

Tears burned behind my eyes. "You know I was just thinking that exact same thing."

"Well—" My dad's voice was suddenly gruff so I knew he'd gotten all emotional on me. "I'll let you go. Have fun."

"'Bye, Dad."

I slipped my phone back into my clutch and pondered the fact that I felt physically brilliant. For the first time in the longest time, I felt like I was breathing free. Although I'd once admitted my fear to Nate that I was somehow, maybe, deep down, harboring some kind of resentment toward my mother, I knew now that it wasn't true. I think what I really feared was somehow disappointing her, and I knew that the only way I could ever disappoint my mom was by not being happy.

It was amazing the kind of relief being happy brought a person.

The pieces of my life were falling together nicely. I had a job I loved, friends I adored, a makeshift family I couldn't be without, I finally liked myself *all the way through*, and I was in love with a beautiful man who loved me back just as much.

Something Nate had set about proving all week long.

Much of that proof of love had been physical, and I swear to God I'd lost five pounds from all the activity. Not that I was complaining.

The bouncer at the doors to Club 39 smiled wolfishly at me, giving me a chin lift as I passed him with a secret smile. My secret smile wasn't for him, though. It was for Nate. After Angus had asked me to work a little later that night, I'd called Nate to tell him to meet me at the bar rather than picking me up. This meant I got to make an entrance for him, but it also ensured that we actually went out, rather than becoming distracted by each other in the bedroom. It was important that we went out tonight, since it was the first night we'd be spending as a couple with our group. Despite not being able to drink, even Joss would be there.

"You're coming?" I'd asked, surprised when she'd called me to confirm the time.

"Hell, yeah. Nate Sawyer brought to heel. Yeah, that's definitely something I want to see for myself."

"I haven't brought him to heel," I'd argued.

"Olivia, he's been screwing anything that moves for as long as I've known him. I've wanted a woman to throw him off course since the first night I met him. Nothing on this earth will stop me from witnessing him drooling over you."

I'd laughed, not wanting to disappoint her by telling her Nate wasn't the drooling kind.

When I walked into the bar I zeroed in on my friends sitting around a table and began to stride toward them, my heart picking up pace at the sight of Nate laughing at something Cam was saying to him. As if he sensed me, Nate turned slowly and as his eyes drank in the sight of me his expression was as close to drooling as I'd ever seen it.

He stood up as I neared, coming around the table toward me.

My welcoming smile was suddenly lost in his hard kiss as his strong arm wrapped around my waist and pulled me against his body. I kissed him back, my fingers curling lightly in the hair at his nape. When our lips finally unlocked, I raised my eyebrows. "That was some hello."

Nate's hooded eyes were trained on my mouth. "That's some dress."

"Your favorite color."

"On my favorite person."

I smiled and gave him another quick kiss. "Should we sit down before we cause a scene?"

"Or we could just go back to your place," he suggested, caressing my hip.

Although I shivered with delight just at the thought of it, I pressed a hand against his chest and leaned back. "I think we can afford to take a tiny little break from the bedroom for a few hours to spend time with our friends."

"An hour."

"Three."

"An hour and a half."

I chuckled and shrugged. "Okay, two."

"Two hours." He gave me one more quick kiss and let go of my waist, only to take hold of my hand. As he led me over to share his seat with him I felt all my friends' eyes burning into us.

After I took my seat I looked around at Ellie, Jo, Joss, Braden, Adam, and Cam, and I had to bite my lip to stifle my laughter. They were staring at Nate as if they'd never seen him before.

"It's a manwhore miracle," Joss breathed, her eyes wide.

I giggled, nudging my shoulder against Nate as he glared at her.

"Seriously." Ellie smiled. "I don't think I actually believed it until I saw it with my own eyes. Nate loves Olivia."

Nate's glare grew darker, but the girls didn't seem to notice.

"I knew." Jo smirked at them. "I knew he fancied the pants off her all along."

"I'm just glad he's finally met his freaking match." Joss grinned smugly at him.

"He did go through a lot of women to find her," Ellie added. "It was a long time coming."

"Men," Nate suddenly growled through clenched teeth, "control your womenfolk."

While Braden, Cam, and Adam laughed, enjoying Nate's discomfort, I attempted to restrain my amusement. It was very hard for me. But it was fun to see someone as laid-back as Nate get wound up over a little teasing.

When Joss opened her mouth, obviously ready to deal out more teasing, Nate cut her a deadly look. "Liv needs no more reminders about my . . . colorful past with women, so can we all shut up and talk about something else, please?"

The group shared gleeful little looks but did as they were asked, and we started discussing the renovations Joss and Braden were making to Ellie's old room in their apartment. They were turning it into a nursery, and once they knew the baby's sex Jo, Dad, and Dee were going to help with the decor.

"I'm getting another round." Nate turned to me. "Want to come up to the bar with me?"

I told him yes, still holding his hand as he pulled me through the crowd to the bar. As we waited I leaned into him, squeezing his hand in mine. "Babe, you know I don't care about your past hookups, right?"

A muscle in Nate's jaw ticked as he looked at me. "I just don't need people reminding you of it."

"Why does it bother you so much?"

He seemed genuinely surprised by my question, as if somehow it should be obvious. "It took me weeks to convince you what I felt for you was real, Liv. I don't need my past messing us up again."

Wow. Nate was worried about losing me?

Pressing against him, I gave my head a little shake. "Nate, those women didn't mean anything to you. They've never worried me."

"You sure?"

"I'm sure. All that uncertainty was about Alana, but that's over, okay? I love you and I'm here with you. I'm not going anywhere."

His eyes darkened with heat and something else I hadn't seen before. "Promise?" he demanded.

I felt concern wash over me as I realized that our separation had caused more demons in Nate than I'd been aware of. It suddenly occurred to me that I'd spent the last week allowing him to drive away any uncertainty I had over the depth of his love for me, when I should have been working just as hard to prove to him that now that I knew he loved me I wasn't going to let anything else come between us.

Reaching up I brushed my lips over his ear. "Let's go back to my place now."

Nate pulled back, his eyes questioning.

"I have a promise to make," I answered on a saucy smile.

Understanding flared in his eyes, and just like that we were moving toward the exit. I texted Jo to let her know we were leaving, and Nate and I hurried along the street in silence until we got to Jamaica Lane.

Upstairs in my bed, where it had all started, I slowly made love to Nate, promising him with every inch of me, that the "after" we'd found together . . . well . . . it was *forever*.

# EPILOGUE

"I really do appreciate you guys keeping me company." Ellie smiled gratefully as she set down a tray of drinks and snacks among all the boxes. "Adam can't stand clutter or chaotic spaces, so I promised him I'd get this place up and running before we move in."

I stood with an ornament wrapped in newspaper in my hand as Joss and Jo dug through boxes. "You can stop thanking us," I assured her. "We're happy to help. You've got a lot on your plate. New house. New job. Wedding plans." I frowned at her, putting down the ornament to reach for a drink. "Did I tell you lately that you're crazy?"

It was a few weeks since our night out with the gang, and Ellie and Adam finally had the keys to their new home on Scotland Street. On top of the stress of the move they were now well into their wedding plans. The wedding was only nine months away.

Ellie laughed. "Well, I thought I'd have help from a certain some-one, but she had to go and get knocked up by my overprotective big brother, who, I might add, barely let her out of the house to help me unpack."

Joss glanced up at her. "Yes. I got knocked up deliberately so I wouldn't have to help with the heavy lifting or bouquet choosing."

"Speaking of heavy lifting," Jo said with a frown, "where is Cole?"

I looked toward the front of the house. "I think he went outside. Want me to haul his ass back in?"

"Aye," she said with a sigh. "Bribe him with food if you have to."

"You didn't have to make him help." Ellie smiled as if in sympathy with the teenager.

"Why?" Hannah suddenly appeared in the hallway, arms wrapped around a box. "You made me help. If I can't escape, Cole can't escape."

"I'll go get him," I muttered, making my way out of the huge living room into the wide, spacious hallway. The double doors were both open against the wall, giving us better access to the property, and as I neared them I heard Cole's voice, followed by a softer female voice. I slowed my steps, quietly making my way to the entrance.

My eyes widened at the sight of Cole standing at the bottom of the front stoop next to a small redhead. It wasn't that the sight of him talking to a girl was surprising; it was his body language. He hovered over her, almost protectively, and the way he was smiling down into her face . . .

The girl laughed at whatever Cole was murmuring to her and I bit my lip at the bright look that entered his eyes. They continued talking in hushed voices in an intimate way, and I decided I definitely was not intruding. On silent feet I made my way back into the sitting room.

Jo looked up from her packing box. "Where is he?"

I grinned. "He's flirting his ass off with a pretty redhead. There's no way I'm interrupting that."

Her eyebrows hit her hairline. "Seriously?"

"Seriously. And by the looks of things, I'd expect a girl to be coming around the apartment from now on, if I were you."

Hannah smirked. "Great. Now I have ammunition."

Ellie nudged her. "Be nice."

"Why? He's always taking the piss out of me. Now I finally have something to torture him with."

We shook our heads at her and continued to unpack.

Twenty minutes later, Cole strode in, a dark scowl marring his handsome face. Worry creased Jo's brow. "Hey, baby boy, you okay?"

He grunted at her and moved toward a box.

I shared a look with his sister before plucking up the courage to ask, "What happened to the girl? The redhead."

Cole jerked as though I'd shot him. Without looking at me he muttered, "She had to leave."

"Well, did you get her number at least?"

He lifted his head and his green eyes blazed into mine angrily. "What do you think?" And at that he stormed out of the room, ignoring Jo's shouts to him to apologize for his rudeness.

"Leave it." I shook my head. "Just let him be."

Before Jo could reply, my cell rang and seeing Nate's face on my screen lightened my mood. "I have to take this." I ducked out of the living room and wandered toward the empty kitchen as I answered, "Hey, baby."

"Hey, yourself." His low, warm voice soothed me. "You about done at Ellie's?"

"Unfortunately not. I'll be a few more hours."

"Okay. Cam and I will just hang out for a bit, then."

"You know, it might be good if you swing by the house and pick up Cole."

Nate snorted. "Bored, is he?"

"Upset. I think something happened. With a girl. So obviously he doesn't want to talk about it with us."

"We'll be right there."

My stomach melted. "You are so getting laid tonight."

He laughed softly. "Don't I get laid every night?"

"Yes, but tonight I'll do anything you want."

"Anything?" he growled.

"Absolutely *anything*."

"Remind me to be a nice guy more often if this is the benefit."

I smiled a little goofily and leaned back against the wall, my body all pliant just thinking about him. "Okay. But don't be too nice of a guy. I do like it when you're bad."

"Do people actually talk like that?" Hannah's voice ripped me back to reality, and I jumped off the wall to see her giving me a wide, teasing smile.

My cheeks flushed and I heard Nate laughing on the other end of the line. "It's not funny," I snapped at him.

"Oh, it's definitely funny, babe," he said on a chuckle. "See you soon."

We hung up and I glared at Hannah. "You could have let me know you were there."

Her eyes twinkled mercilessly. "I could have, but then I wouldn't have overheard your delightful conversation."

I narrowed my eyes on her as I moved to brush past her. "One day, Hannah Nichols, you're going to meet a guy who makes you so gooey you'll end up doing and saying things you never imagined, and then who'll be laughing?"

Hannah's pretty smile widened. "Hopefully we'll all be laughing."

"You have a good answer for everything, don't you?"

"I like to think so."

Chuckling, I wrapped my arm around her shoulders and pulled her with me. "Come on, we've got a house to get in order."

*Eighteen months later*

I glanced at the bathroom door, thinking of the thing I'd left in there.

Okay.

I had to tell Nate.

After a moment I sighed heavily. I glanced at him, then at the movie he was watching, then back to him.

Here goes.

"Whatcha watching?"

I was such a coward!

Nate gave me a look. "The same movie I've been sitting here watching with you for the past half hour. You okay?"

*Tell him.*

I shrugged. "I completely zoned out. Sorry."

Seeming to accept my weirdness, Nate turned back to the movie and we sat and watched it in companionable silence. Well, he watched. I stewed.

Just a little over a year ago, Nate gave up his apartment in Marchmont to move into my tiny little apartment on Jamaica Lane. That day after he'd shown me the tattoo he'd had Cole design for him, we'd worked through everything together. My dad, Jo, Cam, and Nate's parents were particularly happy for us. I'd go as far to say that Nathan and Sylvie were grateful to me. But they weren't the ones who should be grateful.

Although he wasn't perfect—but who was, right?—Nate had tried his hardest to assure me that he was completely and deeply in love with me. He didn't need to try so hard. When I said the tattoo and his speech did it for him, I really meant it. From that moment on, things with us fell back into their usual beautiful pattern. That included Nate spending a lot of time at my apartment. I think if we both hadn't been scared about pushing the other too quickly, Nate would have moved in with me right away, but we didn't broach the subject until six months into our new relationship.

The move didn't just make us happy; it made our parents extremely happy. Because of my insistence—and also because of the heart attack scare—Nate and I visited his parents in Longniddry as much as possible, driving out there at least once a month to spend the night with them. Nathan and Sylvie thought I hung the moon. As for my dad, well, he would always be overprotective, but he'd eased up since Nate moved in with me, especially since Nate had made it clear that he felt it was now *his* job to be overprotective. And boy, did he do that job well.

I wasn't even going to pretend to find it annoying.

I was an independent, capable, strong woman . . . but God, I loved it when Nate got all protective and possessive, because it was usually followed by sexy time.

Sexy time . . . that had led us to our current situation . . .

I was unconsciously staring at his handsome profile, the light from the screen flickering over his features as he watched a prison break.

"What would you prefer?" he suddenly asked. "Life in a maximum-security prison or trapped in Jurassic Park?"

Tilting my head to the side, I pondered his question. "Do I have a social standing in this prison?"

"No. You're just an average Joe."

I heaved a dramatic sigh as if my decision weighed heavy on me. "Then I guess I have to go with Jurassic Park."

Nate smiled at the TV. "Why?"

"Well, I'll have constant fresh air, for a start, and also if I'm going to be anyone's prey, I'm going to be the prey of an animal that's acting out of instinct rather than psychopathy."

His laughter filled our apartment and my chest with its warm rich-ness. "Good answer, babe. As always."

"You?"

He shrugged casually. "If you're in Jurassic Park, I'm in Jurassic Park."

There were moments, like this moment, when sometimes what I felt for him completely and utterly overwhelmed me. "I love you so much—you know that, right?"

Turning his head on the couch, his expression adoring. "Love you too, babe."

We smiled at each other, then turned back to the movie.

The perfect contentment of the moment was broken by the silent taunting of the object in the bathroom.

I swallowed hard. "So . . . what would you prefer? A two-bed in New Town or a three-bed farther out of the city?"

Confusion lit Nate's eyes at my unexpected question. "Why would we want either? We love this place."

My heart began to thump, thump, thump in my chest, and I could swear he would see my pulse throbbing in my neck. "Okay." I took a shaky breath. "I'll be clearer. What would you prefer? A boy . . . or a girl?"

His entire body locked. Frozen.

"Nate?"

Slowly, he turned to look at me, his eyes wide as they silently asked the question.

I bit my lip and nodded.

With my confirmation, the most gorgeous smile broke across Nate's face.

Relief and excitement poured through me. I don't know why the hell I'd been so worried. He'd made it clear in the past that he wanted this for us.

I crawled across the couch until I was straddling him. Stunned dark eyes bored into mine as he wrapped his arms around me. "You're pregnant?"

Dipping my head, I whispered against his lips, "Congratulations. Daddy."

His whoop of laughter filled our apartment, my relieved giggles mingling with it as he held me tight and launched us off the couch, his quick, determined strides taking us toward the bedroom. Usually when Nate was in the mood to celebrate, he'd throw me on the bed and follow me down, but today I laughed to myself as he gently laid me on it like I was fragile.

Grinning up into his face, I asked softly, "Are you getting soft on me?"

"You've got our kid inside you. I've got to watch what I'm doing now."

"I hope not when it comes to sex." I reached for the buttons on his jeans.

Nate grew still, his hands braced on either side of my head.

My heart stopped at the sudden seriousness in his expression. "What is it?"

"I had this plan," he told me, his voice low. "I was going to wait until our two-year anniversary, fly you back to Arizona to visit your old friends, and your mum's grave. You would tell her about us, and after we got back I would propose to you."

A beautiful ache settled across my chest. "Nate . . ."

"But with the baby . . . maybe we should get engaged now?"

I grinned. Huge. "Okay."

His brow cleared. "Okay as in 'yes'?"

I laughed. "Yes."

And then he frowned again. "Shit. That wasn't the most romantic way to propose, was it?"

Smoothing his brow with the tips of my fingers, I promised him, "It was romantic to me."

He smiled into my eyes, pressing a hand to my stomach. "This is not where I expected to be."

"Me neither," I whispered.

"But I'm so fucking glad that someone out there thought this is where I deserved to be."

Running my fingers through his hair, I gently tugged his head down, bringing his lips close to mine. "Here's to 'after,' baby."

Nate pressed his mouth hard to mine, wrapping his arms around me, tightening me against him in absolute agreement.

# ACKNOWLEDGMENTS

When I first introduced Olivia and Nate into Joss and Braden's make-shift tribe, I knew Olivia had to be a librarian. Not just because, during my pre-author years, I always imagined happily working in a library, but because Tammy Blackwell insisted upon it. Okay, so I know you were just cracking jokes, Tammy, but it got stuck in my head. So thank you for inspiring Olivia's career choice, and for giving me insight into the world of librarianship.

Thank you to Paul Gorman at the University of Edinburgh main campus library for taking time out of your busy schedule to show me around the library from the point of view of a librarian. Not only did you provide me with all the invaluable technical info so Olivia would sound like she actually worked in a library, but also you gave me surprising insight into the brazenness of college students. I told you I'd put it in the book.

My deepest thanks to my agent extraordinaire, Lauren Abramo. You always give me genuine encouragement. Anytime I see an e-mail from you in my in-box, I grin huge. You work your butt off every day, and I appreciate it every day. You never fail to rock, my friend.

To my editor Kerry Donovan, a gazillion thank-yous. Your belief in these characters, this series, and me, is mind-blowing. You'll never know how much it means to me. I love working on this world with you. I hope we get to work on many more in the future!

A massive thank-you to my publicist Erin Galloway, and every single person at NAL who has worked hard to see *Before Jamaica Lane* into print and into the hands of the readers.

Also thank you to my editors Claire Pelly and Hana Osman, and my publicist Katie Sheldrake, at Michael Joseph (Penguin UK), for all your hard work.

Moreover, I must say a huge thank-you to Nina Wegscheider and her team at Ullstein for their unbelievable enthusiasm for this series. It's been absolutely amazing to watch German readers fall for these characters, and I thank you for keeping me updated on all the excitement.

As always (and forever), thank you to my family and friends for putting up with my absentmindedness, my disappearances into fictional worlds, and my inability to text back until a really awkward length of time has passed.

And finally, to my readers: Thank you for embracing this series. You make every day a good day.

And don't miss Samantha Young's next book
in the On Dublin Street series,

# FALL FROM INDIA PLACE!

## Available in June

There was an instant connection when Hannah Nichols first met brooding bad boy Marco D'Alessandro, but Marco insisted on holding her at arm's length. He convinced himself that it was for her own good—he didn't trust himself not to break the heart of someone he had come to care about so quickly, and so deeply. And then, one amazing night on India Place, he finally gave in to the attraction. But just when Hannah thought she'd finally broken through to him, Marco promptly left both her and Scotland behind.

Five years later, Hannah has never quite moved on from the only man she's ever loved, the one who broke her heart so completely. And when he walks back into her life, Marco is determined to make things up to her. Regretting his decision to leave her, Marco wants a second chance with Hannah, and he'll stop at nothing until he convinces her they're meant to be together. Despite her misgivings, Hannah soon finds herself falling for him. . . .

Only to be left brokenhearted all over again. She makes a discovery about Marco that unearths a secret she's been keeping from him, and the life Marco thought they were building shatters all around them. The hurt he caused her when he left her all those years ago runs deeper than Marco had ever imagined. . . .

So deep it will take everything he's got to win her back.

Don't miss this bonus novella in the

ON DUBLIN STREET series!

Turn the page for Ellie and Adam's story,

UNTIL FOUNTAIN BRIDGE,

which has only been available in digital format.

# UNTIL FOUNTAIN BRIDGE

*An* ON DUBLIN STREET *Novella*

Ellie has been in love with Adam Sutherland for as long as she can remember. What started as a childhood crush on her older brother's best friend soon bloomed into full-blown infatuation. Unfortunately, it also meant full-blown heartache, as Adam refused to fall for Braden's little sister.

But it took a crisis to make Adam realize he wasted too much time denying his feelings for her. Unwilling to waste a second more, he decided to make Ellie his, no matter the consequences. Now happily settled with the woman he's pined after for years, he's about to find out what their ten-year courtship was like for her, through the journals she kept during their ups and many downs. And though Adam may have Ellie now, he has no idea how close he came to losing her. . . .

# CHAPTER 1

I t was always the same when you were looking for something amongst a big pile of *some things*—the something you were after was at the *bottom* of that big pile of some things. I finally dropped the last box on the other side of the room and wiped a streak of sweat from my forehead.

When I'd moved in with Adam three months ago, I'd promised him that all the boxes of junk that I put in his spare room would be sorted out and put away within a couple of weeks. I'd unfortunately reneged on that promise and wasn't ashamed to say I was still leaning on my tumor scare to get me out of the admonishment that should have followed. I'd been diagnosed with a benign—and yet still terrifying—brain tumor eight months ago; a diagnosis that not only traumatized my family and friends, including Joss, but had kicked Adam, my brother's best friend, in the behind. He'd finally admitted to everyone he was in love with me, and we'd hardly spent a day apart since. Although our relationship had changed, we were still *us*, and Adam tried not to treat me like I was made of glass. However, I'd noticed he let me get away with things he wouldn't have before—such as cluttering up his clutter-free, swanky duplex with all my rubbish—and I didn't know if this was because of the scare or because we were a couple now and he was compromising.

I swooped down on the last box with a grunt of triumph and ripped off the packing tape. Inside I found exactly what I was looking for and I smiled. I'd already upended the box and sent my old diaries cascading across Adam's hardwood floors before it occurred to me that upending a box of diaries might cause scratches. Wincing, I did this silly little dance over the falling journals as if this would somehow, magically, soften the impact of their rapid descent.

It didn't.

I dropped to my knees, picked up the books, and checked the floor for nicks. Nothing. Thank God. Adam was an architect. This meant that he liked his space a certain way, and his way was in pristine condition, especially when his space had cost him a fortune. Hardwood flooring wasn't cheap. Adam had already changed his life for me, doing a three-sixty from being the ultimate player to becoming a devoted boyfriend; from bachelor and proud clutter-free homeowner, to doting partner and proud owner of a stylish duplex covered in weird crap that his quirky, overly romantic girlfriend picked up in random places. He'd literally allowed me to leave my mark on every room, so damaging his floors wasn't exactly a nice way to pay him back. I kissed the tips of my fingers and pressed them against the floor in a gesture of apology.

"Els, what was that noise? You okay?" Adam's deep voice could be heard from across the hall. He was in his office working on his and Braden's current project.

"Uh-huh," I called back, flipping through the diaries to make sure I had every single one of them. I was so lost in what I was doing, I didn't hear Adam's footsteps.

"What are you up to?" His voice was suddenly right above me and I jumped, startled, only to lose my balance.

I heard him smother a snort and glared up at him. "I need to get you a bell."

Ignoring me, Adam crouched down onto his haunches, his eyes taking in the diaries. As always when I studied him, I got a little flutter in the pit of my stomach, and my skin tingled. With his thick, dark hair and great body, honed from daily visits to the gym, Adam was a good-looking guy—but the kind of good-looking that immediately transformed to *hot* when you started to talk to him. He had a wicked smile, intelligent dark brown eyes that twinkled when he was interested in what you were saying, and a rich voice that seemed to take a direct path to a woman's erogenous zones. Those gorgeous eyes of his lifted to smile into mine. "I haven't seen you with one of these in a while."

"My diaries?" I nodded, trying to sort them into chronological order. "I stopped writing."

"Why?"

"I stopped after we got together. There didn't seem to be any point to them any more since they were basically just an outlet for my feelings for you."

His lips curled up at the corners. "Baby," he murmured and reached over to tuck a length of short hair behind my ear. I frowned at the reminder my hair was short. Before the tumor, I had a head of long, light blond hair. I'd loved my hair, and I knew Adam had loved my hair. But the surgeons had shaved a patch of it off my head to cut into my brain unobstructed. I'd covered the patch with a headscarf, but had eventually stopped wearing it as the hair grew back, and I allowed my mother to talk me into getting "a chic pixie cut."

I was horrified when I walked out of the hair salon, and only somewhat appeased when Adam told me he thought my new hair was sexy and cute. I was *completely* appeased when Joss told me anything was better than a tumor.

She was right. If my tumor had taught me one thing about life, it was to not sweat the small stuff. That didn't mean it wasn't damn annoying waiting for my hair to grow back. At the moment, it was barely to my chin.

"So why are you looking at these?" Adam asked, picking one up and flicking through it absentmindedly. I didn't particularly care. I was a pretty open person anyway, but especially with Adam. I wasn't embarrassed by anything I wrote. I trusted him with the very depths of who I was.

"For Joss," I replied brightly, feeling giddy about the whole thing.

The night before, Joss and I had been hanging out at her and Braden's flat—my old flat on Dublin Street—and she'd told me her manuscript was coming along nicely. Joss was American, a writer, and she'd come to Edinburgh to escape a tragic past. Her story broke my heart. When she was fourteen she'd lost her entire family in a car accident. I couldn't even begin to imagine what that must have been like for her. I just knew it had a left a deep mark.

I'd liked Joss immediately when I interviewed her to be my flatmate, but I'd known then there was something broken about her, and I'd decided I wanted to help somehow. She'd been pretty closed-off, but when she started dating my big brother, Braden, I watched her slowly change. She said Braden and I both changed her, but really it was him. He'd helped her so much that she'd even begun to write a story based on her parents' relationship. That was a huge step for her, and she'd told me that she couldn't believe how much she was enjoying writing it. It had given me an idea for her next project.

"Why for Joss?"

"Because inside these diaries is the history of *us*." I grinned at him. "It's a good romance story. I think it should be her next novel."

I could see Adam was dying to laugh for some reason. I had no idea why, so I ignored it. "*Next* romance novel?"

"Next, as in, follows the previous romance. The story about her parents *is* a romance."

"Still, I'm pretty sure Joss wouldn't classify herself as a romance writer. In fact, I've heard her say as much."

"So have I." I tossed my first diary back in the box. It wouldn't aid Joss's research, considering I was seven when I scribbled in it. It was mostly about my Barbies and Sindy dolls and my issues with Sindy's flat feet and the impossibility of her and Barbie sharing shoes. It used to drive me nuts. "And I do believe the lady doth protest too much. She's definitely a romance writer. I've primed her to be a romance writer, subjecting her to so many romantic dramas it would be a miracle if she didn't become a romance writer."

He chuckled, my diary still open in his hands. He asked, "So you wrote about me in all of these?" as his eyes scanned the pages.

Yes, yes I had. I'd had a big crush on Adam since I was ten and he was seventeen. That big crush had transformed into an even bigger crush when I was fourteen, and then just snowballed from there. I threw another diary from my childhood into the box and reached for the next one in the pile. "I've loved you for a long time, my friend," I murmured.

"I want to read about it," he replied softly. The solemnity in his tone made me lift my gaze; brought my eyes to his. They glittered at me, full of the tenderness and emotion that never failed to make me breathless. "I want every piece of you. Even the stuff I missed without even knowing I was missing it . . ." He referred to the fact that he'd spent a good part of my crush being completely unaware of my feelings for him.

I felt myself melt. I was a romantic to the very bone and although it would surprise anyone who knew him, Adam catered to my romantic side with a dedication that thrilled me. He had a way with words that turned me to mush . . . and then usually turned me on, so it was a complete win-win for him.

I gave him a soft smile as I turned to the diaries, and quickly flipped through them until I found the one I wanted. Skimming it, I found the exact entry I was looking for and then held it out to him, holding its place open for him. "Here, start with this. I was fourteen."

Adam raised an eyebrow, I assumed at the thought of reading my fourteen-year-old thoughts, and took the diary from me. I knew exactly what he was reading. I remembered it like it was yesterday.

*Monday, March 9th*

*It's been a really strange day. It started like every other day. I got up just as Clark was rushing out to work, I helped Mum with Hannah since she's got her hands full with Dec at the moment, and I tried to feed myself as I fed Hannah. This meant I had to change my school shirt because Hannah thinks porridge is for decoration only. I wish that had been the only incident today, but it wasn't. As soon as I caught up with Allie and June at the school gates, I just knew something was wrong . . .*

As soon as the bell rang for lunch break, I launched out of my seat and hurried out of Spanish class as if the hounds of hell were nipping at my feet. I tried to hold in the tears. I really tried because I didn't want any of these idiots to know they'd gotten to me, but as I burst out of the main entrance of the school, the floodgates opened.

All the whispering and name-calling . . . It was horrible. I'd never had that happen to me before. Not like that. People generally liked me. *I was nice!* I wasn't . . . I wasn't a "whore."

I cried harder when I heard boys in the year above me laugh at me as I passed them at the gates. Fingers trembling, I pulled out the phone Braden had bought me for Christmas and called my big brother.

"Els, you okay?"

As soon as I heard his voice another sob burst forth.

"Ellie?" I could hear his immediate concern. "Ellie, what's going on?"

"Bri—" I struggled to draw in a breath through my sobbing. "Brian"—my cries continued to interrupt me—"Fairmont . . . he-he's a fifth year, and he-he told everyone he had s-s-sex with me at Allie's birthday p-party on Saturday night." I stopped and huddled against a garden fence now that I was far enough away from the somewhat expensive prep school my absentee father paid for me to attend every year. It was only a twenty-minute walk from my parents' home on St. Bernard's

Crescent, and I was more than tempted to cut school and hide in the house for the rest of the day.

"That little shit," Braden said, his anger actually radiating through the phone and into my hand.

"They're all calling me a whore and a slut, and whispering and laughing at me. Now June isn't speaking to me."

"Why the hell is June not speaking to you?"

"She fancies Brian. I didn't even . . . Braden . . . I spoke, like, four words to him on Saturday night. He asked for a snog and I said, 'In another reality, maybe.' "

"Was there anyone around when you said that to him?"

"His friends were there, yeah." I sniffled.

"So you turned the little perv down and he started a rumor." Braden cursed again under his breath. "Okay, where are you right now?"

"I'm going to go home. I can't take another three hours of this."

"Sweetheart, you can't go home. Braebank Prep doesn't like its students to cut class. Wait at the gates. I'll get this sorted out." I could tell by his tone that Brian Fairmont was about to learn you did not mess with Braden Carmichael's little sister.

I put the phone away and wiped at my face, glad for once that Mum wouldn't let me wear mascara or any kind of makeup until I turned fifteen. Even then, she said I was allowed to wear mascara and concealer, but no foundation—and definitely no lipstick—until I was sixteen.

My friends thought she was weird.

I felt a little better knowing Braden was coming to my rescue. My big brother was really just my half brother. We shared the same father: Douglas Carmichael. Dad was a big deal in Edinburgh. He owned a real estate company and restaurants and a lot of property that he rented out to people. He was loaded, and although he gave time to Braden, he seemed to think spending money on me was a good enough form of apology for neglecting me the entire fourteen years I'd spent on the planet. His neglect hurt. A lot. But I had Braden, who'd helped raise me, with Mum, and my stepdad, Clark. Mum married Clark five years ago, and since the moment he'd come into Mum's life, he'd made it clear he wanted to be my dad. And he was; more than Douglas Carmichael ever would be.

I sometimes wondered how it was possible Braden and I were related to our father. We were both too nice to be his kids. Take Braden, for instance. After purposefully avoiding working for our father, a few years ago he suddenly decided he wanted to take a role in the Carmichael "empire," which meant he worked his bloody arse off to make our father happy.

Not only did my older brother work a lot, he was wrapped up in this girl he was dating, Analise. She was an Australian student and they'd just started dating. Braden seemed to really like her. Still, he always found time for me. Say, to rescue me from hideous situations like the one I was in at school.

"Ellie," a familiar voice, and not the one I was expecting, caught my ear and I turned my head as a car door slammed. My eyes widened as Adam Gerard Sutherland rounded the front of his six-year-old Fiat—a car Braden said was a stupid drain on Adam's finances, considering Adam was a student at Edinburgh University and parking in the city was a nightmare.

I'd had a wee bit of a crush on Adam since I was ten, so I was more than a little mortified that Braden had sent him to rescue me from this situation. Not that I should have been surprised. The two of them had traded that job back and forth since I was tiny.

"Adam . . ." I blanched and started wiping my face to make sure I'd wiped away all the tears.

The way his dark eyes studied me and his jaw clenched, I knew it didn't matter. My eyes felt puffy and red and obviously were. "Braden's sorry. He's in a meeting he can't get out of," he said as he approached. He wore a pristine, wrinkle-free T-shirt and faded jeans. Adam was too clean and neat to show up like a typical grungy student. Even his old banger of a car was tidy inside. "He called me. I have a free afternoon. Come here, sweetheart." Without asking, he pulled me into him and I immediately nestled my cheek against his chest and held on tight, trying not to cry.

"So where is this little shit?"

I pulled back from him, suddenly wary now that he was here and obviously furious. "What are you going to do?"

"He's fifteen?"

"Sixteen."

"Sixteen." He curled his lip in anger. "I can't hit him, but I can scare the absolute fuck out of him."

Braden and Adam cursed a lot, and had no problem doing so in front of me. Mum would be furious if she ever found out how much they cursed. Luckily for them, it had been drilled into me since the age of zero that you didn't curse in front of Elodie Nichols, and I'd never repeated the words Braden and Adam used around me. To be fair, they limited their expressions to the basics—I'd heard way worse at school. Today in fact, and they'd been directed at me.

I felt my eyes start to water again.

Adam saw and his eyes narrowed. "Els, where is this boy?"

I sighed heavily. "Around the back of the building, behind the lunchroom."

"Right." Adam strode in through the gates and I hurried after him, ignoring the curious gazes of my fellow students, and the excited chatter as they guessed that Adam was here on my behalf and that something was about to go down.

My cheeks burned with embarrassment, while my heart pounded in anticipation for a little retribution for the worst morning in the history of my entire school career.

When we rounded the corner of the building, Adam stopped and stared into a crowd of seniors. The fourth and fifth years gradually turned their heads toward us, their eyes widening at the sight of me with Adam.

"Which one?" Adam asked flatly.

"Brian is the one with his blazer tied around his waist."

"The tall, blond kid with the bottle of juice in his hand? The one that looks like a prick?"

"That would be the one."

"Little . . ." Adam growled under his breath and marched toward Brian, who dropped his drink and clenched his hands into fists. Brian's friend nudged him and he turned around to face Adam. Brian instantly paled at the sight of him.

Adam approached and towered over Brian. He titled his head, so his face was close to Brian's, and whatever he said made the seniors around him grow wide-eyed.

"Well?" Adam suddenly asked loudly.

Brian mumbled something.

"Louder, you lying little shit."

"I didn't have sex with her!" Brian cried. "I didn't touch her . . ." He turned and caught sight of me watching and his eyes seemed to plead with me to call Adam off. "I'm sorry!" he said. "I lied, all right!"

A murmur from the crowds drew my eyes past Brian to the lunchroom doors, and my stomach dropped when I saw Mr. Mitchell standing there watching Adam. Adam must have seen him too because his head came up. He didn't, however, back away from Brian.

"Who are you?" Mr. Mitchell asked in a belligerent tone as he walked toward Adam. "You're not allowed on school grounds."

"I was just having a word with Mr. Fairmont here. We're all good." Adam shrugged as if he wasn't a twenty-one-year-old who'd just gotten through threatening a sixteen-year-old.

"Brian, are you okay?" Mr. Mitchell asked.

"Uh, fine, Mr. Mitchell. He took a step back from Adam toward the safe proximity of the geography teacher.

"Adam!" I called out, wanting him gone before he got into trouble.

I drew Mr. Mitchell's gaze and his face clouded over. "Miss Carmichael, you know quite well you aren't allowed visitors during school hours."

"Sorry, Mr. Mitchell."

"I'm just leaving." Adam shot Brian one last warning look and then turned and casually strode toward me, taking his time. Adam didn't like to be told what to do. When he reached me, he put an arm around my shoulder and had me walk him back to the school gate. No one said a word as we passed. They were all looking at me as if I was extremely cool. I mean, I must be, if I had Adam Sutherland's arm around me and he'd shown up at school to scare the truth out of Brian.

I grinned and Adam caught it, his soft laughter making me all warm and fuzzy.

"Feel better?" he asked as we came to a stop.

"Yes. Thank you."

"What were you doing at a party on a Saturday night?"

I frowned at his proprietary tone. "I'm fourteen, Adam. It was a friend's birthday. Anyway, I didn't know seniors were going to be there."

He nodded. "Just be careful."

"Yeah." I lowered my gaze, feeling bad that he'd been dragged into my teen drama.

"Come here." Adam pulled me to him again and pressed a soft kiss to my forehead before he hugged me close. Now that I wasn't bemoaning the stress of my morning and crying on his chest, I was suddenly fully aware of being crushed against him. He smelled amazing, and his body was hard with lean muscle; it felt good against mine.

A weird, tingling feeling erupted in my lower belly and my skin suddenly grew incredibly flushed. I jerked back and tried to cover my awkwardness with a tremulous smile and a goofy wave.

Adam gave me a quizzical smile and then said, "Anytime you need me, you call, okay?"

I nodded.

"Okay, sweetheart. I'll see you later."

"Bye."

He grinned at me again. This caused another wave of tingling to spread over me. As I watched him get into his car and drive away, it occurred to me that my crush on Adam had just intensified. My brain was no longer the only thing attracted to Adam. My hormone-charged teenage body was now too.

# CHAPTER 2

Adam's brow was puckered as he shifted his focus from the diary and gave me a smile. "I don't know how I feel about sexually awakening a fourteen-year-old. It's all a bit Lolita-like."

I laughed at his discomfort. "It's not as if you felt the same way about me back then. Anyway, now that I'm yours, would you really have preferred if some other guy gave me my sexual awakening?"

He glanced back down at the pages. "Good point," he muttered.

"Here." I handed him another diary, open to more than halfway through, and took the one with my fourteen-year-old thoughts out of his hands. "This is from the year after that."

*Saturday, September 23rd*
*I am this close to screaming at Adam to stop treating me like a sister. I'm not his sister! I wish he'd just get that already . . .*

I took a deep breath and pulled the mascara wand away from my eyelashes. Staring at myself in my dressing-table mirror, I exhaled slowly and mentally coached myself to calm down. As much as I tried, I could not stop the wild flutter of butterflies in my belly. I gave up and leaned toward the mirror to liberally apply the mascara, since it was the only makeup Mum would let me wear. I had long, light eyelashes, so no one could tell how long they were until I started wearing black mascara. They were *long* and now that they were black, they made my pale blue eyes seem even bluer.

I'd hoped that the mascara also made me look a little older. Even though I was tall, I was still skinny with small boobs, and had a smattering of freckles across the bridge of my nose that made me feel about five years old instead of fifteen.

I had a date. My first date. It was with Sam Smith. He was a sixth year, which meant that he was two years older than me, and he was cute and cool and I really, really liked him.

I liked him as much as I could like any boy who wasn't Adam.

Not that Adam was a boy anymore.

A knock sounded at my bedroom door as I ran a brush through my long hair for the hundredth time. "Come in!" I called, somewhat agitated since I thought it was probably my mum, who seemed to be at once both more excited than me about the date, and also concerned.

To my surprise, when the door opened, the head that popped in wasn't Mum's but Adam's.

My heart did this little flippy thing in my chest that it did every time I saw him, and I smiled brightly at him. "What are you doing here?"

He stepped inside and closed the door, his brows drawing together in consternation as I stood up to greet him. His eyes traveled the length of me and I saw a muscle tick in his jaw.

I was wearing a white sleeveless shift dress. It had a modest neckline and I was wearing a cardigan to cover my arms, and black tights to cover my bare legs, but I was guessing the short hemline pissed him off. The reminder that he thought of me as a little sister that he needed to protect pissed *me* off. I crossed my arms over my chest, and the movement brought his eyes back up to my face.

"Clark told Braden you had a date tonight. We both wanted to drop by for the momentous occasion. Who is he?"

I rolled my eyes at his overbearing tone. "Just a boy."

"And how old is this boy?" Adam asked softly as he took a few steps toward me.

"Where's Braden?"

"Downstairs. Don't dodge the question. How old?"

"Sam is seventeen."

"What?" He inhaled sharply. "And Elodie agreed to this?"

He didn't mention Clark, since Clark was far more laid-back about these things than Mum. "She's excited for me actually."

"She's chirping like a nervous chicken downstairs."

"That's because Sam will be here any minute." I avoided his eyes, not liking that stubborn tilt to his chin.

"Where is he taking you?"

"To the cinema, then dinner."

"You'll be home before eleven?"

I grabbed my purse off my bed and let out an exaggerated sigh. "Yes . . ."

"And you won't let him touch you."

It wasn't a question.

I froze at his command and narrowed my eyes on him as he took the last remaining steps toward me until he was standing right in front of me, so close I had to tilt my head back to meet his gaze. "It's a date, Adam," I whispered. "Touching is supposed to be involved."

"Not when you're a fifteen-year-old girl. Not when you're you." I flinched back, taking that as an insult, and Adam immediately grimaced. "Els, I didn't mean it like that. I just mean . . . you're not just *some* girl."

"Look, Braden gave me this speech three hours ago on the phone."

"Ellie." Adam gave me a look that clearly meant "shut up." "You're

334 · SAMANTHA YOUNG

special. You deserve a boy who understands that, and a boy who understands that won't try any funny business, okay?"

"Funny business?" I raised my eyebrows at him. "I'm pretty sure Sam won't try any funny business."

"Els, you're a romantic, and you're young. Boys his age . . . they're not romantic. They have one thing on their mind and one thing only. And the little swine isn't getting it from you."

Annoyed at his suggestion that I was some naive little girl, I brushed past him. "Don't you have a comatose date waiting somewhere for you?"

"You cheeky little bugger," he grumbled behind me as I walked out of my room and started heading down the stairs. "I preferred you when you were wee and cute and didn't talk back."

I rolled my eyes and jumped at the sound of the doorbell.

"I'll get that," Adam announced determinedly, but I flung out my arms and blocked his passage.

Unfortunately, I didn't have enough limbs to stop Clark, who darted out of the living room with a glower I'd never seen before.

Uh-oh.

So perhaps Clark wasn't as cool about the whole "first date" thing after all.

"Dammit . . ." I said under my breath as I hurried down the last few steps.

Braden came out of the living room with a bottle of beer in his hand. Eyes wide at his sudden appearance and the darkening of his expression when he saw my dress, I raced by him and collided against Clark's back as he finished greeting my date at the door.

"She's right here," Clark said as I stumbled around him, giving him a questioning look. He was all glaring and intimidating. It was weird.

"Sam . . ." I said, feeling the butterflies in my belly explode at the sight of him. Sam was as tall as Braden, although lanky and slim, and he had messy light brown hair that seemed to have a life of its own. He was famous at school for that hair. All the girls wanted to be the girl who got to run her fingers through that hair. I was hoping that after tonight, that girl would be me.

Sam finished eyeing Clark warily and then threw a dimpled smile my way. "Hey, Ellie. You look great."

"She does not." Braden suddenly appeared behind us. I closed my eyes in actual pain after watching Adam squeeze in beside him. They were both trying to fry Sam's arse with the power of their eyeballs. "She looks fifteen. You remember that."

*Oh, God. Kill me. Kill me now.*

"If you touch her, I'll make sure you lose all sense of feeling. Permanently," Adam warned darkly.

"What he said," Braden added.

When I dared to open my eyes, my heart in my throat, it was to find Sam's ashen face staring at Braden and Adam as though they were Viking marauders who'd come to cut off his head.

"What is all this?" Mum's voice sent a rush of relief through me. "Get away from the door." Adam and Braden were gently nudged aside, and my mum, Elodie Nichols, was left standing alone. Tall and willowy, my mum was still gorgeous, and right now she was an angel.

"Thank you," I whispered gratefully.

She read the expression on my face and threw a dirty look over her shoulder at the retreating men. It appeased me somewhat to know that when I left on my date with Sam, the three of them would get a verbal tongue-lashing that would make their threats to Sam seem like child's play.

When she turned back around, she held a hand out to my date. "Elodie Nichols. It's lovely to meet you, Sam."

"You, too, Mrs. Nichols," Sam replied quietly, clearly not recovered.

"Well, I'll let you two get on." Her eyes now glistened a bit as she tucked my hair behind my ear and leaned in to press a kiss to my cheek. "Have a great time, darling. Be back before eleven."

"Thanks, Mum."

"You've got your phone?"

I nodded and quickly stepped out onto the front stoop, gently pressing Sam toward the street. He didn't say a word as we walked away, heading for the bus stop.

"Just ignore them," I finally advised. "They're just messing with you."

He gave me a weak smile and then checked his watch. "Film's starting soon. We better hurry."

I slammed the door shut behind me, trying to mentally decimate the angry tears that were determined to spring to my eyes.

"Is that you, darling?" Mum called from the living room.

Miserable and needing a mum-hug, I moped down the hall and entered the room.

It was ten thirty and Braden and Adam were still here.

Mum and Clark were in their armchairs, Braden and Adam on the couch, and all four of them were no longer watching the television; they were staring at me.

I took one look at them and knew why they were here, and angry tears began to fill my eyes.

"How did your date go?" Mum asked, her question faltering as she took in my expression.

"Awful," I snapped out and returned my glare to Braden and Adam. "He's not asking me out again because of these two idiots."

"Good," Braden responded flatly. "You're too young to be dating."

Mum sighed. "She's not too young."

"She's too young," Adam said. "And look at what she's wearing."

"There's nothing wrong with what she's wearing."

"She's fifteen," Braden argued. "She's got plenty of time to go on dates. She should concentrate on school."

"Oh, you sound like an old fart, Braden."

"I can't believe your attitude, Elodie." Adam sighed. "I thought you'd be more careful about this stuff."

"Careful?" Mum repeated. "It was a date."

As they squabbled on, my anger had time to seethe, and my humiliation had time to fester. The nicest, cutest, coolest guy at our school had asked me out on a date, and my brother and his best friend had ruined it for me. "I liked him," I suddenly informed them, quietly but with an edge that halted their conversation. They all looked at me and a tear slipped down my cheek as I said, "I really liked him. You both ruined it and you don't even care," I said to Braden and Adam.

My chest aching with the pressure of my hurt, I raced for the stairs and ignored Braden, who was calling my name.

"I'll get her," Adam told him, which made me move even faster up the stairs. I slammed my bedroom door shut behind me and threw myself on my bed, hiding my face in my pillow as I cried into it.

I heard the knock over the sound of my muffled sniffling and lifted my head just enough to growl, "Go away."

I tucked my head back into the pillow and waited.

Since I knew how tenacious Adam was, it didn't surprise me when he disobeyed my command. I heard my door open and the creaks of the floor as he approached. The bed dipped on my right side and I heard Adam sigh.

"I'm sorry," he apologized, his voice deep with sincerity. "Sweetheart, I'm sorry."

I didn't say anything, my throat burning even deeper when it occurred to me this was the first time Adam had ever hurt me.

"Els . . ."

I turned my head so I could see him. I ignored the worried look on his young, gorgeous face and told him stonily, "Just go away, Adam."

He ran a hand through his hair and moved closer to me.

"Look . . . I feel like shit, Els. I didn't mean to ruin your night. Neither did Braden."

"Oh, I'm sure when you threatened sensory deprivation you had no intention of ruining my chances with Sam."

"Jesus," Adam said. "You are too smart for your age. It's like arguing with a grown woman."

"How would you know what it's like to argue with a grown woman? You never stick around long enough to do something to piss them off."

His mouth twitched at my response and he shook his head. "Jesus . . ." he repeated.

After a minute of silence, Adam looked down at me again. His expression was no longer amused. In fact, he looked deadly serious. "If this kid dumped you because he's not man enough to deal with some familial concern, then he's not the kind of boy you want to be with."

The word "familial" pushed that little button inside of me. I gave him an icy glare and said, "You're not my brother, Adam. Stop acting like it."

I felt a slash of pain across my chest at the hurt expression in his eyes, guilt instantly making me want to cry even more. "I know that, Ellie."

Our eyes met, and my skin instantly began to flush. "Do you?" I murmured breathily.

Something flickered in his gaze and he stood up, suddenly looking uncomfortable. "I'll leave you alone for a bit. I just wanted you to know I would never intentionally hurt you."

When I didn't say anything, Adam exhaled wearily and left.

As he was closing my door, I heard Braden's voice right outside it. "She okay?"

"She's pissed off. Let's just leave her alone for a while."

"I want to speak to her."

"Braden—"

"I'll get you downstairs," Braden said, cutting him off. He opened my door, let himself in, and closed it behind him when he stepped inside. Braden's concerned eyes locked on me as he strode toward my bed.

"Els, sweetheart," his voice was slightly gruff as he sat down. "I'm so sorry."

I immediately burst out crying and launched myself against his chest, and let his strong arms hold me tight and his soothing murmurs calm me.

# CHAPTER 3

"You forgave Braden?" Adam frowned, holding the diary out to me.

I shrugged, took it back, and put it down next to the one from the year I was fourteen. "You hurt me more. Not intentionally of course, but I wanted you to see me as a woman, not a girl."

Adam gave me a look that suggested I was daft. "You *were* a girl. You were fifteen."

"So you never saw me that way then? Not that night . . . in my short dress," I teased.

"Not then," he admitted softly, as if worried he'd hurt my feelings. "You were still Braden's wee sister then."

I wasn't hurt. I had retrospect on my side and frankly I'd find it somewhat concerning if Adam had fancied my lanky, flat-chested fifteen-year-old self. Still, I was curious. "When did it change for you?"

"I'm not telling . . ."

"Why not?"

"Because it's a guy thing that you won't get and it'll probably piss you off."

Now I was definitely intrigued. "I won't get annoyed. Just tell me. Please," I begged sweetly.

"Fine." He eyed me warily. "It was the morning after your eighteenth birthday."

My eyes widened as I tried to remember. *Seriously?*

"The morning on which you oh so casually told me you'd just lost your virginity."

That was the moment he realized he had feelings for me? Jeez . . . Joss was right. Guys could be such cavemen. As that morning came back to me in vivid detail, I let out a little laugh. I realized that Adam had been jealous. *Wow.* That was not how it had appeared to me at the time. "I knew you were mad at me, but I thought it was another overprotective 'big brother' moment."

"Nope." Adam shook his head grimly, leaning back on the palms of his hands. "It was an 'I'm looking at my best friend's wee sister who's just told me she had sex for the first time and I can see her kiss-bruised mouth and her bed hair and I'm getting fucking turned on' moment." His eyes locked on my mouth as he remembered. "My body reacted to what you'd said before my brain did. I suddenly wondered what your lips felt like, how you'd taste, what it would feel like to have your long legs wrapped around my back as I thrust into you . . ." I squirmed, feeling my skin heat up as I pictured Adam thinking those very appealing thoughts so long ago when I hadn't had a clue. "Then I got pissed off—at myself for feeling that way about you. And then at the guy for having tasted you. And then at you . . . for letting him taste you."

Our eyes locked and I felt my breathing grow shallow.

I knew if I didn't say something else we'd end up making love in his spare room before we could finish our trip down memory lane, and frankly, I was enjoying the trip. I cleared my throat, grabbed another diary, and started to flip through it.

I found the entry I was looking for and handed it to Adam. "You should know," I murmured softly, "that it all comes back to you."

*Sunday, April 30th*

*I lost my virginity last night. To Liam. It wasn't how I'd wanted it to be. It hadn't been with who I wanted it to be. It hadn't been with someone I loved like I'd always promised myself it would be. And it hurt, at first. And then it didn't. In fact, it wasn't bad at all. But something else hurt last night and unlike sex, it didn't stop hurting. It hasn't stopped hurting . . .*

The ballroom at the Marriott Hotel was absolutely packed. As I looked around, I realized that there were people there that I didn't even know.

Still, it was some turnout, and Allie had pronounced my eighteenth birthday party a total success—and it wasn't even over yet. Braden had booked the room at the hotel as well as a DJ and caterer. My family had invited more relatives, as well as some friends who invited their friends, and I invited my friends, who invited their friends, who seemed to have invited their friends. It was crowded, the buffet was almost completely picked over, and the dance floor was full.

I watched catering staff come out of the back room with fresh trays of food and I scowled as one of the pretty girls was stopped by Adam as she passed. Whatever he said made her laugh and tilt her head flirtatiously. I watched them, ignoring the burn of jealousy in my throat.

"Have I told you tonight how sexy you look?"

I was pulled backward into a warm body. I lifted my chin and turned my head slightly to look up into Liam Fenton's handsome face. He was smiling down at me, his eyes glittering a little. He was buzzed, but not drunk like Adam, who'd started "getting happy" an hour before the party even started. As per usual, he'd turned up alone. From the cracks I'd heard Braden making for years, Adam was a total player and I'd never met a single girl he'd dated—probably because he didn't actually "date."

Liam, on the other hand, appeared to be trying to keep his wits about him. I think I knew why. He was nineteen, a student at Napier University, and we'd met when I'd toured the campus the previous year. We'd kept in touch, emailing back and forth, until Liam—seemingly out of the blue—asked me out on a date. We'd messed around a little bit (and he'd given me my first orgasm), but I'd been reluctant to have sex with him. I'd filled my head with so many romance novels and movies, I was convinced that my first time would be with someone I was in love with. Although I liked Liam and I was attracted to him, I wasn't in love with him yet. However, I think he thought because I'd turned eighteen that tonight was going to be the night. I'd assumed that was why he was trying to stay as sober as possible.

I felt a little nervous about how I was going to dissuade him of that notion.

Smiling up at him, I gave him a shy nod. "You may have mentioned it once or twice."

Liam grinned, his hands sliding down to rest on my hips. "It's worth mentioning more than once. Every guy in here thinks I'm a lucky bugger, and they'd be right."

His lips touched mine and it was nice. Really nice. But since my first kiss with Pete Robertson at a Friday bowling night with friends a few months after my disastrous date with Sam, I'd never felt what all the romance books talked about. I'd kissed five guys since then, and not one of those kisses made my skin hot and my body vibrate and my stomach flutter. I was beginning to think romance novels might be leading me astray . . . .

"Don't mean to interrupt, but I'd like a dance with the birthday girl."

I immediately broke away from Liam at the sound of Adam's voice and turned around to find him standing in front of me, giving Liam a "you have five seconds to get your hands off her before I break your face" look. It had been two and a half years since I started dating, and Adam and Braden still rejoiced in scaring the crap out of my boyfriends. Thankfully, Liam didn't scare easily.

He squeezed my hips. "I'll go get you another drink. I'll be over with Allie and the guys."

I nodded at him, watching him saunter away through the crowd.

A warm hand on my wrist drew my gaze back. Adam was grinning at me as he pulled me into him. As soon as my body brushed his, I felt that familiar tingling again—the feeling centered between my legs as Adam's arm caught me around the waist; his other hand caught my hand and laid it against his chest. I rested my other hand on his shoulder and swayed with him to the music. Being this close kind of hampered my breathing and I tried very hard not to let him see that. His fingertips brushed the bottom of my back and since I was wearing a backless dress it was a skin-to-skin touch. My body reacted to it in a way I recognized, and I ducked my head, unable to look at him.

I'd been in Liam's dorm room two weeks ago and we'd been making out and touching. The touching got a little more involved than I was used to, but I was curious, so when he slid his hand under my skirt and pushed his fingers under my underwear to touch me, I'd almost fallen off the bed. I felt it between my legs and I felt it in my breasts. He'd settled a thumb on my clit and played me as my body slowly started to fracture until it eventually broke into this amazingly pleasurable explosion.

Adam didn't even need to put a hand between my legs. All he needed to do was touch me, and those familiar tingles would vibrate throughout me.

"Enjoying your birthday?"

I turned to gaze at him, my face close to his. I was five foot nine, so usually only a couple inches shorter than Adam, but that night I was wearing four-inch heels, so I was actually just little bit taller than him. He gave me a quick once-over and grinned, shaking his head as I replied, "Yeah, it's been good."

"Have you opened any presents yet?"

"No. I was going to later, but I think everyone is a bit too drunk to care. Including you."

"I'm not drunk. I've got a buzz going, that's all." His eyes narrowed. *"You're* not drunk, are you?"

I rolled my eyes. "Adam, I'm legally allowed to drink now."

"Is that a yes or a no?"

"I've had a couple of shots."

We were quiet a moment and I actually allowed myself to relax against him. That was until he flexed his fingers against my back and an involuntary shiver rippled over me. Adam tensed, as if he'd felt my reaction, and I quickly looked at his face for confirmation. His dark eyes glittered in a way I'd never seen before.

My mouth felt dry.

He studied me a moment and I found myself pressed even tighter against him. My fingers curled into his shoulder. His next words almost blew me off my feet. "You're the most beautiful thing I've ever seen, Els," he said, his voice thick with emotion.

My eyes opened wide with shock at his announcement, my heart began to thud inside my chest. *Adam thought I was beautiful? No, not just beautiful: The most beautiful thing he'd ever seen.*

Wow.

My chest began to rise and fall a little more rapidly. "Adam . . ." I replied softly, unsure whether he meant that in a strictly platonic sense or if he was finally opening his eyes up to see I wasn't a little girl anymore.

"I worry about you all the time," he confessed. "You're so sweet and kind—too kind sometimes. I worry someone will hurt you and I won't be there to stop it."

It was true that I had a tendency to look for the best in everyone, and I had a bit of a hero complex (I wonder where I'd picked that up from), but I wasn't incompetent. And I was a woman now. I could take care of myself, and I told him so.

Adam frowned. "That's not what I mean. You get a lot of male attention, Ellie, and sometimes it's difficult to weed out the wankers. For instance, the guy you came with tonight. He flirts a lot . . . with everything that has tits and a pair of long legs."

Glowering at the insult to Liam, I tried to press back. "Liam is a nice guy."

"Liam is after one thing. I should know—"

"Right, you've been hogging her enough." Braden was suddenly standing beside us, grinning. "I want a dance with the birthday girl."

Adam tightened his hold on me, and then as if it had just occurred to him what he was doing, he threw Braden a smile and let me go. We shared one last look and then he was gone and I was in Braden's arms.

*What the hell had just happened? Had Adam Sutherland . . . Was he? . . . Was that more than friendly advice?* The way he touched me, the things he'd said, the way he'd looked at me. It had felt different. My heart was racing, a bubble of giddy hope starting to float up inside of me. Poor Liam was forgotten as I let myself be distracted by my own longing and fantasies.

"I'm proud of you," Braden told me gruffly, bringing me out of my head, where I was already picking wedding dresses and deciding who would be my maid of honor.

I smiled at my big brother, curious about his declaration. "What for?"

"For many reasons. For getting into Edinburgh Uni. For taking care of Elodie and Clark, and for being a good sister to Hannah and Dec. And for being a great wee sister to me. It's been a tough year, Els, and I'm grateful for all your help."

I hugged him close for a second, my heart hurting all over again for him. After falling for and marrying his Australian wife, Analise, Braden had filed for divorce when he walked in on her and his old school friend having sex in one of Braden's empty developments in New Town. The bitch had put him through the ringer for the last nine months of his marriage and then she'd cheated on him with his friend. It was the ultimate betrayal. Worse, our dad had been the one who'd cottoned onto it and he'd set Braden up to find the traitorous couple. That was Dad's way. Rather than pulling his son aside and letting him down easy, he let Braden walk right into it. Braden didn't seem to mind. It surprised me that Braden was actually grateful to our father. I, on the other hand, thought he was an insensitive arsehole.

As if he'd read my mind, Braden sighed. "Dad's sorry he couldn't be here, Ellie. I'm sorry too."

"Don't apologize for him." I turned my face away, and looked up at the ceiling to try to stop the tears. You would think after eighteen years of complete neglect I'd be over the hurt. Unfortunately, the hurt never went away. I just couldn't understand what Douglas found so unlovable about me, or why he deliberately shunned me time and time again. It was my eighteenth birthday for God's sake, and he couldn't get up off his rich arse for half an hour to pop in and wish me a happy birthday.

I heard Braden curse under his breath. He had a fairly good relationship with our dad, and I didn't want to be the cause of any problems between them, so I gave him a squeeze and smiled at him. "I'm fine. I'm more than fine. I'm surrounded by friends and family who care about me, Braden. And that's all *I* care about."

We shared a hug and the music changed to something more up-tempo again, and Mum and Clark descended on us.

I had a dance with the two of them, giggling as they pulled out moves that hadn't been seen in at least two decades.

As the night continued on, I mingled with friends and family, but my eyes kept wandering through the crowd in an attempt to find Adam again. My stomach was a riot of butterflies, and I couldn't get his voice out of my head.

*"You're the most beautiful thing I've ever seen, Els,"*

I was with Allie and Liam, watching them laughing away, but I had no idea what the conversation was about. My head was stuck in rewind.

When the room began to feel too hot, I ordered a bottle of water

348 · SAMANTHA YOUNG

from the bar and slipped out of the back of the room and found an exit. It was the fire door that led out to the back of the hotel where all the rubbish bins were stored. I stepped outside quietly, sucking in a huge gulp of air and enjoying the peace. It could give me a moment to wrap my head around what had happened—and if what I thought had happened had actually happened.

I felt a giddy smile start to stretch my lips when a grunt followed by a moan made me freeze. The large bins were situated between me and an alcove of the building, and the sounds were coming from there. My heart picked up a little bit as I guessed what the sounds meant and what I'd stumbled upon. When another grunt sounded, I covered my mouth with my hand to keep in the giggle that was threatening to erupt.

"Yes," a female voice groaned. "Adam, oh, my God."

The giggle instantly died as blood rushed in my ears. I felt a burn in the bottom of my throat as some dark, masochistic thing inside of me made me tiptoe around the bins.

All the hope I'd been feeling exploded and disintegrated all around me.

As I watched Adam screw one of the female catering staff against a brick wall, I realized what an idiot I was. What a childish, naive idiot.

And then the anger settled in. And the frustration. And the thought that somehow I wasn't good enough—not good enough for Adam; not good enough for my father.

My eyes narrowed. There was one person who thought I was good enough, so what was I holding out for? For flowers and sonnets and a man on bended knee? That wasn't going to happen. This was reality. Sex was sex. There was nothing magical about it.

Clearly.

I wasn't naturally an angry person, but the burn of jealousy coursed through my veins and I turned silently back to the hotel. As soon as I was inside, the image of Adam moving against the catering girl kept flashing before my eyes. I felt sick. Chugging back more water, I made a decision. I needed to wipe that image out of my brain.

I found Clark talking to his brother in the ballroom. Thankfully, Mum wasn't anywhere to be seen, because what I was going to ask she'd probably not be happy about.

"Els, what do you want to do with all these presents?" he asked, pointing to a table that had been set up at the back.

"Can I ask you and Mum a big favor?"

He smirked, guessing what that favor was. "You want us to take the presents back home for you?"

"My friends and I want to go on to a club, if that's okay."

Clark studied me for a moment and then sighed. "Go on before your mum sees you. And be careful."

I nodded and gave him a quick kiss on the cheek. Leaving him to it, I pushed my way through the crowd on the dance floor and found Liam and Allie dancing together. I pulled Liam off to the side and threw Allie an apologetic smile.

"What's up?" he asked, giving my hip a squeeze.

I looked into his eyes, feeling my stomach flip as I said meaningfully, "Let's go."

His body tensed and his eyebrows drew together. "Just me and you?"

"Yeah."

"Where do you want to go?"

I pressed close to him, making my intentions very clear. "Where do you want to take me?"

Liam's breathing stuttered. He seemed to swallow hard. "I could get us a room."

"Okay."

We left quickly, slipping away from the party before Mum or Braden could see. My nerves kicked in as we made our way through the hotel to the reception desk, and I fought hard not to throw up as Liam booked us a room.

Every inch of me was trembling as the lift took us up to the first floor, and as soon as we were inside the room and Liam started kissing me, he could feel me shaking against him.

"Are you sure about this?" he whispered.

The image I was unsuccessfully trying to bleach from my brain flashed before me again. I wanted tingles and excited butterflies, I wanted flushed skin and passion. I wanted trust and safety, I wanted affection and laughter. I wanted loyalty and friendship. I wanted love.

Unfortunately, life had played a cruel joke on me and I'd fallen in love with the one person in the whole world I couldn't have.

Just because I couldn't have him, however, didn't mean I shouldn't live. None of my friends were virgins anymore. What was it really but a nuisance? It used to be a gift. Or at least I liked to romanticize that it was a gift. I supposed what it really used to be was a mark of ownership, but this was the twenty-first century. No one owned me. My virginity was something I could give to whomever I pleased.

"Yeah," I whispered back, reaching up to unknot the halter tie on my dress. "Yeah, I'm sure."

Thankfully, Liam took his time. He made me come before he put on a condom and pushed inside of me, so I was as ready as I could be. Still, it hurt. After a while, the pain diminished and it felt okay. Liam enjoyed himself. He tried to hold off until I came again, but I didn't. I couldn't stop thinking over and over again as he moved inside me that I'd well and truly buggered everything up for myself.

I'd promised myself since I was fourteen years old that the first time I made love, I'd be in love.

Instead I was lying in some hotel room while a guy I merely liked, casually took the gift I offered, and I casually let him. I felt a heaviness settle on my stomach when Liam was finished.

I stayed awake listening to him snore beside me and cursed at myself for letting anger and jealousy get the better of me.

·   ·   ·

I lay there for a couple of hours and eventually decided I couldn't stand to stay in the hotel room. Just past four in the morning, I snuck out of there and had the concierge call me a taxi. The woman at the reception desk took one look at my mad hair and revealing dress and knew exactly what I'd been up to. The smirk she gave me made me feel cheap, and I realized quickly that the only reason I felt cheap was because *I* thought I'd acted cheap.

I tried not to cry as the taxi took me home, and I definitely tried not to cry as I quietly let myself inside. I was just creeping toward the staircase when a head popped out of the kitchen and startled me completely. I took a deep breath and clutched a hand to my chest in fright.

Adam stood in the kitchen doorway and crooked a finger at me. It wasn't a surprise that he was in Mum's kitchen. He and Braden often crashed at my parents' after a family night out because Clark made a huge breakfast in the morning as part of a hangover cure. What *was* a surprise was to see Adam still awake and waiting up for me. As I approached him, I saw that image again of him and catering girl and the anger returned.

I followed him into the kitchen and he closed the door behind me. I studied his face and saw his eyes were bloodshot. The smell of coffee filled the air and I noticed a grilled-cheese sandwich sitting on a plate. He was obviously getting a jump start on the hangover cure. I was so busy analyzing these things that I didn't notice *his* anger.

"Where the hell have you been?" he hissed at me.

I glowered at him, momentarily blaming him for the loss of my virginity. "Out."

"Where?"

"Just out."

He narrowed his eyes. "With who?"

"Liam."

Adam's face instantly darkened and he took a step toward me, his eyes moving over my messy hair and then focusing on my mouth. They stuck there until I touched my lips, wondering what was so fascinating about them. "What were you doing?" he finally asked, his voice gruff.

And that's the point in the interrogation that I lost my temper. "I'm eighteen, Adam. I can have sex with my boyfriend."

His body jerked, like I'd shot him. "Sex?" he choked out.

I shrugged as if my heart wasn't hammering against my rib cage. "It was a present to myself."

His eyes roamed over me again. "Are you telling me . . . you lost your virginity last night?"

I nodded slowly, hearing an edge in his voice that I was a little bit afraid of.

Adam's eyes narrowed after taking in my confirmation. I stood there squirming as he drank me in from head to foot. I flushed at his appraisal, not quite sure what was happening. And then he made it clearer by turning on his heel and pushing the kitchen door open. Without thinking of anyone who was still sleeping, Adam stormed out of the house and let the front door slam shut behind him.

I exhaled deeply as I began to figure out what was going on.

Adam thought of himself as my big brother. No big brother wanted to hear that their little sister had "gotten herself some." More than that, I wondered if he was as disappointed in me as I was in myself. He knew me. He knew I believed in stars and sunsets and "happily ever afters." I'd compromised my own beliefs by having casual sex with a guy I barely knew.

Then tears came, and I ran to my room with blurry vision. I grabbed some fresh underwear and pajamas and took them into the bathroom with me. For half an hour, I remained in the shower, crying the entire time.

*At least I learned a huge lesson*, I told myself.

I'd learned there were some things in life you could never take back.

# CHAPTER 4

$A$dam put down the diary and looked up at me with something like regret in his eyes. I didn't want him to feel badly, I just wanted him to know that even if my first time hadn't been with him, I'd always wanted it to be.

"Baby, I'm sorry," he whispered.

I frowned and shook my head. "Don't. That's not what . . . I just wanted you to know that it's always been you."

"But your first time should have been special, Els. It should have been romantic."

I shrugged. "In the grand scheme of things, it's not the worst thing that happened. Dad—"

"Douglas died a few days after your birthday," Adam murmured, finishing my sentence.

"Yeah," I whispered back, remembering how mixed up I'd been over my father's death. I'd grieved, but I couldn't figure out if I was mourning the *idea* of a dad or if I was mourning Douglas Carmichael. To make matters worse, he left me a boatload of money and it took me a while to come to terms with how that made me feel. And I struggled, for a time, with the thought that he died while I was mad at him.

Adam slid across the hardwood floor, put his arm around me, and hugged me close. "Ellie, I thought you stopped feeling guilty about that. He was a shit dad. You had a right to be angry at him no matter what happened."

I nodded and snuggled closer to Adam, inhaling the scent of him and his aftershave. He smelled good. He always smelled good.

We sat in silence for a while until Adam said, "I barely remembered what I did with that catering girl, just so you know. And I had no idea I said that to you at your party—calling you beautiful and telling you I worried all the time about you. Fucking mixed signals. I was pretty drunk that night."

"I know. But you were right about Liam. He ended up cheating on me with Allie."

Adam tensed. "That's why you stopped talking to Allie? Why didn't you tell me?"

"Because you would have beaten the shit out of him."

"True."

I smiled. "Always fighting my battles for me."

"*With you*, baby. With you, not for you."

Liking that a lot, I turned my head and kissed him, loving the familiar press of his mouth against mine. I pulled back and cocked my head in thought. "I thought the year you started to see me differently was the one *after* my eighteenth."

"The one after?" Adam's eyebrows drew together in thought for a minute and then instantly relaxed as he remembered. "The *almost* kiss."

While he'd been reading about the night of my eighteenth birthday, I'd found the entry I'd expected him to allude to as to the moment he started to see me as more than Braden's little sister. I held another diary out to him and he took it with a smile as the memories flooded back to him.

*Friday, July 5th*

*Tonight I had my first truly grown-up, sophisticated and, well, HOT, date. I'm just not sure who I had it with . . .*

As Christian helped me out of the taxi, I had to wonder if this was going to be "it." Christian was handsome, charming, a total gentleman—and he had class. He had yet to make me laugh, but I was sure that would come as we became more comfortable with each other.

He smiled at me again as I pushed the hem of my black dress back down. It had shimmied up while I was sitting in the car. "You look stunning."

I flushed. When he looked at me like that I *felt* stunning. I was wearing a plain black sleeveless dress that should have been somewhat modest, considering its high neckline and mid-thigh hemline. However, the dress hugged every inch of my body leaving little to the imagination. It was a sophisticated dress with a splash of "hot."

I'd bought it earlier that day, specifically for Christian.

We'd met in the student union. Christian was pre-law, two years older than me, and from an obviously wealthy and well-to-do family. They had an estate in the highlands. That had nothing to do with what attracted me to him, of course. I was attracted to him and how he'd acted upon our first meeting—with a fresh and open honesty that really appealed to me. It made me feel like I could be just as open with him. It made me feel like I could be myself.

Christian had told me that although his family had the estate, they also had a home in Corstorphine, a busy suburb west of the city. His parents had bought it when his sister had moved to Edinburgh and started popping out children. She was pregnant with her third and the entire family was living in Edinburgh to be closer to her. I thought that spoke volumes about them, and was more than a little excited to meet them.

To my delight, Christian had booked us a table at La Cour for our first date. I didn't even get a chance to tell him it was Braden's restaurant. He inherited it from our father.

As we entered, I opened my mouth to tell him, but Christian started speaking about the menu and what he thought I should order. I was going to tell him I knew what I wanted to order, since I'd eaten at La Cour more times than I could count, when I heard Adam call my name.

Christian and I drew to a halt as the maître d' led us to our table, and I turned my head to see Adam sitting in the center of the restaurant across a small table from a gorgeous brunette. I ignored the flare of jealousy and reminded myself I was on a date with a fabulous man, and that the gorgeous brunette was just one of many sexual partners for Adam. He was a manwhore.

But he was *my* manwhore, and I couldn't help but walk over to him, with Christian at my side and a huge smile on my face, because as always, I was delighted to see him.

Adam grinned up at me, his smile dimming slightly as his gaze flickered to my date. He gave Christian a once-over and then turned those beautiful eyes of his back on me. He perused me with a slight smile and when his eyes hit mine they were full of tenderness. "You look absolutely stunning, Els."

I didn't just flush at his compliment, I absolutely burned. "Thank you," I murmured and then gave his date a polite smile. "Hullo."

She glared at me.

*Oh, well.*

"Adam, this is Christian."

Adam gave Christian a taut nod and then flicked his hand to his date. "This is Megan."

"It's Meagan," she corrected him waspishly, pronouncing it like "mee-gan" instead of "meh-gan."

I saw Adam stifle a long-suffering sigh. Uh-oh. His night obviously wasn't going well.

"We better get to our table." Christian gently pulled on my elbow.

I gave Adam another smile. "Enjoy your evening."

"You, too, sweetheart." I moved to follow Christian but had only taken a step to walk away when I felt a tug on the hem of my dress. I glanced down and watched Adam pull off the price tag. I blushed as he winked at me.

I closed my eyes briefly. I'd left the price tag on. I was always doing stuff like that. God, I hoped Christian hadn't seen it. Opening my eyes I deliberately ignored Adam's date and mouthed a heartfelt "thank you." He grinned at me and I smothered a laugh at myself before catching up with Christian at our table across the room.

"Who was that?" Christian asked casually as we were seated.

"My brother's best friend," I replied equally casually. "We grew up together."

Christian nodded and then ordered us white wine. I preferred red.

We chatted as we waited for the waiter to return, and Christian told me all about a charity he was organizing. He stopped talking when the waiter came back and he began to order my food for me. Choosing to think this was charming rather than overbearing, I informed him this was my brother's restaurant and that I knew what I wanted. He was impressed that Braden owned La Cour and for five minutes I told him about Braden's other businesses.

After that we were back onto Christian.

By the time the second course arrived, my hopes for this being "it" were diminishing rapidly. Not once did my date appear to take any real interest in me, and the more I realized how self-absorbed he was, the more aware I became of Adam sitting across the room from me. Adam, whose eyes glittered with interest every time I opened my mouth.

I had just picked up my fork to take a bite of my steak when a phone rang. Debussy. *Really?* Even his ringtone was pretentious.

Yes, by this point the shine had definitely worn off.

Christian pulled the phone out of his pocket and answered it, his eyes going wide. "I'll be right there." He put the phone back in his pocket and stood up.

I stared up at him in absolute shock. *Was he about to leave me? In the middle of a date?*

"My sister just went into labor," he explained, and I watched as he threw a wad of cash on the table. "Stay. Finish your meal." He leaned down and pecked my cheek. "I'll call you." And then he was gone.

I couldn't exactly hate him because he'd abandoned me on our first date to go be by his pregnant sister's bedside. I slumped against my chair. Christian was obviously a good person. He just also happened to be incredibly self-involved. It occurred to me he'd been the same way at the student union last week, but I'd twisted it in my overly romantic little head and called it open and honest.

I looked at my food glumly.

A hand came down on the back of my chair and a shadow appeared above me. I glanced up to find Adam leaning over me with a scowl on his face.

"Where the fuck did he go?" he growled.

*God, I loved him.*

"His sister just went into labor."

Adam relaxed, but didn't move.

"I'm okay," I promised him. I wasn't okay. I wanted to cry. And he knew it.

He straightened up and called out to one of the waiters by name. "Can you move us to a larger table?"

"Of course, Mr. Sutherland."

"Adam, no," I protested. "I'm not crashing your date."

He grabbed my hand and pulled me up. "You got all dressed up, sweetheart. At the very least, you're going to get to finish your meal."

Holding my hand, Adam led me to the new table and gave a jerk of his head to his date to tell her to come over to us. He sat next me as Meagan took the seat across from him, her green eyes flashing with annoyance.

"Ellie's joining us," Adam informed her, his tone brooking no argument

"Sorry," I mumbled apologetically to her.

"Don't apologize," Adam replied firmly. "You've got nothing to apologize for."

The waiters quickly brought over our plates, and as we dug in Adam asked me about Christian.

"Well." I sighed after swallowing a piece of tender meat. "Up until forty minutes ago, I thought he was perfect. Forty minutes ago, I didn't know he'd try to order my food for me or talk incessantly about himself."

Adam grinned. "Was it about his hair? I bet he could get a good forty minutes out of how long it took him to get that quiff just right. What styling mousse he uses and why, the amount he uses in order to get just the right amount of height and curvature . . ."

I was giggling as he continued to tease me. It was true. Christian had a rather large quiff. Forty minutes ago, I'd thought it spoke of his individuality and style. Now, I was guessing Adam was right. The man probably spent more time on his hair than I did—and that was never a good thing.

Throughout the meal, Adam made me laugh until I forgot all about my ruined evening. It wasn't until the waiter came to take our plates away and offer us the dessert menu that I remembered Meagan was even there. She reminded us by scraping her chair back and glaring at Adam. "I just remembered I have an early morning tomorrow. Thanks for dinner, Adam. I'll see you around."

Before Adam could say anything, she'd turned on her designer heels and stormed out of the restaurant.

I instantly felt terrible. Adam and I hadn't included her in our conversation at all. It was such a shitty thing to do.

Adam must have recognized my guilty expression because he shook his head at me. "Don't feel bad, sweetheart. She started complaining the moment I picked her up. If I was rude, it was only in retaliation."

I gave him a sympathetic smile. "Looks like we saved each other from crappy dates."

He grinned. "Looks like." His eyes dropped to the menu. "Now, what are you having for dessert?"

"We don't need to," I told him quietly. "We could just pay up and I'll go home and let you get on with your night."

His eyes rose to meet mine and he gave me an "are you daft?" look. "Els, shut up and pick a dessert."

I tried to hide my smile and lowered my eyes to the menu.

We stepped out into the warm summer night, and Adam took my arm and tucked it in his. "Where to next?"

I blinked in surprise. We'd finished our meal and I'd just assumed I'd be going home. "Um, where do you fancy?"

"The Voodoo Rooms is only a five-minute walk away. I know the bartenders, so we'll get a table."

I nodded, trying to stop my heart from taking off. Adam was taking me out for a drink. He'd never taken me out for a drink just the two of us before. Sometimes he, Braden, and I would meet up for a drink or two, but it was never just Adam and I.

As I walked down the street with him, arm in arm, I allowed myself the fantasy that we were a couple. *That's what other people would see when they passed us.* My chest burned with utter longing.

Unrequited love wasn't nearly as romantic as the books made it seem.

"Who don't you know in this city?" I teased in an attempt to appear normal around him.

Adam grinned. "There are a few people I've yet to meet."

I chuckled at that. Adam and Braden called Edinburgh "their city," and they almost meant that literally. They had acquaintances everywhere, and whenever I was out with them, we spent half our time greeting people they knew. Some might say that Adam would never have had that kind of relationship with the city if he hadn't grown up as Braden's best friend.

Unlike us, Adam didn't come from a well-off family. His mum and dad were ordinary folks who never really gave the impression that they'd wanted to be parents. Adam had been an accident. Although they'd never been neglectful or cruel, his parents had been distant, and he'd spent most of his childhood hanging out at Braden's and bemoaning the summers when Braden was off in Europe with his mother.

As soon as Adam turned eighteen and moved into student housing that put him into a lot of debt, his parents had gotten on a plane and moved to Australia. He heard from them about once a month. Incidentally, Braden had paid off Adam's student debt as a graduation present, something he proudly wouldn't accept—until Braden had gotten him drunk and recorded his slurred acceptance on his iPhone. I'd heard the recording. He'd said, "Love you, mate. You're beautiful" so many times to Braden, I'd almost peed my pants with laughter.

Adam's difference in background, however, didn't mean anything. Even if he hadn't had Braden there opening all these doors, I believed that with his charm and charisma, he'd still be a guy that a lot of people knew, liked, wanted to be, or wanted to sleep with.

When we got to The Voodoo Rooms, dinner service was just finishing up and the place was crowded.

"Adam!" a bartender called out as soon as we walked in. "I'll get you a table."

We followed him as he claimed a table and wiped it down with a wet dishrag. The guy eyed me as I slid into the booth and gave Adam a smile of approval that made me blush to my roots.

"What can I get you?"

"I'll have a Macallan and ginger ale. Sweetheart, what do you want?"

"I'll have a mojito, please."

Adam settled into the booth with me, his arm sliding along the back of the seat behind my head. For some reason I felt incredibly awkward and I struggled to find something to say.

"Sorry your date was rubbish."

Adam shrugged. "I'll just celebrate with you."

"Celebrate?"

He gave me a small grin, looking boyishly pleased about something. That look hit me between my legs. I needed help. "I'm now a registered architect."

My lips parted and I impulsively threw my arms around him. "Congratulations!"

He chuckled against my ear and I shivered, loving the press of those strong, creative hands against my back. "Thanks, sweetheart."

"Does Braden know?" I asked, pulling away.

"Yeah. He congratulated me by giving me a permanent contract."

I laughed. That was so Braden.

Adam had gotten his practical experience to complete his qualification by working alongside Braden's architect. This last year, however, he'd been doing the work himself and having now achieved all the qualifications and experience he required, he'd applied to the Architects Registration Board.

"I'm really happy for you."

"I know. That's why I'd much rather be here with you than with Megan."

"*Meagan,*" I corrected.

"Whatever," Adam muttered.

Our drinks came and I asked him about the project he and Braden were working on. Adam then asked me about my classes. I had chosen to study History of Art and Fine Art with grand hopes of becoming a gallery curator one day, but while at the university, I was falling in love with the idea of a career in academia.

Clark, who was a professor of classical history at the same school, was extremely proud and excited that I wanted to follow in his footsteps. When I told Braden I was thinking of doing a PhD in Art History he'd given me Adam's "are you daft?" look, but then kissed me on the forehead and told me to do whatever made me happy.

The night seemed to speed away from us, and before I knew it I was on my third mojito and snuggled much deeper into Adam's side, laughing as he regaled me with stories of his and Braden's antics at work and elsewhere.

To the outside world, the two of them were extremely mature young men in their mid-twenties.

I knew better.

I wiped tears of laughter from my eyes and reached for another sip of my drink. "You two are idiots."

"Shh, that's a secret."

I grinned back at him and the smile he gave me suddenly froze.

"What?" I breathed, my heart stopping.

He swallowed and shook his head. "I just sometimes wonder where the time goes."

"I know. We're all grown up now," I teased.

His eyes searched my face, his expression enigmatic. "Yes, we are," he murmured, and something about the way he said it made the air between us suddenly become electric. I could swear that I stopped breathing altogether. His eyes were dark and focused, and I felt the heat of his look slide sensually down the center of my body. Nervously, I licked my lips and his gaze dropped to my mouth.

My gaze dropped to his.

I don't know which one of us moved. Whichever one of us it was, our faces were so close that our lips were almost brushing. I could feel his breath on mine and he obviously could feel mine on his. The smell of Macallan and Adam played chaos with my hormones. My chest began to rise and fall with excited nerves and hopeful anticipation.

I moved my head that little bit closer and our lips brushed. Infinitesimally. Still, that slightest touch sent a bolt of lust straight through me.

Adam made a sound in the back of his throat and I swore he was about to close the distance between us . . .

But I'd never know for sure. His phone rang in his jacket pocket, throwing a bucket of ice-cold water over the moment. I jerked back and watched his face cloud over as he realized what had almost happened. Jaw clenched, he reached into his pocket and pulled out his phone. It had already stopped ringing. He lifted his eyes to me and told me darkly, "Braden."

I guessed he meant that Braden had been the one who'd called him, but I also imagined it had a double meaning. I knew I was right when he quickly paid for our drinks and put me in a taxi, abruptly ending our night together.

I was Ellie, Braden's little sister. To Adam, I would always be Braden's little sister, and that meant I was off limits.

When I lay in bed that night, I cursed Adam Sutherland to hell and back. If he hadn't already ruined things for me before, he definitely had after tonight.

*A brush against my lips.*

One tiny touch and I felt that spark I'd been waiting for since I was fifteen. Whichever guy came next had a lot to live up to.

# CHAPTER 5

"I was freaking out," Adam admitted. He threw me a wicked smile. "I've never been so hard in my life from an almost kiss. I wanted to fuck you every time I saw you after that."

I shoved him playfully and blushed. Adam was often deliberately crude because he knew it made me equal parts embarrassed and turned on. I'd always hated when people used the f-word to describe sex, thinking it emotionless and casual. But after Adam and I became a couple, I'd discovered that when you were in love with someone and you knew they loved you back, there was a wide spectrum of sex. At one end, there was the tender, sweet, slow sex that I would call "making love," and at the other end of it there was the rough, wild, can't-get-enough-of-you sex that was definitely the f-word. Adam was more than proficient in both kinds.

I thought about what he'd said and frowned. "You did a good job of hiding it."

He sighed. "I don't know about that." He looked back at the diary and frowned. "What ever happened to that Christian guy, by the way?"

"I let him down gently when he called to reschedule our date."

"I would say 'poor guy,' but I had to endure five years of wanting you and not having you."

"That was entirely your own fault." I picked up the diary I wanted and opened it up to the specific entry I was looking for: It was a night I would not likely ever forget. "Nine months before Joss showed up . . . It's a perfect example of it being entirely your own fault."

> *Sunday, October 23rd*
> *That's it. I give up. I'm humiliated. Confused and humiliated. And hurt. God . . . Hurt doesn't even begin to describe it . . .*

I was supposed to be spending my Saturday evening with Jenna and a few girls from uni sipping cocktails and talking about anything else but our degrees. Instead, I was in a taxi heading to Adam's duplex apartment in Fountain Bridge. I could have walked there, but I felt a sense of urgency to get there and make sure he was okay.

And I really needed to thank him for having my back, as he always had.

The last week had not been a particularly good one. That was putting it mildly.

I'd been betrayed. *Again.* But this time it was worse than ever. For the last five months I'd been dating Rich Stirling. For the last five months I'd thought I was dating a nice guy who worked in Glasgow for a recruitment agency. Then I discovered that he was, in actuality, a corporate spy for a competitor of Braden's in Edinburgh. This property developer was so desperate to outbid Braden on a piece of coveted land down by Commercial Quay that they'd enlisted Rich to get close to me, to get close to Braden, to unearth Braden's bid, and have his company offer more money for the land.

I wasn't in love with Rich, but I'd let the sleazeball into my life and into my bed—and I'd given him a piece of me. I don't think I'd ever felt so completely stupid in my entire life. All of my friends and family kept telling me I was too nice, that I didn't have good intuition when it came to people, that I let arseholes into my life. I was finally starting to believe they were right.

I knew I could close down, refuse to let people close; be smarter, more selective . . . but that wasn't me, and that was somehow letting Rich win. So I refused to change and there was a tiny sense of victory in that.

It still stung like a mother, though, that I couldn't do anything, couldn't take some kind of retribution. So when Braden turned up at my flat—this gorgeous property on Dublin Street that he'd renovated and then gifted to me—to tell me he and Adam had bumped into Rich out on the town the night before, I'd held my breath, knowing exactly what was coming.

Sure enough, Braden had had to haul Adam off of Rich and take him home to calm him down and ice his knuckles. Apparently, Adam had let the whole world know how he felt about anyone betraying me and Braden. He didn't like it. And when he didn't like it, he'd acquaint your face with his dislike.

As soon as Braden left, I buzzed around my flat in a tizzy, wondering what I should do. Should I call Adam and thank him? Should I go to his place and thank him in person? Should I berate him for using violence to make a point? No, that last one definitely wouldn't wash with him. He wasn't a violent person. In fact, although he could be intimidating and had warned off a number of bullies when I was younger, this was the first time I knew of that he'd actually gotten physical with someone on my behalf. I'd half expected him to go after Rich. Adam had exploded and stormed out of my mum and Clark's house when Braden relayed the news to them all. Braden had told them after he told me, but my throat was still tight with tears as I had to hear it a second time.

After Braden's departure, I finally made the decision to cancel my night out with the girls. I took a long shower, blow-dried my hair straight, and threw on a long skirt with a low waistband, my Uggs, and a woolly turtleneck with a cropped hem. I wanted to be casual, but whenever I knew I'd be seeing Adam, I liked to remind him in some way that I was a woman with a woman's figure—not that it seemed to make any real impact. Despite evidence that he checked me out sometimes, Adam had been carefully platonic in our interactions since our lips brushed at The Voodoo Rooms three years earlier. I had dated three guys in an effort to get over him. It never worked. The guys just paled in comparison to him and the relationships fizzled out.

With a mind to the cold weather, I'd thrown on a short wool jacket over my top, along with a scarf, and I'd flagged down a taxi outside my flat. It was only as the cab was pulling up to Adam's place that I thought maybe I should have called to warn him I was coming over. It was a Saturday night.

*He might have company.*

My stomach lurched unpleasantly at the thought. The last time I'd visited Adam unannounced had been four months prior, and I'd walked in on him with a girl called Vicky. Not only was I horrified once more to play witness to one of his sexual interludes, but I'd been shocked to realize that he and my brother shared women. Not at the same time, thank God. I knew Braden had gone out with Vicky too. In an effort to soothe my severely bruised romantic notions, Adam had explained *ex post facto* that Braden and Vicky had been really casual and when Vicky had said she fancied Adam, Braden had mentioned it to Adam and—*la, la, la, la, la, la, la!* I didn't hear the rest of the explanation because I had indeed stuck my fingers childishly in my ears and tuned him out completely.

Sex was not casual to me. Not only was I annoyed that my brother, who had once been a secret romantic, had turned into a serial monogamist who showed no signs of settling down, I was even more annoyed at Adam for encouraging it. I couldn't even describe how angry I was at Vicky.

After asking the cabdriver to wait a second, I pulled out my phone and called up to Adam.

"Hey, sweetheart," he greeted me, his rich voice filled with concern. He was clearly still worried about how I was coping with Rich's treachery.

"Hullo," I replied quietly, letting the warmth of hearing his voice fill my chest. "I'm downstairs. Are you okay for me to come up?"

"Of course. I'll buzz you in."

I hung up, paid the taxi driver, and hopped out, my heart racing as I hurried to the entrance. Adam let me in.

My palms began to sweat as the lift took me up to his floor. It was strange but my reaction to being alone with Adam had only gotten worse over the last few years. Every time was like a first date, and yet I knew him better than I knew practically anyone.

When the doors opened, my eyes met Adam's. He was standing in his doorway across the hall, his arms crossed over his chest as he leaned his shoulder against the doorjamb. He wore a plain white T-shirt and a pair of old jeans; his feet were bare, his hair mussed, and he needed a shave.

He was so bloody hot it was a wonder I didn't start hyperventilating on the spot.

I crossed the hallway to him and held out the bottle of wine I'd brought. He took it with a quizzical smile and I sighed. "It was either a bottle of wine or a slap on the wrist." I eyed his bruised knuckles pointedly.

Adam's lips twitched. "Wine will do."

I followed him into the duplex, my eyes drinking in the well-designed flat. A large staircase greeted you at the front entrance, leading up to two spacious bedrooms, a bathroom, and an office. Beyond the staircase on the ground floor was just wide-open space—a massive sitting area with floor-to-ceiling glass windows covering one wall, and at the very end of the room you'd find a stylish kitchen with an island, breakfast bar, and a dining table and chairs.

It was a luxurious property—and one he could more than afford. Not only did Braden pay him extremely well, Adam had invested in his own rental properties these last two years and it supplemented his income nicely.

I took another look around the large space, smirking. Unlike my flat, Adam's was completely clutter-free. Everything in it was carefully chosen and had a proper place. In fact, if I didn't know firsthand that he was the straightest straight guy ever (well, with the exception of Braden), Adam's duplex might have convinced me otherwise.

"I think I'll crack this open . . . I feel a lecture coming on." His voice was teasing as he wandered to the kitchen area.

As I shrugged out of my jacket and took off my scarf, I tilted my head and watched his delicious arse walk away from me. The man had the most perfect bottom in the history of all bottoms. I wandered toward the kitchen and watched as he pulled two glasses out of a cupboard and began to pour wine into them. Adam turned just as I reached him and I saw his eyes flicker over the bare skin between the hem of my top and the waistband of my skirt before quickly shifting away. I gave myself a secret smug smile. *Good wardrobe choice.*

"Here," he said somewhat gruffly, handing me a glass.

Our eyes met as we each took a sip of wine. I lowered my glass and told him solemnly, "I came here to thank you."

Adam shook his head. "Ellie, you don't need to thank me." His face darkened. "It was my pleasure, believe me."

"Braden said he had a hard time pulling you off of Rich."

"He fucked with you, Els. I mean, he really fucked with you."

"Literally," I murmured, and Adam stiffened.

"Don't—" he warned me. "I'm this close to finishing the scumbag off."

I felt a small thrill go through me at the sincerity in his voice. I loved that Adam cared this much. He might not be willing to see me as anything but Braden's wee sister, but it was a nice consolation to know he had *some* feelings for me. "I should be reprimanding you." I reached for his free hand, using his wounds as an excuse to touch him, and brought it closer to me for inspection. His knuckles weren't just bruised, they were swollen, and the middle one had a small gash in it that was scabbing up.

I inhaled deeply. "How many times did you hit him?"

Adam moved closer, staring at his hand in mine. "I hit the wall next to his head as a warning shot. He didn't heed the warning, said some shit he really shouldn't have, and I think I got in four really good hits before Braden pulled me off."

I lifted my gaze to his face, no longer feeling the thrill. "Did you leave him conscious?"

"Barely." Adam's eyes narrowed. "Do you care?"

"I don't want you to get in trouble."

His expression softened and he gently tugged his hand free from mine. "Don't worry, sweetheart. According to sources I was nowhere near New Town or Rich last night. We've got a dozen witnesses who will all claim that I was at Bar Kohl last night at the time of the said attack."

I nodded in acknowledgment, but worried my top lip with my teeth.

"Els, how are you really?" Adam asked softly, tentatively.

Instead of answering right away, I turned around and slowly made my way toward his comfy sofa, listening to him follow behind me. I settled myself comfortably and Adam sat down close to me, relaxing his arm along the back of the couch. Finally, I met his gaze and shrugged. "I'm an idiot."

Adam's eyebrows puckered and his mouth got tight. "You're not an idiot."

"I'm an idiot," I insisted. "I'm stupid and naive and . . . humiliated."

He slid closer to me, his fingers touching my wrist gently in comfort. "You have nothing to be humiliated about. He's a prick who played you. He's the idiot. He's the stupid fuck who's going to look back and realize that for five months he was the luckiest bastard on this planet to be with you. He'll regret this, baby."

*Baby.*

For a moment I forgot how to breathe. Adam had never called me "baby" before. There was something intimate about the endearment. I liked it. I liked it a helluva lot.

I smiled at him. "You always know the exact right thing to say."

"Because I only ever tell the truth. You're one of a kind, Els. Any guy would be lucky to have you."

I gazed into his eyes and felt his words like a caress across my body. As I stared, his gaze flickered over me again, surreptitiously checking me out before he took another sip of wine. It occurred to me that perhaps all Adam needed was a push.

Yes, I was Braden's wee sister, but I was also Ellie, the girl he apparently thought the world of and admitted he thought was beautiful. Blame it on the wine or the fact that he'd stood up for me once again, I wanted him and had decided impulsively that I was tired of hiding the fact.

I let Adam make me feel better as we finished off our glasses of wine. An hour had passed before I knew it, and I had kicked off my Uggs and curled up on his sofa, sitting close to him. His arm still rested along the back of the sofa and every time I laughed, I touched his biceps or squeezed his knee. I was an affectionate person, tactile and open, but it was more than that, and Adam knew it. I could see it in his eyes as we chatted and I hoped my plan was working.

You would think hurt and betrayal would make me shy away from opening myself up, but I just didn't have it in me to close myself off. It wasn't who I was, and I definitely didn't want to be that way with Adam.

As the hour drifted into two, I became more determined than ever that things were going to change between me and Adam. I was sick of dating guys I couldn't seem to fall in love with, and even sicker of being duped by them.

Adam was in the middle of telling me about the Skype chat he'd had with his mum a week prior, and his parents' plans to return to the UK for a few weeks in April, when I stretched my arms up, pretending to need to crack my back. The movement pulled the hemline of my top up, baring my flat stomach, and it also pushed my breasts out. When I brought my head back down and relaxed, Adam had stopped talking and I could see a muscle ticking in his jaw.

"Ellie, what the fuck are you doing?" he asked hoarsely, his voice quiet.

Although my face burned with the possibility of rejection I shrugged nonchalantly. "Stretching."

His gaze drifted down my body and I watched his own tense. "You know what I'm talking about. The touching, the flirting, the stretching . . ."

With my heart pounding, I shifted closer to him on the couch until my knees touched his outer thigh. I licked my lips, nervous but completely turned on just by the mere thought of him touching me back. "I think you know," I whispered.

Our eyes met and locked. The air thickened between us. Adam swallowed hard. "Ellie," he whispered.

Holding his gaze, I reached a trembling hand out and placed it on his thigh and slowly I moved it up, caressing him. I had almost reached the heat of his crotch, where, to my utter satisfaction and delight, I watched his erection strain against his zipper, when his strong hand grabbed mine tightly.

I'd barely let out a surprised gasp when he tugged on my wrist, yanking me against him. I collapsed on him and he used my momentary disorientation to his advantage. He gripped the nape of my neck and slammed my mouth hungrily down on his.

I melted against him.

My fingers sank into his hair, and I rearranged my legs so I was straddling his lap. My body sank into his. My mouth sank into his.

It was everything and more than I'd always imagined.

My skin burned and my nerve endings sparked and I was tingling all over. Adam tasted of wine and heat and . . . home. I purred into Adam's mouth, and his arms tightened around my waist, somehow drawing me even closer. The kiss shifted from passionate to dirty in a nanosecond. It was suddenly biting and wet, our tongues tangling and licking and learning every inch of each other's mouth.

It wasn't close enough.

Everything was lost in a fog of sexual chemistry so electric I would never again doubt romance novels. I felt his rough hands on my ankles, coasting along the skin of my calves, and up the back of my thighs as he drew my skirt free of our tangle and bunched it around my waist. Those hands of his caressed my bottom, giving me a squeeze that sent a streak of heat down my spine and made me gasp.

Adam groaned and put pressure on my hips. He pushed me down on his lap so his hard-on rubbed me directly between my legs—nothing between us but denim and the thin cotton of my underwear. I sought the delicious friction, riding him until our mouths parted in brief increments to catch our breaths.

I needed him closer; needed him inside of me.

I sank down on him and dug my fingers into his shoulders as I rubbed harder.

Adam growled and broke away from me to tug my top off. I raised my arms, our movements hurried and frantic as he divested me of my top and then my bra. He cupped my breasts in his hands and I arched my back into his touch.

"So perfect," he murmured hoarsely. "So fucking perfect." He took my nipple in his hot mouth and I cried out at the rush of pleasure that coursed through me, pushing me closer and closer to orgasm.

My being so turned on seemed to fire Adam up. I cried out and found myself flat on my back on the length of the couch and watched through hazy, lust-blurred vision as Adam whipped off his shirt and pulled down my skirt and panties. The muscles of his ripped abs flexed deliciously and I felt a rush of wetness between my legs.

He was so goddamned beautiful it wasn't fair.

Our lips met again as he braced himself over me, my hard nipples brushing his naked chest, my legs spread to fit him between them. He still wore his jeans, and the coarseness of the denim was sensual torture against my naked skin.

As our kisses grew even more desperate, I sought what I wanted from him. My fingers undid the button and zipper on his jeans. I tugged at his boxers, my hand sliding inside to grasp him and pull him out. He was throbbing and hot and hard and I couldn't believe this was actually finally happening. Now I knew *everything* about him.

"Fuck," he groaned against my mouth, his hips thrusting as I pressed the mushroomed head of him against my clit. I let go of him to grasp his lower back, tilting my own hips up as he teased me. He kissed me again, hard, and I felt his erection slide down . . .

I spread my thighs wider and smoothed my hands down his muscular back to push his jeans farther down. I grasped his buttocks and pulled him to me. "Adam, please," I begged. "Adam . . ."

He froze. Instantly. His name on my lips bringing him out of the magical sexual fog.

Our eyes met as he pulled his head up, his body hovering over mine, his muscles trembling with tension. While I imagined my expression was one of confusion, Adam's was one of horror.

It was a look that made me want to crawl inside of myself.

It hurt like nothing I'd ever experienced before.

He scrambled off of me, pulled his boxers and jeans up, and tossed my skirt to cover up my nakedness. "Ellie, we can't." He shook his head and practically jumped off the couch, grabbing his T-shirt and yanking it back on.

I was feeling a mixture of things—confusion, hurt, sexual frustration—and so I was slow in sitting up.

"For fuck's sake, Ellie, get dressed," Adam snapped harshly.

It took everything within me not to flinch—not to cry.

As I pulled on my clothes with trembling hands, Adam exhaled. "Sweetheart, I'm sorry, I didn't mean to . . ." His voice was heavy with regret.

I didn't say anything. I just straightened my clothes and reached for my Uggs, trying to hold myself together. I couldn't fall apart in front of him. I just couldn't.

"Ellie?"

Finally I looked at him as I stood. He seemed almost as heartbroken as I felt. It was a small kind of consolation.

"Ellie, you're Braden's wee sister. I can't . . . We can't . . ." He gestured helplessly to the couch before running a hand through his hair.

And that's when I realized something absolutely tragic. While I thought what was happening was something born out of affection, attraction, and—yes—love, to Adam what had almost happened was something born out of lust. He didn't want to make love to me. He wanted to screw me.

Pain lodged itself in my throat and I knew I was five seconds from bursting into a big, fat, hopeless, teary wreck. I spun away from him and rounded the back of the couch, my long hair covering my face as I grabbed at my jacket and headed to the door.

"Ellie!" Adam called out in panic, but I was already yanking his front door open. "Ellie. Fuck!" I heard him curse as I slammed the door shut behind me and bolted down the stairwell, knowing the lift might not arrive in time for me to make my quick escape.

The tears were pouring down my cheeks as I raced down the stairs, trying to hold in the gusty sobs that were ready to blow.

"Ellie, please!" Adam was suddenly in the stairwell, his footsteps pounding hard behind me.

I ran faster, ignoring his shouts for me to come back and talk to him.

By the time he made it out of the building, I was already racing across the street toward a bus that was about to pull away. I got on it and the doors closed behind me. I sagged down onto a seat in relief and glanced absentmindedly at the route number.

I didn't care where it was going as long as it took me far, far away from the biggest mistake I'd ever made.

There had been a few times in my teen years I'd cried myself to sleep. A couple of those times had been over Adam. But when I was a teenager, like most teenagers, anything remotely negative seemed like the complete and total end of the world. Thankfully, that flair for the dramatic usually disappears as you enter adulthood. It did for me, anyway. So when I say I sobbed myself to sleep that night, it was without a sense of faux melodrama. The pain inside of me was real. It was genuine. It was raw.

For a good eight hours, I believed that not only had I been given absolute proof that Adam Sutherland didn't love me the way that I loved him, I also believed that I'd ruined us and destroyed one of my favorite things in the whole world: my friendship with him.

I barely slept and woke up early to make myself tea, alone in my big flat and puffy-faced, wearing mismatched socks.

A pounding on the front door made me jump and sent hot tea over the rim of my mug and onto my lap. I bit back a curse and placed the mug carefully on the coffee table. I walked out of the room and into the darkened hall.

"Ellie, open up!" Adam shouted through the thick wood. "Ellie!"

I wanted to talk to him. I wanted to somehow fix things and rewind the clock, but I knew that if I let him inside the flat he'd take one look at my face and realize that I, Ellie Nichols Carmichael, was completely and utterly in love with him and that the previous night had devastated me.

So I didn't open the door. I leaned against the wall in my hallway and slid down until I was sitting on the cold hardwood floor. I listened as Adam pounded on my door and called my name. I listened as the phone rang in my bedroom. I listened as Adam left a message on it. I listened as he cursed and walked away . . .

When I woke up I was curled up on the cold floor. I blinked, trying to get my bearings and as I did, everything came flooding back. I didn't have time to dwell on it, however, because I realized what had woken me up was my phone ringing. I got to my feet with a groan, my back and neck hurting from my awkward sleeping position, and I ran into my room to pick it up. According to the display on my phone, I'd been asleep for just over two hours.

My stomach flipped at the sight of the picture of Adam on my phone. I sucked in a deep breath and answered it.

"Ellie, thank fuck," he exhaled in relief and I could just imagine him tugging at his hair in anxiety. "I came by earlier."

"I was sleeping. I had more wine last night, so I was kind of dead to the world," I lied.

"Els, I don't even know where to start. I'm so sorry. God, I'm so sorry."

"Adam—"

"I can't lose you, Els. I can't believe I fucked up like this but you have to forgive me. I can't lose you."

When he said stuff like that it made it hard to hate him. Worse, it made it harder to get over him. But I knew from now on that I really needed to try—and not just say that I was going to try. I *had* to try. I couldn't live my life pining after him. So I made my decision to do just that. "Adam, it's okay," I promised him softly. "It was a mistake. We got carried away in the moment. And I'm sorry for running out on you. I was just embarrassed, that's all."

I heard his heartfelt sigh of relief and attempted to force the sting of tears out of my nose. "Els, you've got nothing to be embarrassed about, okay."

"Okay."

"So"—his voice grew even quieter—"we're good. We're still us?"

"We're still us," I managed, blinking back tears.

"I don't want there to be any awkwardness between us."

"There won't be. I won't let there be if you won't."

"Good, sweetheart. Good. We'll just forget this. It didn't mean anything."

I choked back the pain. "Right. It didn't mean anything."

# CHAPTER 6

"It's like a car crash . . ." Adam sighed, rubbing a hand over his face as he passed me back the diary. "It's painful reading this from your perspective, but I can't look away." He pointed to another diary. "I want to know more."

Not liking the strain etched into his features, I shook my head. "Adam, we're past all this. I didn't mean for this to be painful. I just thought . . . well, now that I have you, I can take a step back and look at the pieces of our history without it hurting. And you know me." I shrugged. "The angst of it all seems romantic." Then I frowned. "But you're obviously not taking it that way, so I'm going to put these away."

He clamped a large hand down on mine as I moved to pick up another journal. I glanced up at him and he shook his head with a small smile. "It's painful to read how my stupidity hurt you at the time, but I like being inside your head. I like knowing that while I was struggling with the fact that I had fallen in love with my best friend's little sister, she loved me back more than I could ever hope to deserve."

I grinned at him. "One: You deserve it. And two"—I gestured to the diaries, to the story of us—"it *is* totally romantic, right?"

Adam laughed at my single-minded determination to turn us into a romance novel. "Maybe. But don't tell anyone I said so. It'll ruin my reputation."

I sorted through the books, looking for the familiar purple leather cover of the last one. "Baby, you ruined that reputation when you told Braden Carmichael you were in love with me."

"Cocky bastard knew all along," Adam muttered unhappily. "Could have saved us a couple of months of worry."

I found the diary and paged through it. "You mean, a couple of months of you being a mercurial pain in my arse?"

"Such a nice way to put it. But let's not forget I wasn't the only pain in the arse."

"All I did was start dating again, and it took me ten months to do it after our little couch scene. You got off easy." I thrust the diary at him and he took it with a scowl.

"I was staking my claim."

"No, you were marking your territory without *actually* staking a claim."

He chuckled and focused on the last page without responding. We both knew I was bloody right.

> *Sunday, August 13th*
> *I haven't had time to write anything down for a few days, partly because of studies and partly because my seething anger has been taking up quite a lot of my time. It all started on Friday afternoon when a casual conversation with Nicholas ended in me wanting to strangle Adam . . .*

As Joss and I walked toward The Meadows, where we were meeting Braden, Adam, Jenna, and Ed for a picnic, I considered telling her what I'd discovered about Adam yesterday while I was having coffee with my fellow student and friend Nicholas. I hadn't gotten the chance to tell her yet because she'd been working at Club 39. I knew Joss would be pissed off on my behalf. I needed that fire—that motivation—to put Adam at a distance and see how he liked it.

It had taken Adam and me several months to get past the awkwardness of almost having sex, and even then, things weren't the same. The truth was that things hadn't been the same for a long time, probably since the lip brush incident when I was nineteen.

It was obvious that Adam had slept with other girls since he'd had me on his couch, and it hurt worse than I could ever explain. The whole incident made it difficult for me to move on. I hadn't been on a single date in ten months.

That was all about to change, however. After making a crack to Nicholas about my dry spell, he'd told me maybe I'd have better luck getting a date if my friend Adam would stop going around intimidating men who might want to date me. Surprised and a little confused by this comment, I'd asked him to elaborate only to discover that Nicholas had wanted to ask me out months ago. Knowing how close I was to Braden and Adam, but thinking that Adam was the safer choice, Nicholas had called Adam and asked him for advice on where to take me out. Adam's response had been, "Stay away from Ellie or I'll break your face."

*What the hell was that?*

*Seriously?*

I couldn't even begin to process how not cool that was. I never knew that Adam had been warning perfectly nice guys to stay away from me. *He was allowed to manwhore his way through Edinburgh, but I wasn't allowed to go on a single date?* I didn't think so.

I wanted to tell Joss all about that. Despite being incredibly secretive about her past, Joss had proven herself to be a straightforward friend. I needed her to tell me if it was okay or not to play a little dirty with Adam. Honestly, I was just so tired of being the nice girl that he could just walk all over, knowing I'd still love him in the end. His actions had proven that he could be possessive of me, which meant he thought of me as "his" in some small way. I wanted to show him that I *wasn't* his, that I would never be his unless he decided he wanted more than a one-night stand.

All this I wanted to confide in Joss that sunny Saturday as we strolled to The Meadows, but Joss was distracted by something, so I decided it wasn't a good time. I was curious whether Joss's distraction had something to do with Braden. She'd been acting strangely around him, strangely enough for even me to notice during the aftermath of one of my headaches. We'd been book shopping with Hannah when it happened. The headache hit me out of the blue like it had been doing for the last couple of months. It was horrible and usually accompanied by tingling and numbness in my arm. When it passed I was exhausted. In fact, lately my energy levels hadn't been great. I kept meaning to go to the doctor but every time I got this ominous churning in my gut, and I put it off, promising myself I'd make an appointment the next day.

Anyway, the headache hit and Joss was concerned—she didn't fool me with her "I don't care about people" rubbish—and taking me to get some food in me. We bumped into Braden and Vicky. While I was pissed off that Braden had slept with her again and brought her back into our lives (and Adam's orbit), I still noticed the tension between Joss and Braden. Admittedly, when they'd first met, I'd had hopes of playing matchmaker, but recent revelations had spoiled those intentions. However, Braden still asked an awful lot of questions about Joss and he stared at her (a lot). I was beginning to suspect that despite denials from both of them, something was going on. I didn't know how to feel about that now that I knew Joss wasn't keen on being in a relationship. It was difficult to pin down her true feelings about anything and I didn't want either Braden or her to get hurt.

Deciding to bite my tongue about a lot of things, I kept my conversation with Joss light and cheerful as we approached our friends in the park. Braden, Adam, Jenna, and Ed were there, sitting on a large chenille blanket with two picnic baskets beside them. My eyes immediately went to Adam and then quickly moved to Braden when I discovered Adam was watching me.

I laughed as Joss teased Braden upon our arrival, something not many people outside of our family dared to do. I think that secretly my big brother did too. Without thinking about it, I flopped down onto the blanket beside Adam. His strong arm came around me instantly and he squeezed me affectionately against his side. "Nice to see you, Els."

The whole point of the picnic was to catch up with Adam and Braden. Since they'd been working so hard on the new development, we'd barely seen them at all. I missed them both, but I missed Adam in particular. Inhaling the familiar smell of him and feeling his strength pressed against my right side, I almost forgot for a moment my earlier resolve. *Almost.*

"Yeah, you too." I gave him a halfhearted smile and pulled casually out of his embrace. I turned to Jenna and Ed to greet them properly, ignoring the sudden tension radiating from Adam. He knew me too well, and he immediately understood something was wrong.

*Good.*

I saw Joss reading a text message and overheard her telling Braden that she needed to take a rain check on the picnic. I gazed up at her in concern, suddenly wondering if there had been more to her distraction than I'd previously thought. "Is everything okay? Do you need me to come?"

Joss shook her head and waved her phone at me. "No, I'm okay. Rhian just really needs someone to talk to. It can't wait. Sorry." She seemed to be avoiding Braden's eyes and when I glanced at my brother, I found him studying Joss in a weird way. *Did he not believe her?* Rhian was Joss's best friend. She stayed in London and had been having personal problems lately, so it was completely plausible that she needed to talk.

"See you later." Joss walked away, her long ponytail swaying across her back.

Looking back at Braden I watched him watch her in a way that unnerved me. It wasn't just the fact that he had that determined, focused expression he got on his face when he was going after something—usually a development property, and rarely a woman—it was the glimmer of excitement in his eyes. I'd never seen him look at anybody that way. The romantic side of me was happy. The practical side of me worried her lip between her teeth, thinking Joss and Braden were either the perfect match or a disaster waiting to happen.

Later that afternoon, after having frozen Adam out to the point of seriously pissing him off, my suspicions over Braden's interest were confirmed when he pestered me all the way home about Joss. I knew by the time he'd dropped me off on Dublin Street that he was going after her, and I knew from having grown up with him that when Braden really wanted something he was absolutely relentless—especially when he was reaching for the impossible. I could only hope Joss didn't hurt him while he tried to reach for her.

I'd spent the picnic catching up with Jenna and laughing at Braden's and Ed's jokes. Maybe once in the entire three hours we hung out did I speak directly to Adam, and I avoided his gaze at all costs. That was difficult, considering he was constantly trying to catch it. Thankfully, there wasn't a quiet moment for him to ask me what the hell was wrong with me, so my form of torture worked out even better than I'd planned.

I was gratified to discover it *was* a form of torture because by the time Braden and I left the park, Adam's expression was dark. Normally, Braden would have noticed our behavior, but much like Joss, he was kind of distracted.

I was even more pleased to discover later, after having a discussion with Joss regarding Braden, that she agreed with me: Adam needed to be taught a lesson. If he didn't want to be in my life in a romantic sense, then he needed to butt out of my romantic life. I was determined to continue my torture that evening.

. . .

Braden, Adam, and I were going out for drinks with Darren, the manager of Braden's nightclub Fire, and Darren's wife, Donna. I wore a black top that was backless. It was held together by a silk ribbon across the middle of the back, while the front was demure with a high neckline and draped chiffon panel that fell a good three inches past my waist. I'd matched the top with black skinny jeans that were so tight they might as well have been painted on. My hair was pulled up into a messy bun to give maximum impact to the top, and I was wearing four-inch silver heels to match my silver teardrop earrings.

It was a little more femme fatale than I usually went for, but I know it did the trick. Adam's eyes flared when I turned around after greeting Donna, his gaze burning as he took in the full effect of my outfit.

That pissed me off.

What pissed me off even more was Braden's choice of going to Club 39 that night. Knowing what he was up to regarding Joss, I didn't feel comfortable letting him unleash his plan while she was busy working. However, Braden wouldn't listen to me and Donna wanted to check out the bar.

My annoyance level increased when Adam held me back as we walked along George Street.

"Are you going to tell me what's wrong or am I going to have to guess?" he asked, his words clipped.

I shrugged, not looking at him. "I don't know what you're talking about."

"Ellie, don't. Being a bitch doesn't suit you."

I flinched and kept walking. "You know what else doesn't suit me? Being single. But apparently that's not my choice."

"What the hell are you talking about?" he said, his voice low since we'd gotten closer to Braden.

I kept my voice quiet, too, as I illuminated him. "You know exactly what I'm talking about, you overbearing arsehole."

"Everything okay?" Braden asked.

I nodded sharply and hurried forward to walk beside him. As we approached Club 39, I sighed and said, "Braden, I hope you know what you're doing."

He shot me a wicked smile. "Always do. You know, Darren knows the doorman here." Turning to Darren, Braden set his devious little plan in motion. "Darren, why don't you go on in ahead and gets us drinks from the bar. We'll find a table."

Darren nodded and ignored the complaints from people standing in line as he made his way down the narrow steps to the basement bar. He greeted the big guy at the door and they spoke for a few minutes. He turned and pointed up to the street where we were standing and the next thing was we were being waved down the stairs. Darren disappeared inside the club and I watched Braden take Donna's arm.

I glowered at his back. Donna was an attractive brunette and Braden was hoping to use her to make Joss jealous. I knew how Braden worked. He liked this idea because it meant that he could use a woman to make Joss jealous without actually getting entangled with another woman. My brother liked reaction, and I was guessing he wanted a big reaction from Joss. Part of me hoped she'd deal with it with her usual admirable self-confidence.

Unfortunately, my hopes were dashed. As soon as we got inside Club 39, I found Joss behind the bar and I watched her expression harden as Braden leaned down to whisper in Donna's ear. He looked right through Joss and I saw a flicker of something I didn't like pass in her eyes before she quickly turned away.

I really wanted to bash my brother's head against Adam's.

More than anything I just wanted to leave the two of them to themselves. But Adam wouldn't let me. He pressed me forward as Braden managed to find us a table. I brushed off his hand, still playing it cool. I strode after Braden and stopped as he and Donna, followed by Adam, slid onto a couch. Standing over them, I couldn't decide which one frustrated me more.

"Ellie, sit your arse down," I heard Adam snap over the music.

I narrowed my eyes and shook my head.

Adam's expression darkened and before I had a chance to maneuver away from him, he reached up, grabbed my arm, and yanked me down beside him. I felt his body pressed to my side and struggled to get away, but was halted by the sensual brush of his fingers across my bare back as his arm wound around my waist. His hand clamped down on my hip and he forced me closer, his mouth at my ear. "If you stop acting like a petulant child, I'll stop being overbearing."

I stopped resisting, but held myself tense so he'd know I was still angry with him. For the next hour, he kept me held against him, his grip possessive and definitely more than friendly.

Braden didn't even notice. His eyes were burning holes in Joss and her colleague Craig, who had started the night off by sharing a kiss, flirting, and having fun.

I liked this side of Joss.

Braden apparently did not. He did in theory; he just didn't like that she was this way with another guy. The mini-drama playing out before me almost kept my mind off my own, but when Braden, who'd clearly had enough, got up and approached the bar when Joss went on break and somehow managed to talk the other bartender into letting him into the staffroom, I was forced to consider my own situation.

Darren and Donna were up at the bar getting more drinks.

Adam and I were alone on the couch.

He caressed my hip soothingly, obviously trying to get me to relax. "So," he spoke into my ear again, reinforcing the feeling that we were in our own little bubble inside the bar. "Are you going to tell me why you're being a bitch to me?"

"Stop calling me that," I snapped, turning my head so our noses were almost touching. I stared into his dark eyes and lost my breath so badly I had to look away.

"Stop acting like one."

"I'm annoyed," I explained. "I'm allowed to be annoyed."

"Would you fill me in?"

I turned to him again, and this time I don't think I managed to mask my hurt and confusion over his actions because his own expression softened with concern. "Why did you threaten Nicholas with physical violence when he came to you for advice about asking me out?"

Understanding dawned in his eyes and he sighed heavily. "He's not good enough for you."

"That's not up to you to decide."

His fingers dug into my hip as they curled in reflex to my response. "It's up to me to protect you."

I closed my eyes, his words hurting me. "I'm not yours to protect."

We sat in silence for a moment.

The silence was broken when his arm loosened its hold around my waist. I was looking at him questioningly when I felt the touch of his fingers against my upper back. Slowly, torturously he skimmed them down my spine and I flushed feeling my nipples harden visibly against the fabric covering my chest. "You sure about that?" he murmured hoarsely in my ear.

My eyes widened as I stared into his, a flurry of confusion rioting in my head. When Donna and Darren took a seat next to us with our drinks, Adam's arm came back around, his hand resting gently on my hip, and I sat there stunned, wondering what the hell he'd meant.

# CHAPTER 7

Adam winced as he looked over at me. "I really did send you some pretty mixed signals."

I giggled. "You think?"

He smiled sheepishly. "I'm sorry, Els. You pissed me off. I was trying to make a point that you *were* mine. It wasn't fair."

I shrugged. "You were torn. I forgive you. Especially since it makes a really good story." He laughed as I reached for the diary again, flipping through the pages to find the next entry. "That night at Club 39 wasn't nearly as bad as the night at Fire."

Adam groaned. "Damn, I don't know if I want to read this from your point of view."

"I get quite detailed."

He quirked an eyebrow at me. "Detailed?"

I nodded and felt my face redden.

He saw my blush and grinned, pulling the diary out of my hand. "Baby, that's hot."

*Sunday, September 16th*

*I'm done. It's over. I don't care what history lies between me and Adam . . . It's finally over . . .*

I hadn't been looking forward to the night at Fire because it meant being stuck in a club and having to watch Adam flirt with everything that moved, but it was a big night for Braden: He was holding a special event for Freshers' Week, the week first-year students descended upon university in the city, and I promised him I'd be there.

As per usual, he and Joss were so wrapped up in their own stuff they didn't notice the tension between me and Adam. It was this horribly awkward tension, mixed with sexual frustration, and it had sprung up between us after our clash a little while after the eventful night at Club 39.

It had happened when I accepted a date with a guy called Jason that I met in Starbucks. Jason was hot and seemed nice and I saw no harm in grabbing a drink with him. Except, Braden had informed Adam of my plans and Adam had spent the entire night calling me up with stupid questions. He ruined the date. It was immature and completely outrageous.

Even more so was the fact that, as Joss so bluntly pointed out, I had rudely kept answering the phone instead of switching it off. The truth was I'd been enjoying Adam's jealous reaction.

Somewhere along the line I had forgotten my vow to move on from him after the night at his apartment, and I was playing our stupid game again. I wanted a reaction from him and I got it. But after chewing him out, Adam had gone from hot to ice cold. He tried not to be alone with me and when he was alone with me, he only spoke about things you'd chat to a perfect stranger about.

It had been wearing on my nerves for weeks. That, along with my worries about school and the recurring headaches I couldn't seem to get rid of, I found myself wanting to lay all my frustrations at his feet. Everyone else would get nice Ellie, sweet Ellie, the Ellie everyone knew and liked. Adam would get crabby Ellie, tired Ellie, the Ellie with the bitter, broken heart.

While Braden detained Joss for a little alpha-male skirmish about her dress, Adam led me up to a private booth across from the bar. I slid in and was surprised when Adam sat down quite close to me.

"Careful," I warned him dryly, "I think you're breaking your one-meter-distance rule with me."

He curled his lip, unimpressed. "Don't start. Not tonight."

"Not any night."

His eyes flashed. "You know why I don't date, Ellie? So I don't have to put up with this shit. It's like being in a fucking relationship without the benefits."

I felt hurt by his declaration and gave him the dirtiest look I could muster. "No, it's like being in a friendship *you* broke."

Having successfully spread my hurt to him, I felt awful, and feeling awful made me even angrier. I didn't want to care that I hurt his feelings.

Adam was about to respond when movement drew our attention and we saw Joss approaching the booth. He gave her a look that told her to plant her bottom down beside us and save him from me.

I was almost as relieved as he was when she sat down on my other side.

"Braden's having drinks sent over," she said, her eyes taking in all the guests. "I didn't realize he had other friends appearing tonight. I thought it was just us and random people."

"No," I replied absentmindedly, my bad mood causing the rope bridge between my brain and mouth to snap. "Some of his exes as well as his previous friends-with-benefits girls love clubbing. He invited them and a few of his guy friends."

It wasn't until Adam snapped, "Ellie, what are you playing at?" and I turned to see him gazing pointedly at Joss that I followed his gaze and saw Joss had frozen at my careless comment.

Mortified, I hurried to assure her apologetically, "Oh, crap. Joss, I didn't mean anything. I mean, those girls don't mean anything."

"Let's get drunk," she announced overly cheerily, and I felt unbelievably guilty for making her uncomfortable and uncertain of Braden.

"I don't think that's a good idea. Let's just wait for Braden," Adam insisted.

However, Braden spent an awful long time flirting and chatting with guests. The tension at our table grew so thick we all sought to escape it. Joss and I headed for the dance floor, and I kept her company for a while until I headed to the bar to get some water. As I approached, I caught sight of Adam and felt that familiar burn in my throat. He was wearing a black shirt, rolled up at the sleeves, with black trousers. It was simple; it was hot. He always looked hot. And tonight he looked especially hot as he leaned into a girl who was sitting on a stool at the other end of the bar. She had her head tilted back while Adam braced one hand on the bar and leaned in to whisper in her ear. She laughed and he lifted his face so they were almost close enough to kiss. Whatever he murmured to her made her laugh soften to a flirtatious smile and I felt that burn in my throat transform into a lump of tears.

As if he sensed my gaze, Adam's head lifted and our eyes met. I'd never found it easy to hide my emotions when I was feeling something deeply and I quickly looked away before he caught it.

"What can I get you?" One of the bartenders finally approached me.

"Bottle of water," I replied, my voice hoarse with pain and he had to lean in for me to repeat the order. Just as I handed him money for the water, I felt a hand on my lower back and his cologne hit me seconds before his mouth brushed my ear.

"Els," Adam said quietly, his voice thick with emotion.

I didn't know how to respond. My eyes fixed downward on the bottle as I tried to control myself, knowing that every day I was getting closer and closer to forcing our situation into some kind of resolution by putting the truth out there.

"Sweetheart, would you look at me?"

I did as he asked, searching his face for answers I knew he wasn't ready to give me—answers he may never be ready to give me.

He lifted his hand from my back and brushed his knuckles tenderly along my jaw, his eyes following their movement. "The prettiest thing I've ever seen," he murmured.

The words stung because they signaled another ride on this roller coaster of mixed signals. I reared back from his touch, grimacing. "Don't."

He dropped his hands. "Ellie—"

I gestured to the girl at the other end of the bar who was now throwing invisible daggers my way. "Did you say that to her too?"

"El—"

A surge of shocked murmurs and shouts interrupted him and we both turned to look over his shoulder to see Braden rearing back from hitting someone. "Gavin," I gasped.

Adam immediately took off to be by his friend's side and I followed, my heart racing for Braden. Gavin had been his and Adam's friend at school, but he'd grown up into a prize arsehole. Braden, for some reason, felt loyalty to him and kept him around. That was until five years ago, when he'd slept with Analise and betrayed Braden.

"*That* is Gavin." Braden threw Joss a disgusted look. "The friend who fucked Analise. Why the hell were you talking to him like you know him?"

*Oh, dear God, Joss knew him?* For a moment I felt absolute panic take over me at the thought of history repeating itself for my brother. But I remembered this was Joss, and despite her flaws, she would *never* be disloyal. I only had to watch the shock fall across her face at the discovery of who Gavin was to realize that whatever was going on, it was a big misunderstanding—at least on Joss's part.

"He's a trainer at my gym," Joss explained. "He helped me once." She looked up at Braden and she swore that she had no idea who Gavin was.

She also let her feelings for my brother all hang out. I knew she probably didn't realize it, would even be mortified if she thought for one second she was making herself transparent. However, I was glad to see it and wished Braden wasn't so riled up because he didn't even notice it.

"Looks like you moved on to better things, Bray." Gavin peered at Joss in a way that made my skin crawl and I saw Adam's shoulders tense up in front of me. "Here's hoping history repeats itself because I've wanted between her legs for fucking weeks. How about it, Joss? You fancy shagging a real man?"

I'd never witnessed my brother hit someone, but he was on Gavin before anyone could stop him. Adam tried his best, but I knew there was a part of him that didn't want to pull Braden off the sleazy little traitor. But he did, only just managing to keep a grip on Braden when Gavin said something so crude that *I* almost threw a punch.

By the time security came to drag Gavin out, I thought Adam was going to let Braden go just so his own arms were free to start to swinging. And poor Joss. I watched with concern as Braden, bristling with adrenaline and anger—the likes I'd never seen in him before—hauled her out of the room and up the stairs into his private office.

I didn't even want to know what was about to happen in there.

I stood there, still shaking from the whole episode, as the crowd returned to enjoying their night. Adam and I were on the dance floor staring at each other; we were both trying to work out where we were at, and what the hell had just happened.

The girl from the bar strolled over to him in a tight jersey dress that showcased her bombshell figure. She was shorter than I was, but had more hips and ass. I suddenly felt dowdy in my shapeless, shimmery shift dress. Stopping in front of Adam, the girl placed a proprietary hand on his arm. "Let me buy you a drink after all that."

When Adam glanced over at me, I was desperate not to bleed as openly as I had earlier, so I took a deep breath and told him flatly, "Go. I'm leaving anyway."

I brushed past him before he could reply, pushed through the crowd, and made my way to the street level. A hand suddenly curled around my biceps as I was about to step outside and I looked up in surprise to see that it was Adam, with his jacket on.

"I'm making sure you get home okay."

"You don't need to."

He didn't reply and he didn't let me go. I was too tired to struggle, so I let him hail me a taxi and I sat in absolute silence with him as the cab drove us to Dublin Street.

When we arrived at my building, he paid the driver and followed me out and up the front stoop. He waited patiently as I got out my keys and opened the door to my dark flat. I took a few steps into the hall, flicked the light switch, and kicked off my heels. "You can go now."

Instead, Adam slammed the front door shut behind him and stared at me.

I sighed softly, tired of fighting. Mum had always joked that I was a lover, not a fighter. She'd even bought me a T-shirt that said it. "You can leave now, Adam. Thank you for seeing me home."

"What do you want from me?" he asked, his voice husky with anger.

I backed away, hitting the wall, and watched warily as he stalked me. My chin tilted, my lips parting in surprise as he placed his hands above my head on the wall and caged me against it. He lowered his head, his nose sliding along mine until his mouth rested just above my lips. I swallowed, finally finding my voice. "What do *you* want from *me*?"

His answer was to crush my lips beneath his.

Like the last time he'd kissed me like this, the world just disappeared, taking reality and all the important stuff with it. I wrapped my arms around his neck, my fingers curling into his hair, my breasts pressed hard against his chest as we devoured each other.

Adam eased our carnal kiss, releasing my swollen mouth to press soft kisses along my jaw and down my neck as his hand slid up my thigh. I sank against the wall with a throaty moan, my eyes closed as he kissed my lips again, his tongue teasing mine. His fingers slipped under the fabric of the lacy lingerie I was wearing under my dress and I groaned into his mouth at the pressure of his fingers pushing inside of me.

Adam pulled back, his breathing as shallow as mine as he toyed with me. I closed my eyes again, the pleasure building. I gripped his arm as he pushed me toward it. "Adam," I pleaded.

"Look at me," his words rumbled over my mouth and I immediately opened my eyes to find his blazing into mine. "I want to watch you come."

I felt my cheeks flush even harder at the demand, but I held his gaze as his fingers worked me, my hips undulating against his hand, my gaze turning drowsy. Adam's breathing grew harsher and harsher as he watched me, and when he pressed down on my clit with his thumb and I broke apart, clinging to him through my orgasm, he swore loudly and rested his head in the crook of my neck.

My legs were trembling as I came down from my high, reality settling in. Confusion overwhelmed me and I felt tears in my eyes. Adam's warm breath caressed my skin as he lifted his head to whisper in my ear, "I almost came just watching you."

I shivered, tingling all over again.

"You make me so goddamn hard," he confessed, and he gently lifted my hand to press it to his erection straining against his trousers. Triumph melted the confusion away for a second, a powerful feeling of victory taking over me as I caressed him and felt his groans of pleasure against my ear. *At least he wanted me. At least he was in torment over that.*

"If you don't stop, baby"—he peeled my hand away with a regretful sigh—"I'm going to blow."

Our eyes met and he saw the tears shining in mine and pushed away from me with another curse. Running his hand through his hair, Adam sighed heavily and said, "I shouldn't have done that. Els, I'm sorry." His face crumpled and I saw the self-flagellation in his expression.

"Why?" I asked softly, needing to know once and for all what was happening to us. "Why shouldn't you have done it? Why can't we . . . ?"

Those gorgeous dark eyes of his lifted to mine in surprise, as if he couldn't believe I didn't understand. "Because of Braden, Els. He's my best friend. He's family. I can't take the risk that he won't forgive me for . . . ." He gestured helplessly to me.

The warmth from the aftermath of the orgasm he'd given me was destroyed by the chill his words created in me. I stepped away from the wall and tried to control a burning lump in my throat. "But I'm willing to. I'm willing to because I'm in love with you. You know I'm in love with you."

The lack of surprise on his face was confirmation.

I shook my head, laughing bitterly as I wiped at tears that had begun to fall. "All these years, even now, you've told me all you ever wanted to do was protect me from getting hurt. And yet you say things and do things to confuse me, to make me think you might feel the same way that I feel about you, and then in the next second, you're cold and you flaunt other women in front of me." The tears fell fast now and I could see Adam's own eyes starting to shimmer with pain. I didn't care. I had to get this over with. "The only person who's ever really hurt me is you. And I keep letting you."

"Ellie . . ." He sounded wounded as he took a step toward me. "I do love you," he admitted, and instead of feeling joy at those words, the last piece of me holding on to hope crumbled.

I shook my head. "But not enough."

"You know that's not true. Els, you of all people have to understand. If you and me start something and it all goes south, I lose Braden too. I'll lose the two people in the world who mean the most to me."

I wanted to understand him. I tried to understand the reasons behind people's actions because I wanted to believe the best in everyone. But all I knew was that I loved him enough to risk it all—to risk our history—for something more, and the fact that he wasn't willing told me he couldn't possibly feel the way I felt about him. I didn't want to be in a relationship with someone I loved more than he'd ever love me.

"Go home, Adam," I replied softly. "We're done."

His eyes widened in shock. "Ellie—"

"I'll pretend for Braden. When we're all together, I'll pretend for Braden that nothing has changed between you and me." I held his gaze, attempting to be strong as I ended us. "But whatever this is, it's over. Everything. Don't call me, don't visit. Just don't. I don't want you near me when you don't have to be. It hurts too much, and if you care about me even just a little bit, you'll stay away from me."

I didn't let him reply. I couldn't. I turned and strode down the hall into my bedroom, closed the door behind me, and leaned up against it as I tried to catch my breath.

There was silence in the hallway for what seemed like forever, and then finally I heard the front door open and close quietly.

The burn in my throat burst out into sobs, and I slid down the door trying to catch my breath through the pain . . .

# CHAPTER 8

"Most miserable bloody weeks of my life after that." Adam turned the pages, scanning my sparse entries after that night.

I slid my hand around the nape of his neck and gave it a squeeze. "Me, too, honey."

He lifted my hand from his neck and brought it around to give my knuckles an absentminded kiss. "The night at Jenna and Ed's wedding was fucking torture."

I agreed with him completely. We'd both taken dates. I went with Nicholas, just to be particularly annoying, and Adam had taken some random girl with him. Although I'd flitted around the wedding, acting my cheery self and steadfastly refusing to look Adam's way, it was one of the most painful experiences of my life.

Adam threaded my fingers through his and rested our hands on his lap. "Here it is." He held the diary up.

"What?" I frowned, trying to read my writing.

"I'm fast-forwarding to my wake-up call."

*Monday, December 17th*
*I'm writing this as quickly as I can because I can see Adam is*
*about to rip the pen from my hand and use whatever means at his*

*disposal to bring my attention back to him. Since I like the means he will use, I need to get this down. It's been an utterly exhausting weekend but today I woke up feeling stronger than I have in a while. This morning I woke up to something beautiful, and I swear after the last week I've had, I didn't think that was possible . . .*

Focusing on a crack in my ceiling I attempted to push the fear and desperation back. There was this buried part of me that kept trying to push up and grip my chest from the inside out to pull me to it to whisper desolately, "I'm not ready to die."

*Stop it, stop it, stop it, stop it, stop it, stop . . .*

I couldn't think like that.

But it was what I'd been hiding from for months. When my doctor told me I needed glasses, I'd ignored my own instincts and focused on that solution with utter relief.

Still, the headaches kept coming and the exhaustion worsened as the anxiety I kept hidden from everyone grew.

I'd had a seizure in my kitchen. I was terrified but also strangely relieved as I sat in the hospital and waited for an MRI. I was sick to my stomach with fear, but relieved that I was going to know once and for all what the hell was wrong with me.

*A tumor; a brain tumor.*

I tried to catch my breath. We'd waited ten days for the results. It was a brain tumor and they wouldn't tell me anything else. I had twenty-four hours of waiting to find out if I had brain cancer or not.

I wanted to handle it graciously, not just for me but for Braden and Mum and Clark and Hannah and Declan. I wanted to handle it graciously for Joss, knowing it would be difficult for her.

A tear slid down my cheek as I thought about Joss's reaction. I'd watched the panic in her face and then she just shut down. She left me when I needed her the most.

Braden was furious and panicking about me and about her and trying not to. His anxiety was making me feel worse, so I told him to go and speak to Mum and Clark. Understanding I needed just a little time to myself, he gave me it.

I couldn't think of the worst. I wouldn't be like Joss. I mean, I wanted to be prepared, but I wasn't a pessimist. And surely, I was too young. You never think something like this will happen to you. It feels like a dream; it's so surreal, like you're watching someone else's life play out in a movie.

My phone rang and I turned my head on my pillow to eye it on my bedside table.

*It was Adam.*

I breathed through the tightness in my chest and reached for the phone. Since I landed in the hospital ten days prior, Adam had reneged on his unspoken promise to stay out of my life. He called me every day and came by to see me as much as he felt I'd let him get away with. Too exhausted to fight him, I *did* let him get away with it.

"Hullo," I answered, and even I could tell I didn't sound like myself.

There was a crackle down the line as he let out a heavy sigh. "Braden just called."

I tensed, hearing the roughness in Adam's voice, the brokenness in his tone. "Yeah."

"God, Ellie," he groaned as if in agony. "Sweetheart—"

"Don't." I shook my head and bit my lip to try and stem my emotions. As soon as I felt I could speak without crying, I continued, "We don't know anything yet."

"I know I need to come to you. I'll be there in ten minutes."

"No, don't," my voice was sharp as I sat up, my heart pounding at the thought of having him here to hold me through this. "I don't want you to."

"Fuck, Els."

I winced at the hurt in his voice. "Please, Adam."

"I need to. I need to be with you. I love you, Ellie. I'm fucking in love with you."

He was crying.

I'd never heard or seen him cry before. At his tears and outright confession, I started to cry harder and collapsed back on my pillow, squeezing the phone tight to my ear. Finally I whispered, "Just stay on the line with me, okay."

Adam cleared his throat, his voice breaking as he replied, "Anything, baby."

I sighed and snuggled deeper against my phone. "We don't know anything," I repeated.

"It could be nothing," he added.

"Whatever it is, I'm going to fight it."

"I'll fight it with you."

"Shh," I hushed him softly. "No promises. Not like this."

"I'm done wasting time, Els."

I smiled sadly, too weary to go there. "Just waste a little more time for me. Please."

He was a silent a while and then he replied quietly, "Only a little, baby. Only a little."

Adam stayed on the phone with me for two hours and we hardly spoke at all. I just listened to him breathe as he listened to me breathe. We finally hung up when Braden returned, but Adam refused to let me say good-bye; it was the first time I heard undiluted fear in his voice when he begged me not to say that word.

It was a lot. It was huge. But it was one thing for him to admit to me again that he loved me, and an entirely different thing for him to admit that to Braden. I needed to get through this crisis before I could deal with me and Adam.

I watched television with Braden for a while, snuggled up into his side as he stroked my hair soothingly. Mum and Clark had gotten into a huge fight with him because they wanted to come to me, but Braden insisted there was nothing they could do right now and while I was stuck in limbo it would be best if I had peace and quiet and didn't have to worry about how they were coping with this. I gave them a quick call so they could hear my voice and I could ask them to take me to my appointment the next day. They were okay at first but then suddenly Clark had to say a quick good-bye when Mum started to sob. Of course that set me off for a while, and then I calmed, and then as it got darker outside and the evening began to pass, the fear over what I might hear from the doctor the next day hit me.

Braden laid me back on my bed and curled my hand around a mug of hot water and whisky. He sat on my bed as I drank it, and he watched me until my eyes finally fluttered closed.

They shot open at the sound of my bedroom floor creaking. I was curled up in a ball on my bed in the dark, and through the moonlight spilling in through the large window I saw Joss standing at the foot of my bed.

Surprised that she had come to me, but still gripped by hurt at her defection earlier, I gazed at her silently.

At a breathy gasp, my eyes grew wider as I realized Joss was crying. *Joss.* I knew she'd deserted me earlier because of the baggage she carried around about the deaths in her family. I'd known that on some level that fear had sent her running from me, but actually witnessing her tears, I realized it all meant that she cared about me. She was frightened of losing me.

The tears slipped down my cheeks and moved Joss to action. She crawled up onto my bed and as she settled in beside me, I turned on my back. Joss immediately rested her head on my shoulder and shifted closer to me. She took my hand and held it between both of hers.

"I'm sorry," she whispered.

"It's okay," I promised her and meant it. "You came back."

"I love you, Ellie Carmichael. You're going to get through this."

*I'd won the love and affection of someone as lost as Jocelyn Butler?* For me that was a whole lot of light in a whole lot of darkness and it overwhelmed me. I tried to swallow my sobs as I whispered the truth back to her, "I love you, too, Joss."

Braden had woken us up that morning and he'd made us breakfast. Even with the appointment with the neurosurgeon looming over me, I could tell something had gone horribly wrong with Joss and Braden. I discovered they'd broken up and I attempted not to feel guilty. *I failed.*

They'd clearly broken up because of me—because of Joss's reaction to what was happening to me. Hearing Braden's deadly cool voice with her and seeing the pain in Joss's face, I wanted to intervene, I wanted to fix what I had inadvertently helped break, but they wouldn't have it and I was ushered out of the room and into the shower.

At one point I heard their intense voices over the sound of the running water, and then a plate crashing followed by more shouting. Worried, I switched off the shower and clambered out, but the voices had quieted to a murmur. I pulled on a bathrobe, ready to put myself between them if need be.

Instead, as I walked quietly down the hall I heard Braden confessing that he loved Joss and that he wasn't going to stop fighting for her. He promised her that he would be relentless. The romantic in me almost passed out on the spot.

"You're insane," Joss said to him.

"No," I disagreed, coming to a stop in the kitchen doorway, giving them a smile. "He's fighting for what he wants."

"He's not the only one."

I turned my head in shock at the sound of the familiar voice, and watched with a pounding heart as Adam strode toward me. He looked like hell with dark circles under his bloodshot eyes.

Tired and unshaven, he was still absolutely beautiful, and the way he was gazing at me, like I was something precious just dancing out of his arm's reach, was absolutely beautiful.

When he stopped before me he took my hand and raised it to his mouth, squeezing his eyes closed as he pressed a kiss against it. My breath caught as he opened his eyes and I saw the tears from yesterday were back again, shimmering in their depths. I also knew from the determined fire blazing in his expression that he had really meant it when he said he'd only waste a little more time for me. As in, less than twenty-four hours.

That's why when he tugged me by the hand and drew me into the kitchen as he faced up to Braden, I let him. I knew that in a few hours I'd discover whether or not I had the biggest fight of my life on my hands, and even after everything, the only person I wanted fighting by my side was Adam Gerard Sutherland. We had a history, and I wanted to keep adding years to that history.

"I need to tell you something." Adam faced Braden and I could feel the tension vibrating from his body.

*He was doing it. He was really willing to risk it for me.*

I squeezed his hand tighter.

Braden crossed his arms over his chest, his eyes moving from Adam to me and then back to Adam again and I knew he knew but he wasn't going to make it easy. "Go on."

"You're like a brother to me. I would never do anything to hurt you. And I know I haven't been what a brother would consider good material for his wee sister, but I love Ellie, Braden. I have for a long time now, and I can't *not* be with her. I've wasted too much time as it is."

I don't think either of us breathed at all as we waited for Braden's response. After a minute's contemplation, he finally turned to me, his gaze softening. "Do you love him?"

Adam looked back at me and I was surprised to find a glint of insecurity in his eyes. Silly man. I gripped his arm tighter to reassure him and then smiled at my brother. "Yes."

And then quite casually, as if Adam and I weren't tied up in knots over his possible reaction, Braden just shrugged and leaned over to switch on the kettle. "About bloody time. You two were giving *me* a headache."

My muscles tensed in reaction. *He'd known all this time?* Adam and I had put ourselves through pain and heartbreak these last few months and Braden had known all along how we felt about each other . . .

"You really are a know-it-all pain-in-the-ass," Joss said to the three of us. She pushed past Braden and stopped to say more softly, "I'm happy for you," to me and Adam before she flounced down the hall to the bathroom.

Braden laughed softly. "She loves me, really."

The bathroom door slammed at that and Braden laughed again. Adam narrowed his eyes on him. "I hope she puts you through hell, you cocky bastard."

Braden smirked and shifted his gaze to me. "I had to make sure you were willing to fight for her. She's worth the fight."

Adam sighed and put his arm around my shoulder, drawing me into his side so he could kiss the top of my head. "I know that better than anyone."

I closed my eyes and inhaled, thanking whatever divine being out there that had added another glimmer of light into my darkness.

For a moment I just lay there, my smile pressed into my pillow. Not only had I awoken to the heat of Adam curled into my back, his forehead pressed against my nape in sleep, his heavy arm draped across my waist, and his right leg caught in between mine, but I'd awoken to the lightness of relief. I'd awoken feeling stronger than I had done in what had felt like a very long time.

Although I knew from the look on his face he wanted to come with me, Adam remained at my flat—along with Braden, Joss, Hannah, and Dec—while Mum and Clark accompanied me to my appointment with the neurosurgeon.

Dr. Dunham was a pleasant man in his early forties who shunted the fear of God out of me and my parents with five words: "There's nothing to worry about." He assured us that the cause of the physical symptoms was actually a large cyst attached to two very small tumors, and the cyst was causing pressure. He told us it had to be removed and because of its placement—on the surface of my brain—there was very little risk to the surgery. He'd also told us that there was little chance of the tumors proving to be cancerous, but that they'd be sent off for biopsies to be sure. He'd scheduled me in for surgery in two weeks' time. While I was scared as all hell about going under the knife, the relief of knowing that there was a massive chance I was fighting a small fight and not one for my life was still overwhelming and draining.

When I'd returned home to give everyone the optimistic news, Adam had surprised me by kissing me right there in front of my parents. I was even more surprised to discover *they* weren't the least bit shocked. Afterward, we'd all gone next door to the pub to gather our thoughts and try to unwind from what had been the most horrendous twenty-four hours I'd ever remembered experiencing. I sat in the pub with Adam on one side and Hannah curled into me on the other, and, despite everything, I felt incredibly lucky as I gazed around at my friends and family.

Mum and Clark eventually took Hannah and Dec home, Braden reluctantly left to give Joss some space, and Joss disappeared, to give me and Adam some space. We ordered some takeaway, which I ravenously ate when we got back to my flat.

Adam and I hung out on my bed and talked for a little while, but there was so much to talk about it and I was too exhausted to give us the focus we needed. It seemed Adam was, too, because he disappeared with our leftovers and returned only to cuddle up to me in the bed and reach out to switch off the light.

When I awoke to soft morning sun pouring in through my curtains, I was feeling strong and ready to take on anything, and Adam Sutherland was spooning me.

It was kind of beautiful.

I felt his hair tickle my neck as he moved and his arm snaked across my waist. "You awake, baby?" he murmured, sleep making his voice extra sexy.

My grin got bigger. "Yeah." I lightly caressed his forearm. "You know in all the years I've known you, I've never slept near you. You make noises."

I felt his chest move behind me in laughter. "Noises?"

Twisting around, so I could look into his eyes, I grinned up into his face as he leaned over me. "You make 'mmm' noises."

Adam grinned back at me. "What are 'mmm' noises?"

"You know 'mmm' noises. Like when something tastes or sounds good."

He grimaced. "Like 'yum' noises?"

"Exactly, but you say, 'mmm . . . '"

"I think I just took a hit to my masculinity."

I burst out laughing and stroked his jaw. "Don't worry. I liked it. I just imagined the 'mmms' were for me."

I turned over and Adam wrapped his arms tighter around me as he pulled my leg over his hip. His eyes grew drowsy and heated as he stared at my mouth. "They were for you."

"How could they be for me if you didn't even know you make them?"

"Because I dream about you," he answered instantly, and I stilled in surprise. He felt it and gave me a squeeze. "I've been having these dreams about you for a few years now."

"What am I doing in them?" I asked somewhat breathlessly. There was a rising tide of warmth in my chest, and an even hotter heat tingling between my legs at his confession.

His hand slid down my waist to caress my bum and then he pulled my lower body against his and I could feel his morning erection pressing against me. I felt my nipples tighten in reaction, and drew in a breath. "Sometimes we're making love, other times we're fucking."

I lifted my eyes to his, my smile dimming. "I don't like that word."

His mouth twitched. "You think it's unromantic."

He knew me too well. I shrugged unsurely.

"Els, wanting to fuck you doesn't mean I don't love you."

Needing more clarification, I slid my hands down from his face and settled them lightly on his chest. "What does it mean?"

His voice was hoarse now. "When I want to fuck you it means I'm in the mood for rough and hard."

To my utter shock his words were turning me on. I squirmed a little against him and felt my cheeks flush. "I don't think I've ever been . . ." I still wasn't sure if I could say the word. I'd admonished Joss so many times for using it because it was so tawdry sounding but when Adam put it like that.

"Say it," he whispered across my mouth. "I want to hear it from your sweet mouth, baby."

I gulped and bravely met his eyes. "I've—I've never been fucked," I whispered.

If it was possible, he grew even harder against me and when his hand slipped between our bodies and beneath my underwear, his fingers thrusting gently but easily into me, Adam groaned. "Baby . . ." He leaned into me, his mouth brushing mine, his tongue just touching the tip of mine. "I think you like the thought of me fucking you."

In response I kissed him. It was a deep kiss, one I meant to encourage him, but instead it turned soulful and desperate.

Adam rolled me onto my back, pressing my legs apart so he could settle between them, and when he broke our kiss it was to look into my eyes with such adoration I couldn't breathe. "I'm not going to fuck you this morning, baby. This morning I'm going to make love to you. We'll leave the rest until you're recovered and at full strength." His eyes darkened with promise. "You're going to need it."

I grinned up at him, suddenly realizing that Adam was here, in my arms, talking about our future together. It was a thirteen-year-old dream come true. "You have no idea how much I love you."

He nodded slowly, pushing my nighty up my body. "As much as I love you."

It was the first time he'd said it that I could allow myself to really feel it. Those three words poured out of him and pooled in my chest. As I raised my dress over my head, lying almost naked for his perusal, I smiled shyly up at him. "You know, I don't mind what we do this morning. You can do whatever you want to me."

To my surprise this caused Adam to groan and he dropped his head on my shoulder.

"Baby?"

He turned his cheek and pressed a kiss to my bare skin, his hands coasting up my ribs to cup my breasts. I arched into his touch with a sigh as he replied, "How did I get so lucky? Smart, funny, sweet, beautiful, passionate—and she tells me I can do anything I want to her . . ." He chuckled now. "There has to be a catch." I blushed deeply and Adam smiled. "Fuck, I forgot modest."

"Stop it." I pushed playfully at his shoulders but really I needed him to stop or I was going to start crying.

He laughed again, the rumbling against my chest doing happy things to me down south. Adam gave my shoulder another quick kiss and sat up, straddling me as he pulled off his T-shirt. I drank my fill of him, biting my lip as my eyes took him in. I'd forgotten how beautiful he was—broad shoulders and lean muscles. Abs to die for.

His eyes never left me as his hands went to the buckle on his belt. I shivered with anticipation as he drew the zipper on his jeans down. "This morning I'm making love to you because our first time should be about that. Plus, no matter how great you're feeling, and I can tell you're feeling a lot better, your body must still be exhausted. We're taking it nice and slow." He pushed down his jeans and underwear and my breathing stuttered as his erection sprang free, jutting up and out, hard and throbbing. Now I knew why the bugger was so confident. He was walking around with *that* in his trousers.

"You're making 'mmm' noises," Adam told me with laughter in his voice as he turned to shimmy his jeans clean off.

"I am not!" I protested, blushing again, and realizing I'd been so lost in staring at him that there was a great possibility I *had* been making "mmm" noises.

"You were. It's fucking adorable." He reached for my underwear. I tilted my hips to help him ease them down my legs, and as he did he stopped every now and then to kiss my bare skin. He pushed my left knee up and I watched him with growing heat coiling in the pit of my stomach as he trailed kisses up my calf, across my knee, and along my inner thigh. "Your legs go on forever," he whispered, his eyes lifting to meet mine. "I can't wait to have them wrapped around me while I'm inside you."

"Adam . . ." I was completely at his mercy.

I repeated his name when his head descended between my legs and his tongue licked gently at my clit. He worked me with his mouth, kissing and licking and sucking until I came fast and hard against him.

I was still crying out to God as Adam kissed his way up my stomach and then stopped to draw my nipple into his hot mouth. He played with me a while, all the time murmuring compliments and words of love, until eventually I was wound so tight I begged him to come inside me.

At the pressure of him between my legs, I tensed momentarily. Feeling it, Adam threaded his fingers through mine and held my hands down on the bed while he stared into my eyes, anchoring me to him in every way he could. His lips parted on an exhalation as he pushed inside me and sank deep. I gasped and lifted my hips in instinct, causing a delicious frisson of pleasure through us both. Adam studied me, his expression tender. "I love you, Ellie Carmichael," he whispered, his words heavy with sincerity.

I nodded and moved my hips again, panting slightly as I replied, "I love you, Adam."

His grip on my hands became almost painful and he slid out of me nearly entirely before gliding back inside. I undulated against him, and we caught a wave, a slow rhythm that grew and grew until I was desperate for the finale. My legs were wrapped around him now, my thighs squeezing him tighter, begging for more.

"Adam," I cried out, pushing against his hands, wanting to touch him, wanting to grasp him against me. "Harder, please."

He growled low in his throat and he pulled out only to slam back into me. I started murmuring nonsense, mostly saying the word "Yes" over and over again as he continued to slam into me.

"Come for me, Els," he demanded, his eyes on my face. "Come for me, baby."

And like I'd been prone to doing for years, I gave him what he wanted. The rhythm hit its crescendo and I broke apart with a scream as Adam pressed his cheek to mine and tensed. I floated around in postorgasmic space and he shuddered hard against me as he came.

We were both panting heavily, both clammy with sweat. I grinned up at the ceiling. That was what happened when you had the most amazing sex of your life. *"Wow,"* I whispered, sliding my arms around his back now that he'd let my hands go.

Adam lifted his cheek from mine, his features relaxed with satisfaction. His dark eyes, however, were glittering intensely. "Wow doesn't even cover it," he replied. "Been waiting my whole life for that."

I bit my lip because hearing that was so nice, I wanted to cry.

He picked up on my emotions, smiled, and gave me a soft kiss. When he pulled back he frowned. "That was a bit of both."

"What?" I frowned back at him in confusion.

"I started out making love to you but it's your fault I ended up fucking you."

"My fault?"

"'Adam.'" His voice went amusingly breathy as he imitated me. "'Harder, please.'" He shook his head as I laughed. "I'm a man of great self-control but that . . ."

I squeezed my thighs around him again in delight. "Are you admitting I have power over you, Adam Gerard Sutherland?"

His eyebrows puckered together as he shook his head in denial, a shake that quickly turned to a nod as I giggled beneath him. He closed his eyes in what appeared to be pleasured pain and suddenly he captured me around the waist and flipped us so he was on his back and I was lying on top of him. He held me close and I relaxed against him. I understood: He just needed to hold me for a moment and remember I was okay.

Once again I was overwhelmed by the realization that he was in love with me. I smiled and snuggled closer to him.

After a while he murmured, "You're on the pill, right?"

"Shouldn't you have asked that before you took me oh so wildly?"

He grinned up at me. "I wasn't really thinking about anything but the need to take you oh so wildly."

"Well, not to worry. I'm on the pill," I assured him and settled back on his chest.

"Wouldn't have mattered anyway," he murmured, stroking my hair.

I tensed. "Meaning?"

"Meaning if an accident happened, it wouldn't matter. An accident with you is a kid with you."

Shock held me completely frozen as I processed this. How many times had I heard Braden joking with Adam about how terrified he was of getting a girl pregnant? It was one of the reasons Braden suspected Adam never slept with the same girl twice. In his twisted male logic, he thought it meant it lessened the chance of an accident, or at least it lessened the chance of a girl liking him so much she'd force an accident.

"You'd want a baby with me?" My throat croaked on the question.

I felt his knuckles brush down my spine in a caress that made me shiver to the tips of my toes. "Ellie, I want everything with you."

Tears glimmering in my eyes, I lifted my head and replied softly, gratefully, "I never knew you could be so romantic."

Adam's lips twitched in response and he shook his head against the pillow. "I'm not, but I reckon I'd do anything for you and since that has included sitting through more romantic comedies any man should have to endure, I know you're a romantic. I just want you happy. I've got a lot to make up for." He brushed my hair back from my face. "And you make it easy." He pulled lightly on a strand of hair, his expression suddenly serious. "But if you breathe one word of it to your brother, or anybody for that matter, there will be consequences."

I smiled and shook my head. "I won't tell, I promise. I like knowing something about you no one else does."

"Then we're even."

"How do you mean?"

He flipped me again and I squealed with laughter as he wrestled me back on the bed. Once he had me captured with my legs wrapped around his waist, he kissed me and drew back to murmur, "I'm the only one who knows sweet little Ellie Carmichael likes it when I talk dirty."

Once again I felt my skin flush with embarrassment, but I didn't contradict him. I couldn't because he was so damn right.

# CHAPTER 9

"Okay, I've decided you can't give these to Joss." Adam slammed the diary closed. "In fact, you may have to burn them."

I took the journal from him and added it to the pile. "Why?"

"Because you go into a lot of detail, Els. Not just about sex, but also about what I say to you before, during, and after sex."

I tried not to laugh and failed miserably. "You mean the romantic stuff?"

He gave me an unimpressed look. "You are *not* giving that to Joss. She'll tell Braden and I'll never hear the end of it."

"You know Joss tries to be considerate, since Braden's my brother, but sometimes things slip and what slips is that he can be a romantic too."

Adam's eyebrows rose and I saw his mouth start to curl mischievously at the corners. "Romantic how?"

I smiled at him. "As if I'm going to tell you and give you ammunition to torture him."

"It's only fair if you're going to give him ammunition to torture me."

Chuckling at the fear that my brother would discover Adam's softer side, I shook my head slowly and answered casually, "I'm not."

"What do you mean you're not?"

"I've decided not to give Joss the diaries."

Cocking his head in confusion, Adam's eyes asked the question for him.

I shrugged. "I was going to up until that last entry. Reading it all just reminded me how much we felt, how much we feel, and how much a part of us it all is. It doesn't belong to anyone else, and I guess I don't want it to. It's ours. Our history. Our story. And in a way, our future too. As much as I love her, you're right. I can't give that to Joss. I can't give *these* to her." I gestured to the diaries and then got up on all fours in an effort to clean up the piles of books, but I was stopped abruptly by the pressure of Adam's hands on either side of my hips.

I looked back over my shoulder, my eyes widening slightly at the sight of him on his knees behind me with the most carnal and possessive look on his face. My lips parted as he pulled my arse into him and I felt his erection rub against me. "What are you doing?" I asked on a whisper.

In response, he slipped his hand around to the zipper on my shorts and tugged it down as his other hand tugged the zipper down on his jeans. "In a little while, we'll go upstairs to make love, but right now I'm going to fuck my future wife on top of our history."

Somehow Adam managed to get the f-word into the most romantic sentence ever, and I didn't care. Instead I gasped as he rocked against me and hoarsely replied, "What about the floor? We might scratch it."

He stroked my spine, then brought his hands back down to grip my hips and pull me harder against him. "Do you really think I give a shit about the floor right now?"

I shook my head, already flushing with anticipation. "I'm guessing not."

Adam grinned wickedly. "Let's start the next chapter, baby."